The sun blasted against o[...]
We were moving through[...]
Tainted Zone larger than the New Arkham Dust Zone by several orders of magnitudes. Our dust masks and goggles kept the worst of the radioactive sand away but not all.

I was leading Gamma Squad Rangers and carried a T-17 heavy assault rifle in my hands. We were on foot, having left our jeeps to recharge their solar batteries. All of us were carrying more equipment than usual, looking like a collection of walking arsenals. Recon and Extermination missions were usually the most dangerous and we were equipped accordingly, but there was something about this mission which made us double stock on weaponry.

Strangely, the thing I was most aware of was the weathered Stetson on top of my head and the leather duster around my back. The hat was my single most cherished possession, a legacy from my father. He'd been a member of Gamma Squad before me and I'd requested the right to wear his hat. It was stupidly romantic of me, but I sometimes felt his ghost was looking out for us. I felt it was the least he could do after trying to murder me as a child.

"Look alive, Gammas," I spoke into the microphone hidden in my mask. "We should be spotting this 'Black Cathedral' any time now."

Speial thanks or acknowledments

I'd like to acknowledge Jim Bernheimer, Tim Marquitz, Matthew Baugh, Sonja L. Perrin, Thom Brannan, Rakie Bennettt, Rob Pegler, Bobbie Metevier, Devan Sagliani, Shana Festa, Frank Martin, Jeffrey Kafer, Valerie Gibson, David Niall Wilson, David Dodd, Andrea Ball, and all the other people who helped bring this book to print. This includes H.P. Lovecraft and Robert E. Howard for being so kind to share their mythologies with others in their lifetime

Macabre Ink is an imprint of Crossroad Press Publishing
For information address Crossroad Press at 141 Brayden Dr., Hertford, NC 27944
www.crossroadpress.com

First edition

CTHULHU ARMAGEDDON

BY C. T. PHIPPS

DEDICATION

I dedicate this book to my lovely wife, Kat, who was always willing to tolerate my staying up all night to type about monsters.

FOREWORD

What would you get if you crossed *Mad Max* with the *Cthulhu Cycle*?

These are the kind of thoughts you have when you're up at 5:00 am working on your master's degree in college as well as a hardcore tabletop gamer. *Cthulhu Armageddon* was my first novel idea and I've re-written it six (count 'em, six) times since first coming up with the story. In the end, I always came back to the vision of a lone soldier travelling across a wasteland while Great Cthulhu loomed in the background.

It's a very gamer image.

And I am a gamer.

Over the years, I've played ungodly amounts of *Dungeons and Dragons*, *Call of Cthulhu*, and *Vampire: The Masquerade*. I've also played a lot of video games, of which my favorites have included *Call of Cthulhu: Dark Corners of the Earth* and the *Fallout* franchise.

Cthulhu Armageddon is undeniably a mash-up fiction which is brought about from the idea of what it would be like to experience a post-apocalypse survival tale from the perspective of someone who was more akin to the Road Warrior than Giles from *Buffy: The Vampire Slayer* (more typical of Lovecraft's protagonists than Mel Gibson).

For those looking for a traditional telling of H. P. Lovecraft's work about the cosmic horror of humanity in a nihilistic universe where nothing makes sense, I suggest you look elsewhere. This is a work drawn from my own experiences of treating Lovecraft's bestiary as my own personal *Monstrous Manual.*

I love Lovecraft's work even if I suspect my anarchist, pro-racial-equality, pro-gay, theistic viewpoint of the world wouldn't go down well with him. Then again, Lovecraft had quite a few odd friendships, so maybe we would have gotten along on our shared love of monsters.

No, this is a novel which was written with the idea of soldiers and survivors traveling across the blasted hellscape of a planet warped by the rising of the Great Old Ones. It's fantasy-horror at best rather than just horror, and I can assure you many monsters are horribly killed. The cold nihilistic universe of Lovecraft is no friendlier to the Great Old Ones than it is to humanity.

In a way, my book does them a service because this is a world where the Great Old Ones have incontrovertibly won. Earth has been warped beyond recognition and mankind is reduced to scattered bands of survivors. They are survivors, however, who have learned to adapt to their new world, however. While Cthulhu and Yog-Sothoth may rule the cosmos, mankind may be the ants which ruin their picnic.

If you're a Lovecraft purist, this will not go over well, but I'm far from the first man to think the best thing to do when you meet Cthulhu is call the Ghostbusters. Hell, there was even an episode of the cartoon where they defeated Old Batwings. Likewise, Brian Lumley wrote a series of novels (the *Titus Crow* series) where his protagonists beat the living crap out of them with a flying coffin-TARDIS.

This is just my contribution to the genre.

- C. T. Phipps

CHAPTER ONE

The sun blasted against our environment-reinforced uniforms. We were moving through the Great Barrier Desert, a massive Tainted Zone larger than the New Arkham Dust Zone by several orders of magnitudes. Our dust masks and goggles kept the worst of the radioactive sand away but not all.

I was leading Gamma Squad Rangers and carried a T-17 heavy assault rifle in my hands. We were on foot, having left our jeeps to recharge their solar batteries. All of us were carrying more equipment than usual, looking like a collection of walking arsenals. Recon and Extermination missions were usually the most dangerous and we were equipped accordingly, but there was something about this mission which made us double stock on weaponry.

Strangely, the thing I was most aware of was the weathered Stetson on top of my head and the leather duster around my back. The hat was my single most cherished possession, a legacy from my father. He'd been a member of Gamma Squad before me and I'd requested the right to wear his hat. It was stupidly romantic of me, but I sometimes felt his ghost was looking out for us. I felt it was the least he could do after trying to murder me as a child.

"Look alive, Gammas," I spoke into the microphone hidden in my mask. "We should be spotting this 'Black Cathedral' any time now."

I remembered our mission now; it was an errand of mercy. We were performing a rogue operation the Council of Leaders never would have approved of. We were just supposed to scout the area, find out the local tribes' numbers and armaments, but one of their chiefs had persuaded us to look into a series of mass kidnappings. Our team wasn't at full strength, only the six of us remaining from our original eight-man squad, but the Remnant had neglected to reinforce us. We'd just have to make do.

I'd exceeded our orders by taking us on this investigation, but there had been children involved. Children always changed things; they were the one universally precious thing to all of humanity. Whoever was taking slaves from the local villages wanted especially young captives. That was enough to melt even the hardest soldier's heart.

Well, almost.

"I still don't know why we're looking into a bunch of illiterate savages having their brats stolen," Joseph Stephens said behind me. A blond-haired and blue-eyed man's man, Stephens seemed to think he was a purer example of humanity than other members of the squad, ludicrous as that may be. "If we manage to get them back, they'll probably eat them. Then they'll try and eat us."

"You're doing this because I ordered you to," I said in response. In fact, that wasn't strictly true. I'd asked for volunteers and Stephens was the only one to object.

"You're a heartless bastard, Stephens," Jessica said, speaking in a smooth Southern drawl. She was a pretty, brown-haired girl underneath her mask and armor, something which many individuals had noticed on our treks across the Wasteland.

It was fruitless, though. Jessica wasn't interested in a relationship. She might gently flirt but she'd lost her husband only a year ago during the "Color Incident." I felt more than a little guilt for the fact I hadn't been able to pull him out of it alive. There was also what had happened to her children. Frankly, I didn't understand how she continued to function—much less joke around.

"It does not require a majority to prevail, but rather an irate, tireless minority keen to set brush fires in people's minds," Jeremiah "Jimmy" Schmidt said, quoting some figure from Old Earth's past.

Jimmy was the most educated of us despite being the youngest. I was a distant second, understanding roughly half of the references he made. Occasionally, he'd catch flak from Stephens for his African descent. It was one of the reasons why I'd made a number of requests for the latter's re-assignment. Not the least because I was every bit as black as Jimmy.

"This whole cathedral is probably just a hoax. Don't you think we would have noticed a huge stone temple sticking out in the middle of the desert?" Stephens was clearly more nervous than he was letting on; part of that had to be his own superstitious fear of the Wasteland.

I was of the mind that Stephens was more ignorant than actively malicious, but his manner had always grated on me. Still, he was a part of my squad, and that meant he was closer than anyone but family.

"The Wastelands can hide a lot of things," Jessica said, her voice hanging in the wind. "My grandmother once saw a dragon in the Wastelands."

"Your grandmother didn't see no god-damned dragon." Stephens said. "There's no such thing."

"Have you ever seen a dragon?" Jessica asked.

"No!" Stephens snapped back. "I just said that's impossible."

"Then you can't say they don't exist." Jessica stuck out her tongue, a childish gesture but one that made me chuckle.

"That makes no ..." Stephens trailed off as he bumped into my back. Spread out before us was a particularly deep valley in the sands. In the center of the dusty wastes was a cathedral. Not just a temple or an old church but a genuine, honest-to-god cathedral with soaring towers and architecture like the kind humanity hadn't been able to build since before the Rising.

The building stood alone, no surrounding infrastructure or community. It was a testament to its builders' dedication and resourcefulness they'd been able to construct something like it in the middle of nowhere. Yet, I couldn't admire them too much because the building was disturbing in a way no piece of Old Earth architecture could match.

On a very primal level, looking at the alien building made me sick. The color of the building was black, darker than obsidian, with stones seemingly formed from the very night itself. Grotesque statues lined the outside of its walls. The obscene statuary included both Great Old Ones and mutated humans, each more hideous than the last. Its cyclopean walls were covered with stained glass windows made of some twisted organic crystal.

The building itself seemed as much grown as constructed in some places. Every time I blinked, the building seemed slightly different, as though my eyes weren't able to fully grasp its entirety. A disgusting black biomass was growing out of the ground and wrapping itself around the building's towers.

"What the fuck is that?" Stephens said, summarizing the entire unit's opinion.

"Who the hell builds a cathedral out in the middle of the fucking desert?" Jessica asked, staring. I hadn't realized until now she hadn't thought the name was literal.

"Mormons?" Jimmy suggested.

"Very funny," Jessica muttered. "I don't think they've changed that much since my great-grandpappy's day."

I would have guessed the cathedral to be Extra-Biological Entities (E.B.E.s) in construction, possibly mutant or alien in origin, if not for the familiarity of the place. Despite how sickened I was to look upon the building, I felt a definite sense of *déjà vu*. Parts of the building were less inhuman than others, resembling the most ancient of human structures. Yet, its alien components dwarfed those familiar constructions, as if all I could recognize was a pale shadow of what this building's mad architect had achieved. The Black Cathedral was magnificent; it was abominable.

"I can tell you what it is." I loaded up another magazine. "It's our target."

"Are you sure you want to continue, Captain?" Sergeant Misha Parker asked. Parker was a pale-skinned woman with half of her face having been badly damaged by acid but with still-functioning sight. Parker was new to the group but someone I still trusted. She was a survivor of Alpha Squad and came highly recommended from that now-defunct group.

Still, I hated when she questioned my orders. "Yes, Parker. I'm sure."

"I'm ready, Sir. We're all ready," Private Thomas Garcia added, reminding me we were understaffed with only six soldiers. Garcia was a thin but tall man with glasses and a shaved head. He was openly gay, though received no flak from Stephens over it. I suspected that was because they were cousins.

"Speak for yourself, Garcia," Jessica said. "This is weird even by our standards."

Jimmy walked up beside me, pulling out a pair of binoculars

to get a closer look. "Parts of it look Ancient Egyptian and other parts early Byzantine Empire. There are definitely influences of both Mayan and Medieval European architecture as well. A lot more of the influences I can't place though, nor would I want to. For example: the semi-organic motif."

"Thank you, Jimmy." I glared at him.

"You're welcome, Sir."

"That was completely useless." I rolled my eyes.

Jimmy grimaced. "Yes, Sir."

I understood what he was saying, though. The place looked simultaneously influenced by every culture on Earth while being recognizable as none of them. Despite the fact it couldn't have existed before the Rising, it almost seemed to predate humanity. There was a primordial feel to the place. I felt in my bones this building had seen the rise of humanity and would exist well past our extinction. That was impossible, though. Nothing like this had ever been constructed by Pre-Rising mankind, especially not in the middle of the Great Barrier Desert.

Taking out my binoculars, I did a quick survey of the terrain. "I don't see any guards or sentries. But this place is huge, larger than some Old Earth skyscrapers. If the slavers are inside, there could be hundreds of them."

"They're likely to be packing a lot less, Captain." Jessica adjusted her cowboy hat, a relic similar to mine she wore with my blessing. She gave her heavy assault rifle a humorous slap, as if it were a gun from the Old West. Drawing from her courage, Jimmy and Stephens exchanged glances before nodding.

"We should go in," Jimmy said. "This could be a threat to New Arkham and the United States Remnant."

The Remnant consisted of New Arkham and some outlying villages, so saying both was traditional but redundant.

I smiled, proud of Gamma's dedication. "Very well, I suggest we go in quietly and see what we can see."

"Are you sure we shouldn't radio headquarters? The General should know about this," Parker said, looking nervous.

I took back what I'd said about their dedication.

"Kind of defeats the point of a secret mission, doesn't it?" Stephens said, giving her a sideways look.

Parker looked down at the ground.

"Just shut up and keep a look out," I said, feeling strangely drawn to the place. Even more than rescuing the children we'd been sent to find, who were most likely dead, I wanted to go inside. There was a terrible energy bubbling beneath the surface of the Black Cathedral's walls. An energy which, despite how insane it was, felt familiar. Walking forward, my team traveled through the Black Cathedral's broad open doors and we encountered no hostiles.

The insides were no less surreal than the exterior I'd earlier remembered seeing. It was a place bizarre in both subtle and grandiose ways. The doors, for example, were octagonal rather than square, while the columns holding up the domed ceiling above our heads were made of an organic, stone-like coral. The chamber around us was illuminated by a mixture of diffused sunlight streaming in through bulbous windows and free-floating orbs of green crystal. I'd never seen anything like it in my two decades of exploring the Wasteland.

"Fascinating," I could hear Jimmy say behind me.

"Yeah, if you like funhouses," Stephens said.

"I wonder if this is a building belonging to the mythical Pre-Human Elder Things or Yithians," Jimmy said. "It's possible that some force, perhaps tremors from the Rising or deliberate human effort, forced this place up from the underworld where it was buried."

"Jimmy, I love you but maybe you should stay focused," Jessica said. "We're hunting slavers."

"Sorry," Jimmy said, looking uncomfortable as he checked his heavy assault rifle. "I guess I've just always wanted to meet a genuinely intelligent E.B.E.—not the usual psychopathic killers we meet."

"You already know Richard," I said, leaning down to examine the smooth gray stone floor. There were signs of recent passage, human too, by the size and shape of the scuffmarks.

"May I say how uncomfortable I am with the fact the Captain knows a ghoul and hasn't shot him yet?" Stephens said, raising a hand.

"Yes," I said. "You may."

"And if you ever tell anyone about Richard, I'd like to register your remaining life will be measured in minutes," Jessica said, her eyes boring into Stephens. "He's helped us a lot."

"Be quiet, all of you. It's not natural that no one has come out to meet us. Even if the slavers aren't based here, there should be some sign from the inhabitants. The best-case scenario is they're hiding; the worst …" I didn't need to say the rest.

"Orders, Sir?" Jessica's voice became very soft.

"We move in quietly," I said, also lowering my tone. "Nice and quiet. No engaging of targets unless I say so. Our first objective is to establish if the missing children are here. If they are, getting them out becomes our top priority. Stick to the shadows and corners; avoid any and all places where ambushes seem likely. It's possible the slavers saw us coming and moved farther into the temple, so we need to be cautious. Any questions?"

"No, Sir," they all said.

"Good," I said, waving them forward.

Moving deeper into the Black Cathedral, I was immediately struck by how much the place reminded me of a museum. The rooms we passed through were filled with treasures from across the world, most of them Pre-Apocalyptic. It must have taken the owner years to loot enough historical sites and vaults to fill this place.

As we proceeded towards the center, the treasures were gradually replaced by displays of historical sites and battles which grew darker and more perverse with each room visited. The first ones were merely chronicles of humanity's wars but the final ones showed humanity's slaughter by the Great Old Ones.

"Permission to make a comment, Sir," Jessica said to me, hefting her heavy assault rifle before her.

"Granted," I said, trying to hide my disgust.

"The man who owns this place is seriously fucked up," Jessica said.

I had to agree, looking up. There, hanging like we were in some sort of Medieval castle, was a set of green-and-gold banners with the Elder Sign in a circle. The sideways pentagram and eye inside it filled me with a strange sense of unease.

"Take a look at what's hanging over our heads," I said. "Strange to see cultists using that."

"Damned cultists," Stephens grunted. "It's them who brought the Great Old Ones."

"We are pilgrims in an evil land," Jimmy said.

"This is a lot more civilized than your typical set of Wasteland savages," Parker said, looking around. "I mean, who collects antiques after the end of the world?"

"Maybe someone who was around before it," Garcia said.

"Cut the chatter, we've got a job to do," I said. I was feeling uneasy beyond belief. There was a sense of danger in the air. It only grew worse as we reached the central dome of the Black Cathedral, the place where we'd achieve access to the entire building.

The place was almost completely empty, not a soul in sight, which screamed *trap*. Nevertheless, as if supernaturally pulled in a certain direction, we proceeded into the center of the room—ignoring my earlier advice as if all military discipline couldn't hold us back from taking in the sights around us.

The walls depicted a freshly painted mural of particular insanity, showing in blasphemous glory the fall of mankind to the Great Old Ones. It was just one of the hundreds of things on display as the room had artifacts of the various E.B.E. species spread throughout the acre-sized chamber. The centerpiece of the room, however, dwarfed them all. There, one of humanity's greatest foes had been put on display as a trophy.

In the heart of the room, propped up like a skeletal Tyrannosaurus rex, was a collection of bones unlike any other I'd ever seen. Topped with a fish's skull, it was the shape of a man but at least twenty feet tall. An aura of power encircled it, even as it was propped up with wires from the ceiling. At the foot of the great beast was a display stand covered in a little gold plaque reading, HERE LIES DAGON, LEAST OF THE GREAT OLD ONES.

Stephens shook his head. "Seriously, the guy who runs this place is utterly batshit."

"The Wasteland has driven most of humanity's survivors mad," I muttered. "It's why we exist: to protect the Remnant from the rest of them."

Honestly, given how the Council reacted to encountering other groups of survivors, I wasn't sure we were all that much better. Several small nations had emerged on the East Coast, and the

Council was determined to pretend they didn't exist or treat them as hostiles. I'd killed almost as many humans as E.B.E.s during my two decades of service.

Jessica looked at the statue of Dagon with something approaching awe. "Do you think it's really one of the Great Old Ones?"

"If it was one of the Great Old Ones, he wouldn't have been able to kill it." I said coldly, still unnerved by the sight. "It looks like nothing more than a particularly large Deep One. Chicanery, nothing more."

"Chica what now?" Stephens asked.

"It means trickery." Jimmy rolled his eyes. "Seriously, Stephens, you could use a couple more years in Re-education."

"I've got other ways to amuse myself." Stephens chuckled, giving a lewd look towards Jessica and Parker. "If you know what I mean."

"You could never keep up with me, Stephens," Jessica said, surveying the landscape for possible points of entry.

Stephens looked between me and Jimmy. "Aw, I'm just kidding. You girls are like sisters to me."

"That says more about your family than I ever desired to know," Jessica said, snorting. "And we're women, Stephens. Learn to tell the difference and maybe your dating life will improve."

Parker smiled at that.

So did I.

It was weird how casual everyone was being in a potential combat zone. That was when I realized what was going on: someone was asserting a psychic influence over us—forcing us to relax. Martha had tried it during a few arguments over the years, only managing to piss me off more whenever she did it.

"Everyone, shake it off," I said, trying to warn everyone. "It's too quiet for this not to be an ambush."

"You just had to say it's too quiet, didn't you?" Jessica grunted.

"Sorry."

That was when a dozen secret doors opened and a hundred armed Cthulhu cultists poured out.

CHAPTER TWO

The Cthulhu cultists were a motley band of half-deranged psychotics, but Earth had never seen more fearless warriors. Armed with meat cleavers, baseball bats, makeshift spears, and whatever firearms they'd scavenged, the cultists were more of a mob than an army. Their clothing and armor was as eclectic as their weapons, consisting primarily of scavenged sports equipment and bits of scrap metal sewn together.

There were no tactics or strategy to their assault, only sheer numbers driven by mindless ferocity. I had heard legends the cults of Cthulhu used a combination of drugs and ecstatic rituals to drive all fear of death from their warriors. Seeing the way they whooped, hallowed, and rushed eagerly into the jaws of death, I believed it.

"Humans forever!" Stephens shouted one of the traditional battle cries of the R&E Rangers, cutting down several cultists with his heavy assault rifle as we sought cover. Overturning museum cases and knocking down the statue of Dagon, we brought the full force of our weapons to bear.

The first part of the battle, if you could call it a battle, was little more than a slaughter. No matter how brave a warrior, how skilled, he was nothing more than a target for even a moderately skilled soldier armed with automatic weapons. We did not indiscriminately fire into their ranks but selected our targets.

It was a slight delay, one many commanders wouldn't have encouraged their troopers to make, but one I'd drilled my team for often. This method, nicknamed "crowd control" by Stephens, guaranteed a kill every time. It slowed down the enemies' charge and filled the room with corpses.

The tide of Cthulhu cultists managed to use weight of numbers to their advantage, however, getting close enough to engage us in hand-to-hand combat. Despite their reckless courage, this too failed them. Each of my team was more than a match for any five of the barbarians surrounding us. The trick was only engaging that many at a time, an increasing prospect as they came after us in ever-greater numbers.

"For the glory of great Cthul—" one tomahawk-wielding, punk-haired lunatic shouted, wearing an amulet which caused bullets to bounce right off of him like raindrops. He managed to charge right up to Jessica and swing at her head. She promptly clocked him across the face with the butt of her gun before shooting him on the ground and returning to fire into the crowd.

I was impressed.

"These guys are idiots!" Parker shouted so everyone could hear her over all the automatic gunfire.

Jessica pulled close to cover me. "How you handling yourself, Captain?"

"I've been better!" I shouted, cutting down more of the enemy combatants trying to swarm us. When one got close enough to stab me, I smashed his face in with the butt of my gun and shot him with the last rounds of my magazine. Reloading, I brought to bear my weapon to mow down an additional five charging me.

"Fair enough!" Jessica laughed before slamming her machete's edge square into one of the cultists' heads before blasting another in the chest. Some might have called it psychotic glee, but I called it excellent soldiery.

In the Wasteland, you had to train your men to enjoy combat—to love it—in order to survive. I often wondered whether it was the right thing to do, but it was too late to change anything now. I, too, had been trained to get a thrill from battle.

Parker and Garcia covered each other and the two of them made sure none of the Cthulhu cultists got anywhere near as close as the one Jessica had to take down. Their style of fighting was different than the others as they focused on three-round bursts. Stephens and Jimmy fought side by side, the two ignoring their usual belligerence to concentrate on the enemy. By the end of five bloody minutes, both men had saved each other's life a dozen times.

Our caution in bringing so much equipment proved well

justified, as the extra ammunition proved the difference between life and death. Corpses were strewn across the ground by the dozens, some of them having fallen in piles as the horde kept coming over their own dead.

The battle was wearing but, exhausted as we might be, we emerged victorious in that particular struggle. Not a single Cthulhu cultist chose to flee but we'd annihilated them nevertheless, all without a single casualty. Even by Ranger standards, it had been a tremendous victory.

"Well, that was anticlimactic," Jimmy said, kicking a cultist's corpse. "They just ran to their deaths."

"Another triumph for New Arkham, freedom, and superior firepower," Stephens said, giving his rifle a kiss.

"Do you think it's over?" Jessica stared across the battlefield, looking at the corpses of well over a hundred slavers littering the ground. She visibly winced at the battle damage done to several of the display cases, the artifacts inside having been destroyed by gunfire or grenades.

"No," I said under my breath. "No I don't."

The assault by the Cthulhu cultists had been too crude for the mastermind we were investigating. He or she had plotted the removal of hundreds of children from dozens of settlements. His or her minions had done so in an efficient, methodical, and thoroughly well-planned manner. This, by contrast, was the work of someone with no concept whatsoever of strategy.

"Even if we've destroyed the bulk of their fighting force, several hundred children were reported missing. They have to be here somewhere," I said, looking around the room. The place had been devastated by our battle, symbolized by Dagon's bones being scattered about like so much refuse. "It's our duty as members of the United States Remnant to secure their release."

"Yeah, assuming any of the kids are still alive. These crazy psychos probably ate them," Stephens muttered, rubbing the back of his head. Despite his words, I could sense the worry in his voice. Stephens wasn't a sociopath and his disdainful treatment of our mission was a way of divorcing himself from the probable fate of those we sought to rescue. At least, that was what I believed. I had faith in him, despite our disagreements.

"Don't even joke about that, Stephens." Jessica looked at him with a disgusted expression on her face.

Stephens, in fact, was not looking at her. Instead, he was staring at a pile of corpses nearby. "Damn, some of those bastards are still alive."

"That's very ... unlikely?" Jimmy started to say before turning his head to the bodies. Then I saw his head tilt in confusion. Following his gaze, I saw the corpses he was looking at were starting to move.

All of them were starting to move.

"Shit!" Parker said, stepping away from them and pointing her gun down at the corpses around her.

"God dammit, West-boys! Shoot 'em in the head!" Stephens shouted, aiming at the various corpses' skulls and unloading with ammunition.

For once, I believed Stephens had the right idea. "Everyone, we've got Reanimated-class undead! I want you all to fall back into a circle with covering fire on their remains. Aim for either the head or the spine!"

"Yes, Sir!" my squad shouted in unison, spraying the rising monsters with bullets. I just prayed it was enough.

The Reanimated, known as "West-boys" in Ranger lingo, were the single most deadly type of undead to emerge in the aftermath of the Rising. I had high enough clearance to know they were an evil the Remnant had brought down on itself. While I was too young to have participated in the fall of New Boston, I knew it had been the Remnant's experiments which had resulted in the Reanimated becoming a self-propagating plague on humanity.

The "Herbert West Formula" created durable, semi-intelligent, and fearless creatures without any sense of morality or restraint. I'd never fought them before, but my grandfather had told me they were several times stronger than the ordinary "zombies" created by Wasteland sorcerers. There was no telling how the lunatic in charge of the Black Cathedral had gotten ahold of it.

"Captain, do we have enough ammunition to kill them all again?" Jessica asked, continuing to fire in short bursts.

"No," I said, solemnly. "We don't."

All around us, the bodies of the Cthulhu cultists began to slowly pick themselves up and retrieve their weapons. Those who had been damaged in their legs moved slowly and awkwardly but the majority moved faster than they did alive. The fact they seemed to ignore gunfire anywhere but the most vital portions of their body made them nearly unstoppable.

We managed to shoot a number of them in the skull and spine before they rose, but there were at least sixty to eighty in front of us by the time we prepared for our exit. Worse, the Reanimated were between us and the entrance, leaving us effectively pinned down.

"Switch to flamer rounds!" I called. We had only one magazine of flamer rounds each, so it was mostly a choice of *when* we were going to use them than *if*. However, fire might give us a short reprieve.

"You got it!" Jessica shouted, firing the bullets that caused the bodies of several charging Reanimated to catch fire. Jimmy and Stephens soon joined in, the flaming corpses coming at us until they collapsed from the nerve damage. The Reanimated who possessed some limited intelligence seemed to back away from the fire, even if only for a few moments. That bought us valuable seconds as I considered my options.

"How many grenades do we have left?" I asked, firing another spray of bullets into the skulls of a half-dozen Reanimated. Their bodies collapsed and caught fire as the undead behind them fell back only to eventually move around them with ruthless determination.

Jimmy and Jessica responded to my question by hurling a pair of grenades into their ranks. The resulting explosion was neither large nor spectacular but it blew several of our opponents to pieces and thinned their ranks enough to give us a little breathing room. Only a little, since the Reanimated were infinitely more dangerous foes than the cultists they'd been but minutes earlier.

"Those were the last of them, Captain!" Jessica said, right before she was bitten on the arm. "Son of a bitch!"

Parker shot the monster before the injury was anything more than a surface wound, Jessica smacking it across the chin with her rifle butt.

"Does that mean she's going to turn!?" Stephens shouted, knocking another Reanimated away with the butt of his rifle before setting it aflame with the explosive ammunition in his gun. Kicking the flaming corpse away from him, Stephens created a protective barrier in front of him. He was surprisingly cunning when he remembered to use his brain.

"No, Stephens," I sighed as we found ourselves pressed against the back of the central chamber. That was when I noticed a grand staircase was now behind us, a huge marble thing decorated with hanging chandeliers which *had simply not been there before.*

Taking a look at it, I shouted over the blare of gunfire, "Well that doesn't look like a trap, does it?"

"What do we do, Captain?" Jessica said, shooting a few of the Reanimated in the legs to slow down the ones behind them. It wouldn't work in the long run but was the only option we had in such tight quarters. With only a few flamer rounds left between us, the Reanimated were going to overwhelm us within moments.

I didn't have a chance to respond before the reanimated corpse of the bullet-immune cultist charged at Parker and then bit into her throat, tearing it out. Parker didn't get a chance to scream before blood sprayed and she went down.

I pulled out a machete my wife had blessed, then charged forward, cutting the corpse's head clean off before ripping away the amulet. The creature fell over in an instant and ceased to move before I tossed away the amulet and jogged back into formation, shooting the entire way.

"Jesus!" Garcia said, right before a Reanimated on the ground grabbed his leg and pulled him to the floor. It crawled up on him and gouged out both his eyes with its thumbs, tearing away his face with its teeth. Jessica managed to shoot it, as did Stephens, but it was a futile gesture since a half-dozen more Reanimated were already upon Garcia, tearing him apart. There was nothing that could be done for him and he had to be abandoned if we were going to survive.

"Up the staircase!" I ordered, sick to my stomach at our losses. "We'll switch to pistols once we reach the top and try to take them out one by one."

"Murderers!" Stephens cried out, tossing his heavy assault rifle on the ground. The last of his flamer ammunition was expended. He then pulled out a refurbished Desert Eagle and started shooting Reanimated after Reanimated in the head. This was a mission of revenge now for my teammate and I worried I'd lost him.

Jimmy was slower getting his pistol, instead getting overwhelmed by a horde of the creatures when his assault rifle ammunition ran out. Stephens didn't hesitate to throw himself into close quarters combat with Jimmy's attackers, firing the gun into their faces at point-blank range.

"No! Stephens … fall back!" I cried out, lifting up my own pistol as I watched Jimmy crawl out from under the mass of reanimated dead. What happened next was bloodcurdling; Stephens was ripped limb from limb as the monsters chopped away at his arms before pulling him to pieces.

"Son of a bitch!" Jimmy coughed, bleeding from the mouth as he crawled on the ground, pulling his own gun out to shoot a few avenging rounds at the individuals murdering his squad mate.

"I said fall back!" I repeated my order. I snapped the neck of a Reanimated coming within inches of me and fired a few shots into the heads of the ones between Jimmy and me. I'd not lost any squad mates since the Color Incident and it was painful to experience it again. Private Stephens hadn't been my favorite trooper but he'd willingly laid down his life for Jimmy. It made me ashamed I'd ever doubted him.

Everyone finally moved back into formation as we were given breathing room by the burning corpses before us. The fire we'd set, plus all the Reanimated we'd shot in the spines, slowed down the thirty or forty undead remaining to give us time to get up the staircase. We'd inflicted massive casualties on them but at a terrible price.

I was first up the stairs, almost to the top, with Jessica behind me. Jimmy trailed behind us, possibly wounded. A number of Reanimated broke through the fiery barrier and charged up at him. Refusing to leave a man behind, I lifted my pistol up and descended the stairs, shooting one after the other in the head. Five were down as Jimmy passed me. I, for a second, thought we were going to make it.

That was when a lone Reanimated assassin at the bottom of the staircase, a woman missing the lower portion of her jaw, lifted a revolver and fired over my head three times. I didn't even see her until it was too late. Clicking off a final round, I sent her spiraling down to the ground where she joined the ranks of her other forever-dead colleagues.

"Captain!" Jessica cried out.

Turning around, I saw Jimmy had been hit by all three rounds in the back of his head. Both of his eyes had been shot through and so had the back of his mouth.

"Dammit!" I spit, knowing we didn't have time to mourn our losses. I'd gotten my entire team killed but forced that thought from my head. I needed to survive and get my sole remaining teammate to safety. I didn't care if I got killed at this point but I had to cling to the idea I could salvage one of my brethren. "Jessica, keep moving up the stairs! We've got to get a move on!"

I didn't have time to say more because black tendrils descended on us both, throwing us to the ground and sinking into our skin like leeches before lifting us into the air. I was able to catch a brief glimpse of their source at the top of the stairs, a figure standing in front of the gigantic blob-like thing producing the tendrils. It was a white-haired man with skin the color of chalk dressed in a dirty suit leftover from centuries past. I recognized him as Alan Ward, my old teacher and one of the last human scientists left on the planet.

What the hell was he doing here?

I didn't have time to think about it before I passed out.

CHAPTER THREE

The first thing I saw when I woke up was a blinding bright light. My mouth was full of saliva and I had a splitting headache. Attempting to move, I found my wrists and feet were tied to the back of a chair.

"Hello?" a soft female voice spoke in my ear. "Are you comfortable?"

I hated it when captors were polite. The memory of my team's death was fresh in my mind and I was tempted to bite at the throat of whoever was holding me. I was still too weak and in shock to respond with anything but the mildest rebuke, though. "Fuck off. You can go to hell for all you've done."

"I'm lucky I don't believe in hell. You're not a prisoner, though, John, at least not of mine. You're also not in enemy hands."

"What?" I blinked, wishing I could see what was going on. "Where am I? Where's Doctor Ward?"

"Doctor Ward hasn't been part of the Remnant for decades."

I spit the saliva out of my mouth on the ground and tried to get my bearings. "I'm confused. I don't know where I am or how I got here."

"Obviously."

The light moved away from my face, revealing I was in one of the Remnant's hospitals. Most certainly *not* the Black Cathedral. I also wasn't wearing the uniform I'd been wearing when I'd been struck by Doctor Ward's magic. That, briefly, filled me with a sense of relief. Then I realized the person holding me was one of the most infamous interrogators in the Remnant and the attire I was wearing was a gray prison jumpsuit.

Dammit, so much for not being a prisoner. Rather than focus

on my circumstances, I instead looked over my captor. If not for who she was, it wouldn't have been an unpleasant sight to look on. Mercury Takahashi was a thirty-something crimson-haired woman wearing a dirt-smudged laboratory coat, slacks, and an old but serviceable green shirt which highlighted a pleasant-looking body. Thin like most of us but not emaciated, Mercury's almond-shaped eyes, dimples, and soft cheekbones made her quite pretty. Supposedly, that only made her more effective at her job.

"Do you remember who I am?" the woman asked, almost sweetly.

"Yes," I answered her.

"Do you know who you are?" Mercury blinked, trying to read my reactions.

It was a strange question; I knew exactly who I was and didn't understand why I shouldn't. "Captain John Henry Booth, United States Remnant Recon and Extermination Ranger, Gamma Squad leader."

A number of other useless details filled my head—like my address and where I'd gone to school. It was like my mind was fact-checking itself. I must have taken a bad blow to the head. I couldn't even remember how I'd gotten here. It was as if there was this terrible *blackness* in the back of my skull and I couldn't face it.

"Correction, John, you *were* a captain." Mercury interrupted. "You were stripped of your rank three days ago. It's 5-27-2137."

A month later.

Jesus.

"No." I stared at her, blinking. "That's not possible."

"You've been found guilty of murder and treason. As for your squad, you killed them."

"I … Jessica too?"

"So, you don't deny it."

"The Black Cathedral killed most of them but … Alan Ward."

"So you mentioned. The former Director of Arcane Studies is the one who killed your squad?"

I nodded, glad she understood. "Yes. He's built some kind of cult in the middle of a temple in the Great Barrier Desert. Actually, it's more like an army that can come back from the dead."

"You mentioned him in your sleep but the Council wasn't

interested in excuses." Mercury almost sounded conciliatory.

The horrible fragmented images continued to intrude on my conscious mind, driving out all else. I saw shambling mounds of rotting flesh, desiccated husks, and vile caricatures of human beings. The kind of creatures people made up legends to explain. The reality was worse than any horror story could begin to convey. I formed my memories together and recalled the Reanimated and our tragic encounter with them but, in the end, couldn't remember what happened next. There were gaps in my memory.

"God Almighty," I whispered, wishing I could clutch my head in horror. The bindings prevented me from doing so, holding me fast despite my struggles against them.

"I'd be careful about calling on gods. You never know what sort of being will answer," Mercury said, walking to a nearby cabinet. She pulled out a syringe and a clear, fluid-filled vial. Mercury proceeded to fill the syringe in her hand with the vial's contents and walked over to inject it into my arm. "This should help you relax. How badly were you injured out there?"

"I don't know," I said, my mouth dry.

The room wasn't very clean: the tile walls were stained a sickly-yellow color, the floors looked like blood was routinely spilled on them, and the paint on the cabinets was peeling. Much of the scientific equipment was old, dating back to the Pre-Rising period. The rest had been constructed from materials dating back to that time. Worst of all, there was a rotting-fish smell to the place, possibly from the experiments they conducted here on E.B.E.s. A horrible sinking sensation filled my chest, wondering whether my loved ones were suffering for this insane accusation. "My family, what about them?"

"Your wife's been reassigned to another spouse and your children re-purposed to other families." Mercury had an almost reassuring smile. "They'll be fine."

I wondered if she was trying to emotionally claw out my guts or if she was just that insensitive. "Thank you."

"Stay focused," Mercury said, dismissing my concerns with a cavalier wave. "Do you remember what happened on your last mission?"

"Some," I said, sighing. "Not enough. I'm not guilty of killing my squad, though."

"I know, John. No one thinks you did. You were a respected war leader and tragedies happened on the battlefield."

"Then *why*?"

"Politics," Mercury said, taking her equipment back to where she'd retrieved it. "No one wants to admit responsibility for losing another squad and your survival would make you a hero or a villain. They chose villain lest you threaten their power base."

It was pathetic. The Council of Leaders was playing games over who got to control one dying city on a dying world. "What about my wife? Did she go along with this? Did she try and fight this?"

Mercury spared me a look of sympathy. "Martha Booth was the first to denounce you. Her transcripts are rather colorful."

I closed my eyes, trying not to cry and just barely succeeded. I'd save my tears for my squad. "I see. When am I to be executed?"

"You've already been executed." Mercury walked over to a nearby desk and pulled out some extra-large black-and-white photos.

Taking the pictures in my tightly bound hands, I looked them over. I was startled by a grisly series of images depicting my trial and execution. The pictures ended in my funeral and cremation. No one attended my funeral but security: an ignominious end for an otherwise exemplary career. She'd clearly gone to elaborate lengths to get me here. "What is this? Who made these?"

Everything was taking on the surreal quality of a nightmare. Just when I thought I couldn't be surprised by this terrible world, it seemed the universe provided another reason why everything was chaos and disorder.

"I paid your guards off in food rations. They probably think I'm going to perform some sort of ghastly experiment on you."

"Are you?" I was strangely calm about all this.

"Of course not." Mercury leaned down and whispered in my ear, her voice gaining a sultry edge to it. "Though I did let it slip I was considering using you for *recreational* purposes."

I raised an eyebrow. The staggering tastelessness on display here made me wonder if she had some form of mental infirmity. "Excuse me?"

Mercury put a hand on the side of her hip, posing for me. "My assigned husband was seventy when I married him. I bet you would be far more entertaining."

"I do not bed murderers." I remembered the horrible time I'd been a prisoner of the Dunwych. "Not willingly."

Mercury straightened her posture, frowning. "It'll be a wonder if you'll ever breed again then, especially where we're going."

"You've lost me." I stared down at my clothes. I would have to get a replacement set if I was going to get out of here. Already, my mind was working on ways of figuring out a plan of escape.

"How familiar are you with the Wasteland?" Mercury asked me, bluntly.

"Very. I'm the best scout we have." *Was* the best scout they *had.*

"That's not what I asked."

"I know the Wasteland I know it well." I answered her again, growing irritated. "I could survive in them indefinitely."

"What about people?" she asked, her tone a little more desperate. "Are there any people outside of the Remnant?"

Her ignorance was quaint really, though I wanted answers. My patience was rapidly drying up. "There are many groups of humans outside of the Remnant."

"Are they tainted?" Mercury's lip actually quivered. "Cannibals? Rapists?"

I wondered what kind of stories she'd been hearing. "There are tainted, cannibals, and rapists amongst them. The majority, however, are simply people. Now what is this about?"

Mercury took a deep breath. "I want you to take me to what passes for civilization."

I stared at her like she was mad. "I am not in the mood for jokes, Doctor."

Mercury clenched her fists. "This is no joke. I need to escape New Arkham and the Remnant. It is no longer safe for me here. I need your help to do it."

"You're the Council's scourge." I shook my head. "Why would they want to get rid of you?"

"No, I *was* their scourge. Something has happened which will change that very soon." Mercury took a deep breath. "I can't go through what I've done to other people."

I had no sympathy. "It is the one comfort of this cold, vast, and unloving universe that it is equally as uncomfortable and horrifying to the terrible as it is to the good. You have earned whatever is done to you."

"No one earns anything. There are survivors and the dead in this world, nothing more." Mercury raised her hand again as if she was going to slap me. "Don't you want to live, John?"

I was still processing the fact Gamma Squad was dead. Parker, Garcia, Stephens, and Jimmy all killed by the living dead. I'd had a responsibility to bring them home safely so they could help one of the last pockets of humanity survive, and I'd gotten them all killed on a fool's errand for a Wasteland tribe.

I deserved to die.

But I needed to get back to the Black Cathedral.

I needed to avenge them.

"Call me Booth. We're not on a first-name basis." Knowing my family would be safer here than out in the Wasteland, I made a decision. "What do I get if I help you to civilization?"

"Saving your life isn't enough?" Mercury asked, looking exasperated.

"From you? No," I said calmly. "I have other concerns than life now."

I'd taken my job in the R&E Rangers as a form of protracted suicide, really. Everyone who went out into the Wasteland made peace with death. Life in New Arkham wasn't a guarantee; at any point our ramshackle civilization could be exterminated by the horrors beyond, but it was more likely to keep you alive than being among those who scouted the surrounding territories.

No, I wasn't afraid of dying here.

Only of leaving my brothers and sisters unavenged.

A human hand had killed them.

Ward.

A man. Not a monster. Something which could be killed.

"You're impossible." Mercury sighed, looking defeated. "I *need* this."

I was surprised by her display of weakness, half-wondering if it was an attempt to emotionally manipulate me. What sort of life did she really think could be found outside in the Wastelands, anyway? It was a rough, brutal, and unforgiving sort of existence, especially for a woman. "Make it worth my while."

Mercury took a deep breath and stared, her voice cracking. "I'll get you guns, ammunition, and a jeep. Is that enough?"

Her desperation surprised me. "How many people said that to you before you killed them?"

"I was chosen for this job, *Booth*. If I hadn't done it, I would have been shot. What would you have done?"

I remembered shooting a fellow trainee for stealing food during Basic. Suddenly, I didn't feel so righteous. "Fine. I'll see you across the desert, past the Dust Zone, away from the mutants, through Ghoul Pass, and up through the shadow of the Great Idols. I'll take you to Kingsport, which is as close to an actual city as probably exists outside of the Remnant's control."

"Thank you. Hopefully, I can find a position there."

"Yes." I sighed. "You're medically trained, aren't you?"

"I was going to be a physician before they assigned me to Research and Interrogation," Mercury said, hopefully.

"Then you won't have to be a prostitute or a slave." I said, harsher than necessary. I didn't want to help her. "After this, we're done. I never want to see you again. You won't want to be around me anyway; I intend to continue to fulfill my duty after my escape."

"Your duty?" The disbelief in Mercury's voice was palpable. "*What* duty?"

"Blood and vengeance."

It was one of the few things left which humanity could purely call its own.

CHAPTER FOUR

Getting out of Mercury's laboratory wasn't difficult. The sun had set over the horizon and I was used to moving in the shadows. In my gray prison fatigues, I was practically invisible against the similarly-colored buildings of the Remnant. There was also the fact that the Remnant's soldiery was used to watching for people trying to break *into* the city as opposed to the reverse. Still, I'd need a good look at just who was doing what if we were to get out of this place.

Once out, I dodged guards and citizens alike until I made my way to the set of cliffs jutting out from the center of New Arkham. The tiny mountains were an aftereffect of the Rising. Whole sections of the globe had been casually upended by the Great Old Ones; ancient cities unearthed from the ground or re-created as human civilizations were erased with the casual ease of scattering a child's building blocks.

Reaching the top of the peak wasn't difficult and I'd scaled it dozens of times. Taking a series of deep breaths, I took a moment to survey my former home. The runways of the former United States Air Force base were covered in hastily constructed bunkers and adobe-esque huts. Its useless traffic control towers served as homes for rich families.

Lights were on all across the makeshift community, television antennas sticking out of the roofs of houses. A series of worn electric fences surrounded New Arkham, each guarded by heavily defended checkpoints. Each layer of the perimeter had its own scrap metal watch towers, gunnery emplacements, and landmines to supplement security. In other words, escape would be difficult.

A familiar voice spoke behind me, almost causing me to fall over the cliff's edge. "I knew you would come up here. It was always your particular form of madness to look down at the human race from above as though you were one of the gods rather than an ant."

Somehow my wife had managed to make it up the side of the cliff without me being alerted to her presence. Even for a psychic that was impressive.

"Martha," I said, turning around. "I didn't expect to see you up here."

"Why? Because you're supposed to be dead or because I testified against you?" Martha asked.

"Both."

"I see," Martha said.

Martha Anne Booth walked easily up the rocky pathway, one I'd only barely managed to navigate. The shadows parted and I got a good look at the woman I'd been married to since I was seventeen. Martha was "touched" by the Great Old Ones but her inhuman traits fell onto the realm of the exotic as opposed to the macabre. Her skin was the color of marble and her hair a shade of silver. Her almond-shaped eyes were her most striking feature, resembling the predatory yellow ovals of a cat. Tonight, she was dressed in the black trench coat of a Loyalty officer, an outfit which reminded me however much I might have once felt for her, her loyalty was foremost to the Council of Leaders.

I looked away from her, shaking my head. "How did you find me?"

"I have my ways."

She was a psychic. Stupid question. "Right."

"Tell me, do you see a future for these people?" Martha asked, gesturing down to the city below.

It was an odd question given what was going on. "No."

"Did you ever?"

"No."

"Yet, you kept fighting for them. Why?"

I shrugged. "Why not?"

"Easier to die."

That was an odd way to deflect a conversation. "That's not in my nature. This is the Great Old Ones' world now. Perhaps it always was, but that doesn't mean I'm going to roll over and let them take from me what little part I've carved for myself."

"Honestly, I doubt they even noticed us when they woke. Earth's governments used nuclear weapons in the first hour of the Rising but they were like raindrops against the Great Old Ones' skin." Martha then switched subjects. "Tell me, what's your next move? Are you going to try and steal away your children? Perhaps ask me to run away with you as well, treason aside?"

"No," I said, thinking about how I'd been a terrible father who'd missed most of their childhood. "I want to be with them badly but the Wasteland is no place for children, even teenagers. The Remnant is a decaying shell of itself but it's still the safest place in the world for a boy and girl."

"And us?" Martha asked.

"That ended a long time ago."

"True," Martha said, her cat-like eyes almost luminescent in the night. "I was asking for your sake."

I shook my head, annoyed with her attitude. Then again, she was a psychic and they rarely were ones for conversation. "Can you at least tell Anita and Gabe I'm not a traitor?"

"Do not worry, I do not intend for them to grow up believing lies about their father. Though, technically, by all accounts you *are* a traitor. You hate everything the Remnant stands for. I'm surprised you made it as far up the ranks as you did."

I ignored her jab, mostly because it was true. "Why did you do it, Martha? You could have kept silent. They wouldn't dare go against you. The Loyalty Division practically worships you."

Martha stared at me in a way which was almost threatening. I was well over six feet tall and she was only midway past five, making her glare almost comical. Yet, looking into those mutant eyes I felt like she might push me over the side of the cliff with her gaze alone.

"John, you wandered in from the Wastelands naked and covered in dried blood. You were babbling in tongues no one recognized and had apparently walked two hundred clicks in a dust storm. No normal man could have survived that."

I blinked at her description, surprised by the new details it brought to my ordeal. "I wandered in naked?"

Strange how that was the part which bothered me.

"Yes." Martha turned to me. "Even if you had explained the

truth of what happened, they would have condemned you. I could no more protect you than I could myself if I rose to your defense. Something supernatural happened out there and the tiniest whiff of it is terrifying to the Council."

"Alright."

Martha wasn't done, however. "Everyone on the Council believes you to be a monster in human guise. Something out there happened to you, something which changed you. Most of the Council believes you to be no longer human. Those who think you are, believe you to be incompetent; a man who got his entire squad killed."

I tried again to remember just what exactly had occurred, to no avail. "I can't tell you what happened on my squad's last mission. It's mostly a blank. All I know is Alan Ward was involved, somehow. He killed them."

"Consider yourself blessed you cannot remember the details." Martha walked over to press a gloved finger against my chest. "Memory loss can often protect us against what the human mind is not equipped to handle. As for Alan Ward, I suggest you drop it. He was the most dangerous man ever produced by the Remnant. He was more of the Old Ones in the end than human."

"No," I said, my voice lowering. "I'm going to kill him."

Slowly. Painfully. Like a human.

"Your squad mates are beyond caring and your own peace of mind would not be helped I'm sure." Martha's gaze softened and she actually looked concerned, her yellow eyes glowing in the night. "Simply assume the Black Soldier took pity on you and guided you back home. It would be better for everyone."

The Black Soldier was a Wasteland scare legend, one my father had passed down to me from his father and so on since the days of the Old World battlefields where it had originated. The Black Soldier wandered the battlefields of the world, granting curses and blessings. Some days I believed in him.

"I can't do that," I said, staring down at the ground.

"Alright. I'd say good luck but there's no such thing anymore."

I stared out past the city into the desert. The Dust Zone surrounding the Remnant stretched on endlessly, lifeless silver particles having replaced whatever had existed before the Rising. There were people beyond the Dust Zone, people who were every bit as deserving of the Remnant's protection as the citizens below me.

"Thanks."

"I have something for you."

"A photograph of the children?" I asked, half-joking. Film was too rare to waste on such things. It had been an extravagance to use it for my execution. "One last kiss?"

Martha paused, as if the idea hadn't even occurred to her. "I suppose those would have been appropriately sentimental, but no. My gifts are a bit more practical."

"Pity."

Reaching into her jacket pocket, Martha removed two objects. The first was a curved golden blade about the size of a Bowie knife. Carved into the sides of its surface were sigils that seemed to twist and turn as if alive. It was a Deep One rune blade, a creation of ancient R'lyehian magic and considered taboo by "civilized" Remnant citizens. I'd seen only a few in my time and they could carve the flesh of E.B.E.s like cheese.

I looked to the second object. It was a little black leather book, roughly the size of the Bible. I doubted it was a copy of that book, however, as my wife was an avowed pagan. There were also numerous hand-written notes and what looked like a couple of folded maps inside. The book smelled of cinnamon and dust, yet there was a strange weight to it as if the paper's very contents were somehow making it heavier.

"Err, thank you." I reluctantly took both objects. Due to its weight, I took the blade to be made of actual gold. "A piece of gold to melt down and trade as well as a book to read on the way to Kingsport. Both should come in handy."

"You will find this book more valuable than gold or iron in the Wasteland." Martha leaned up to kiss me on the cheek. Her lips were warm, the only part of her that wasn't cold as ice. "It is the only one of its kind left here in the Remnant. Study it well and if you remain sane, it might save your life. Indeed, it might if you don't."

Checking the insides, I saw there were numerous illustrations of indescribable entities and non-Euclidean geometric diagrams. It also contained numerous unintelligible scribblings with translations underneath. I recognized a few as ceremonial languages of the people who had emerged from humanity's scattered bands of survivors, but the majority of the material was foreign to me.

"A copy of the *Necronomicon*," Martha said, as if that explained everything. "It holds secrets lost to even the learned."

"I see."

A lovely parting gift if you were a psychopath or a madman. I had no idea what sort of use I'd get out of a grimoire of pagan sorcery. Yet, it was quite possible Martha was right. Wastelanders put stock in such things, and using their own superstitions against them could mean the difference between life and death.

"I imagine your *companion* will also find its writings interesting." Martha said the word companion like she was cursing.

Her reaction surprised me; I'd long thought her uninterested in my dealings with other women. The fact I had no such interest in Doctor Takahashi made it all it all the more ironic. You'd have thought she'd know better since she was capable of reading minds. "Martha … I …"

My hesitant speech didn't last long. An inhuman screech cut through the quiet of the night, the sound loud enough to shatter glass.

"What the?!" I shouted, grabbing hold of my ears as I stared into the sky. There I saw a terrible shape streaking out from the stars, a vision straight from an abyss worse than hell.

Descending upon us was a faceless man-sized beast. Tall and scarecrow-like, it possessed a long black barbed tail and thin membranous wings that stretched out into the night. Its chest was covered with some kind of thick armored exoskeleton, one which should have prevented it from flying in any rational world. Unfortunately, we were living in anything but a rational world.

"Out of the way!" I shouted at the top of my lungs, ignoring all secrecy as I carried my wife from harm.

Rolling across the cliff face's surface, I heard the beast behind me land with a sickening crunch. Despite its size, its claws tore through the stone like wet tissue paper. The being had no expressions to read but I could feel its hostility, the almost incomprehensible aggression radiating from it.

Staring at its faceless form, I struggled to keep my gaze steady.

The entity seemed to occupy space in an impossible manner. As if it was larger and more vast than the thing I saw. I couldn't really describe the sensation. Like a two-dimensional being trying to perceive something with three or four. A mere glance was enough to make me feel sick to my stomach. Whatever it was, this creature did not belong in our reality.

"A nightgaunt," my wife whispered. "Death has come for us."

"I can see that!" I scrambled for some sort of weapon on the ground, a rock if nothing else. The book she'd given me lay a few feet from us, covered in dirt.

My wife picked up the golden blade I'd dropped, and handed it to me. "Take this, John, it can hurt it!"

"A grenade would have been better," I muttered, taking the knife in my hands.

Down below, I heard alarms going off across New Arkham. The creature's cry had probably been heard halfway through the city. Ignoring the effect it would have on my escape, I moved into a combat position, holding the heavy knife across my chest in a close quarters fighting stance. The beast didn't move for a second, keeping an almost wary pose. It was uncharacteristic behavior for a Wasteland predator. They almost uniformly treated human beings as only a little more threatening than mice.

"Move, you bastard," I said through gritted teeth, hearing another terrifying cry tear through the air before the monster jumped at me. Despite its size, it moved more like a cheetah than a man. Yet, I was already prepared for its attack.

I let the force of its body push the knife up into its frame while I let it knock me down the side of the mountainous path I'd climbed. The creature's cries were ear piercing, threatening to deafen me as I felt a thick acidic ichor dribble down onto my hands from where I'd stabbed it. The pain was intense, almost as if my hands were on fire, yet it only inflamed my desire to kill the creature.

Raising my legs and requiring every bit of strength in them, I pushed the creature off me. The monster weighed more than it appeared. The creature howled once more, slid across the stone and stretched out its wings, readying itself to pounce. I didn't give it time to move though, instead suicidally raising my knife to stab the abomination repeatedly across its torso.

The golden blade sliced through the creature's armored exoskeleton as easily as the monster's claws had carved through rock. I slashed over and over, causing the creature's twisted and blackish organs to spill out onto the ground. The monster did not die easily, however, jabbing its talons through my left shoulder as I continued my attack.

Driving the knife into its faceless skull, I felt weak as I heard Martha speak. "John, you need to stop. You're bleeding to death."

Shit.

CHAPTER FIVE

I stared at the gaping wound in my shoulder. The nightgaunt's claws had torn into the skin and muscle beneath. I was bleeding out over the dead abomination's crumpled form. I'd been lucky to take it down with me. Humans were inherently fragile creatures compared to even the weakest of the Great Old Ones' servitors. Killing the beast was little consolation, however. My quest for vengeance was over before it had even begun.

Martha was at my side, her voice filled with surprising concern. "This wasn't supposed to happen."

"I doubt the nightgaunt took that into account." I began coughing, gasping for air. Falling on the ground, I saw my blood start to pool around me. It was a disgusting but familiar sight to me, as I'd seen many soldiers die of injuries far less severe than the one I now had.

In a futile gesture, Martha tried to stem the tide with her hands. "I'm sorry."

They say your life flashes before you just before you die. I wasn't sure if that was true, but I could feel the barriers in my mind falling apart as the life blood freely flowed out of my body. In an instant, I was no longer there on the mountaintops overlooking New Arkham. I was once more with my squad on our final mission. Perhaps it was God's (or whatever was out there's) way of compensating for the fact I was about to die.

My vision started to break up. A shifting torrent of new imagery filled my mind's eye: my pistol emptying its last round into Jimmy's decaying, undead form, the biomass throughout the cathedral coming after me, a thousand tooth-filled mouths, and a wounded Jessica fleeing out of the door as I desperately held my flamethrower in front of me.

"Ah!" I cried out before launching myself upward, waking from my delirium with a staggering pain in my shoulder.

Despite the agony, I was struck by a single fact: Jessica was alive. I couldn't believe it. Then slowly, I realized it was true. She'd gotten out of it. I didn't fail them all. Even more so, I knew what had killed Jimmy and Stephens was in this so-called Black Cathedral. I had to get back there, mortal wound or not. I needed to find the bastards who'd killed them every bit as much as I needed to find Jessica and bring her home.

"John!" I heard Martha's voice shout in my ear. "Can you hear me?"

"Yes." I blinked, shaking off my vision.

Oddly, it didn't feel like I was dying. I'd been wounded before and the sensations that accompanied it were lacking. There was no pain, no feeling of shock, and I honestly felt better than I had in years. Both Mercury and Martha were beside me, the noise of the base's alarms still blaring in the background. The two women were staring at me like I'd just risen from the dead.

Glancing over at the wound on my shoulder, I wasn't sure I blamed them. They'd removed my shirt, so I got a good look at the damage done to me, or to be precise, the *lack* of damage. My wound had completely healed over, a white handprint in place of the gaping hole which had previously been there. It was as if God or an angel had reached down and pulled me up from death. I had to reach over and touch the wound to be sure it was real.

"What *are* you?" Mercury said, her voice filled with a kind of horrified awe.

My wife spoke, too quickly for my comfort. "I used my powers to heal him."

"You *used your powers*?" Mercury stared at her in awe before it turned to anger. "You're lying. If you had that power, it would have been known about by now."

"We all have our secrets," Martha responded before turning back to me. "How are you feeling?"

Where my hands had once been calloused and worn from years of work, they were now crisscrossed with albino-white scars from where the creature's acidic blood had burned me. Yet, before my eyes, the scars were fading and the flesh returning to its original black color. The handprint on my shoulder was also disappearing, becoming only a scarred outline.

"Fine." I continued to stare. "I feel fine."

Was the Council right? Was I a monster?

Had my father been right all along?

No, fuck him.

Damn him forever.

I was better at being a soldier, being human, than he ever was.

He was *not* right.

Martha snapped me out of my fugue with her next words. "The base has been alerted by now. It won't take them long to realize something happened up here. We need to get going."

It sounded like she was trying to get rid of me. I was surprised to find the creature was already gone. The monster had melted away like a bad dream and no trace remained save the gory ichor on my knife.

"I see your point, Martha. "Mercury, do you have our transportation?"

Mercury blinked as if suddenly realizing she was being talked to. "Oh, yes. I have your jeep, a Mark-7 Light Carrier. It's just a few yards down the path. I also requisitioned enough supplies to get us to Kingsport, I think."

"Good." Standing up, I lifted up my arm and gestured for her to go ahead. "I'll meet you there in a moment."

Mercury nodded. Turning around, she jogged toward the nearby jeep. Somehow she'd managed to get the thing up the narrow path along the cliffs. I could barely make its shape out past the bright glare of the headlights.

The Mark-7s were nothing more than glorified composite vehicles made from the parts of non-functioning Pre-Rising automobiles, but they were serviceable enough. I could make out a number of old transportation barrels sitting on the cargo bed. Hopefully, with a little work, we could make the back into a decent smuggling compartment.

Turning back to my wife, I said, "You summoned that thing, didn't you?"

I don't know how, but I knew it to be true. Her guilty expression confirmed my suspicion. Even without magic some psychics had the power to control E.B.E.s. Martha was one of them. She could bring them across the desert or conjure them from thin air. It wasn't an ability the Council of Leaders allowed her to use often, especially since summoning them was different from controlling them. She could, but only with great difficulty.

"I'm sorry." Martha took a deep breath and exhaled. "The nightgaunt proved stronger than I expected."

I held the golden knife underneath her neck, tempted to slit her throat then and there. "You betrayed me once and I was willing to forgive you. I'd be a fool to do it again."

"Yes, you would be." Martha's voice became low and almost resigned. "You're too soft for the Wastelands, John. You know nothing of the true forces which rule the Earth."

"I know enough," I hissed at her, wondering why she thought taunting me was a good idea at this juncture. Did she really think I wouldn't harm her? Dammit, of course she did. She was psychic.

"No, you don't. The curtain you've pulled back opens to a world where rationality has no place, a world where the old rules of morality and physics are just synonyms for delusion. The fact the creature broke free of my control was unexpected, but so was the fact you killed it. You've survived wounds no normal human being could have. Something happened to you in the Wastelands, something that has made you different from other humans."

"I should kill you for just babbling all that nonsense." It wasn't nonsense, of course. I understood what she was saying, I just didn't know how it applied.

"Then do so." Martha's voice was calm, precise, and ordered. "You're important to the world, more important than me. I can't quite divine the reason but you will buy the human race a few more years before its extinction. However, I sense great troubles in your future. I had to see if you were ready for them."

"So you sent a monster to kill me," I grunted, unable to believe what I was thinking. I still kept the knife at her throat despite knowing I couldn't harm her. "Bitch."

"Yes," Martha whispered. I could hear her voice finally crack, the first hints of genuine shame and guilt now audible in her tone. "I did and I am."

Knowing I was incapable of harming her, I lowered the blade.

"You gave two lives to this world with me. I'm sparing you for their sake. Don't make me do it again."

It was an empty threat. We both knew it.

Martha stared at her shoes, shaking her head almost sadly. "That tender heart of yours is going to get you killed."

"Probably." I sighed. Putting the golden knife in my pocket. I put the book she'd given me in the other one. I started to walk to Mercury's jeep. Just bursting out of the front gates would be suicide, so we'd have to use stealth.

A plan was beginning to form in my head when Martha called from behind. "You called a woman's name, Jessica, in your delirium. Is she your lover?"

I paused in mid-step. "No. I care for her but our relationship wasn't like that."

"Do you love her?" Martha asked, her voice a mixture of curiosity and jealousy.

"I loved all my squad."

"Not what I meant."

"Not that way."

"Then I hope you find her." I could hear the reluctance in her voice. "And I hope she's still human."

"Me too."

As I started down the path down the mountain, Martha said, "John, don't forget the *Necronomicon*."

I turned back to her and stared at her. "I'm not going to need a book out there."

"You will," Martha said, sighing. "More than you could possibly imagine. I'm going to call in the troops to look to the Residential Areas for that creature and divert their attention, but you need to know some things before you depart."

"I don't need lessons on how to survive the Wasteland."

"You do about Alan Ward."

I narrowed my eyes. "What do you know?"

Ward had been my teacher, my friend even, before his banishment. I had considered a career in science before diverting to the military after his exile. Martha, however, had been one of his pet projects. It had been because of Alan Ward's influence she and the other "Touched" were employed by the Remnant rather than killed as in the olden days.

"Alan Ward believed as you do that the human race would never reclaim the planet Earth from the Great Old Ones. That we were doomed to die out on a world which was increasingly no longer ours. He, however, believed it did not have to be that way."

"Then he was a fool."

"Was he?" Martha asked. "Doctor Ward believed it was possible to make humanity as the Old Ones did, free and wild and beyond good and evil. With laws and morals thrown aside and all men shouting and killing and reveling in joy. Then the liberated Old Ones would teach them new ways to shout and kill and revel and enjoy themselves, and all the Earth would flame with a holocaust of ecstasy and freedom."

I looked out to the Wasteland beyond. "I think we're already there."

"He wanted to change us, John. To use the blood of Deep Ones, ghouls, and other creatures combined with the science we've learned from Yithians to make us a new humanity. One which was as immortal as the other species and capable of surviving the New Earth. He learned the sorcery of the Dreamlands and spells of that book in your hands to help make it happen."

"What happened?"

"They exiled him for it, obviously. They destroyed his research and kept only those, like myself, who were too useful to discard."

I walked up to her. "All the more reason to track him down and put a bullet in his head."

Martha looked at me. "Actually, I'm arguing you may be the product of his research. If he's continued it, then maybe there is hope for our species."

It was a disgusting accusation, one which was worth killing a man over whether in the Wasteland or in New Arkham. All humanity had left to cling to was an inflated sense of genetic purity. My ancestors had no trace of monster running through their veins and the accusation of such thrown at my mother was enough to get my father to kill her before trying to kill me. Martha knew how hurtful such an accusation would be to me but she'd thrown it in my face anyway.

Harlot.

Witch.

Abomination.

I stared at her, opened my mouth, closed my right fist, then looked away. “I don’t think we’re going to see each other again.”

I walked away.

Then I heard her chuckle. “Never say never, John.”

CHAPTER SIX

The entire base was on high alert, the sound of klaxon horns audible across the city. Guards were probably combing the city up and down for the nightgaunt. It was a justifiable concern but couldn't have come at a worse time. Eventually, no matter how good I was at hiding, they'd find me. Our only option was to escape *now* and I'd hastily laid out a simple but time-honored plan to get us out of the city.

I was lying in the back of Mercury's jeep underneath a makeshift false bottom. Above that was a collection of waste barrels carrying food and water amongst other supplies. It wasn't elaborate camouflage but there was elegance in simplicity. Focusing my attention on our escape allowed me to put the incident with Martha behind me, at least for the time being.

"Let's just hope the guards are as corrupt and inefficient as I remember back when I was a grunt," I muttered and sucked in my breath, as we pulled to a stop. Everything would depend on Mercury's ability to talk herself past the gate.

If worse came to worst, we could probably make a break for it by shooting our way past the perimeter guards, but I didn't relish the prospect. These soldiers were my family, after all. Still, it was *possible* we could fight our way out if that became necessary. Beside me, in the smuggling compartment, was a small arsenal. There was a heavy assault rifle, grenades, pistols, and plenty of ammunition. Mercury had done extremely well in arming us for our journey, I gave her that much.

I stopped strategizing when I heard a guard speak, signaling the most important part of our escape had begun. "Hello, Doctor Takahashi, what are you doing out here?"

"I'm transporting hazardous biological waste out of the base," Mercury said, responding with a smooth confidence.

"What?" The guard asked in disgust. "You're kidding."

"I never kid about my work. It contains E.B.E. corpses and human testing remains." Mercury maintained her chipper attitude, probably unnerving the men further. "You know, the usual."

"Doctor Takahashi, the base is on alert. There's a possible E.B.E. incursion. We can't let you out when we're still searching for it. It'd be too risky." The guard had adopted an almost flattering tone, probably hoping to kiss up to someone close to the Council of Leaders. Apparently, whatever was driving her to flee from the Remnant wasn't common knowledge yet.

Mercury didn't miss a beat, reacting as if it was just another night at the office. "That's why I'm moving the barrels outside of the base. It's possible the creature is being attracted by biohazardous material's scent. I'm going to observe whether or not they attempt to follow the trail I'm leaving."

As lies went, it seemed pretty safe. After all, what did the average soldier know of the habits of E.B.E. hunts? I barely knew anything and I had clocked more combat time with them than anyone.

"Ma'am, we're going to have to inspect these barrels." I could hear the disgust in the guardsman's voice.

"That's certainly your prerogative. Have you had all your shots?" Mercury had that same pleasant tone to her voice she'd used when speaking to me. It was the kind of tenor which had probably broken a dozen or more hardened soldiers during interrogation.

"Shots?" I could hear the bewilderment in the guardsman's voice.

"Vaccinations against mutation and contamination when handling hazardous materials, of course," Mercury said, sounding almost bored. "You don't want to be touching this stuff unless you've had them. Not unless you want a couple of extra fingers or eyes."

"Ugh. Just go," the guardsman said, disgusted.

With the screech and rumble of the East Gate sliding open, I felt a mixture of relief and annoyance: relief at our successful escape and annoyance at the amateur behavior of the guardsman. It was a shameful day for the Remnant guard, arguably for the armed forces as a whole. Still, I held my breath until we passed the remaining checkpoints and started traveling across the terrain outside the base.

About ten clicks later, I felt the jeep pull to a stop. Seconds later, I heard Mercury laboring to remove the barrels above me. Grunting and breathing heavily, she removed them one by one. Mercury wasn't a particularly strong woman, so I had to admire the speed with which she worked.

Within minutes, the barrels had been removed and I pushed the plywood cover away. Mercury stood above me, wearing an outfit I hadn't had time to appreciate earlier. Mercury had changed out of her dirty laboratory coat into a pair of khaki pants and a plain white button-down shirt. A red scarf was tied around her neck, accenting her hair and face. Her attire was more suited to an afternoon's work in the sun than traveling across the Wasteland. Still, I couldn't really blame her since she had almost no survival experience. It was up to me to get her to her destination.

"Thank you," I said sincerely. Getting away from the Remnant was like a great weight being lifted off my back. "I wouldn't have been able to escape without you." As much as I held nothing but contempt for her past actions, I did owe her my life.

Mercury, however, didn't seem to be paying attention. Her gaze was squarely focused on my bare chest. Whether from sexual attraction or because she was looking at my unnaturally healed wound was anyone's guess.

"Are you alright?" Mercury whispered, raising her hand to my shoulder.

I took her hand from my shoulder. "The wound is gone but I feel queasy, like the insides of my body are burning."

I rubbed the handprint scars left behind by my unnatural healing. Disturbingly, my own hand fit into the print perfectly. I briefly tried to think about possible explanations before realizing I didn't have enough information to start guessing.

Stepping out of the jeep, I took in the vastness of the desert around me. The terrain outside of New Arkham was a bleak, dusty, and cold ruin of an environment, with many small mountains torn up by the Great Old Ones' passage. The moon was high in the sky, stained red and no longer an object familiar to men of every age, as huge chunks of its surface were now missing. Sometimes, I wondered what it must have been like to live in a world in which some things seemed eternal.

A few albino rats with deformed heads crawled across the sands beside us. They were one of the many new animals which had emerged on Post-Apocalyptic Earth. Most normal animals had died in the ensuing disasters, with the survivors transformed forever. Others seemingly hailed from whatever world the Great Old Ones originally hailed, having slumbered beside them. It made the resulting ecology ... interesting to say the least.

"I'm sorry," Mercury said, reaching into the back of the truck and pulling out a First Aid kit. "I've packed a lot of painkillers. I figured they'd help with the locals."

"Thinking of becoming a drug dealer?"

"Yes."

"Good idea."

Mercury sighed, sticking me in the bicep with her hypodermic. "Not primarily, though. I intend to use my knowledge for the betterment of mankind."

Flexing my arm a few times, I sighed. "If you think it'll help. Humanity is in its final hour. We only have a few generations left before it's all gone."

"I don't believe that," Mercury said. "I think we'll eventually claw our way back to a place on the midsection of the food chain, if not the top. Ants survived in a world with humans, we can survive in a world with the Great Old Ones."

It was strange to have this conversation now, especially after having a similar one with Martha less than an hour ago, but I could tell Mercury was uneasy about entering the Wasteland. She wanted to believe there was hope.

I wished I still did.

"We should go now," I said.

"I'm sorry for offending you," Mercury said. "Here, have a fresh suit of clothes. Your others are still, well, blood soaked."

It was a pair of jeans and a military-issue gray shirt. "Thank you. You're surprisingly nice for a torturer."

Mercury's eyes narrowed. "I didn't choose this life. It was chosen for me. What made you want to be a soldier, anyway? The glamour and glory of getting slaughtered by monsters?"

"Hardly," I said, reluctantly pulling on my new gray shirt. "It was mostly because of my father, I suppose. I wanted to prove myself worthy of his legacy."

"Your father who tried to kill you?" If there was any doubt that tact was not one of Doctor Takahashi's virtues, it was laid to rest.

"Yes." I answered her question, savoring the clean desert air around us. "I just always wanted to make him proud. I admit, though, there was also my desire to spite him. Becoming an R&E Ranger allowed me to illustrate who the better man was."

"He wasn't your biological father, you know. It was in your file." Mercury talked like her bringing it up was the most normal thing in the world.

"I know," I said, wondering where she got off thinking this was an appropriate topic for us to discuss.

"Sorry. Do you know who your real father is?" Mercury asked almost immediately thereafter, apparently having no concept of privacy. "I mean, did you ever try to find him?"

"My real father is Marcus Booth," I snapped, a little too harshly. "He deserves that title as opposed to the bastard who slept with my mother." Though, technically, I supposed it was I who was the bastard.

"Again, sorry." Mercury raised her hands defensively. "I didn't mean to pry."

"You're failing miserably." Closing my eyes, I shook my head. "It's alright, really. It's an old pain, but one that has never entirely healed."

"I was pulled out of class when I was barely an adult to become a torturer, Booth." Mercury bit her lip, her voice having the same twinge of desperation she had earlier. "I can barely remember what normal human reaction is sometimes. My husband was certainly no help there. The only reason I married him was because the whole selection process is fixed."

That was one of the more poorly kept secrets of the Remnant. Old and powerful families could select the best mates for their children and themselves. Politicians, especially, got the most attractive spouses available. In a way, I'd been lucky to end up with Martha instead of a seventy-two-year-old Councilwoman.

"You rescued me, *Mercury*," I said. I reluctantly used her first name instead of her title. "I owe you my life. That doesn't mean we're going to become friends on this trip. I have … other concerns which will take me away thereafter. We should probably avoid getting to know one another. Keep things professional."

Mercury lowered her gaze. "Fine. If that's the way you want to be, we'll just sit here in total silence."

I stepped into the driver's seat of the jeep. "Good."

Mercury took a seat beside me, leaving behind my dirty clothes in the middle of the desert as we started off once more toward our destination. Noticing her miserable expression, I decided to speak to her. It was the least I could do, after all.

"Alright, we can talk. Just not about my past."

"Good," Mercury said. "Tell me about Kingsport. What's it like?"

"I have no idea." I admitted, smiling at my little bit of misdirection.

"What?" I could hear her enthusiasm deflate in an instant. "You said you could lead me there!"

"I can. I didn't say I'd actually been there, though," I said, a wide grin on my face.

Mercury looked stunned by my words. "You bastard!"

Remembering our earlier conversation about my parentage, I said, "That would be literally true, yes."

Mercury cursed up a storm thereafter.

I chuckled and pulled the jeep to a stop to take stock of our situation. The sun might come up in a few hours, or the night might last another ten. Night and day no longer functioned as they used to, the nature of reality having fundamentally changed with the Great Old Ones' rising, but the darkness was our friend.

The Remnant would undoubtedly send someone after us; the loss of a military-grade jeep was too great for them not to. However, they would hesitate to do so in total darkness. The Council of Leaders' arrogance extended only so far when regarding the dangers of the Wasteland. As long as only the stars and moon illuminated our path, we could travel in relative safety.

"So you mean you've never actually been?" Mercury was still having difficulty wrapping her head around the fact she'd been tricked. "You played me?"

"That would be correct," I said as I pulled out a pair of

goggle-equipped masks from the glove compartment and tossed her one. "Here, put this on."

"What's this?" Mercury stared at it blankly.

"A dust mask," I replied nonchalantly before affixing mine. "They're standard issue for R&E Rangers and scavengers. We'll need to get proper coverings for the rest of our bodies before we get too far out into the desert. We don't want to be caught in a wind storm unprotected."

"Oh." She looked at the hideous thing before reluctantly putting it on. Her voice was slightly lower once it was firmly affixed to her face. "Why the deception? You could have told me about a dozen other locations instead."

I was tempted to say, *because you had me tied to a chair where I was at your mercy.* Instead, I just pulled my dust mask on with one hand and said, "I didn't lie to you. I've done reconnaissance of the city's exterior and I've spoken to a number of its citizens. I just neglected to tell you I've never actually been inside the city limits."

The truth was the Council of Leaders had been less than pleased to discover Kingsport was a thriving community with a population rivaling New Arkham's. They'd suppressed the information and there'd even been talk of war. Their ridiculous overreaction had been one of the major reasons I'd lost faith in the Council. What sort of leaders felt more threatened by their fellow humans than E.B.E.s?

"What *do* you know about Kingsport, then?" Mercury was trying to hide her annoyance, which wasn't difficult since the dust mask obscured most of her features, presenting only leather, rubber, and a pair of glowing green lenses. The mask's night vision would provide us with additional visibility while we made our trek across the desert.

"It's a rebuilt city. The original populace died of war, plague, famine, and all the other usual ailments that followed the Rising. However, a number of enterprising warlords took over the ruins and fortified them. Somehow, they managed to regain electricity and other technological marvels. Strange lights constantly blink over the city, hence the name. It's a place of cults, commerce, gambling, prostitution, science, slavery, and trade."

"That's quite an assortment." Mercury whistled, staring into the night, though that just might have been the goggles. "Are you sure this is the best place to take me?"

"I can always take you back to New Arkham." I gestured with the wheel, briefly turning it as we passed over a sand dune.

"No!" Mercury pointed at me, her eyes blazing. "Don't even *joke* about that, Booth."

Her reaction was a bit extreme for a woman who had, until recently, been one of the most securely placed citizens in New Arkham. "Alright."

"Will we get there tonight?" I could hear the anticipation in her voice; despite everything, she was excited about getting away from the Remnant. I wished I shared her enthusiasm.

"Not a chance." I said, my voice sounding somewhat sinister through the re-breather attached to the part of the mask near my chin. "The solar cells won't hold out until then. Besides, we have to take our journey slow through infested areas. They're too dangerous to go through at top speed. We'd run the risk of bandits, mutated desert predators, or voracious E.B.E.s."

"Oh. Couldn't we just outrun them?"

"No," I replied, unhappy with an untrained civilian at my side. "Not the ones I know. Don't worry, we won't be camping out in the middle of the Wasteland. If our battery holds out, I'll get us to Scrapyard before morning."

"Scrapyard?" She turned her head to stare out into the desert. "Did all naming convention go out the window when the world ended?"

"It's a scavengers' village, just outside the desert. You'll love it," I replied, grinning under my mask. I was actually sure she'd hate the tough but insular community. "It's between Mud Flats and Shit Town in Ghoul Pass."

"You're making that up."

"I wish I was."

"Why there?"

"It's a good place. I admit, though, I'm going there for another reason."

"Which is?"

"I need to consult with a ghoul."

CHAPTER SEVEN

"You know a ghoul?" Mercury asked, sheer disbelief in her voice. "Like a dog-headed, baby-stealing, flesh-eating, ghoul?"

"I don't think Richard does any of those things. He is dog-headed, though."

Ghouls were one of the largest near-human species which inhabited the world we now lived in. They were a divergent race from humanity, having interbred with things from other worlds or been altered by them, so they were immortal and possessed powers akin to a werewolf (albeit never changed shape). They knew many things about the Great Old Ones and were not hostile to humanity.

They did, of course, eat dead human bodies but that was because fresh meat was hard to obtain nowadays. At least, that was the argument Richard put forth. New Arkham's other soldiers killed any ghouls they encountered, which wasn't many or their race would have long since destroyed us. My friendship with Richard, by contrast, had yielded many dividends.

"It has a name?" Her tone changed to one of complete disgust.

"*He* has a name," I corrected her. "Richard Allan Jameson. Richard grew up human but changed when he reached adulthood. A changeling."

Sometimes ghouls kidnapped human children, raised them as their own, and then sent them out to serve as agents among us. The ghoul children they left appeared as human until their mid-thirties. It was paranoia-inducing to say the least, as something about their instincts always won in the end.

"Booth, you realize knowing an E.B.E. on a personal level is treason." She might as well have been reminding me water was wet.

"Good thing I'm already a traitor."

Mercury was silent for a long time thereafter. Curiosity eventually won out over disgust, however. "So what's he like?"

"He's a mechanic who likes music from the Pre-Rising era and loud Hawaiian shirts." I leaned back in the jeep's artificial leather seats, feeling the worn springs beneath.

Mercury blinked twice. "Uh-huh."

I paused, wondering how to explain my friend in a manner that would be believed. "You'll meet him soon enough. The people of Scrapyard have a cordial relationship with the ghouls. They don't bother them, and the ghouls don't eat anybody who isn't already dead."

"Charming," Mercury said, looking disgusted.

"I've seen worse arrangements." I was serious. People did what they had to do to survive, no matter how personally distasteful. I was no fan of the ghouls but their relationship with Scrapyard was less exploitative than most. "In any case, Richard is a mystic of sorts. If anyone can help me find out if Jessica is still alive and what happened to my squad in the Black Cathedral, it's him."

"The Hawaiian-shirt-wearing ghoul." Mercury repeated my description like she hoped it would sound less insane the second time around.

"The Hawaiian-shirt-wearing ghoul," I repeated. It didn't sound any less crazy the third time around.

Mercury paused, turning her attention back to the road. "What's Hawaii?"

"Some sort of Pre-Rising island paradise." I'd seen a picture of it once. "The men and women wore flower necklaces."

"I've never been to an island," Mercury said, clearly realizing there wasn't much left to talk about in this particular conversation.

"Neither have I," I replied, staring out into the Wasteland. We'd finally come out of the Dust Zone and for that I was tremendously grateful.

The land outside of the Dust Zone wasn't much better but it was slightly less hellish. Brownish grass and sickly yellow-looking cacti dotted the landscape along with the occasional mutated animal. Doctor Takahashi took a particular interest in a two-headed-coyote pack that hunted a hairless rabbit litter.

Surprisingly, we didn't have any conflict with bandits or hostile nonhumans along the way. The way was unusually clear, especially for this time of year.

Eventually, we started coming across ruins. Ancient dilapidated structures once inhabited by Pre-Rising humanity. They were an inescapable part of any Wasteland journey. Most Recon and Extermination Rangers cut their teeth on these particular ruins, looking for mutant stragglers or bandits hoping to intercept Remnant convoys.

These structures, which included everything from gas stations to schools, were a mixed sight. Most were half-collapsed at best. Others were eerily perfect, as if their owners had just stepped out for the night. Driving past them on decaying roads and shattered streets was always a sobering experience, however. Everywhere were reminders of the days when humanity had been great and powerful.

A couple of ruined towns we passed showed signs of the most insidious of fates to befall Old Earth humans: becoming *tainted*. These places still stank of rotting flesh and unnatural matter a century after terrifying mutations had taken their citizens. Their buildings showed signs of having been rebuilt with *unclean* materials—human bones and substances grown from the corpses of otherworldly monsters.

Thankfully, they were almost certainly uninhabited. The Remnant had slaughtered their residents in my grandfather's time, leaving nothing alive which could remotely be called inhuman. Intelligent Mutants were not necessarily evil but a vast number of them were unable to handle their transformation—becoming enemies to humanity and everything else that lived. We had enough problems without having to deal with them.

We were passing through the remains of something called a suburb, a seemingly endless row of identical houses each shattered in a different way, when Mercury asked me a strange question. "Booth, do you really think we don't have a chance of making it?"

"I wouldn't be taking you if I didn't think we'd get there."

"No. I mean the Rising." Mercury stared at the horizon as a glint of light began peering over the edges. The sun was rising in the east, on time for once.

"We already survived the Rising," I muttered. "The fact we're here is proof enough of that."

"This isn't surviving. This is slowly dying out." She gestured toward a billboard, still legible despite all odds. It said, "WELCOME TO BLOCK SPRINGS: A MODEL COMMUNITY."

"I think we're doomed, yes." It wasn't something I liked admitting but I wasn't going to shy away from the facts either.

"I was an interrogator, John. I can tell when you're lying. What are you hiding?"

I remembered Martha's words about Doctor Ward's experiments and couldn't help but wonder if they were true. Had he discovered some way to change humanity into something which could survive? The West-Boys were nothing more than Reanimated cannon fodder but I'd survived the nightgaunt. What if he could save us? My men would have willingly died for something like that but I couldn't bring myself to care. I wanted to kill him and the fact it would save the human race was meaningless to that fact. God, was this why we were doomed?

"I think we *could* survive," I said, clenching my teeth. "I just question whether the price would be our humanity."

"I see," Mercury said.

"You asked."

"I did, didn't I? Let's move on. How many ruins are like this?" Mercury asked, thankfully distracting me from that line of thought.

"You get used to seeing them after a while," I lied again. "You shouldn't worry so much about it."

"If I don't worry about it then who will?" Mercury said.

She had a point.

The car then passed through an old half-ruined tunnel jutting out of a set of copper cliffs. The moment we exited the other side, I lightly applied the brakes. We were arriving at our destination sooner than we should have. What lay beyond was gorgeous.

Stretching before us was Ghoul Pass, a place whose name did not encapsulate its loveliness. The canyon in which it rested was huge, stretching outward for at least a mile and a length closer to twenty. Far below in the valley, created by some Great Old Ones' passage, were trees. Not the sickly brown or leafless things that sometimes clung to life in the Wasteland, but gorgeous green things that stretched up into the air in defiance of the world's end. A few trails of smoke emerged from the villages inside the valley, tiny enclaves of man in the otherwise wilderness-filled enclosure.

Mercury's mouth hung open in awe. "I don't believe it. It's … dreamlike."

"Dreams live in this world," I said, agreeing with her. "For better or worse."

"I've never seen so much green in my life," Mercury said.

I rapidly put our vehicle in park and watched her step out to look over the cliff's edge into the valley before.

"People live there?" Mercury asked.

"Yes." I nodded, getting out of the car. "They're a vassal state of the Dunwych tribes to the East. I don't approve of them entirely. Their rites to their gods can get a little extreme. However, they're overall a very ecological and self-sufficient people."

In fact, I had a very complicated relationship with the Dunwych. They'd held me prisoner for months and I'd learned to both respect and loathe them since they'd tried to make me one of them with the threat of death hanging over my head if I refused. I'd been forced to comply with the desires of their priestesses, forced to kill their enemies, and forced to put my mind so deep into their mindset I sometimes forgot I hated them. I'd managed to get away and back to New Arkham but the consequences still haunted me.

"There's so much *life*," Mercury whispered.

"Yes." I took position beside her, having picked up a pair of binoculars before exiting the jeep. Removing my dust mask, I slid it into my pocket before scanning the horizon. "They've already started planting the seeds of their trees beyond the borders of the valley. Something about the valley's foliage is remarkably durable. They attribute it to the blessings of their goddess Shub-Niggurath."

"Finally a god who does something good." Mercury couldn't help but continue to stare at the sight before her. I couldn't really blame her; I'd had much the same reaction when first viewing Ghoul Pass. It existed in defiance of the Rising, showing life continued and would continue to do so in the face of Armageddon. Noticing the intense look on my face, she asked, "What are we looking for?"

"Danger."

"Surely there can't be anything hostile in this place. It's like paradise."

"There are things worse than serpents in this garden," I replied. "The locals were only semi-friendly to my team at the best of times. The only reason we were accepted that much is I had my team offer up sacrifices to Shub-Niggurath."

"Who or what?"

"Don't ask."

Surveying the landscape, I searched for the tiny little paths which existed between the trees. Despite its appearance of being a wild and untamed wilderness, Ghoul Pass was anything but. Its pagan settlers had carefully cultivated it, making it a source of food and protection for its human population. I'd charted every one of the paths for New Arkham, despite knowing they'd never bother to send trade delegations or even attempt to enforce some form of sovereignty over the place.

"Do you see anything?" Mercury asked, impatiently. "Do you think they have apples? I've never had apples. They look delicious in pictures."

"Quiet."

My eyes rested onto an unsettling sight. A caravan of travelers on foot mixed with mutated, splotchy-skinned bears pulling carts was moving down the path from Scrapyard. That wouldn't have drawn much concern if not for the fact that the travelers were heavily armed, tattooed, and deformed bandits flying a gold-and-green banner containing the starfish-like Elder Sign.

The mark of Cthulhu was on several of their animals. It was a strange combination since the Elder Sign was a traditional ward against the Great Old Ones' influence. Were these Ward's people? More of the Reanimation-capable tribesmen? My concern over their paraphernalia vanished when I saw the contents of their carts. The crude vehicles contained cages filled with children, dozens of children. There were a few adults mixed in but most were adolescent or younger.

Leading this dread procession was a priest wearing a homespun robe and a crudely stitched together brown leather mask with tendrils hanging down the front of his face. Riding on the top of a hideous pale horse, the figure held up a staff tipped with a jewel-covered human skull.

"Shit," I cursed.

"What?" Mercury said, "What's going on?"

"Slavers," I practically spit the word out. "Cthulhu worshipers, too."

"What? Them? Fuck."

"Yes," I said.

Mercury had a layman's knowledge of the Wasteland and only clinical knowledge of the Great Old Ones—but everyone knew the name of Cthulhu. Countless cults to the Great Old Ones existed in the Wasteland, but the worst were the devotees of that particular monster.

The cults of Cthulhu engaged in every form of perversity imaginable and claimed to possess supernatural powers of the highest order. All of this despite the fact none of them could produce any evidence that their god even knew they were alive, let alone approved of their actions.

"Damn," Mercury said as I handed her the binoculars. Taking a look at what I'd been gazing at, she sighed. "Poor bastards."

"Not for long." I returned a few moments later, carrying a sniper rifle she'd packed.

"Booth, what the hell are you doing?" Mercury stared at me while I placed the rifle on a tripod over the edge.

"I'm about to snipe someone," I answered, stating the obvious. "Preferably, a lot of someones."

"I can see that," Mercury said, confused. "Why?"

"They're slavers." It should have been answer enough for any rational person. Traffickers and peddlers in flesh were the lowest of the low, below even the fact they were worshipers of the Great Old Ones.

"And?"

"They're *slavers,*" I repeated, a little forcibly. "Deranged cultists, too. The fate that awaits their prisoners if we let them go is nightmarish. You haven't seen true horror until you've seen the aftereffects."

"I've tortured people." Her voice held more than a little hint of scorn. Oddly, her attitude didn't reflect someone genuinely remorseful, which either meant she was a sociopath or she had remarkable skills at compartmentalization. Then again, who was I to judge? I'd done plenty of things to survive in this world. The sounds of tribal peoples' screams as I gunned them down for trying to loot food from New Arkham caravans filled the back of my mind.

Deciding to take Mercury at her word for the time being, I said, "Then I suggest you consider whether or not it's time for you to start paying humanity back for your actions."

Mercury blinked, apparently processing what I just said. "Go kill the bastards."

"Thank you."

I put the leader of the caravan in my sights and proceeded to start shooting.

CHAPTER EIGHT

Sniper training was something every R&E Ranger underwent. Bullets didn't always kill what you faced in the Wasteland but when they did, you wanted to be as far away from your target as possible. The slavers below were, at least at first glance, human. That meant it should have been easy killing them all. Somehow I knew it wasn't going to be.

It went well at first, my first shot going squarely through the lead slaver's masked skull. I then focused on a woman in a leather jacket. She wore a necklace of finger bones, marking her as a trophy taker. She, too, went down easily enough. Following her was a man covered in blood-colored tattoos, sporting a Mohawk, and wearing a belt covered in scalps.

I enjoyed killing them. It made me feel more human.

"This is justice. The only justice which exists in this world. The one I choose to deliver," I said, giving a grim smile as I shot a chubby-looking man who had filed his teeth down to razor-sharp incisors.

"Uh, Booth ..." Mercury leaned down and tapped me on the shoulder. "Something's happening."

"Not now," I said, focusing in on the banner carrier for the slaver gang. He was running around confused, not fully aware of what was going on but desperate to find some cover. Unlike the rest of the gang, he hadn't yet found any. I mercifully relieved him of his life, taking a head shot which sent his body spiraling to the ground.

"Damn, the rest of them are behind their carts and slaves," I grumbled, falling back to find a new firing position. It was unlikely they could hit me from this point, but all of my efforts would be for nothing if they were able to get away with their cargo.

"Booth!" Mercury called out. *"Something's happening!"*

"What?" I looked up at her. That was when I noticed the light was disappearing from the sky. Whereas once there was a clear morning sky, a black set of clouds covered the entirety of the pass now. The air crackled against my face, now charged with static electricity. I knew instantly what was happening: a summoning. Not a small one, like the one my wife had performed, but something *big* from the Dreamlands or a distant world.

Rotating my sniper rifle, I looked through the scope at the chief slaver's corpse. Despite having a visible hole through his head, he'd gotten up off the ground and was chanting. Waving his skull-tipped staff around, I realized I'd underestimated the magic of the Wasteland.

"Bastard," I muttered before snapping the rifle's magazine into place and running back to the jeep. There, I grabbed a case of flamer rounds. They hadn't been all that effective against the Reanimated but they were all I had right now. Reloading, I ran back to where I'd been lying before.

I took position to aim at the magician, intending to finish the job I'd started moments before. The next shot took most of the chief slaver's head off, a second shot hitting him in the heart. From there, the man's body became a mass of fire. As his robes burned off of him, I saw hideous wormlike figures moving in the flames. Whatever it was, it wasn't remotely human. Eventually, the worms collapsed into several disgusting piles and continued to burn. Unfortunately, it was too late to stop whatever the inhuman slaver had been doing earlier.

"Booth, it's still coming!" Mercury shouted. I could hear her scrambling for a weapon in the back.

Spinning around, I saw the ground underneath the jeep begin to crack. The Mark-7 was carelessly thrown to the side as a huge slimy, tapeworm-like creature bashed itself up through the ground. The top of its mouth opened up four separate mandibles to expose the vicious, gaping maw it possessed. I had never known a worm to scream but that's what it did, letting forth a cry into the air. Once it broke loose from the ground, it kept rising until it was close to fifty feet in the air.

"Yeah, that's bad." I made the understatement of the decade, staring up at the creature. I knew instantly what it was, one of the Demon-Beasts of the Abyss Beyond Time, an Earthmover.

I'd seen Earthmovers before. I'd witnessed the mammoth creatures devour whole regions of scrubland, transforming whatever they passed through into empty desert. This particular specimen was only a baby, yet it would destroy all of Ghoul Pass and anything else in the immediate area if it was left unchecked. Even worse would be what happened if it tasted human flesh. Once Earthmovers did, they entered a blood fury not quenched until they were destroyed. Unfortunately, I'd just killed the only person capable of sending the Earthmover back where it came from.

"What's the plan?" Mercury shouted as the creature reared its head and prepared to bring its mouth down upon me. She had a pistol in her hands which, sadly, wasn't going to be of much use. Still, she got points for effort.

"Run away!" I shouted, rushing out of the creature's path, watching it descend on the edge of the cliff and snap it off into the valley below, clearly trying to swallow me whole.

"What!" Mercury shouted, seeking refuge behind the jeep that had just been turned over.

The creature seemed to be disorientated, as much as you might discern the opinions of a slime-covered worm from another reality. That was about my only advantage as the Cthulhu cultists' bullets bounced off against the monster's thick hide. Earthmovers, unfortunately, definitely fit under the category of things bullets didn't affect.

"Running away is the plan!" I shouted as I grabbed Mercury by the arm and ran for the tunnel, watching the Earthmover grab the jeep with its mandibles and push it down its throat. It took only seconds to digest the remains, forcing it down its long tube-like body. The creature was still half-inside the cliff face, either partially still in its own home dimension or burrowed in the ground beneath our feet.

"Yeah, this is bad," I muttered, realizing there was no way to get away from this thing. Earthmovers could be miles in length.

"Oh no," Mercury said, looking at it.

Handing her the sniper rifle, I nodded to her. "Shoot at it!"

"Are you insane?"

"Probably!" I made a running dash to where the jeep had been overturned. A number of items had spilled out of the ground when it was knocked over, valuable items that just might mean our salvation.

Mercury, showing she had courage to face the horrors of the Wasteland, fired repeatedly. It didn't take much skill not to miss such a thing but each shot bounced off against its otherworldly hide. That was expected. I just needed her to distract it while I made a grab for a bandolier of grenades which had fallen nearby. With the creature's attention focused squarely on Mercury, I pulled out a pill, and hurled them all simultaneously at the base of the Earthmover's sixty-foot stalk. They were designed to detonate if one exploded, a feature meant to kill E.B.E.s rather than people. I had about three seconds before it swallowed her whole.

It turned out, I only needed one.

The explosion was tremendous, causing a rumble through its body as bits of slimy flesh were thrown left and right. Six grenades going off more or less at once wasn't enough to kill the thing; instead it just caused it to lose mobility. The mammoth creature fell over the side of the cliff face, its wounded body no longer able to support its weight. Now it was flailing about and doing its best to survive, a futile gesture given how much damage it had sustained. I ran over to Mercury's side and held her steady. She was clutching onto the sniper rifle, still firing from its rifle magazine.

Even wounded, the creature lived several more minutes, finally ceasing its struggles as it bled out from the wounds I'd given it. I couldn't hate the creature. It had been brought here against its will and undoubtedly had been more confused than malicious, yet I wasn't sorry to see it perish. Earthmovers were too powerful to live on the same world as humanity. They belonged in whatever strange and distant realm they had evolved in.

"Is it dead?" Mercury huffed, looking shell-shocked from both her first battle and the appearance of a being far above humanity.

"More likely, it's regenerating back on whatever world it was drawn from. We only saw a small portion of it." I shook my head. "The question concerning me now is whether the slavers are still alive."

Mercury shot me a furious look which was justified since I'd just gotten all of our supplies destroyed. "Who gives a *damn* about the slavers?"

"The slaves," I replied.

I'd always had something of an eerie calm around the monsters of the *Cthulhu Cycle*. Some had speculated that it was because there was something fundamentally wrong with me. Others believed it was a function of humanity finally adapting to the horrors around it, though few others displayed any such inclinations in the Remnant. For me? I believed it was exposure to the blackest parts of humanity as a young child. My father's betrayal had shattered any sense of safety I might have had early on. There was nowhere to go but up.

Mercury took a deep breath, calming her down. "Fine. Go check on your natives."

"Of course," I said, thinking it strange it had only taken a few decades for the Remnant's citizens to start thinking of their fellow Americans as backward primitives unworthy of anything but scorn. That was one area where we were worse than the monsters and far from the last.

Taking the sniper rifle from her hands, I looked through its scope back at the slavers' caravan. I discovered the remaining cultists had fled. I shouldn't have been surprised; seeing their leader killed and the arrival of an Earthmover was probably more than the average cultist of Cthulhu was prepared to deal with.

Leaving Mercury behind me, I started walking down a path carved into the side of the canyon's walls. Hopefully, it would take me directly to the path they'd been traveling. Scattering the cultists wasn't enough; they could always just return later to reclaim their "cargo."

The slaves needed to be returned to their village and the remaining slavers hunted down. If I was going to make a difference in this world, I had to start with the human evils rather than the inhuman ones, mostly because the inhuman ones were too powerful for humanity even at its height.

Hoisting my sniper rifle, more than a little angered I no longer had any of the other weapons we packed, I hoped I wouldn't have to engage any of the slavers at a short distance. The pathway was long and hard but not treacherous, which meant Mercury was able to catch up to me quickly. We were about halfway down when she started talking again.

"That was … interesting," Mercury said, walking close behind me. She seemed almost exhilarated now—which was insane given what the Earthmover could have done to us. "I've seen the Great Old Ones' servant races before, but that was the first time I've seen a genuine extra-dimensional being. That mutant we encountered in the Wasteland was nothing compared to it."

"An E.B.E. is an E.B.E." I muttered the erroneous Remnant adage before using my scope to scan the valley treetops one more time.

If we went any farther down, we'd lose the high ground and any visuals they afforded. I didn't see any of the cultists through the thick foliage, which didn't mean they weren't there. I'd only killed a small portion of the slavers and it wouldn't take more than the element of surprise to return the favor if the survivors came back. Dammit, I hated unknowns.

"So, why did you do it?" Mercury asked, surprising me.

"Do what?" I said, holding my rifle before me as we finally reached the Pass's surface. The trees were less magnificent up close. Instead, they were ominous. Despite the fact the valley's growth was less than a century old, all of the trees looked positively primordial. The tree trunks were twisted and creaked as a wind passed through their leaves.

Most were covered in moss, ignoring the old scout adage it only grew in the North. A few sprouted fruit from their leaves but it was no recognizable human fruit, often resembling some bizarre hybrid between apples and oranges.

"Intervene," Mercury said, trying not to show how the environment affected her. Where I was wary, it was clear everything around her was a source of fascination. She actually paused to walk over and poke a four-foot-tall mushroom, ignoring the fact doing so could be dangerous in the extreme. "I mean, you didn't derive any benefit from it. It also exposes us to considerable danger. Is it because you've made some pact with the locals?"

"It was the right thing to do."

"No, seriously," Mercury said, patting me on the shoulder. "You can tell me."

I remembered briefly being a slave of the Dunwych and the indignities I'd been exposed to. Indignities they'd expected me to be honored by. Mine was an empathy born of shared experience combined with the fact I liked killing. The Remnant also kept slaves, though we called them workers, and I had no true moral high ground. Still, it was these lies which kept the human animal from fully comprehending its true darkness. "I'd rather not talk about it."

Unusual sounds emanated from the surrounding woodland. I'd been in Ghoul Pass on numerous occasions but I'd never entirely trusted the mutated forest. There was an old Wasteland legend the woods had been created through the blessings of Shub-Niggurath, one of their so-called Awakened Gods. Doctor Ward had named her as one of the Great Old Ones. If she had blessed this place, it was touched by forces well above humanity's comprehension.

"If you don't want to, that's your business. Just don't get me killed in the process."

I could tell there was real concern in Mercury's voice. I was a person to her, not a thing which could be casually discarded. It was more empathy than most of my countrymen had been willing to show me. I wondered how she could feel that kind of connection to a person she'd only known a few hours and do the things she'd done as the Remnant's chief torturer. It was a paradox of humanity I hadn't solved.

"Fine," I said. "I'll do my thing and you do yours but I'll make sure you're not killed before I bring you to Kingsport."

"*We're* not killed," she corrected.

"Of course."

Eventually, the two of us managed to find ourselves on the same path the slavers had been walking. There, I saw the remains of the men I'd slain, mixed in with fresh kills. Scattered across the caravan's remains were five or six men slain by spear or ax. The children I'd seen imprisoned were no longer held in cages, but were even now being freed by a pair of individuals I recognized.

The first of them was a brawny man who stood even taller than me, quite the accomplishment since I was considered something of a giant amongst the Remnant's men. Handsome and intelligent-looking, Peter Goodhill had shaved his head since the last time we'd met. His tanned olive skin was also marked with crimson Dunwych tattoos, a Van Dyke mustache adorning his face. It was almost enough to disguise the fact he was a Remnant deserter.

Despite having apparently joined the Dunwych, Peter still looked a great deal like the soldier he'd once been. Wearing camouflage pants but no shirt, a pair of dog tags hanging down from his neck. In his hands was a submachine gun confiscated from one of the dead slavers, making any encounter between us one to handle delicately. In our last meeting, I'd tried to kill him for desertion.

The fact he was still alive was testament to his skills or the fact I hadn't been willing to die to kill him. I honestly wasn't sure who was the better between us. Peter was another one of the Remnant's soldiers who displayed no hesitation in killing or fear of the monsters. Indeed, like me, he was more comfortable with them than with regular humanity. It made his banishment a sick joke as a punishment.

Beside him stood a woman I believed to be one of the most alluring in the world. I was no man attracted to frail weaklings and Katryn's taut yet distinctly feminine body had entranced me from the first moment I'd laid eyes upon her. A true-born Dunwych woman, her skin was bronzed by the Wasteland sun but otherwise Caucasian, while she wore homemade leathers in place of re-stitched Old Earth clothing.

Like Peter, Katryn bore the tattoos of her tribe, though she sported many more. Each marked a particular deed of valor in their Post-Apocalyptic culture. Yet, despite her exotic attire, she bore a stark reminder of the family I'd left behind. Her silvery white hair was the same color as my wife's, hanging down freely over her chest past her breasts.

"I hope you know these people," Mercury said, leaning over.

"That may make things worse," I whispered. "Hello Peter, Katryn."

Mercury blinked. "I wasn't being *literal*."

Katryn's response to my appearance was to draw a knife and throw it at me. I didn't move or react as it buried itself in the tree behind me. Looking at her, I raised an eyebrow. "I see you're still upset about my leaving you after the blood rite."

"If I was still upset, Booth, you would be dead," Katryn said. "You helped us, though, and I am willing to let the past rest."

Katryn had been one of those who had misused me while I had

been a prisoner of the Dunwych. She had thought herself honoring me with her presence. There had been times I had wanted to kill her and would have if not for the fact I had been fascinated by the Wasteland lore she'd taught me. The Dunwych were a subset of humanity far better adapted to this world than the Remnant and I'd used what I'd learned upon my return.

From her tense stance, I imagined it pricked her pride to realize I cared only about her as a resource and no longer could muster the emotion to even hate her. Both hers and Peter's presence here smacked of conspiracy, but for me or something else? Were they plotting some mischief against the Remnant? It was no longer my concern. Only my squad and revenge mattered now.

I would die to kill Ward, not these two.

"John Henry Booth." Peter lifted up his submachine gun, an Uzi variant that had clearly been custom built from a half-dozen other guns. "I should kill you where you stand."

"You can try," I said, nonplussed. If he'd joined the Dunwych then he was subordinate to Katryn now. Their priests held power even greater than their warlords.

"Well, this is a friendly meeting. Are you this popular everywhere?" Mercury asked.

Peter looked at her funny. "Is that who I think it is?"

"Doctor Takahashi." I nodded. "Yes."

Peter smiled in admiration. "A pleasure to meet you, I'm a big fan of your work."

Mercury's expression was even. "That makes one of us."

Peter frowned. "I see."

"Are you going to try to kill us, Peter?" I asked.

"Are you the guy who killed the Earthmover?" Peter looked between us.

"Yes," I said.

"Then no," Peter replied. "Unless Katryn wills it."

Katryn looked at the worms on the ground and stomped on one with her wrapped foot. "Not right now."

"I'm glad that's resolved." I nodded to Katryn before turning to Peter. "What are you doing here?"

"Hunting," Katryn said, staring at me. Her unnatural blue eyes, completely lacking in whites, seemed to look directly into my soul.

"The servants of Dread Kaithooloo came to Scrapyard and killed the Sheriff. They then began burning houses, demanding a dozen children as a tithe. We agreed to go with them as slaves, intending to free them at a later date."

Cthulhu worshipers taking children all but confirmed this was part of the same group we'd tracked to the Black Cathedral. I would have loved to interrogate the surviving slavers, but Katryn had made sure that was impossible. I wasn't entirely displeased with that as I didn't just want Ward dead, I wanted all of his associates killed as well.

Peter kept his machine gun ready. "We broke out of our cage when someone started shooting our captors, including the High Priest. What are you doing here?"

"Passing through." I wrinkled my brow. "I think I may have been tracking these slavers beforehand. I seek the Black Cathedral."

"Why?" Katryn said, her expression revealing nothing.

"To kill everyone inside."

Katryn nodded. "Then our purposes are aligned. I will spare your life until the time we have revenged ourselves on the Necromancer who leads them."

"Good," I said, not trusting her in the slightest. "We have an accord then."

For now.

CHAPTER NINE

Checking the children's health was our first priority. The lives of the next generation being paramount were one of the few areas on which New Arkhamites and Dunwych agreed. A quick examination followed by a short series of questions told me much. They were a mixture of boys and girls of primarily Hispanic descent between the ages of eight and fourteen.

They were all in reasonably good condition, if traumatized. The children had been forcibly separated from their parents at gunpoint and forced to watch a battle. That would leave scars on any psyche. With time and love, however, they would survive. Children were more durable than most people gave them credit for.

Afterward, our group proceeded on foot toward Scrapyard. Katryn and Peter took point while we covered the rear. The children walked in-between us, as safe as they could be given the circumstances. Scrapyard wasn't far but it was a potentially hazardous journey to the unwary. Even in relatively settled woods of Ghoul Pass, there were many dangerous predators and toxic plants.

Mercury was a loud traveler, her feet crunching against the leaves on the ground. The children also moved loudly, signaling our presence to all the individuals around us. Despite that, Katryn was almost completely silent moving through the foliage. Peter and I split the difference, moving as R&E Rangers were trained to do.

Softly.

As we walked, I thought about the slavers' curious choice of prey. For obvious reasons, slavers preferred attractive adults or ones capable of skilled labor. Children were usually taken with their families and sold at a discount, if at all. There were a few groups which bought children, to be raised by communities or sacrificed to the Great Old Ones, but their involvement only raised more questions.

The second issue I had with the situation was Katryn's and Peter's presence. Ghoul Pass was technically under the control of the Dunwych, but their territory was vast—consisting of nearly the entirety of the Eastern Grasslands. The odds of encountering two people I knew well were low. The odds of them being on a quest similar to mine were almost nonexistent. Katryn would call it destiny; I called it suspicious.

"John, can I ask you a question?" Mercury asked.

"Yes?" I sighed, getting used to her inappropriately timed questions.

Mercury leaned up to my ear. "What *the hell* were you thinking?"

"I don't know what you mean." I really didn't. I'd made a lot of recent questionable decisions.

"Taking us into their group." Mercury gestured to Katryn and Peter. "I won't be a Dunwych slave."

"I won't let that happen to you, I promise." I let her fill in the blanks. I would slit her throat before she was taken and go down fighting first before I returned to the life I'd escaped. The Dunwych had not been worse than death, few things were, but I wouldn't let myself be distracted from my quest.

Mercury looked at me like I'd just asked her to leap into a pit of rabid wolves. I was about to say more when my eyes caught glimpse of a colorful feathered serpent, a Coatl, one of the deadliest killers in the Wasteland. Its venom would kill a man instantly, melting him from the inside out.

The creature lowered itself from the top of a branch, ready to pounce on one of the girls in an unnatural display of aggressiveness. Grabbing it by the base of its jaws, I squeezed the animal so tight with my bare hands it couldn't squirm free, then watched it die, before tossing it away.

"Beautiful!" An eleven-year-old, red-haired girl with pale skin stared up at me. I hadn't meant for any of the children to see me handle the danger to them. I feared it would cause a panic. "Where did you learn to do that?"

"Advanced training," I said, seeing the Coatl come back to life then slither away. "What's your name, girl?"

"Jackie. Jackie Howard." The girl smiled, showing her surprisingly prominent teeth. "Are you an R&E Ranger? My Dad told me they were the greatest warriors in the world."

"Something like that," I said, smiling. Miss Howard reminded me of my daughter, Anita. Anita was nearly a woman now, sixteen in January, but she'd always be a little girl in my eyes. I'd missed her last two birthdays. "Don't worry, we'll get you back to your parents."

"My parents are dead." Jackie stared at the ground, her voice strained. "I have no one in Scrapyard."

"I'm sorry," I said, seeing Katryn take us off the path into a denser part of the surrounding woodland. From what I gathered of her position, it would shave considerable time off our journey.

I agreed with her decision. Speed was more important now than comfort, especially with children in our ranks. "Mercury, you have good reason to trust Katryn and Peter as long as we're with them."

It was a lie but I didn't want to offend our temporary allies. The Dunwych were too dangerous an enemy to irritate and I couldn't do harm to Peter as long as he was one of them.

"Why's that?" Mercury huffed, clearly not liking how the power dynamics had shifted in our relationship.

"Because you need me and I can't beat them," I responded. "Weirdness going on with my body aside."

If you could call coming back from the dead weirdness. Perhaps I now had more in common with the Coatl I'd just killed than humanity.

Disturbing thought.

Mercury stared. "I see."

I didn't want to deal with allaying her fears but there was no point in putting it off. "If it makes you feel any better, I can tell you where I met them."

"Will I trust them more?" I could hear the uncertainty in her voice. The encounter with the Earthmover had shaken her, appropriately so. Right now she needed the comfort of a friend. Unfortunately, all she had was me.

"Maybe," I said. "They rescued me from the Color. For some definition of the word rescue."

"The Color?" It was clear she had difficulty processing the concept.

"Yes, the Color, a terrible, indescribable thing from another world. You would think I'd be used to such things but something about it frightened even me." I could still remember the mission in my darkest imaginations. So much horror and death, it was a wonder I was still sane—if I ever was. "It all began about a year ago when a meteor shower struck the city of New Ipswich. Do you remember?"

"Sort of hard to forget, Booth. Every man, woman, child, and dog was killed. Even the plant life was reduced to ash. A whole city gone within hours of the first distress calls," Mercury said, before shaking her head. "That relates to your story?"

"Yes," I said, coldly. "I was there, so was Peter. We were both assigned to the R&E squads sent to investigate." Compared now to what had happened in the Black Cathedral, it was not the worst mission I'd ever been on. Yet, before, I would have called it the most terrible struggle of my life. "You can't describe it as something physical, Mercury. It wasn't flesh, metal, plant, or animal. It was just a color: a color that human eyes cannot view on the spectrum of light. Something not from this world or any world that humans could possibly imagine."

"I believe you," Mercury said.

She didn't understand, couldn't really, even after her encounter with the Earthmover. Some things had to be experienced firsthand.

"When we arrived in New Ipswich we saw it had been destroyed ... wiped completely off the map. Everyone reduced to powder, as if the life had been sucked from their bodies. In the center of the town there were ... meteorites," I continued, remembering the devastated remains of the city and its vampirized populace. "From those fallen stars raised a collection of tiny lights which twinkled in a beautiful but sickening way. Maybe they were drawn by the Rising, maybe they just arrived here by accident. I don't know, but they formed a swarm which drained the life of anything it touched."

"What happened?" Mercury asked, her voice finally becoming understanding.

"We fought, or tried to. Our weapons couldn't harm it; it was on a world with conditions totally unlike our own." I lowered my head. "Our entire backup perished, and then we started to die one by one. All except those who chose to run—just run."

Like Peter. I left his name unspoken. I'd never forgiven him for that act of desertion. Still, he'd stayed long enough to show he was a capable soldier. Only Gamma Squad had emerged from the battle unharmed but those who'd fought beside us that day were the best of the best. Anyone who survived even a short time proved his mettle.

I still had nightmares about that day. You'd have thought the other missions would have drowned out the horrors of it through sheer numbers by now. "Those that stayed continued to fight. Beta and Gamma teams were devastated, their courage and skill meaning nothing against it. I would have died too if not for Gamma Squad's leader. General Ashton-Smith managed to temporarily scatter the Color with a set of radiation grenades."

Temporarily.

"Wow, that's horrible," Jackie said, surprising me. I realized, to my horror, she and every other child was listening to my story with rapt attention.

I blinked, taking a deep breath as I flushed with embarrassment. "This is not the sort of story for young ears."

Peter shouted from the front of the line. "Oh come on, John, keep telling us your story. You're doing a wonderful rendition of a half-mad soldier."

This entire situation felt *off*. Peter had forgiven me far too quickly. He was plotting something, I was sure of it. "In any case, I don't see why you can't finish the story. You were there as well."

"I left that part of my past behind," Peter said. "You seem to have, but I can tell you're still carrying it on your back." There was something hesitant in his voice, as if he was trying to hide his emotions under a false façade of cheerfulness. I knew the feeling. There was also a glimmer of hate in his voice. I knew that feeling, too. Due to my report, Peter was exiled from the Remnant. I'd almost killed him and he'd nearly done the same, the two of us shooting up a section of these very woods, but a group of feral ghouls had been attracted by the noise and forced us to part ways. I'd hoped they'd finished him off, but they'd obviously done no more to him than me.

"What a bastard," Mercury muttered under her breath. "Why don't you go on with your story?"

"There's not much left to tell. With the Color temporarily scattered, we found ourselves wandering across the desert supply-less and alone. A Dunwych war party found us, Katryn was its leader. We were defeated and taken captive."

"What, really?" Mercury's astonishment was clear. Looking at Katryn's backside, she tried to put her surprise into words. "But she's uh … you were soldiers, armed soldiers. I mean she's got a *spear*, John."

"A blessed spear is more effective than firearms against many creatures of the Wasteland," Katryn answered Mercury's unspoken question. "The Dunwych do not disdain technology, though we do not embrace it either. Better we forge a new life than exist forever picking over the ruins of a dead civilization."

"John, were we just insulted there?" Mercury blinked.

"Yes," I said, not concerned about it. "The Dunwych may be descended from a bus of tourists that got marooned on some surprisingly durable farmland near Sentinel Hill, but that doesn't mean they're not capable."

"You're kidding," Mercury said.

"Yes, because I'm such a kidder." I rolled my eyes.

"Yeah, you are," Mercury surprised me by saying. "In a dry-wit sort of way."

Katryn interrupted, perhaps not enjoying having her racial heritage summarized so. "To continue John's story, my people have had encounters with monsters from the sky before. The seeing stones read that John Henry Booth would be able to find a way to defeat the indescribable thing from the stars. We decided to spare the survivors' lives and not take them as slaves if they agreed to help us avenge our losses. The Color from the Sky had killed a Dunwych village hours before; it had simply returned to its nest thereafter."

"What did you do?" Jackie, of all people, was the one to speak. I was appalled she'd been listening to our grizzly tale.

"We lured the swarm to an abandoned mine and detonated a nuclear warhead, one of New Arkham's remaining six. It destroyed the enemy." I allowed them to think the Color was dead. I had to do it, despite the terrible truth thatit could not be killed. I knew on some instinctive level it had just been buried under a thousand tons of rock. Someday, the Color might leak into the groundwater or rise through the cracks in the rubble above it. That day, humanity would meet its end.

"That's incredible." Mercury said, genuinely impressed. A fact which confused me— after all, I'd just described how the three R&E squads had been almost completely helpless against an E.B.E. and how we'd won only through blind chance.

Katryn finished off my tale, covering a part I was uncomfortable with narrating. "I sealed the creature beneath the mine with a dozen spells and the lifeblood of traitors who had run away during the final battle. I invited Captain Booth to become a member of the Dunwych. We stayed together for a short time but there was no fruit from our union. He disappeared soon after, an affront to the gods."

"I thought you didn't bed murderers?" Mercury asked, biting her lip. "Pretty sure she qualifies."

"I said willingly."

"Oh," Mercury muttered.

Katryn sniggered, an unexpected reaction.

Peter, by contrast, looked annoyed.

"Are we almost there?" I asked, anxious to break the silence.

"Yes." Katryn pointed, moving aside some tree branches. From there, I caught a glimpse of Scrapyard. A town literally made of junk. Much of the remaining Pre-Rising machinery had decayed to unusable refuse, even when humanity struggled vainly to keep it perfectly intact. That meant gathering new examples from the ruins of humanity was a thriving business.

Scrapyard positively reveled in this trade, stacking countless bits of antique garbage left over from Old America around them. If something was irreparable, more common than not, it might provide a glimpse about how to construct something similar. Houses were made of welded-together metal sheets, cars, and pieces of shattered houses slapped together. Piping ran through the entire town, hundreds of twisting and spiraling bars linking up to the town's tiny windmill power plant. It was ghastly and beautiful at once.

The children, upon seeing their home, didn't waste any time in running inside. The townsfolk, a strange collection of tribals and tinkerers, immediately rushed out to greet them. Alone, Jackie stayed behind. She just looked at the town with a mixture of sadness and longing. I understood her feelings.

We were both without a place in this world.

CHAPTER TEN

Scrapyard was officially a holding of the Dunwych tribes, which meant its warriors occasionally came by to say, "Send us tribute or we'll kill you."

As a result, Katryn and Peter were treated with a wary respect by the locals. Likewise, I was a known quantity in Scrapyard. It was a small enough community that everyone remembered me from my previous visits. The town's salvagers didn't necessarily have any love for Remnant soldiers, but we'd done favors for them and brought trade. The invisible unacknowledged trade which the Remnant depended on and the people of Scrapyard had benefited from.

As the children were gathered in the town square, they were picked up one by one. Parents and relatives collected them, sometimes with tears of joy and other times with a cold, sullen resentment, but collect them they did. During the process, I hoped some noble soul would come and collect Jackie. Yet, after all citizens of the town had visited with us, Miss Howard stood alone.

In small towns like Scrapyard, blood ties ran deep. If you couldn't find a person's parents, you were able to find someone related to them. Grandparents, uncles, or cousins could usually be counted on to take care of a child if something happened to their parents. Even when whole bloodlines were wiped out, due to plague or blood feud, neighboring families were usually willing to take in a child. The fact that Jackie wasn't taken spoke volumes about how she was treated here.

Mercury, tactful as ever, observed this. "You're not terribly popular around here, are you, girl?"

"Mercury!" I snapped.

Jackie answered her question without offense. "My mum got pregnant collecting fruit in the valley. No one knew who the father was and my mom died giving birth before she told anyone. They thought it might be a mutant or a ghoul or something. That scared them. Only the Sheriff, my Da, was willing to take me in. The others, they were happy to give me up after the slavers killed him."

"I see," I said, unsure how to respond. I couldn't help but see parallels between her situation and my own—which frightened me since I'd have seen the villagers' actions as reasonable not long ago.

Katryn leaned over and put a comforting hand on Jackie's shoulder. "Do not worry child, we will hunt down any surviving slavers and spill their blood on the fields."

"Good," Jackie said before looking up and smiling weakly.

I expected Mercury to recite some bullshit statistic about how, anthropologically speaking, it was probably safest to reject Jackie from the community. Instead, she raised a fist. "Booth, I have to take care of this child."

That got a single-word response from me. "What?"

"Anthropologically speaking, it's good cultural instinct to adopt children without parents." Mercury pointed to the air, as if lecturing. "They can be taught skills from a young age, which strengthens their chance of survival."

"Uh-huh."

Jackie looked up, uncomfortably. "I don't know how I feel about that ..."

"You should help me, Booth," Mercury suggested. "After you murder everyone at the Black Cathedral."

"There is no after."

"Ha!" Peter let out a hearty laugh. "Escape one family and immediately get another. You have no luck, do you, John?"

My response was simple. "Fuck you, Peter."

Turning back to Mercury and me, Katryn said, "If the girl proves too difficult for your journey, my tribe will offer her sanctuary. We have ways of discerning if her blood is mutated or of the old races. You have my word by the Old Gods that if it is, I will deliver her to her true people. If not, she may stay on as a member of our tribe."

Jackie looked terrified rather than reassured. The Dunwych were a bigger boogeyman than the Great Old Ones to the people of Scrapyard. Let alone the promise to hand her over to what Jackie undoubtedly thought were monsters.

Taking a deep breath, I knelt down so I was nearly eye level with Jackie, trying not to smile at the display. This was a serious subject. "I will find someone to care for you; you have my word."

"Thank you," Jackie said, staring up into my eyes. They were big and innocent despite what she'd endured.

That would not last.

"With the exception of one incident, John Henry Booth is an honorable man." Katryn blinked her deep blue eyes and nodded solemnly, ignoring what the girl was saying. "You would do well to believe in him, child."

"Yeah, John is really honorable." Mercury nodded. "Except for the whole treason, lies, and revenge thing."

I glared at her. Everyone trotting over the girl's grief was obscene. "I may have lied to you about visiting Kingsport but I will get you there."

"I'm holding you to that. In any case, I want her to come with us until you find an acceptable alternative guardian," Mercury said, patting the young girl on the back. "That is, unless you want to accompany me to Kingsport. I'll teach you how to do medicine and you can become a doctor. Eventually, with our superior knowledge, we can rule the Wasteland!"

Jackie smiled, probably respecting the sentiment even as she was even now looking at Mercury like she was insane. "That's nice … really."

Thankfully, Katryn changed the subject. "I would have words with you, John. If your quest actually means anything to you, we must share information."

"I have every intention of doing so, Katryn." I trusted the Dunwych priestess about as far as I could throw her, but she knew more about what was going on in the Wastelands than I ever would. "However, my feeling is a matter which takes precedence."

"Yeah, Booth has decided he needs to meet with a Hawaiian-shirt-wearing ghoul." Mercury didn't bother to conceal her disbelief. I was beginning to wonder if someone had ever explained the concept of tact to her.

"Ah, yes, Richard Jameson." Katryn nodded her head solemnly, tightly clutching her spear. "The Dream-Walker."

Mercury blinked. "He wasn't making that up?"

Ignoring her, I turned in the direction of Richard's workshop, near the far edge of town. Jackie then grabbed hold of my pant leg. "Can I come, Mister Booth?"

I looked down at her, wondering why she was so panicked. Then I saw the eyes of the people around us: they were accusatory, distrusting, and occasionally even hateful. It was a monstrous reaction to a girl whose father had just been murdered. If Jackie was left alone, she might not survive. It seemed only the former Sheriff's protection had kept her alive before. "Of course, young one."

"Uh, Booth ..." Mercury paused, "I'm not sure taking her with us to see a ghoul is wise."

"I don't mind Mister Jameson," Jackie said. "He treats me like family."

That was unsettling. "I see."

Silence reigned until we reached our destination on the other side of town. Jameson's Salvage and Reconstruction was a unique building in a town composed of unique buildings. It was, in many ways, a castle composed of junk. The original Pre-Rising garage was still visible in the central "courtyard" but it was surrounded by a fortress of pipe and steel.

Concrete smokestacks had been constructed to handle the interior smelting furnace, as thick walls made of abandoned cars surrounded the place. The strange building stood in the direct shadow of the town's windmills with a number of power lines running toward the garage's rooftop.

Despite this connection, it was clear Richard didn't rely on the town's own meager supply of electricity to satisfy his energy needs. He had his own windmill and a large number of solar panels lining the top of his roof—he probably had more power than the rest of the town put together.

The dweller had a rather pungent odor, a mixture of stench from nearby pigpens mixed with an earthy corpse-like smell. Mutated hairless rats popped in and out of the wall erected around his home, all of them hideous and red-eyed. Arriving at a thick wrought-iron gate, I wondered how I'd begin our conversation. *Hello, Richard, long time no see. Would you mind working some sorcery on me*? That was a conversation I was not looking forward to.

"This is not what I was expecting," Mercury said, staring at the place.

"What *were* you expecting?"

"Something more … cyclopean."

Many noises were coming from within his shop. Today, in addition to the din of tools at work, there was the sound of old Earth rock and roll coming from within.

"What is that ghastly din?" Mercury looked vaguely horrified by it. "Ghoul music?"

Katryn corrected her. "I believe it is called 'Gas on the Lake.'"

"'Smoke on the Water'!" Richard's voice called from inside the building, apparently able to hear us from forty feet away.

That was when the shocking figure stepped out, the sun illuminating a figure of absolute terror.

CHAPTER ELEVEN

The nightmarish figure stepping out caused Mercury to seize up in horror, choke, and look ready to vomit. I, Katryn, Peter, and even little Jackie had more subdued reactions to Richard's arrival. We merely looked uneasy, even if every instinct in our bodies told us to run away screaming. I was surprised to see Jackie was so good at it given her young age. Most children her age would have screamed, cried, and run away.

Hell, most adults as well.

Ghouls were a hideous sight by human standards. They had claws, fur, pointed ears, ugly hoof-like feet, and warty yellow-green skin. Their faces were the most unnerving thing about them, being an unnatural cross between a man's and a wolf's. Worse was how *expressive* they were, showing all of the emotions a human could, but in a twisted fashion.

Richard was a particularly repulsive example of his species, standing closer to the middle ground between man and monster than most. He was a walking, talking reminder of how close the relationship between our two species was.

As if to compensate for it, the ghoul wore outlandish attire. Today, it was a bright red shirt covered in pineapples, jean shorts, and sandals. It was such a ridiculous sight that for a moment, the dissonance seemed to relax Doctor Takahashi.

"Howdy, neighbor!" Richard said, walking up to the gate between us. I'd often wondered why Richard chose to live amongst humans of Scrapyard despite the prejudice he must endure. The only answer I'd ever gotten from him was, "Ghouls are immortal but only humans know how to live."

"Hello," I said, giving a pleasant wave to Richard, trying to hide my revulsion. "It's good to see you."

Finally, Mercury managed to say, "Hello, uh, Richard."

"Hey, Mister Jameson!" Jackie waved to him, unafraid.

"Why hello, Little Jackie!" Richard leaned down to look at her square in the eyes. "What are you doing here?"

"My Da died," Jackie said. "He was killed by slavers. These folks killed them."

Richard looked down at her as if processing the information. "Uh-yeah, I heard some commotion in the village square earlier. I decided it wasn't any of my business. I'm sorry."

"It's okay," Jackie said. "They're weird but I like them."

Uncomfortable, I coughed into my left fist before saying, "Richard, I have need of your peculiar expertise."

"First, introduce me to your companions. I have to be wary of strangers," Richard said, smiling his demonic-looking canines. "Monsters aren't always obvious."

"Yes, I agree," I calmly answered. "You know Katryn. This is Doctor Mercury Takahashi."

"Nice to meet you," Richard extended his hand to Mercury.

Mercury looked at the inhuman clawed grip. "Um."

"Right." Richard chuckled sadly, pulling his hand back. "So, what have you been up to, Katryn?"

"Hunting individuals who have been kidnapping children so I can crush their skulls and turn their teeth into jewelry," Katryn answered.

"So, the usual," Richard said, grinning. "I was wondering when you'd return. Honestly, given the condition you left in, I wasn't entirely sure I'd ever see you again."

I blinked, unsure if I'd heard that correctly. "I was here?"

"Yes, you and Jessica."

I reached through the gate's bars, grabbing his shirt. It was a ridiculous gesture since Richard could rend me limb from limb. "Tell me *everything*."

"You wandered in here, extremely delirious, with the girl." Richard tried prying my fingers off his shirt, failing until I released him.

"So Jessica …" I said, still stunned. "She's *here*?"

"Yeah," Richard said, looking down at me with his deep, soulful eyes "You two mounted an escape from the place where you were imprisoned. Jessica was badly injured, some sort of infection."

"Go on."

"I've been treating her with the old black magic. So far, no luck. Jessica just keeps getting worse and worse."

"I see," I said, feeling stricken. "I've found her just in time to watch her die."

"It happens." Richard said, spitting his cigarette onto the ground. "Oddly, John, I thought you were the one who was going to die for the longest time. Then, one day, you just got up in the middle of the night and wandered into the desert."

Another piece of the puzzle fell into place. It didn't explain how I'd gotten to New Arkham, though. That was almost eighty miles away. "Please, Richard, bring me to her. I beg you."

"Okay, sure, John," Richard said, opening the gate and letting us through. "But remember, you owe me. What did you come here for, anyway?"

I still needed to find out who'd done this to her; there was a chance she wouldn't be able to tell me. "I need another favor."

"Lovely. The tab just keeps running up," Richard said.

"Please," I whispered.

"I didn't say I wasn't going to do it," Richard said. "Just note immortal things remember what humans do not."

"How did you two guys meet, anyway?" Mercury asked. "You're, uh … not exactly the sort of people who would normally hang out together."

Richard started back toward his workshop. "What with him being a Recon and Extermination Ranger and me being the exterminated?"

"Yeah," Mercury said sheepishly.

Jackie took Mercury's hand and walked beside her as we reached the entrance to Richard's garage.

"He was a friend of General Ashton-Smith, my mentor," I said, recalling another person I would never see again. "The General always had unconventional ideas about how exactly to protect the Remnant. Richard and I struck an odd friendship after being introduced."

"Yeah, just a boy and his dog-man," Richard said. "Watch your head."

The sounds of Old Earth music continued to play in the background as we ducked under the half-closed garage door. The song currently playing was one I'd heard before, an ethereal melody called "Dark Side of the Moon."

The inside of Richard's workshop was a wonderland if you were interested in Old Earth technology. The place was dark, greasy, smelly, and covered in soot, but there were more innovations going on here than in most of human civilization. There were stacks of recycled paper covered in charcoal scribbles of machinery parts, clay tablets preserving lost knowledge, and even technical diagrams written on the wallpaper. Hundreds of Pre-Rising homemade items had been disassembled and looked at closely under glass-blown magnifying glasses, while stacks of identical machines showed Richard's methodical devotion to his craft: the craft of tinkering.

Scrapyard lacked the infrastructure to maintain or repair most of the more complicated pieces of machinery it salvaged, but Richard had taken it as an affront to humanity losing any of its technology. So far, he'd managed to construct items up to the 1960s in complexity and was slowly building his way up. There was even a half-completed plane hanging from the garage's ceiling.

"Is that a computer?" Mercury blinked, pointing at a strange, hybridized thing with a greenish-tinged screen. "You have *computers* out here?"

"Yeah, I mostly use it to play old video games. I used to be able to watch movies on it before the drive busted and the monitor failed. Still, it was an experiment which taught me quite a few things. Once we get computers back, it'll be smooth sailing." Richard took position in front of a door marked EMPLOYEES ONLY. Pointing, he said, "The girl is in here."

"Ghouls are interested in computers?" Mercury showed little interest in Jessica's fate, not that I expected her to.

"No, but humans are. I used to be one, you know." Richard chuckled before a look of pain passed across his face. His face was similar enough to a human's that I could recognize the emotion. "I know. It's hard to tell."

Not hesitating, I rushed past my friends through the doorway. Inside was a crude medical station equipped with some salvaged hospital equipment. It was inferior to a Remnant hospital but not for lack of trying. IVs, monitors, sterilized equipment, and so on had been placed inside the room, while the place smelled of antiseptic. Richard had done his best to see Jessica was taken care of, for which I owed him a huge debt.

There, lying on an ancient, rusted hospital gurney was Jessica. She was naked under a well-washed, frayed white sheet with a tube injecting homemade morphine into her arm. Her long brown hair trailed over the side of the bed while a couple of strange humming machines kept track of her life signs.

"Thank you," I said, grateful for what Richard had done.

"Save your thanks for when she makes it out of this alive," Richard said. "*If* she makes it out alive."

My relief at finding her died in the pit of my stomach as I saw a marking on her shoulder. My joy was short-lived however, turning to a disturbed awe, as I saw a handprint made of scars on her right shoulder. It was identical to the one on my own.

"Richard, what's wrong with her?" I had to ask, a horrible sensation welling up inside my stomach. "You know things we don't even know we've forgotten."

"John …" Richard trailed off.

I gritted my teeth. "Tell me what's wrong with her."

Richard looked sympathetic but nevertheless answered. "As far as I can tell, John, *you are*."

"Explain," I said. It was more a command than a request.

Katryn stepped past Richard and moved to press her hand against Jessica's scar. "The Dream-Walker does not have to. I have seen this before. It is the Hand of Nyarlathotep."

"Just once, I swear, I wished there would be a Wasteland god or monster with a name that wasn't unpronounceable," Mercury muttered, looking in on Jessica. She then switched topics and said, "She's pretty, got some good genes there. No sign of mutation."

"Your observations aren't helping," I said, before looking between Richard and Katryn, trying to regain control over my emotions. "Could you explain? Why is she like this?"

Richard stood in the doorway, his larger than normal frame blocking Mercury and Jackie from entering. "The tribal lady seems to understand more about this than I do. All I know is she was getting better until this morning when she suddenly took a turn for the worst."

A sinking feeling filled my chest. I was not a believer in coincidence. "Did it start happening about six to seven hours ago?"

"Yeah, how did you know?" Richard looked perplexed, as much as a human canine hybrid could at least.

Because that was about the time I was impaled by the nightgaunt. I didn't say it aloud, but I could see it on Mercury's face she was thinking the same thing. Somehow, there was a supernatural connection between Jessica and me, one that was slowly killing her. I had to figure out some way of stopping it, no matter the cost.

Even if it was at the expense of my own life.

Katryn took her hands up to my chest and slowly removed my shirt, exposing the handprint. "You have been marked by the God with a Thousand Forms, John. The one you call the Black Soldier, who we call the Trickster, and who is known by countless other names. Some dreadful sorcery has been worked, feeding your life with this woman's own. When you suffer, she suffers. Yet, as long as she has life left to give, you will recover from even the worst wounds. This is the nature of the Hand of Nyarlathotep."

I felt sick to my stomach, stunned at such a horrible thing's possibility. What sort of mad sorcerer had worked this enchantment on us? Was it Ward? If it was, I needed to find out so I could rip off their head and put it on a pike.

"Sounds like a pretty sweet deal to me. Too bad it has to be such a hot young thing," Richard said, shrugging his shoulders. "No wonder I wasn't able to get her to wake when you left. You crossed the Dust Zone without any clothes or water. I'm surprised she didn't die a dozen times getting you back home."

"Wow, that's even more tactless than my usual comments. You should be proud, Mister Jameson," Mercury said, shaking her head.

"Just doing my part," Richard said, smiling a mouth full of sharp teeth. "I can sound human even if I'll never be so again."

I felt helpless and in need of something to shoot.

Mercury reluctantly squeezed passed Richard's thick, furry form. "Let me have a look at her, I'm a doctor."

"Is she?" Richard sounded impressed.

"Something like that," I corrected, not at all happy Mercury was getting near Jessica. Unfortunately, she was the only one here with any real medical expertise. I wanted to say more, but I was still in shock and couldn't think of anything else to add.

"How do I break the spell?" I asked, deciding to focus on what was important.

"She's quite beautiful." Katryn's eyes lingered over Jessica's fallen form. "But you need to think pragmatically. A true warrior would be willing to die for their leader. If you truly wish to kill the Necromancer, I suggest you allow her to serve as your shield. She will give you the strength you need to destroy him."

"I was her Captain. *I still am,*" I snapped, disgusted by Katryn's words. "I'm not going to use her as some sort of ... battery. It's my job to keep her safe. Do you understand? *It's my job!*"

"Actually, I'm pretty sure it's the job of soldiers to complete their mission. At least, that was how it was back in Old Earth. I was a mechanic in the Korean War, you know. Seriously, it sucks my life became about living underground and eating carrion when the Summer of Love was just getting started," Richard blathered on. I think he was trying to distract me from my troubles, but he was doing a very piss-poor job of it.

"John, I would like to have words with you." Katryn's voice was as commanding as mine had earlier been. "We need to discuss what you know of the Necromancer and what I know. Destroying him should be the guiding focus of our efforts."

"In a moment, Katryn. I'm speaking to Richard." I raised a hand, trying to be as respectful as possible to my former lover. "My squad mate's safety comes first." I wanted revenge against Ward if he was the one responsible for my squad's death and Jessica's current condition. However, if it became a choice of her health versus Ward's death, I would choose her survival every time.

"As you wish, for now. Afterward, we must speak, though," Katryn said. "Not a second longer, though."

"So be it," I said, nodding. "I am pleased you respect the bond between me and my men."

"Man, I miss when people talked like normal folk." Richard sighed, shaking his head. "The English language has seriously regressed since the Rising. You guys sound like you're from a different century."

"We *are* from a different century than you." Mercury pointed out. She'd already started taking notes on a chart that Richard had set aside.

"Touché," Richard said. "Anyone want some kidney pie? I just opened up some poor sucker and the organs are especially fresh!"

Mercury opened her mouth in mute horror.

"Ha!" Richard said. "Old ghoul joke."

CHAPTER TWELVE

Certain there was nothing more I could do for Jessica here, I looked to Richard and asked him for the favor I'd mentioned earlier—with an added caveat. "I need you to break the spell binding me and Jessica. I also require a Dreamlands vision-quest. You've said it's possible to travel the mists of time through ghoul ceremonies to this place. I have lost memories I need to recover. The spell breaking the connection between me and Jessica takes priority, however. If we can break our link, maybe she'll have the strength to recover."

It was a lot to ask of my friend; Richard was only a hedge magician and I'd never seen him do anything remotely comparable to what I was asking. Yet, I wasn't sure if I could ask Katryn to do it. Even if she was capable of such magic, things had ended ... badly between us.

Richard coughed and raised his hands defensively. "You're talking some serious juju here. The dream-walking is easy enough. I can do that with just the right smoke and mirrors. Breaking an invocation to Nyarlathotep, though? That requires ancient Pre-Babylonian 'Age of Sorcerer Kings' stuff. I'd need to get things from the elders underground for that."

"Can you do it or not?" My voice rose, I was about ready to snap. I had to know; if not, I'd find someone else.

"Yes." Richard grinned, and it was highly unsettling. "The issue is *cost*, John."

"I see." Nothing came free in the Wasteland, even from friends. I was disappointed in Richard, though not by much. Thankfully, I had something to barter with. It was another reason I owed Martha. "I have a copy of the English translation of the *Necronomicon*, Richard.

It has the original Arabic text included. I will allow you to read it if you do this for me."

Richard stopped motionless, his posture suddenly threatening. "Don't lie to me, John."

I pulled out the book and opened it, flashing Richard a couple of pages. Specifically, a despicable set describing how the Great Old One Dagon lay with human women in order to sire the debased Deep One race. That particular set on pages had numerous illustrations on how to perform spells designed to attract them.

Richard's eyes grew wide, taking in the reality of my offer. "Uh … well now… that's … big."

Pleased by his reaction, I asked, "Is this enough?"

"Easily. I'll go get the necessary stuff. See you in five or six hours." Richard spoke no more and left.

Little Jackie, who had been silent for much of the conversation, stared at Jessica and then glanced up at Mercury. "Is she going to live?"

"The facilities are crude but sufficient. If there's a scientific basis for this life-transfer phenomenon, which there has to be, then it's mostly a case of getting her strength built back up," Mercury said, looking positively tickled to have a patient before her.

"So, yes?" Jackie asked.

"Yes."

I hoped she was right. "Are you alright staying here for the time being, Jackie?"

"Sure!" Jackie said, more enthusiastically than expected. "Mister Jameson is awesome! I once was dared to sneak into his place but my father smacked me for it after the fact. He's got some nifty stuff here."

"Good," I said. "He's the only person I really trust here. It's only temporary, though. I promise."

"I don't like it," Mercury said. "We should take her with us."

"You're going to assist her in regaining consciousness?" I ignored Mercury's objections; it was becoming the chief way I dealt with her.

"As soon as I make sure that won't adversely affect her health, unless you have any objections to a 'professional torturer' helping your friend?" Mercury said, looking up at me with a strained expression on her face. She looked genuinely hurt by my earlier words, something I was unprepared for.

"Just do it. If you can, I will speak no more ill of you," I said, leaving the room, trying to catch my breath. Seeing Jessica in her current condition, knowing it was my fault, was too much. I also didn't want to watch Mercury working on her given how I'd treated her. Despite all the things she'd done, I owed her my life and soon I would owe her my squad mate's life. She deserved better.

"I need a minute alone," I muttered, talking to myself. I decided Richard's guest bedroom was the best place to do so. I'd stayed there a couple of nights in the past.

Heading inside, I felt someone coming up behind me. Slightly moving my head to the left, I saw Katryn's fist coming at the back of my head. Immediately, I ducked underneath her blow.

Barely.

"What the hell are you doing!?" I asked, turning around and backing into the room. Katryn was ready to fight, that much was easy to see from her battle-ready stance and flaring eyes.

Katryn spun around with her bare foot moving to spin-kick me in the stomach. I managed to catch it and proceeded to sweep her other foot out from under her.

Katryn moved with an effortless grace, somersaulting out of my grip onto her feet. Her fighting style was reminiscent of Brazilian capoeira, more dance-like than my own training.

I raised my fists defensively. "I thought we were going to hold off on killing me until after this Necromancer business was settled."

"Fighting you is not killing you," Katryn said, tossing her spear to one side.

"I'm glad that distinction is being made!" I said, annoyed. I didn't have time for this. Jessica was dying and Katryn wanted to fight? What was *wrong* with her?

Katryn continued her explanation, her movements graceful yet deadly. "You have a way of showing up when most needed. I am not one to question the will of the gods, but I need to know if your reflexes are still as capable as they were a year ago."

"There are easier ways to test my reflexes!" I said, my frown turning into a smirk. It was hard not to think of our time together. It had been four years into the disintegration of my marriage; she'd been both forward and exotic, two things I loved.

"You gave up that right when you left the mating circle," Katryn said, coolly. Her words held hints of her own attraction, however. Just the way she spoke them said that she still wanted me as much as I wanted her.

"I didn't have a choice to enter it!"

Jumping up, she attempted to knee me in the face. I managed to grab her by the arms and tossed her on the ground. That proved a mistake as she somehow reversed my hold and sent me flying up against the wall. By the time I was looking up, she was already moving to bring down her foot onto my face. I barely managed to roll out of the way before her foot slammed into the ground beside me. The dust of the floor was now flying up from our athletic contest, covering us both.

"You're lucky I'm holding back." I moved my hands up in front of my face, guarding it against her attacks.

In truth, I wasn't, but psychological warfare was the only edge I had. The Dunwych valued strength as much as they did honor. I had called into question both by leaving her, showing myself to be weak-willed and an oath-breaker. It was now up to me to prove I still had the personal fortitude to be a worthy ally. I had no intention of disappointing.

"If you were holding back, I'd know it." Katryn proceeded to pull a knife from her leather outfit.

I was surprised by that, less because of her willingness to escalate our conflict than because hers was not the most concealing of garments. It opened up all sorts of questions as to where exactly she'd been hiding it.

Slashing toward my chest, I avoided each of her blows before making a move for her knife. I could have drawn my R'lyehian blade, but I intended to prove I didn't need it. "Maybe you overestimate yourself."

"Show me." Katryn anticipated my attack and immediately spun around to kick me in the chest. It was here the general discrepancy of our body weights proved to my advantage. Most men could not stand a blow from Katryn and remain standing; once they were down, she killed them with one easy blow. If I'd had any less of a pound advantage, I'd be on the ground crippled.

Still, it hurt like hell.

Ignoring the pain of her blow, I managed to pull the knife from her hand and brought it up against her throat. Another second and she would have been able to turn the situation to her advantage, but the battle favored me this time.

"Yield," I said, holding the knife steady at the base of her throat, "or die."

No sooner had I done so than I found myself going over her shoulder with the knife pulled from my grip. A second later, I was on the ground with the weapon once more in Katryn's hands. She had it pressed against the tip of my Adam's apple, a single motion ready to slit my throat at the slightest movement.

"Well," I coughed out, stunned by my defeat. "It seems my reflexes *have* dulled somewhat."

Katryn let out a tinkle of melodic laughter, a great contrast to her normal seriousness. "Perhaps I have merely grown faster."

"That you have."

Katryn snorted and assumed a combat-ready position a couple of feet away, apparently ready to continue our battle. "You're skilled enough for me to believe you're still a worthy ally. The care you show to your subordinate makes you soft, though. I do not know why warriors from your homeland are so sentimental. It is a weakness."

Realizing this contest was now a friendly one, I went to the guest-room door and shut it tightly before locking it. The chance to spar with Katryn was a rare opportunity.

"I've been accused of many things, but being sentimental is not one of them," I said. "Even so, most of my fellow soldiers don't feel as I do. Surely, you've learned that from your lover."

"My lover?" She seemed genuinely surprised by my words.

"Peter," I said, letting a hint of jealousy taint my words as I entered into a combat-ready pose. It was an affectation since I couldn't help but feel only trauma recalling our time together, but I had to let her think otherwise. I needed her help to take down Ward and that required her thinking she had a hold on me. No matter how disgusted I was by all this.

Katryn stared at me for a moment, her eyes seemingly searching me for some hint of irony. After a second, she let forth a torrent of stunned laughter.

"Is something funny?" I asked, already suspecting the truth.

"I'd sooner bed a Deep One." Katryn delivered a playful series of blows toward my face, ones I blocked one after the other. The combat had become slower paced, more like a practice session than genuine combat. "He is an oath-breaker, one who has no honor."

"You accused me of that, too." I would never regret the fact I'd chosen to flee Dunwych territory, it had been for my family after all, but I'd always feel a bit of sadness over doing so.

"You are an oath-keeper, John, even when circumstances prevent you from fulfilling the letter of them. You left me because you still loved your wife and children. I suspect you left the Remnant because you love your squad. I see how their absence tortures you now." Katryn's voice took on a sympathetic tone.

I loved my children but I'd been a horrible father to them and an even worse husband to my wife. I'd left because I loathed the Dunwych. What Katryn was saying was nothing more than the product of her mind trying to rationalize my departure. I needed her to play on her justifications. "I never meant to hurt you."

"Spare me the sentimentality, John. You may need it but I do not," Katryn said as her next kick went a little high and I was able to easily dodge it. She continued to talk as I watched her motions closely, trying to guess her next move. "Blasphemer or not, I might be able to forgive you. Peter, on the other hand, left my people as soon as you did. He started selling his services to the highest bidder, serving everyone from Kingsport's gangsters to Arizonian slavers."

"He's a slaver?" That shocked me. Desertion was one thing, slavery was another. I could no more work with a slaver than I could a cannibal or child-murderer.

"Peter came as close as humanly possible without actually becoming one himself. He guarded their caravans, directed them to villages willing to sell their members, and killed those who would strike out against them. Only recently has he returned, claiming to have seen the light." The suspicion in her voice spoke volumes about her opinion of the man.

The Dunwych were brutal and efficient conquerors but they had their own set of ethics. Like the Remnant, it seemed they could look down on slavery as long as they didn't call it that. "Why accept him as a member of your tribe, then?"

"We need every warrior we can get. The Necromancer grows stronger every day," Katryn explained, right before I managed to successfully toss her onto the ground. She smiled, pleased at my getting the best of her even temporarily.

"Who is he to you?" I decided to hold on to what I knew for the time being. I knew of Alan Ward's identity a decade ago but not what he'd been doing since.

"A wizard, a priest, a scientist, a warlord, and everything in between. Rumors attest he wandered in from the desert like you have been described doing. Boiling down corpses to their essential salts, he raised them from the dead. He also displayed other powers, like healing and making crops grow."

"I take it his benevolence had a darker side?"

The two of us began practicing other holds, close ones. It burned me to have Katryn so near and not wrap my arms around her in more intimate ways. I should have been thinking about the Necromancer, but as we grappled with one another, my mind wandered to other things. The stress of everything I had endured longed for a release, a release which could only come from the union of a man with his lover.

Katryn pulled my arm around my back, shifting her weight as she put me into a painful wristlock, an action which momentarily dulled my emerging feelings. "Soon, reports of corpses stolen in the night were whispered. Women were sent to him and their bodies were found elsewhere, drained of blood. His followers were joined by Deep Ones and those who worship Kaithooloo. Whole villages were enslaved or exterminated at his command, their children taken away for some evil purpose. One of the Dunwych's outlying villages was amongst them. We don't have a name for him, though, if he has one."

"Alan Ward."

"You encountered him, encountered him and survived." Katryn let go of her wrist hold.

"Yes." I took a deep breath. "I just can't remember *how*."

"We will find out," Katryn said, walking close to me. She took my face into her hands and pressed her lips against mine.

Pulling away, I said, "We shouldn't."

I pretended to be reluctant because I knew it would drive her to desire me more. I hated the thought of her touching me, though. "I need you sharp and alert, John," Katryn said. "You are a warrior in distress and we still made oaths to be with one another. It is my right."

"I ..." I trailed off. "Alright."

CHAPTER THIRTEEN

The sex was joyless but passionate, pushing me past the limits of my endurance. I had to think of Jessica, my wife, and even Mercury to finish, but if Katryn suspected I was in any way reluctant, she gave no sign of it and seemed responsive enough. Afterward, Katryn rested her head on my shoulder as if our past differences mattered not at all. I fell asleep against my will.

In my dreams, I saw an ancient cluster of worlds in a distant galaxy. Eventually, its sun died and the star system's impossibly old, advanced races traveled from their homes in forms not quite physical and not quite intangible. Whether these were Cthulhu and his ilk, I could not say, but they settled down upon this Earth and merged with its soil. They warped the existing primordial life repeatedly, destroying and rebuilding what was evolving until they could place the consciousness of their offspring in their frames. This had gone to create races like the Deep Ones, ghouls, Earthmovers, shoggoths, and yes, humanity. I saw one ancient thing take the form of a man and lie with my mother.

No. It was not true.

Just a dream.

My revulsion carried me to more recent memories that I had suppressed. I was naked and strapped to a table in the Black Cathedral's upper levels. There, Alan Ward, the Necromancer, stood above me. He looked no older than twenty-six—the same age he'd looked when he'd taught me, despite being over forty, yet he was all the more terrifying for his essential youth and beauty. Platinum-haired, tall, slender, pale, and delicate of feature, he looked like a human from the Pre-Rising days.

A closer look at his face showed his appearance was slightly "off" in subtle and profound ways. There were a few extra rows of teeth in his smile and his grin was a little *too* wide. Both sides of his face were identical, possessing none of the distinctiveness normal people possessed. Even Ward's lily-white skin was cursed, being not just pale but dry and papery. It was as if he was an exceptionally well-preserved corpse.

Only his eyes were fully human, human but mad. A madness born from researching too long into things man was not meant to know. Walking around the table wearing a stylish business suit from the early 20th century, a fashion so ridiculously anachronistic it only added to his settling presence, he began speaking. "You are the beginning, John."

"Leave me alone. Please." My voice was unable to rise above a whisper. I was helpless as a newborn babe, my body unresponsive to my commands to it. I could neither flee nor fight, just lie there in paralyzed agony.

Ward ignored my pleas. "You and Jessica are the beginning of a new humanity. For that, however, you must both be purged—through pain."

Ward lifted his fingers and poured forth a torrent of black unnatural lightning. It was not composed of electricity, however. Instead, the lightning was made of literal cracks in the fabric of reality. Each of these cracks tore into my flesh with a fury fiercer than any attack I'd ever endured, biting and sucking away my life with every strike.

I screamed.

The bolts felt akin to hot hooks tearing away bits of my flesh. It only grew worse over time. I saw other things as I relived the suffering of my torture, something I knew to be a memory now rather than a hallucination. I saw a vast gladiator arena where I was forced to do battle with abominations of sorcery, a golden pair of revolvers I used to shoot into the folds of a terrible amorphous multiform horror, and the sight of children in cages stacked one on top of the other as if for storage. In my dreams, I remembered it all.

I found I could think in my dream, struggling to grasp at the memories that were so close to the surface of my thoughts. Endure, dammit, endure! Just a few seconds and I'd remember everything. I could regain all of my memories and know what terrible things had been done to me and my squad. I'd know where to find Ward and what weaknesses he had.

"John!" A shout woke me up from my slumber with a start.

I sat up from where I lay, a cold sweat covering my body. By my side was the sleeping form of Katryn, looking content from our lovemaking. Knocking at the door was Richard, his unnatural strength making even light rapping sound like a great pounding.

"Dammit, just a little while longer and I wouldn't have needed that stupid ritual," I grunted.

My hands shook from the memory of my torment. You weren't supposed to feel pain in a dream, yet the experience I'd relived in the dream was every bit as horrible as the real thing. I took some small comfort in the fact Ward had been forced to torture me and I hadn't willingly assisted him in any way, but the fact I'd been so helpless before him galled me.

"I'll kill him, I swear," I coughed, in between ragged breaths. "No matter how long it takes, no matter who I have to kill to do it."

"John, I mean it." Richard's voice carried through the door. "I've gone through a lot of shit to get this weird-ass stuff. If you're trying to stiff me, I'm going to sell it to the next half-insane soldier who wanders in from the desert."

"I'm coming." I got up from the bed and opened the door, not bothering to dress.

Richard was on the other side, wearing the same clothes as earlier but now covered in cavern dust. A number of strange arcane artifacts were in his hands: candles, bags of powder, stone tablets, dolls, and objects I couldn't even begin to identify. I had no idea where he'd gone, though the most likely answer was the deep network of caverns the ghouls had dug underneath the Earth's surface.

The ghoul took one look at my form and averted his eyes. "Dammit, John, could you put some pants on?"

"You asked me to open the door," I said. "Next time you should be more specific."

Richard snorted and sniffed the air, looking over at Katryn's naked form. She was waking up.

Richard snorted and said, "A word of advice, John, when you're a guest in someone else's house, it's polite not to leave their rooms hot and sticky."

"I'll bear that in mind," I said, uninterested in dealing with the ghoul's prejudices. "You have the materials necessary to perform your spell?"

"Yeah," Richard juggled the pile in his arms a bit. "I got your whatzits."

Katryn stretched her arms and slid out of bed, walking up behind me without bothering to get dressed either. "Dream-Walker, I would like to review your preparations. I know something of the eldritch arts myself."

Richard stared, gazing up and down her naked form. "Okay, forget everything about what I said. You can do whatever you like in my place, whenever you want."

"Avert your eyes, ghoul, or lose them," Katryn said, tossing her hair behind her head.

Richard turned around, looking as embarrassed as a half-man/half-canine could. "Hey, it's not my fault. You stick that in front of me I'm going to look. Do you know how long it's been since I've had sex? Ages! I'm telling you, ghoul women give new meaning to the word dog-faced."

Against my will, I smiled. "You are a true friend, Richard. However, I'd avert your eyes for your sake."

"Yeah, yeah," he said, turning his head.

"Thank you." I could never repay him for what he'd done. "Thank you for all of this. You are the greatest man I have ever known."

Richard seemed bothered by my statement, not speaking for several seconds. Finally, giving a halfhearted smile, he said, "It's been a long time since a human has said that to me. Now put some frigging clothes on!"

Needing no further encouragement, I picked up my clothes off the floor and slipped on my undergarments before doing the same with the dusky black-and-gray clothes I was forced to wear. I would have to barter or borrow a change of clothes before I left Scrapyard. I didn't intend to travel all the way to Kingsport looking like I was from the Remnant.

Katryn retrieved her own clothes as well, quicker than I expected. She was usually less modest, caring little if individuals admired her body. Then again, most individuals weren't Richard. He was more polite than I expected during the process, only sneaking a few peeks as she did so.

Once Katryn and I were dressed, the three of us exited into the workshop outside. Jackie was sitting in the driver's seat of a strangely beautiful midnight-blue car without a top. A convertible, I believed they were called. It was unlike any other vehicle I'd ever seen.

When I'd first arrived, the vehicle had been covered with a dusky-gray sheet, but it was now revealed in all its glory. Richard had affixed the automobile's trunk with solar panels and a number of spare batteries, but the vehicle otherwise looked identical to what it must have resembled when first built, probably in the 1960s or so.

God, Richard must have spent decades restoring the thing. I'd never before seen a car that wasn't a composite or a crude reconstruction. This was the first original, or at least semi-original, I'd viewed outside of a history tape or yellow-paged magazine. I was so entranced by the machine I barely noticed Peter Goodhill was leaning up against it. Staring directly at Katryn then me, he asked, "I take it you two had a good time while I was gone?"

Katryn had said she and Peter weren't together, but I wondered if Peter knew that. Putting my arm over her shoulder, I said, "Yes. Yes, we did."

Jackie smiled, honking the horn of the vehicle. "This is great! I've never been in a real car before! Well, one that works."

Richard put all of the various bits of occult paraphernalia on the back of the trunk, before sticking his used cigarette from earlier back in his mouth. "I call it the Blue Meanie. Don't ask me to explain, it's before your time. I figured if you were going to give me a look at the *Necronomicon,* assuming it proves to be legit, the least I could do was give you a way to get to Kingsport."

"What?" I blinked, unable to believe what I was hearing.

Richard just shrugged. "It's got a fully charged set of batteries and some weapons in the trunk. Decent ones, not that cobbled-together crap you use in the Remnant."

I blinked, stunned by the generosity of my friend. "Richard, this is a princely gift."

Taking my arm off Katryn's shoulders, I stepped to the car's side and ran my fingers along the edge of its frame. I'd never owned anything like this in my entire life.

"Yeah, I'm a regular Prince Charming. Only Sleeping Beauty would have woken up screaming if I'd kissed her." Richard coughed violently then lit another cigarette.

"You know, those things can kill you," I said, not bothering to look up from the car.

"Two hundred years and no cancer," Richard said, puffing. "I'll take my chances."

I turned around the shop, looking for any sign of Mercury. I didn't see her amongst the group assembled.

"Where's Doctor Takahashi?"

"She took off," Richard answered.

"What?" I asked, my eyes widening.

Richard raised a reassuring hand, seeing my immediate distress. "I think she's over at the bar getting drunk on the local mud beer. She finished up with Jessica and walked out in a huff as soon as I came back. Were you two involved?"

"No," I said firmly.

"Maybe she's just trying to get to know the locals then," Richard said, shrugging. "She'll be fine. Mercury's human after all."

"So noted."

Katryn surveyed the convertible, pacing around it as if it was hers. Which, given her rank in the Dunwych, she could probably make happen. "You have an excellent vehicle, Richard. Peter and I have our own transportation but this should allow you to meet us in the city."

I blinked, glancing up at her. "The city? You're going there, too?"

"The Dunwych are amassing an army," Peter said, gritting his teeth. "They're going to attack the Necromancer's stronghold head on."

"I see." The Dunwych never did anything halfway.

"Yeah, Aragorn here is going to take Gondor up to the Black Gate. It's suicide," Richard said, shaking his head.

"What?" I asked.

"Long story. I'll be busy for the next half-hour." Gathering up all the occult artifacts he'd assembled, Richard walked through the guest-room door and slammed it behind him. "Don't disturb me unless you want to get eaten by something unmentionable which isn't me."

"What a strange man," I muttered.

Katryn nodded in agreement. "We know the approximate location of the Black Cathedral, but no details about its defenses. If you can recover your memory, we will have a substantial advantage."

Something told me Richard was right when he described a direct assault as suicide. I kept my mouth shut, however. "I will do what I can. Hopefully, I will see you in a day or so."

Reaching around, I placed a warm kiss on Katryn's lips. I could feel Peter's eyes boring into the back of our heads and the cold hatred which came with intense jealousy. In a way, it was almost comforting. Jealousy was a purely human emotion, something born and bred in the soul of every man. How ironic it was for a relationship I couldn't stand.

Katryn pulled away first, smiling brightly. "Stay safe, John."

Jackie watched the two of us from the car seat, fascinated by our romance. "Aw."

"Oh, John," I heard Peter speak behind me. "I have something for you as well."

"What's that?" I asked, turning my head.

"This." He then threw a punch at me, his fist covered in a brass knuckle he'd slipped on.

Huh, apparently I'd been right on the money on him being jealous.

CHAPTER FOURTEEN

As with Katryn, I saw Peter's swing coming before it connected. This gave me time to duck under it, albeit just barely. Peter wasn't the same caliber of warrior as Katryn but he was still an R&E Ranger—the best of a hungry and violent race of survivors. So I didn't feel guilty about jabbing my fists up into his ribs, a cheap shot to repay a cheap shot.

"Oof!" Peter choked, before recovering quickly. Kneeing me in the gut, he punched me across the face with a fierce blow that sent me spinning backwards. Hitting the ground with a thud, I threw a punch at Peter's abdomen and then head-butted him across the chin, recovering my resolve.

Katryn reacted first, her outrage over the display clear. Pointing at Peter, she shouted, "As your priestess, I command you to stand down!"

"No. This one is mine," Peter growled. Reaching over to a nearby bench, he grabbed a tire iron. "You both disgust me. He's not even a person."

"You'll pay for that remark," I said, seeing his weapon. Our encounter had gone from a brawl to a life-and-death struggle.

Katryn seemed stunned by his stupidity, momentarily senseless. "You have sworn away your life."

"Leave him to me," I said, rising up. "I'm going to enjoy killing him."

That was when Peter came at me with his newly acquired weapon. Grabbing some sawdust off the ground, I threw it in his face, temporarily blinding him.

"Monster!" Peter shouted. His blow missed and I promptly pulled the tire iron from his hands before throwing him into a nearby pile of machinery.

"And proud of it," I said.

If Richard heard our struggle, he wisely decided to stay out of it. The door to the guest room remained firmly closed, limiting our conflict to the garage.

Peter immediately got up, charging at me and beginning another series of brutal swings at my face. His attacks were wild and emotional, in direct defiance of his CQC training. Had I not been overwhelmed with anger myself, I could have easily disabled him and sent him painlessly to the ground. Instead, I blocked each of his blows before starting to punch him in the face with purely the intent to hurt.

Jackie and Katryn looked on as Peter regained some of his senses, his mouth dripping blood from my earlier blows. Jabs, kicks, and grapples followed as we sought to beat each other senseless.

Peter wasn't as strong or as skilled as I, but he was faster and his blows were unrestrained by mercy. There was darkness inside him that was almost palpable, a darkness driving him to hit harder and faster than he normally would have.

Peter's anger was a distinct advantage as I held myself back, pulling my punches when they could have shattered bones. I wasn't sure I wanted to do him any permanent lasting harm and that was hurting my chances.

Then he picked up a wrench.

"Fuck it," I said, grunting in rage. Seeing him swinging it toward my face, I quite simply went nuts.

Blocking the wrench with my tire iron, I kicked him savagely in the stomach before ripping the weapon from his grip. I then struck him across the face with my weapon. He was lucky he wasn't killed instantly. Instead, he just hit the ground like a sack of potatoes.

"I'll …" Peter started to speak, spitting out teeth.

"No, never again," I said. My shoulder started burning again as I felt a hate within me I couldn't remember feeling before but seemed to drown out all other feelings.

Pulling him up by the dog tag and lifting the wrench over my shoulder, I was ready to kill him. Then I began to hear music. Not the retro tunes of Richard's jukebox, but something from another world: a weird, alien piping mixed with unnatural-sounding flutes and surreal stringed instruments which drowned out all other sounds.

In the background, there was chanting. The voices were not all human, each speaking the same word over and over again: *Azathoth, Azathoth, Azathoth, Azathoth, Azathoth.*

Azathoth was the name of the Dunwych god of creation and destruction. Supposedly, he'd created the universe in a fit of madness. I had no idea why I thought of him and the terrifying music devoted to his glory. Yet, I could feel the music running through my body as my shoulder burned. The act of murdering Peter was like an action sacred to that dread god.

Dropping the wrench from my grip, I blinked. Slowly, the bizarre music quieted and eventually faded away. What the hell was happening to me?

Realizing I was still holding a nearly senseless Peter, I ripped the dog tags free from his neck. "You do not deserve these. You are a disgrace to the United States Remnant and the city of New Arkham. You are a horrible example of a human being, a slaver and scum. Get out of my sight. If I ever see you again, I'll kill you."

Peter looked up to me and spit blood against my chest, defiant to the end. His courage didn't last long however, because he immediately ran off afterward. Watching him flee like a coward, I wondered why I'd spared his life. A smarter man would have killed him then and there.

I couldn't do it, though. Not when I didn't know if it was me that wanted him dead or something *else* inside me. The fact I couldn't tell the difference frightened me more than I could put into words.

"You should have killed him," Katryn said, watching him leave. "Now you'll have to do it later, if I don't get to him first."

"I know."

Jackie looked at me from over the edge of the convertible, her eyes briefly looking like Richard's. For a second, as the last of the music faded away, I swore I could see the canine visage of a ghoul superimposed over her human features. I saw her red hair growing out of her ghoul-like head, a hideous sight given her normal cuteness.

Shaking away the hallucination, I took several deep breaths to calm myself. "I'm sorry, Jackie. A girl like you shouldn't be witness to that sort of violence."

"It's okay, Mister Booth. I saw my Da kill plenty of people

before," Jackie said, looking at me with a dissonant cheerfulness. "I'm sorry you didn't kill him."

"Me too," I muttered.

What the hell was wrong with me? I didn't get a chance to think about that because Katryn took my hand and whispered, "When you were about to kill Peter, I saw something in your eyes. What did you see?"

"Nothing," I said, pulling away.

Katryn half-closed her eyes. "Do not lie to me, John. You had the look of a high priest in your eyes. Either that or a man who has the blessing of the Awakened Gods upon him."

I gave her a sideways glance. "I don't feel blessed."

"Blessed or cursed is relative." Katryn took a deep breath. "Tell me what you saw. You can trust me."

I couldn't but I'd invested heavily in our alliance. "I heard something, music and strange voices. They were chanting the name of your creator god."

"Azathoth, the Creator and Destroyer. The Blind Idiot God has taken notice of your quest." Katryn sounded awed. "Him or his messenger, Nyarlathotep. Perhaps a sorcerer did not place that mark on you, but the gods themselves."

"Blind Idiot God?" Jackie asked.

"Azathoth is the maker of the universe according to Dunwych mythology, but he's a gibbering, mindless abomination. They believe he will eventually destroy the universe as effortlessly as he made it," I explained, remembering all I'd learned from the *Necronomicon* and my earlier conversations with Katryn.

Jackie's eyes widened. "Wow, the Dunwych have awesome gods."

"I'll try and keep my enthusiasm contained."

Katryn's eyes became so cold, I believed she was about to kill me. "Do not mock our faith."

"I'm not," I said, lying. "If you say I am blessed by alien gods, I will take your word for it."

I had my own suspicions about what had happened, too. I'd died at the hands of the nightgaunt, genuinely died. Somehow, this had activated the Hand of Nyarlathotep that had been placed on my skin long ago. Jessica was currently having her life-force drained to heal me and somehow this was also putting me in touch with eldritch forces, possibly ones associated with the Dunwych's so-called gods. If my theory was true, it was all the more important that I break the bond between me and Jessica. The Mark could be doing irreversible damage to me, making me into something … less than human. Worse still, I could be becoming something *more*. It was better than the idea I'd always had something *other* inside me, but not by much.

"Are you okay, Jackie?"

"Oh yes, I love it here," Jackie said. "Can I stay?"

I thought about that and decided, increasingly, she was half-ghoul and doomed to become like Richard. Death would be a kindness but I wouldn't be able to do that to a young girl. Better she be with her own kind. "I'll think about it."

"Whatcha thinking about, Mister Booth?" Jackie asked, obviously seeing I was deep in thought.

"Nothing important," I said, smiling.

Katryn leaned in and gave me one last kiss, this one long and lingering. Pulling back, she gave me a slight nod before walking out. "Keep the spear, John. You may need it. Also, be nice to the one you care for. You will need her."

"Do you mean Jessica or Mercury?"

"Yes," Katryn said. "Watch over the child, Jackie as well. I feel your fates are intertwined."

I was now more confused than ever. "Alright."

I walked back into the guest room, my eyes giving one last glance toward her as she disappeared out the front door. Inside the chamber, Richard had drawn a mystic circle on the ground with pig's blood. The symbols inside seemed to pulse and shift like the ones on my knife. Once more, the sight of the spellwork made me ill, causing me to look away.

I'd seen more than my fair share of debased rituals in the Wasteland. Spells designed around summoning horrific monsters, assuming unnatural forms, and even raising the dead. More often than not, these enchantments enacted a horrific toll on their casters. Those who dabbled in the arcane arts usually ended up deformed, insane, or both. It bothered me I had to seek the assistance of sorcery to save Jessica's life, even sorcery worked by someone I trusted as much as Richard.

"I hate magic," I muttered, shutting the door behind me and locking it.

"Yet, you own a copy of the *Necronomicon*," Richard pointed out. "Can't get much more magical than that. It's the Koran of the Creepy. The Bible of the Black Arts. The ..."

"Knowledge isn't magic," I interrupted, keeping my eyes closed before sitting down on the ground beside Richard. The *Necronomicon* contained a great deal of useful information beyond the spells inside.

"Sure it is," Richard said, starting to draw pictograms in blood on my forehead. "All knowledge is magic. The problem is that knowledge is power and power corrupts. So, by definition, knowledge corrupts!"

"You just made that up," I said, staring at him.

"Of course, I made it up. Who else would say something so wise? I was able to get the spell I needed from the ghoul elders living a few miles under the valley, but this is *not* going to be easy. I can't just wave my hand and remove the bond between you and Jessica."

"Just tell me what I have to do." I waited for him to finish before shifting positions to Indian style on the ground.

"We need to go talk to an Elder Thing," Richard explained, assuming a position identical to mine.

"An Elder ... Thing," I repeated, taking the same skeptical tone as Mercury had during our conversation regarding the Color. I vaguely remembered reading about these Elder Things in the *Necronomicon* but I'd been hoping they had some other name to refer to themselves by. Seriously, did I just walk up to them and call them *things*? It seemed rude.

"Don't start with me." Richard poked me in the chest with a clawed finger. "Their actual name is unpronounceable by humans. They're big, powerful, and almost as old as the Great Old Ones. If anything in the universe can break this spell and restore your memories, it's one of them."

I wasn't about to argue with him. "What are they doing in the Dreamlands?"

Richard shrugged. "Safer than remaining on Earth, I guess. Once they were the top dogs on our planet, millions of years back, ruling the world in their arcane tentaclely fashion. Then the Great

Old Ones came from the sky and kicked them off their throne. The Elder Things had human slaves and shoggoths to look after them and lasted as a viable culture until the end of the last Ice Age. The few remaining ones fled from Antarctica to the Dreamlands about a century and a half ago."

"That recently?" I was surprised the Old Earth's governments hadn't detected them.

"Humans are a dumb, unobservant species. You'd be surprised at how much shit was going down without anyone realizing it," Richard huffed. "Er, no offense."

"None taken," I said. "My opinion of my fellow man has never been particularly high. How are we going to persuade this being to help me?"

"I have no fucking idea." Richard coughed into one hand. "That's your problem. Stop asking so many questions. You're about to enter an alternate dimension through astral projection; most people would be fascinated by the shit we're doing."

"Fair enough," I said. I then removed my shirt so Richard could start drawing more symbols on my chest. He also lit a set of candles which filled the air with a strange pungent aroma. I recognized the smell as Ghoul Dust, a powerful hallucinogen the underground race traded with outsiders. Its use was often said to cause insanity and death.

Great.

"What can you tell me about the Dreamlands?" I asked, as I started feeling a bit woozy. I knew very little about the place, other than it was a place priestesses like Katryn and psychics like Martha visited regularly. Professor Ward had speculated it was a quantum dimension adjacent to our reality, affected by the now-proven phenomenon of psychic resonance. Richard and apparently all ghouls everywhere considered it just as important as the physical world, which told me jack shit about what to expect.

"It's the collected mental diarrhea of the universe. Every little thought you have is reflected there and so are the thoughts of everyone you've ever met. All of humanity's puny little gods along with every little fool who's ever been so foolish as to believe in an afterlife exists in the Dreamlands," Richard said, pulling a leather wineskin out from under the bed and handing it to me. "Drink this;

it'll put hair on your chest. Admittedly, not as much as mine."

"Doesn't sound so bad," I said. Taking a drink, I found myself coughing violently. The substance inside tasted like octopus ink mixed with blood.

"It wouldn't be if it was just humanity's delusions of self-importance and masturbation fantasies. The problem is it's also every single terrible thought and nightmare every species in the universe has had. Let me tell you, the most miniscule thought of Cthulhu could destroy the collective dream worlds of an entire planet of lesser beings—you know, folks like us."

"How depressing," I said, coughing again.

"Hey, I didn't make the world. I just try and live in it." Richard shrugged.

I was tempted to ask when the spell would begin, only to have myself start going into convulsions. My mouth foamed over as my eyes rolled back into my head; every part of my body felt alight with fire. Finally, after several moments of agonizing pain, the entire world faded away. For a split second, I thought I was about to die.

Then, almost immediately, I found my eyes opening to an alien sky.

CHAPTER FIFTEEN

I stared up at the alien sky, blinking my eyes.

No, not an alien sky, it was the sky of a world long dead. Everything was a surreal blue color. There were strange puffy white clouds and the air was fresh. The sun was shining, the color yellow, and I could hear birds chirping in the distance. It was a place I had only seen in my dreams, a bright and beautiful place the Great Old Ones destroyed long ago. I was in the shadow of Old Earth's glory.

"Wow, this is totally not what Earth's sky looked like," Richard said, walking up ahead of me. "What's that smell in the air, oxygen? Geez, man, you have got some weird ideas about what the twenty-first century smelled like. It was mostly carbon monoxide and poison."

"Please be quiet, Richard, I want to appreciate this." I ran my arms through the dirt around me, making an angel, before standing up. I was no longer dressed in camouflage, but instead in my R&E uniform. My father's leather Stetson was affixed prominently to my head along with his weather-beaten duster to my back and I saw my heavy assault rifle nestled up against some nearby rocks.

Amazing.

In what was becoming a running theme in this trip, I saw I was once more on the side of a cliff face. This one overlooked a vast sweeping vista consisting solely of gravesites. They were marked with swords, guns, and other weapons of war in place of headstones. In the center of the seemingly endless military cemetery, a spiraling tower stood, which spun infinitely into the air. The tower vaguely resembled the same architecture which compromised the Black Cathedral, but was majestic as opposed to ominous.

"Where are we?" I asked, stunned by the sight.

"The Dreamlands. Specifically, the Fields of Blades," Richard said, glancing over the cliff face and taking in the somber landscape. "The Jungian archetypal representation of the endlessness and futility of war. Wow, John, your subconscious is a real vacation spot."

"I don't put much faith in psychology." I took a deep breath. "What does the tower represent?"

"It's a tower, John. It's probably where the Elder Things live. Remember, we're just using your dreamscape to find them."

"Anyway, why are you here?" I had been under the impression this would be a solo mission. Then again I knew very little about the Dreamlands; he probably thought I needed a guide.

"No way am I leaving you out here—oh shit." Richard pointed in the direction over my left shoulder. "On your six!"

Looking over my shoulder, I saw the decaying form of my dead father. "Shit."

The rotted corpse was dressed in a tattered version of the uniform he was buried in. Half of its face was blown off by the shotgun blast which had killed him. The air reeked of its rotting stench, as if it had been dead for a week. I was surprised I'd missed it while breathing in the fresh Dreamlands air. Spinning me around with its desiccated hands, the zombie-like creature proceeded to grab me by the throat.

"Not my son!" it gargled through a twisted, mangled jaw. Its grip was tight and vice-like as I struggled to pull its fingers free from my neck.

"You're not my father!" Pressing my hands against the creature's face, I struggled to push it back before pressing my thumbs into its eyes. Both fingers slid straight into the soft tissue, the half-rotted orbs collapsing beneath the pressure I applied.

The monster emitted an inhuman growl before pulling back, clawing at its bleeding eye sockets. I tried to maneuver myself out of the way but the monster proceeded to slam one of its huge arms against my face, sending me to the ground.

"Not my son!" it screamed again, charging its eyeless body at me. Tackling me to the ground, it once more tried to strangle me.

"Need help?" Richard said, acting as if there was nothing to be concerned about.

"Shoot it!" I screamed, struggling to maneuver my hands around its neck. Each breath was more difficult. In a few moments, I'd be dead if Richard didn't intervene. I was not going to give this bastard the chance to finish what he started three decades ago. "Shoot it, now!"

"Fine," Richard muttered before walking over to where I'd once stood and taking up my heavy assault rifle. The weapon proceeded to fill the creature's chest with holes. Despite being undead, it seemed pained by the action. With a quick motion, I snapped its neck and sent the monster spiraling to the ground.

"Feel better?"

"Give me my gun." I extended my hand towards Richard, looking at the strange dream creature on the ground.

"Sure." Richard handed the gun to me.

I proceeded to aim it at Richard, not bothering to look from the corpse on the ground. "Never joke around when my life is in danger. I wouldn't do the same with you. If you ever do something similar again, I'll kill you."

I meant it, too. As beneficial as I found our partnership, I wasn't about to risk my safety. I would kill whoever I had to in order to get to Alan Ward. He would pay for killing my squad and if I had to sacrifice others to do it, well, then, so be it.

"Sorry, was just a joke." Richard shrugged before glancing down at the corpse. "Take a look at it."

Slowly, but surely, its features began changing from a deformed representation of my father to something else entirely. The final result was a creature the size of a small horse. It stood taller than my father, at least eight feet, and was a mass of deformed muscle. It possessed claws more akin to knives than talons and a mouth that looked like it made up eighty percent of its face. Below its waist was a pair of kangaroo-like legs, ending in cloven hooves. If Richard was hard to look at, this creature was absolutely ghastly.

"A ghast," Richard appropriately named it, pinching the ends of his snout. "The ancestral enemies of ghouls."

"Do they normally assume the form of loved ones to stalk someone?" I asked, appalled at the intimacy of the violation.

"No." Richard looked distinctly uncomfortable. "They're ghasts, John. They don't do the whole 'fascinated with humans' thing my race is famous for. They eat, sleep, fuck, and kill."

"Like humans," I said, struggling for breath. "So this creature is unlikely to have assumed my father's form on his own?"

"You could say that. Of course, they also die in sunlight so I'm not sure what the hell is going on with this particular one."

"Interesting," I said, struggling to get as much oxygen down my bruised windpipe as possible. "Go on."

"If it's protected by magic, whoever set this stuff up has some serious juice behind his or her spells. That kind of magic has not been seen since the days when Atlantis, Mu, and R'lyeh were only half-sunk." Richard reached down and parted some of its fur, revealing tattooed sigils to the Elder God Hypnos.

I'd read about Hypnos during my studies under Doctor Ward. He was a deity of sleep and dreams, equally likely to do good or evil. Supposedly, only the most powerful sorcerers attempted to harness his power since one could never tell whether one's entreaties would be met with favoritism or retribution.

Richard then said, "Yep, this is big-ass sorcery here. You don't call on this guy unless you're absolutely sure you know what you're doing."

"So you're saying someone *sent* this thing after me? Dressed, for lack of a better word, as my father?"

"Someone who knew you were coming to the Dreamlands, yes," Richard said, blinking his large dog-like eyes. "Got any suspects?"

"One." Dammit, things had just gotten a whole lot more complicated. "What now?"

Richard looked out to the tower. "We walk."

"How long do you think it will take?"

"As long it takes."

CHAPTER SIXTEEN

"As long as it takes" turned out to be seven weeks, three days, and eleven hours. The travel time bothered me until Richard explained it would only be seconds in the real world. Either that or we'd starve to death and our problems would be over anyway.

In the end, there was plenty of food and water to be found within the Dreamlands if you knew where to look. We traded with a tribe of nomadic Horned Men, fought several winged horrors from Leng, enjoyed the hospitality of several cloven-hoofed succubi, and paid our respects to the many warriors whose dreams were buried here.

By the end of our journey, we were exhausted and worn to the quick but perhaps a little bit wiser. Standing less than a yard from the Elder Things' tower, we both stared upward as if to try and catch a glimpse of the tower's top. A futile gesture since the tower appeared to be literally infinite in its height.

Far away, the tower had looked like it was a gargantuan but comprehensible structure that was only a few miles away. Now that we had reached it, we saw the tower's true nature was unfathomably greater. The building's mass defied description and we were less than ants compared to its Olympian presence. Even the Great Old Ones would have felt terribly small at the foot of the enormous building. The staggering fact was, there were doors and windows built into the tower for beings who would not even see us for their height. I could not imagine the mass of the beings inhabiting this tower, what sort of life they lead, or how they would react to us.

If they noticed us at all.

"You know ..." Richard looked down and started to roll a cigarette, having stolen some Ulthar tobacco from the Horned Men we'd met. "That is one big fucking tower."

"Yeah," I said, not looking away. "It really is."

"Getting through the front door is going to be tough," Richard said. "And by tough I mean impossible."

We were right in front of the tower's single visible door; unfortunately, there was seemingly no way to open it. It would take unimaginable force to budge it even a few degrees. Had a small crack existed under the door, we could have easily fit underneath it, but no such space was present. It was hundreds of feet high and probably dozens of feet thick. I saw no way to break it open, especially not with the minimal equipment in our possession.

"This is going to be difficult," I said, taking a deep breath. "Were the Elder Things this big?"

"I don't think so," Richard said. "I've never actually met one, mind you, but they used to live in Antarctica. I'm pretty sure this place would be visible from Earth on Jupiter."

"You have a point. The fact something like this can exist baffles me," I shook my head. "So how are we going to get in?"

Richard shrugged his shoulders. "Not my problem."

"Thank you," I said, sarcastically. "I'm glad I can count on you."

"Hey, I'm just being honest." The ghoul threw his hands up in the air. "I have no idea. You're the brains here, Soldier Boy. I'm just the guide."

"Maybe we should just knock?" I suggested, not really having any answers for tackling a problem of this magnitude.

"Somehow, I don't think that would work." Richard pointed between us. "Dress code and all."

Richard's Hawaiian shirt had mostly rotted off him, leaving him looking more like a regular ghoul—naked and animalistic. The rain and the yellowish spores we'd encountered had mostly eaten it away. My own clothes were now covered in mud, thread-worn, and looking like they'd been through hell and back.

"Fine," I said, trying to think of other options. Then I remembered an old saying my father had taught me: *The only thing infinite that can be held in a man's hands is a thought*. It was a Zen koan he'd picked up from a Wasteland mystic named Carter. Now, I could see the wisdom in it, especially here. "Richard, close your eyes."

"Why?" Richard suddenly tensed. "What are you planning?'

"Just do it." I tried to focus on the fact this was my dream. Even if it somehow linked up with a greater "Uber-Dream" all beings shared, it was still formed by my thoughts and ideas. That meant I had the power here.

"Okay." Richard finally obeyed my command, shutting his furry eyelids.

Doing the same, I imagined Richard and I were tall enough to walk into the tower through the front door. I stepped forward, putting my hands out, believing I had enough force to move mountains. Everything would depend on my believing the impossible, something I tried to do at least six times a day.

I was rewarded by the feel of the stone giving way, slowly at first but gradually more deliberately. The tower didn't become any smaller but its proportions shifted, as if the universe was re-orientating itself to my vision. Did the Great Old Ones see the world this way? If so, did that make the physical universe their dream? I wasn't sure I wanted to know the answer. My musings ended when I felt the stone fall forward as if pushed down. It struck the ground with a titanic but not ear-splitting thud.

"Huh. It worked," I said, opening my eyes. We were now standing in a tower built for beings only slightly larger than ourselves. If we had gone down the rabbit hole, we'd now just drunk from the bottle labeled DRINK ME.

"John, what you just did is impossible. The Dreamlands don't work this way." Richard looked almost offended at what I'd done. "If they did, I would have advised you to *dream us up a damn plane*."

"I had considered that," I admitted. "On my first day no less."

"*You might have mentioned that!*" Richard's voice was shrill and I actually heard growling in the back of his inhuman throat.

"I just figured you'd have told me if such a thing were possible. Besides, I was enjoying the journey," I said, shrugging my shoulders. "I got a lot of thinking done while I was out. I think I solved a number of philosophical riddles I'd been long pondering. Like, 'Why do good things happen to bad people?' and 'Where do my socks go when I put them in the dryer?'"

"Next time, save your weird-ass walkabout for when I'm not potentially starving to death in the physical world." Richard looked about ready to tackle me. I admit, it felt good to pay him back for what he'd done during the ghast attack.

The interior of the tower was surprisingly homey, albeit not in a manner most human beings would find comfortable. The hallway was circular and uneven, as opposed to square, often looking like a size-shifting worm had dug its passages. There were torches along the walls, but each was tipped with a coral-like crystal instead of fire. What was recognizably furniture was present as well, but for bodies unrelated to any hominid ancestor.

"I'm not sure if I should be unnerved or reassured at the similarities," I said, taking a moment to soak in the alien architecture.

"The Elder Things are carbon-based beings." Richard warily began walking in. "That's rarer than you think. I suppose in the grand scheme of things that makes them closer to our race than say, the Great Old Ones' species or species-es. What's the plural form of species?"

"Species. You said *our* race?" I asked, enjoying his crisis of language.

"You've adopted one of our kids; you're an honorary ghoul now. Just don't expect to win any beauty pageants." Richard slapped me on the back.

His words confirmed something I'd expected for a long time. Little Jackie was a ghoul-human hybrid and doomed to undergo the same transformation Richard had undergone. "Richard, was … it painful?"

"The Change?" Richard's voice grew very cold, almost sad.

"Yes."

"Excruciating." Richard's voice, still human despite his canine mouth, changed only a little as he said that one word. That tiny change in his voice, however, spoke volumes.

"I'm sorry."

The two of us soon found ourselves at a strange, twisting staircase, one which rose high up toward a star-shaped doorway. Beyond it, strange noises echoed and weird lights flickered on and off. We both paused at the base of it, not ready to make the trek up, even if our quarry was close at hand.

Richard took a moment to think before he started speaking again, "Listen, if you want some advice about Jackie, the best thing—"

And then he was dead.

The nature of combat is a violent, swift, unromantic thing. That was the first thing I'd learned as a soldier. One moment, you were standing next to someone you thought of as a friend and brother-in-arms, the next you were cradling their dead body. In Richard's case, he was struck by a bolt of strange alien energy which passed through the front of his chest and out the other side like a gunshot. A massive, gaping hole was created by the blast, killing him instantly.

I had only a split moment to react before a second bolt was discharged in my direction. Reflexes are faster than conscious thought, however. I was able to maneuver out of the way of where my assailant was aiming. Long enough to privately vow I would kill whoever had taken my best friend from me.

Staring up at the top of the stairs, I saw the Elder Thing. It was not as sanity-blasting as some of the creatures I'd seen in the Wasteland. Yet, the creature was still alien and terrifying. It was a creature from another world, whose race had colonized the Earth when it was nothing more than boiling seawater. The Elder Thing stood eight feet tall with a barrel-like chest and starfish-esque appendages where its head and feet should have been.

It had other inhuman qualities which unsettled me just looking at them, such as stalks for eating and seeing in ways humans could not appreciate, but none of these interested me. The only things that did were the crystalline rod it held in one of its tentacles—the weapon which had killed my friend—and the fact it was Richard's murderer.

"Murderer!" I screamed at the top of my lungs, forgetting all thought of how the creature might help me.

Lifting my heavy assault rifle, I poured the dream-based ammunition into the creature's weapon. The monster didn't seem to understand what I was doing, only moving its weapon to fire again as the tendril holding it was promptly shredded.

The Elder Thing let forth an inhuman shriek as blue and greenish fluids poured out of its wounds. The crystal rod shattered seconds later, disarming it. In that moment, a red mist came over my eyes, drowning out all reason. I continued firing into the monster's chest, wounding it further until the magazine was empty.

The Elder Thing was badly injured from my assault, bleeding from multiple holes spread across its chest while letting forth wails of pain which no terrestrial animal could duplicate. Grabbing my rifle by the barrel, I charged up the stairs and slammed my body squarely into the Elder Thing's chest. The creature possessed strength no human could match but the intensity of my anger drowned out all difference in our sizes.

The Elder Thing was thrown to the ground, its frame sliding across the polished surface of the tower's floors. I could tell by the shrieking and wailing it made that it was stunned by the ferocity of my attack.

Good.

"Butcher! Beast! Creature!" I screamed at the top of my lungs, bringing the end of my rifle around and smashing it against the tendrils sticking out of the top of its octagonal body. The tissue there was soft, and pieces broke off with the first blow.

The thing had no eyes or face to read emotions from, but I could sense its fear as I brought down the butt of my weapon into its head tentacles again and again. Its wounds sprayed me with the Elder Thing's neon-colored internal fluids, dying my attire a shade of luminescent orange. The same unstoppable rage I'd experienced fighting Peter once more consumed me, driving me to beat the Elder Thing to death. I once more heard the music of Azathoth's court.

This time, I embraced it.

"You have no idea what you've destroyed!" I shouted, hearing the sound of my weapon bash against its head. "One of the last true humans!"

It was an insane comment and in all likelihood, the Elder Thing had no idea what I was saying; still, it made me feel better.

By the end of my penultimate attack, its upper appendages were a brutalized mass of fluids and gore as I saw its eye-like sensory stalks look at me. Lifting my weapon up a final time, I prepared to crush the monster's head in and end its life. The music in my head reached a crescendo, signaling it was time to send the beast to whatever hell awaited it.

That was when I heard a voice in my head, a telepathic plea that sounded almost human despite its peculiar stereo-like quality. Its words were the only things that might stay my hand from finishing it off. *"Please, don't harm the children!"*

What?

The otherworldly music in my head grew louder, as if compelling me to crush the Elder Thing's upper torso despite the Elder Thing's dying plea. Forcing myself to resist the urge, I managed to drive out the accursed music. It took every ounce of my willpower; I dearly wanted to kill the beast and avenge Richard's death, but I did it. I would not become a man who orphaned children if I could help it.

Stopping the descent of my weapon just a few feet above its head, I asked, "What did you say?"

The Elder Thing moved up one of its protruding stalks, possibly what passed for its eyes. What it said next with its telepathic speech sounded almost surprised. *"You can understand me? Impossible. Humans do not have the mental capacity to understand the language of the Elder Race."*

I lifted my weapon again, holding it over the tentacles which existed in place of its face. "Think again."

God, I wanted to kill it. Taking several deep breaths, I managed to calm myself, albeit barely. If the creature showed any sign of treachery, I vowed to smash it to a gory pulp of alien goo—children or not.

One of its outgrowths raised in an almost pleading gesture. "I apologize. I have not seen any of your species since the dying days of my people's civilization, when the southern continent dwellers worshiped the snake god Yig-Seth and the northerner continent dwellers prayed at the altar of Crom Cruach."

I aimed my makeshift club at its tentacles, uncaring about the creature's reminisces. "You said you had children?"

It was ridiculous to pull back now. Nothing this thing said could change the fact it had murdered Richard, one of the few people in my life I called friend. Yet, I couldn't bring myself to kill the beast if it was just trying to protect its offspring. Enough sympathy existed within me to understand that was an urge that united all races.

At least, I hope it did.

"As your race defines them, yes. You are not here to destroy my clan's egg clutch?" the Elder Thing said, its telepathic voice causing me as much of a headache as my recent memory flashes.

"No."

"I am sorry. I presumed you were with the Necromancer." The Elder Thing had no emotions which could be read on its nonexistent face, yet I guessed it was probably feeling guilty. Probably. Its telepathic "voice" lacked the inflections that would have told me for sure.

Nevertheless, I listened as it continued to speak, *"I bear your species no harm. Yet, one member of it has transcended the limitations you possess. He has destroyed several other Dreamlands clans, seizing their technology and homesteads. I assumed you were his agent."*

"No, his enemy." I put my weapon down, though still kept my grip tightly around its handle. "I know we invaded your home but we came in peace. We only wanted to ask for your help."

I doubted Elder Things possessed the capacity to appreciate irony or experience bitterness at the vagaries of fate. Yet, if the aliens had an equivalent, I suspected it would be feeling them. *"I will assist you in any way possible, if only for the fact you are a highly dangerous organism and I wish you out of my domain."*

It was almost enough to make me laugh. This whole thing was absurd—tragically, horrifically absurd. "Believe me, I don't want to be here anymore than you do."

"I somehow doubt that." The being continued to twitch on the ground, still badly wounded from my attack. Unlike other entities I'd encountered, apparently Elder Things didn't regenerate. *"Since you can communicate, I would like to know how you broke the proportion-warping effect we worked around our hatchery. It should have made the tower impossibly formidable to look upon."*

I bit my lip. It had all been an illusion. Richard would have found that funny. "Luck, I guess."

"That is an insufficient answer," the creature responded. Its cold and clinical manner made me want to kill it, any earlier sympathy largely evaporated.

"I saw through it." My grip tightened around the barrel of my gun. I desperately wanted to believe Richard was still alive, that he'd just woken up when his astral-self had been killed, but something told me that wasn't the case. He was dead and it was my fault, all because of my insane need to find out more about my last mission.

Staring at the creature, I hoped against hope there was some arcane magical solution for what had just occurred. "Can you raise my friend back from the dead?"

The Elder Thing twitched a second before responding. *"Resuscitation of non-Elder Race life-forms does not fall within my area of expertise. No."*

No, of course not, that would have been too easy.

I pulled out a spare ammunition magazine, one I imagined was in my pocket before it appeared. I then placed it in my weapon's chamber. It was an experiment to see if I could still bend reality, the size of the tower being an illusion aside.

So far, so good.

Holding the weapon up to its head, I put my finger on the trigger and contemplated just sending the Elder Thing to whatever afterlife awaited plant-sea creature hybrid aliens. I then asked, "Can you remove a spell?"

The creature was clearly distressed and I wondered if it was scared. Could Elder Things even feel fear? If they could, I was glad. I would hate this thing forever for killing Richard. Still, I needed it to finish my mission. That was the only way I could sort through my grief right now.

Noticing it was hesitating, I put the gun straight to where I guessed its central nervous system laid. "Answer me!"

"I do not know what a spell is," the Elder Thing finally admitted. *"Your mental projections regarding them just come off as nonsensical, irrational imagery."*

"It's a connection, between me and something called Nyarlathotep." I kept the gun aimed at it, fully intending to kill it if it couldn't help. "It is a god, if you know what that is."

Would it be murder? Probably, but murder was something you became used to in the Wasteland. I'd never executed someone without good cause before, but the death of my friend was pretty damn good cause in my mind, mistake on the Elder Thing's part or not.

"Ah. I am familiar with the Dreamlands' personifications of the universe's laws." The Elder Thing moved its tendril over my chest. *"Strange, this seems to weave in and out of your body."*

"Just break it."

"You are not entirely divorced from this power. If I remove it, it will not change the fact you are not entirely dissimilar to my race, at least mentally," the Elder Thing said.

"I have no idea what that means."

"I am unsurprised. Despite your ignorance, you may be quite useful to my people, especially if this Nyarlathotep is the same being we call K'Tharl'tak." The Elder Thing seemed almost … cocky. *"You are evolved on a sturdier level than the humans I recall. You are different from them on a fundamental level."*

"I'm human, just human." I didn't like the way this conversation was going.

"Yes and no, which is why you are fascinating to me." The Elder Thing forced its presence against my mind. A stinging pain passed over me, one which threatened to kill me. For a moment, I thought that was the creature's intention but its presence was violently thrown out of my mind as if my brain was defending itself.

"It is done." The creature sounded almost impressed. *"I am surprised your mind could handle my psychic surgery."*

I tried to push down my suspicion of the creature. "Gee, thanks. Will the person I was connected to recover now?"

"Perhaps," it responded.

The Elder Thing was really starting to get on my nerves. I then told it, "There's one more thing I want you to do."

"Of course." The Elder Thing seemed almost annoyed. *"Humans always require more. You are not that removed from the primates we elevated you from."*

I was actually pleased the Elder Thing stooped to the level of petty insults. It showed the creature wasn't so far removed from humanity. "I'm also missing memories: memories that would help me fight the Necromancer you fear."

The Elder Thing lifted one of his outgrowths, the thing wiggling a bit in the air. If Elder Things had an equivalent of amused disbelief, it was showing it. *"The Necromancer is not remotely human, not anymore. It is close to a Great Old One, like the human who became one before named Carter."*

Normally, I would have asked more about a human becoming a Great Old One, but I needed to remain focused on my objective. *I can kill him. I have to. I just need to have my missing memories back so I can know what he did to me.*

The Elder Thing moved another one of its tendrils over me, *leaving a slimy trail up the front of my uniform. "Your collection of neurons is not a difficult pattern to follow, unusual as it may be, nor is it difficult to correct the disrupted pathways."*

Almost immediately, I felt its terrible psychic presence once more force itself into my brain. This time, the agonizing pain was located squarely in my mind.

I struggled to hold onto my rifle, slowly falling back a few steps while my vision blurred. "I don't ... remember anything, yet."

"The damage will take several more of your minutes to heal." The Elder Thing seemed to grow slightly more confident. *"Do not struggle. We do not intend to kill you. You are an anomaly which must be studied. It will assist my species in its survival while also aiding yours in its. This is a noble cause and should not take more than seventeen hundred cycles."*

I realized what the Elder Thing was talking about seconds later. Two more of its race stepped forth through the doorway before me, both wielding the same crystalline rods which the first had used to kill Richard.

They were lumbering forward, moving at an extremely slow place which was, nevertheless, menacing. They looked almost like demons with tentacles for heads, drawing on the most primordial racial fears of humanity.

"Son of a bitch," I said, falling back down the stairs as I aimed my assault rifle straight at the fallen Elder Thing's upper body. Firing, I watched its brain-matter equivalent splatter across the steps. It wasn't going to help me survive but it felt good to avenge Richard's death.

The remaining Elder Things proceeded to fire a series of luminescent green globes at my feet. The blasts exploded on the stairs beneath me, sending fragments of stone and dust up into my face. Falling down the staircase, I rolled out of the way of their next attack.

From the erratic nature of their blasts, I determined the Elder Things were not trying to kill, but instead disable me, probably for the sick experiments the dead one had spoken of. I wasn't about to let that happen. Climbing to my feet as another blast exploded behind me, I made a break for the door. The creatures continued their assault, forcing me to duck and dodge like I was playing football. Finally reaching the bottom of the staircase, I felt my leg burning from pieces of stone shards embedded in them. Staring down at the wound, I saw it was bleeding badly.

Great.

Continuing to shamble down the hall, I finally exited into the Dreamlands outside. There, the sky had once more filled with disturbing unnatural storm clouds. Instead of their earlier familiar faces, they took the form of hideous malformed monsters: things which resembled combinations of Elder Things, Great Old Ones, and humans. The rain pouring down from them had also changed, becoming a mixture of blood and gory chunks of flesh.

"Never trust an E.B.E.," I coughed. Now drenched in blood, I threw myself onto the ground and took up a defensive position. Holding my assault rifle in hand, I waited for the Elder Things to burst through. My rifle had been almost useless against the first of their kind, and I privately wished I had a bazooka.

Amazingly, the heavy assault rifle began to morph and twist in my hands. Almost like it was clay shaped by a child's hands, the weapon slowly became a bazooka. I concentrated and focused my will, transforming it into a specific weapon. Not a bazooka, but something packing a bit more punch, a P21 rocket launcher. The P21 was the only Post-Rising Anti-E.B.E. ballistic weapon ever created and it was damned good at its job.

"I'm starting to like the Dreamlands." I grinned, watching the two Elder Things through the open doorway. The infinite tower was no longer remotely infinite, now merely the size of a moderately tall skyscraper.

Firing my rocket launcher, the rocket sailed between them and exploded into the center of the hallway. For a brief moment, I thought they were both dead, their bodies consumed by the fire I'd created. It would have been a fitting funeral pyre for Richard, a way to celebrate his life by killing more of the beings who'd taken it.

Unfortunately, my predictions of victory were premature as neither of them had perished. Like the mythical phoenix, both emerged from the tower doorway covered in fire and looking decidedly pissed off.

"Dammit," I muttered, imagining another round for my rocket launcher. It was a hard and exacting process, conjuring things from nothing in the Dreamlands. Yet, the creatures weren't going to wait and I struggled to do it anyway.

Letting forth an unearthly and terrifying roar, like nothing ever produced on this Earth, the Elder Things smashed through the Tower's doorway and flew into the bloody rain with their crystal rods raised. That was when I got a good look at them, the flames around them dying out. The monsters weren't completely unharmed; their skins were covered in a gray flaky film that might have been the outer flesh seared by the force of my explosion.

At least I had managed to wound them.

"Shit," I muttered, watching the rocket I'd been conjuring twist to become unusable dream stuff. I'd let my attention wander and it had ruined the entire effect, giving the monsters time to attack. "This is going to hurt."

Two spiraling globes of energy shot forth and exploded at the base of my feet. The detonation was like a mine going off beneath me, throwing me in the air along with a pile of dirt. When my body struck the ground, I couldn't hear a thing through the ringing of my ears and the shaking of my body.

In all likelihood, I was suffering numerous internal injuries that would claim my life without proper medical attention. That is, if my legs hadn't been completely blown off by the blast; I couldn't tell at my current vantage. I struggled as I reached over for the rocket launcher. Despite my hands feeling like they weighed a hundred pounds, I tried desperately to reach for it. It was several feet away though, and I had to start pulling myself over towards it. The weapon was unloaded but I could just dream up ammunition.

I wasn't going to go out without a fight, maimed or not.

That was when the sky opened up and lightning poured down upon both. Not just a single bolt of it but a storm of electricity, hundreds of bolts hitting them one after the other. The terrible torrent didn't stop until both were little more than charred, ashen shells of their former selves. The Elder Things had no skeletons per se but their ruined interiors were similar enough that it gave me a little thrill. They were dead; there was no question about it. The question was *how*?

My answer came in the form of a silver-tipped cane pressing against the top of my abdomen. "Ah, John, fancy seeing you here. I knew you would eventually make your way into the Dreamlands, but in the company of Elder Things? Tsk-tsk. You should have told me you shared my passion for destroying the beasts, we could have arranged a hunt."

I recognized the voice.

Alan Ward had arrived.

CHAPTER SEVENTEEN

Staring upwards, I saw the figure of Alan Ward in all his demented glory. He stood over me, leaning on a silver-handled walking stick. The tip of the walking stick was shaped like an idol of Cthulhu. The disgusting octopi-headed demon-dragon thing possessed ruby eyes which seemed to glow with an unholy inner fire. He was dressed in an old Pre-Rising, black business suit which seemed pristine despite being at least a century old.

Around his neck hung a strange necklace, resembling a large warped starfish in a circle with an eye over it. I was so badly shaken by my experience that it took me a few seconds to realize it was the Elder Sign. Alan Ward had created his own syncretic religion combining worship of the Elder Gods and Cthulhu, despite how the two were usually depicted as opposed.

"Ward ..." I hissed through ragged breaths. More than ever, I wished I still had my rocket launcher. Putting a missile straight up his ass would have pleased me immensely.

"That's my name, yes," Ward said, pulling forth a sword from the end of his walking stick. It was long and made of a moon-colored metal that I could not identify. "I'm sorry it's come to this, John, but you've made a rather expansive mess."

"You killed them! You killed my friends! Tortured me! Kidnapped children and murdered more!" I spit out blood from where my lip had busted open. I tried to spit in his face but the saliva barely left my mouth as I struggled to move. I wanted desperately to strike out at the man, yet I had expended every last ounce of my strength fighting the Elder Things. I had nothing more to give, not even when faced with my squad's killer.

"Oh, don't act like that," Ward said, taking aim with his blade. "I bear you no ill will. However, there are always winners and losers in these things. That's assuming you even remember anything about our last fight—I'm afraid I left you a bit banged up after our last encounter."

Oh lovely, he'd decided to be *chatty*. "Go. To. Hell."

Ward tightly clutched his hands around his sword's handle. "There's no such place, John. The true gods care nothing about sin or redemption. Only humans do and we are as insignificant as rays of light caught in a black hole's gravity. I hope your next life proves more illuminating to the universe's truth."

"I'm going to kill you," I said. It was an irrational thing to say, I knew, but I said it anyway. Somehow, against all odds, I had faith it was not going to end this way. I had to believe it; otherwise, all of this had been for nothing.

"I sincerely doubt that," Ward moved his sword directly over my heart. In that moment, I realized I had to play on his arrogance. I wanted to live and I needed to buy time to avenge my squad. For that I was willing to do anything.

Watching him raise the sword to strike, I had the dubious honor of regaining my lost memories. The Elder Thing's psychic surgery finally took hold, restoring what I'd forgotten just as I was about to die. Just my luck, I was going to remember everything I needed to know to kill Doctor Ward when he was about to kill me.

One moment I was seeing the Necromancer's blade descend, the next I was once more his prisoner. I was naked, strapped to a vertical metal table, and inside a chamber of horrors. To call it a laboratory was stretching the definition. Surrounding me were strange, humming Elder Thing devices, human-constructed machines straight from the imagination of Nikola Tesla, and freakish half-dissected monsters resting on metal trays. Instead of a sterile environment, the walls were made of stone. Really, the place resembled where Doctor Frankenstein created his monster more than anything else.

Across from me was the equally naked form of Jessica. She was breathing heavily, having apparently woken before me. My thoughts regarding her were protective, worrying about the kind of treatment a woman might receive at the hands of the Black Cathedral's insane residents. It was a pointless worry; there was nothing I could do to prevent her assault. Yet, I would've gladly died a horrible death if it meant sparing her from such pain. Not that it was likely I'd get the chance. In all likelihood, we'd both be executed after extended torture. It was how things worked in the Wasteland.

"Jessica, are you…?" I hesitated before asking more; "alright" seemed like a tremendously stupid thing to ask.

"For now, Captain," Jessica said before taking several deep breaths. "I haven't been tortured if that's what you mean."

I breathed a silent prayer of thanks. "I suppose we can be grateful for that, at least."

"Grateful?" Jessica asked.

"We'll get out of this, Jessica, I promise." I wasn't sure if it was true but I would damn well try to make it so. "How long have you been up?"

"A few minutes," she said, blinking, looking ready to laugh at the absurdity. "One of the cultists told me they're going to let us watch some movies until Doctor Ward is ready to see us."

I blinked at her. "What?"

A pair of Alan Ward's Reanimated walked into the room, carrying a projector and a collapsible screen under their arms. I almost vomited when I realized they were Stephens and Jimmy, or what was left of them. Stephens's body had been stitched back together, metal grafts visibly sticking out of his shoulder and legs. Jimmy, on the other hand, possessed neither eyes nor tongue. Where those things should have been, the holes were sewn up in a grim mockery of a human being.

The pair carried out their labor wordlessly, reacting to neither Jessica nor me until they finished. Turning on the movie projector, the two Reanimated soldiers bowed before departing.

"The word 'sick' doesn't even begin to cover this, does it?" Jessica said, looking at them.

"No," I said. "It doesn't."

The next six hours were spent watching—I cannot really describe this without sounding deranged even to myself—Pre-Rising horror films. The incongruity of watching moving pictures in such a grotesque environment may strike a person blackly humorous. Reliving my memories, I briefly had enough self-awareness to wish I could give a gallows laugh. I laughed at the start of the first film, screamed obscenities throughout the whole of the second film, and then silently watched the third for lack of anything better to do. We were in the hands of a madman and I was unable to do anything about it.

As the third movie reel finally ended, I heard a rustling coming up from a nearby stairwell. Stepping into the room was Doctor Alan Ward, now dressed as an Old Earth gardener with a white apron over plain work clothes. In his left hand, he held a trough that he was cleaning dirt off with his fingers.

"I'm terribly sorry for making you late, but you did catch me at a somewhat bad time. The Mandragora strains I'm cultivating in my gardens are nearly ripe. The screams they unleash when they are pulled are enough to kill a full-grown man at eighty paces." He merrily waved his trough at us. "I hope you have not been too uncomfortable."

Jessica proceeded to unleash a torrent of profanity with such speed and hatred it would take several minutes to recite all of the insults she hurled at Doctor Ward, despite taking no more than thirty-five seconds to say them all. I did not consider all of the things she accused him of being to be insults, especially regarding his sexuality and race, but the intent was clear.

The final bits were especially ironic, given some of the insults. "… evil, murdering, Nazi piece of shit!"

Alan Ward blinked behind his bifocals, briefly pausing to wipe some spittle off the end of them. "My dear, the Elder Sign and my appreciation for their efficiency aside, I'm not the one who hails from a purity-obsessed fascist state. The only Nazis present, I fear, are you and Mister Booth. I, by contrast, am a more cosmopolitan sort—open to any and all perversities and species provided they amuse me."

I would have argued with Alan Ward, if only because New Arkham did not discriminate on race, but he preempted any discussion by snapping his fingers. Instantly, Jessica started to bleed from her nose, convulse violently, and then pass out. It was as if he had the power to control her body with his mind.

"That was unnecessary." I swallowed my anger and decided to interact with him on a rational level. I had dealt with several psychopaths before, mostly petty warlords and cult leaders. The key to successful negotiation was making sure you treated them as if they weren't the monstrous little egomaniacs they were.

"Necessity is in the eye of the beholder." Ward spread out his hands, smiling. "Manners are always important."

Treating him as a rational human being was going to be more difficult than I thought. "That's not what I meant."

"I know. Don't worry, she won't die. I have great plans for you both, and neither involves your deaths." Alan Ward removed his apron and placed his trough on a nearby table.

"What do you want?" I asked, trying to maintain my decorum in the face of my squad's murderer.

"You still think this is a conversation, don't you?" Ward looked at me for several seconds, apparently trying to determine if I was joking. "Oh, John, I'd forgotten how amusing you could be. I'm centuries old and you're easily the most interesting person I've ever met, exempting Randolph Carter."

"The Alan Ward I knew was a man of honor. He wouldn't be party to the taking of children." I was flattering him now. He'd killed friends and no matter our past relationship, the moment I was free, I would kill him for it.

"You didn't know me very well, then," Ward said, sighing. "I have always been willing to do whatever it takes to save humanity."

Jessica interrupted my attempts to talk him down. "Save humanity? Is that what you call those things out there? You animated a bunch of corpses to kill us! You killed our squad, you killed our friends."

"I've killed many members of the R&E Rangers, although you probably don't realize it, and hundreds of Remnant citizens besides. I control much of the wildlife outside of New Arkham, the cults as well. What started as a disaffected group of mutants and savages living in ruins, I have forged into an empire. The Color was summoned by me and I brought down other horrors as well."

Jessica's eyes blazed with hate.

I closed my eyes. "I don't believe you. No one can control the horrors of the Wasteland. We are subject to it, not its masters."

"In a world where there are few gods who care for us but many who don't, the universe is as cruel to the Great Old Ones as it is humanity." Ward closed his eyes. "New Arkham is irrelevant to my activities, but I needed test subjects and they were a ready source. I'm sorry it's come to this but we're all expendable in the grand scheme of things."

I abandoned any pretense of negotiation. "You're a sick man, Ward. What is your plan anyway? Do you intend to make your own little empire out here? Raise all these children to worship you as a god?"

"Close enough," Ward said, opening his eyes. "Humanity is a sick, dying, weak species. The Elder Things envy our will to survive but we are on the road to oblivion. We need a new humanity to rise from the ashes and I have created it. It will not be a mankind which carries the failures of the Old Race, though. I want to raise the better half of man to godhood, not its monkey side."

"You intend to experiment on these children," I said in a hushed whisper. "Turn them into something like the Deep Ones."

Martha had been right.

"Don't be ridiculous, John. I've *been* experimenting since before the Great Old Ones rose. In previous lives, I studied alchemy and necromancy in hopes of finding ways to overcome death. I learned the secret to taking over the bodies of my descendants before mankind was performing open-heart surgery. Only now with the technology of the Elder Things have I *perfected* my science." He shook his fist in the air, his eyes gleaming. "Do you understand what I'm saying?"

"That you're crazy?" Jessica said, not helping our situation.

Ward ignored her and stared into my eyes. "You know what I can achieve, John. You've seen my early work."

"Your current results are … what exactly?" I couldn't help but ask.

"John!" Jessica shouted, betrayed.

"The bowels of this temple are filled with the half-alive foul abominations my earlier failures created, but I have at last found perfection in the arcane sciences. The children I've taken will eat of the fruits of my labors, becoming as eternal and undying as the Old Ones."

"And they'll still be human?"

"More or less, yes," Ward snorted in derision at my questioning look. "Once I have fostered my children to the next stage in our race's evolution, we will take to the stars through the Dreamlands and bring forth a world where we can live in peace."

A part of me wanted to believe he could do it. That there was a terrible, possible hope for humanity to survive. In the end, I couldn't bring myself to accept humanity had a future. "You can't just change the nature of humanity."

"As if there was something special about our race of upjumped chimps," Ward said.

Jessica continued swearing at him, trying to gain his attention and promising violence should she get free.

"Leave me out of it," I said. "I won't help you. Willingly or otherwise."

"Not even immortality and immunity to disease can persuade you?" Ward crossed his arms, raising an eyebrow.

"No."

"Then I fear I have to take what benefit of your body I can. If you will not be my body, you will be spare parts." Ward began unbuttoning his shirt. "You see, the unfortunate side effect of magic is that every use of it exposes you to potential catastrophic side effects. I coined the term 'M-Rads' to draw a parallel to nuclear radiation. The results, however, are arguably worse."

I began pulling against my bands, weakening them, while Ward exposed his bare chest. All across his chest were mouths, mouths with sharpened inhuman teeth and *tongues*! Wiggling, slithering tongues! In between those inhuman maws were eyes, both human and inhuman, by the hundreds!

They blinked and stared at me, clearly aware and sapient as any eyes on a human face. I was almost too shocked to continue my plan, the sight of his disgusting mutations freezing me in place.

"My God." I almost vomited then and there. "*What are you?*"

"A work in progress," Ward said softly. He slowly began buttoning up his shirt, flicking one of the long pointed tongues sticking out towards me. "Once I become like the Great Old Ones, my current state will cease to be an issue, but I do not want to take any chances."

I was almost ready; I could feel the restraints beginning to buckle. Even so, I stuttered with fear. I hadn't reacted like this since I was a child. "I-I don't see how this applies to me."

"Your slut of a mother may well have conceived you with my seed. It's a long shot but my current form is incapable of breeding a new body should this one fail. I like to *hedge my bets.*" Ward said, reaching over to pat me on the cheek. "Do you *understand*?"

It was the aspersions on my mother's character which gave me the strength to shatter my bonds. The leather straps around my wrist, chest, and legs snapped in quick succession before the mad sorcerer-scientist's astonished eyes. Before he could bring up a spell to defend himself, I socked him across the jaw with more force than I'd ever struck a man.

Doctor Ward possessed power equivalent to the gods, rivaling the sorcerers of Old Earth myth like Merlin or Eibon, yet he was still human. Kicking him in the hideous mutant mouths growing out of his chest, I shattered several of their teeth before grabbing a nearby beaker of glowing fluid and smashing it against his face. Whatever bizarre alchemical substances it contained, it burned the demonic doctor's face like acid.

As he screamed, I lifted him high in the air above my head and hurled him into some nearby electrified machinery. A titanic explosion followed with his body lying in the rubble of the machine's remains, tortured and shocked. Some sort of evil god must have been on his side, however, because he continued to breathe.

Searching for some sort of weapon to crush the man's skull and end his evil reign of terror, I found a thick steel rod that I lifted over my head. Doctor Ward could do nothing to stop me, having been knocked unconscious by my savage attack.

"Goodbye, Doctor," I said with a smile on my lips. "It's been a pleasure."

My sense of victory was premature. No sooner was I bringing down the rod than someone struck me across the back of the head with a blunt instrument. Hitting the ground hard, my vision became woozy as I glanced over my shoulder at the figure behind me. It was Peter Goodhill, the coward who'd betrayed Gamma Squad and whom I'd failed to kill in our last encounter.

Peter was not yet covered in his Dunwych tattoos, instead wearing military fatigues and a green beret affixed with the Elder Sign. In his hands was a wooden baseball bat covered in my blood.

"Traitor," I coughed, staring up at him.

"Shut up," Peter replied, bringing his boot down on my face. Once more, I hit the ground unconscious.

This was getting to be a bad habit.

CHAPTER EIGHTEEN

For a brief moment, I was aware of my present state in my flashback. The discovery that Peter Goodhill was a servant of Ward made me think about my encounter with him in Richard's garage. Peter working for "The Necromancer" explained a great deal, from his unusual friendliness to why he'd suddenly decided to join the Dunwych after a post-desertion career of self-serving behavior. Peter was nothing more than a plant by the old sorcerer-scientist.

Peter was a means for Ward to gain information on any plots the Dunwych might be formulating against him. Any guilt I felt towards nearly beating Peter to death evaporated, replaced only by the regret that I did not finish the job. I had precious little time to think on the revelation because my memories resumed with a feverish dream-like quality.

I remembered being punished for my almost successful assassination of the insane scientist. Doctor Ward was a master of inflicting ungodly pain upon a human body. When he was not doing so, bizarre medical tests involving injections and spellwork were performed.

I had read of encounters with "Grays" and the Plutonian Mi-Go species, where men were abducted and subjected to traumatizing scientific experiments. Those stories were the closest thing I could think of to compare my experience to. Blessedly, Ward feared me so much that he kept me doped up on a cocktail of drugs so strong I could barely feel much of what I endured.

There were other things too, things I could barely recall because Ward began to experiment with possession. Scattered images filled my head of elaborate gladiator contests. Battles where he wore my body like a suit, using golden revolvers to fight various monsters of his own creation.

I vaguely recalled Jessica fighting in these contests as well, something which only increased my hatred of Ward. I took no pleasure in the victories I remembered; each one signaled the doctor gaining a greater control over my form. It was close to eight days before I regained control of my body. It took that long for the drugs to pass from my system and to recover enough mental strength to drive Ward's presence from my mind.

I could not say for certain what gave me the willpower to perform this feat. I believe, in part, it had to do with my desire to protect my family and see again those I loved. Also was my care for my surviving squad mate, Jessica, and the knowledge a terrible fate awaited her were I not to break free.

When it finally happened, a primordial scream escaped my lungs, filling the room. "Ahhhhhh!"

A female voice whispered in my ear, "It's alright, John. I'm here."

I did not immediately look to the source, instead taking in the chamber around me. I was in a dungeon, a genuine one unlike the laboratory I'd been imprisoned in before. The room was surprisingly spacious, albeit filthy. I was in a single large chamber with a row of iron bars separating it from rows of similar chambers outside.

Surrounding me were several ancient corpses, fossilized by the epochs of time and magical radiation. Given the Elder Things had no reason to keep human prisoners, this place had probably once housed slaves.

There was a single guard standing in front of the bars, a debased-looking Cthulhu cultist who had tattooed himself with hundreds of Elder Signs. He was not a particularly formidable-looking fellow, looking somewhat diseased and wretched. Given Ward had spent the past week brainwashing and drugging me, he'd probably thought it unnecessary to provide someone more skilled.

Fool.

I shook my head and turned to look at the woman behind me. "Jessica?"

"Yes, Captain, it's me." I saw she was dressed in rather ridiculous attire. Covering her form was tight-fitting cowgirl attire. It was like none of the practical clothing worn by the Wastelanders outside of New Arkham but more like something you'd see in Pre-Rising art.

"Jessica, why are you dressed like … that?"

"Ward made us dress in these outfits when he had us fight for his cultists' amusement." She looked as disgusted as I felt confused. "I'm just glad he hasn't forced us to do anything else."

"Us?" I noticed I was wearing a male variant of the exact same thing. "I don't believe it."

"I wish I still had this option," Jessica huffed before slowly helping me to my feet. "Did you actually know this guy?"

"He was my mentor for a few years, back when I thought I still might be a scientist."

"Damn," Jessica replied, patting me on the back. "I take it your course wasn't Crazy-Ass Experiments?"

"No." I leaned up to whisper in her ear. "Have you any idea how to get out of this place?"

"There's a transport garage nearby," Jessica whispered back. "The problem is this place is crawling with cultists and weird-ass monsters. I swear, I think Ward's inner circle is composed of vampires."

I bit my lip, looking at her skeptically. "Vampires don't exist, Jessica."

"Have you seen any?" she asked, raising an eyebrow.

"No," I sighed. "I haven't."

"Then don't contradict me." Jessica wrinkled her nose, smiling. It was a sad smile, though. "I miss Jimmy, Garcia, and Parker. Stephens, too."

"I miss them all as well." I took a deep breath, then stood up. I looked at her, taking in her soft features and missing my wife more than ever. Though we were estranged, I still thought of her every day. "Is there anything else I should worry about?"

"Ward has a dragon?"

I said, speaking a little louder than I should have been, "Jessica, you know how much I hate to agree with Stephens, but that's just ridiculous. There's no such thing."

"I've *heard* it, John," Jessica hissed under her breath. "It doesn't roar, so much as make a thousand terrible noises all at once. The thing sounds like the pipe organ from hell, but it's real. It's big, nasty, and slithering down beneath us. A few times, I've felt the whole cathedral shake."

I knew better than to contradict Jessica; she might be prone to the occasional flight of fancy but if she said she heard something then I believed her. I didn't believe in dragons but there were aliens undoubtedly as large and dangerous. "Alright, there's a dragon."

"Thank you." Jessica breathed a sigh of relief. "I'm glad you believe me. There were times I was sure I was going mad. The sounds it makes, they scare me in ways that Doctor Ward and his experiments can't even begin to compare to."

I placed my hand on Jessica's arm, barely resisting the urge to embrace her. Right now, we needed to work together to get out of this. Years of training together had made us like a pair of twins, in tune and aware of each other's surroundings. We could get through this. "I think we need to use Plan 23 to get out of here."

She nodded and asked, "What's Plan 23?"

"You'll figure it out when you see it," I said, giving her a halfhearted smile. Clutching my stomach, I raised a hand, "Guard … I think I'm sick. Oh God, I'm going to throw up!"

The guard turned to look at me. "Idiot. I don't think anyone has ever fallen for that in their …"

That was when Jessica broke a leg bone across her knee and jabbed the jagged edge of the larger piece into the left eye of the Cthulhu cultist. He was dead before he hit the ground.

"Is this what you had in mind?" Jessica said, walking over to the corpse. "'Cause if you actually intended him to come in to help, I've lost all respect for you."

"It proceeded more or less how I pictured it in my head. Never underestimate the power of a good distraction." I smiled, waiting for her to unlock the door. "Our other option was for you to try and seduce our guard before I overpowered him."

Jessica snorted, shaking her head. "That plan is only slightly better than the stomach virus one."

"We could have done it the other way if he was so inclined," I said, searching the body of the deceased cultist. There I found a crude powder pistol. It was better than nothing, though not by much. "We now have to proceed to that transport garage, hopefully arming ourselves. We'll go in silently and deadly. Hopefully, we can convince the Council of Leaders this place is a threat."

"Oh, they'll bomb the place to the ground, I'm sure of that. Never have I been more grateful the Council is a bunch of paranoid old egomaniacs," Jessica said, laughing. "Let's go, Captain."

"Affirmative."

The interior of the Black Cathedral was still stunning to travel through, even with the sense of fear and unnaturalness that clung to its alien architecture. The Elder Things, who I knew almost nothing of back then, didn't strike me as the most religious of people, but they had constructed a vast temple to their otherworldly gods.

Everything was built to many times the size of humans, despite the Elder Things being only twice that. There was a sense of grandiosity largely lacking from human design. I had to admire them, even knowing what sort of cruel logic-driven beings they were.

"I'm not seeing much of the locals," Jessica said, clinging close as we moved from hallway to hallway. "Do you think it's a trap?"

"Traps are for people who are not completely in your power," I said.

Jessica grimaced. "Right."

I gestured for her to be quiet and moved into a nearby passageway as a group of Cthulhu cultists came around the corner. They were, like the others we'd killed, dressed in scavenged attire and outlandish tattoos. It made me wonder what Doctor Ward had been thinking recruiting them. All of them were carrying small arms, however, which made their elimination vital.

Signaling Jessica to stay quiet, I counted down from three as they passed by. When we hit zero, the both of us moved behind the two closest to snap their necks. Jessica had difficulty with hers but still disabled him within seconds. It left only a single short red-haired cultist wearing a pair of glasses; he was also conspicuously wearing a set of flamethrower canisters on his back.

"For Great Cth—" a battle cry he started, before I stabbed him in the eye with the same bone Jessica had used to kill our jailer.

"Why do they always shout before they fire?" Jessica said, arming herself with the guns on the ground. "The whole point of a good battle cry is that it should be done *while* you're attacking."

"I don't think logic is the main concern of these people. Make sure to stab each of the heads, just in case. We don't want any more Reanimated coming after us." I started removing the flamethrower from the deceased cultist's back.

"You're actually going to use a flamethrower? You do realize those are horribly impractical weapons, right? Flamer ammunition is much superior." Jessica's Southern drawl slipped for a bit, revealing the New Arkham accent we all shared.

"You make do with what you have, Corporal," I said, checking the weapon for leaks. "Are we close to where you saw the motor pool?"

"Motor pool may be giving it too much credit. These cultists don't seem to have too much in the way of vehicles. Still, we're not far. Only about two or three hallways, I think." Jessica checked the magazines of both the semi-automatic pistols now in her hands. She then added, "Captain, I want to thank you."

"Thank me?" I asked, wondering if now was really the right time to get sentimental.

"For distracting Doctor Ward; the entire time he was focused on torturing you, he wasn't able to do anything to me. I know that was your doing." Jessica patted me on the arm, giving me a look of deep gratitude.

"I'm pretty sure that's not what happened, Corporal." I took a deep breath, testing the flamethrower by launching a brief burst of flame in front of us. "I think I just annoyed him more than you. Nothing deliberate about it."

"Well, I owe you one."

"We owe each other. More times than I can count."

"How about you let me buy you twenty or so rounds at The Radioactive Cowboy, anyway? I'm starting to warm to Scrapyard's mud beer."

"That makes one of us, but I'll take you up on your offer anyway. I'm sorry I got you into this."

"You didn't."

"I'm pretty sure I did."

"If you're going to blame anyone, blame the Council of Leaders." Jessica spit on the ground. "They're the ones who let Ward loose in the desert. They're the ones who got my husband killed fighting a giant evil Crayola. Hell, they're the guys who keep sending us out against situations we have no idea how to handle."

"We can't choose our leaders," I said.

"So much for democracy, eh?" Jessica snorted.

"Yeah. I suppose so," I replied, realizing what I'd said. "Just note, I've always got your back."

"Always."

Jessica shook her head, unconsciously reaching for her hat that was no longer there. "God dammit, if I wasn't going to kill him for wasting Jimmy and Stephens, I'd kill him for taking my hat."

I was about to say we had bigger things to worry about when a noise threatened to split our eardrums. It was an explosion of noise so loud it echoed throughout the halls around us several times over. If this was the thing Jessica described as "a thousand terrible noises," then she was a master of understatement.

"The dragon!" Jessica shouted, grabbing my arm. "John, we need to make a break for it!"

"I …" I hesitated for a second, processing the sound. "I think you're right, Corporal."

At the end of the hall we'd just come from, I caught the sight of what was coming after us. If it didn't resemble a dragon, then it certainly possessed all of its intimidation value. I had never seen such a malevolent looking *thing* in my entire life. If I lived a thousand years, I'd probably never see its like again.

It was death incarnate.

Rolling down from an archway on the floor above us, seeping over balconies and hallways, was a shapeless black creature composed of amorphous bio-mass. Much like the growths on Doctor Ward's chest, it was covered in mouths and eyes that had no business belonging on anything but a face.

Its thousands of mouths spoke together, shouting nonsensical alien words in a mind-blasting chorus of pipe organ-like voices. Its protoplasmic body slithered and moved in ways no oozing thing should have been able to, smashing aside stone columns in its path as if they were a child's building blocks.

One moment it moved like an amoeba, the next it possessed all the fluidity of water, and then it became solid as steel. The gigantic thing had not even begun to finish its entrance by the time it filled the entirety of the Black Cathedral halls behind us. I could see it was hundreds of feet long, more vast than any subway train or building I'd encountered in the Wasteland's ruins.

Given we had no idea how far the Black Cathedral really

extended given its space-bending properties, the creature could have well been a mile in length or longer. Though I did not have a name for it on the day I first encountered it, Abdul Alhazred had written of the dreadful entity in the *Necronomicon* a thousand years prior. He had given it the name *shoggoth.*

Eons ago, they had been creations of the Elder Things, only to destroy their vast supernatural kingdom, destroying all of the ancient beings' advanced technology and devouring the majority of them. They were made of matter culled from multiple dimensions and were immune to nearly all weapons.

Had the shoggoths been so inclined, ages ago, they could have annihilated all other life-forms on Earth. Instead, they'd just kept to the ruins of the Elder Things' once grand empire, gurgling obscene blasphemies and thinking whatever twisted thoughts shoggoths did.

"Run!" I shouted to Jessica, firing the flamethrower's juices onto the creature's form. The fire seemed to only tickle it, dancing melodically alongside its tar-like form before being absorbed into its greater frame.

Jessica didn't bother to run behind me, instead only tugging on the back of my shoulders before the shoggoth formed a hammer-like shape within the folds of one of its tendrils, bringing it down towards me. Only Jessica's movement saved me from being crushed as the Elder Things' treated stone shattered like thin glass before the force of its blow.

"How about you take your own advice!" Jessica shouted in my ear, pulling on my arm.

I ignored her insubordination again and took off running. Pulling off my shoulder straps, I tossed the useless flamethrower behind me, only to have it consumed by the hungry shoggoth trailing behind me.

The monstrous creature extended hundreds of tendrils forward, their movement almost like little baby chicks gestating within the folds of the monstrosity, ready to be fed by their mother. I could not help but think if Doctor Ward was nursing this creature to birth more of its kind, that he was even madder than I thought.

Running as fast as our legs would allow, we were still only able to barely keep ahead of the seemingly endless tidal wave of blackness rushing behind us. When we arrived at the transport garage of the Black Cathedral, we were already beginning to feel winded, while our pursuer was only picking up speed.

Unfortunately, the transport garage was no refuge. The place definitely had the transportation necessary to escape the cathedral. There was a vast collection of rebuilt cars, piles of rusted oil drums containing probably the last substantive stockpile of oil left in the world, and a surprising number of weapons. The exit, however, was sealed over with a huge pair of stone doors that would prevent any escape. There was also a collection of two dozen cultists, all heavily armed, looking toward us as we ran in.

The universe was mocking us.

"Shit!" Jessica shouted.

The shoggoth poured into the chamber as I threw her to the ground, rolling across the floor, out of the way of the cultists' line of fire.

"Truer words have never been spoken," I spoke to her as the creature let forth another alien cry.

CHAPTER NINETEEN

The Cthulhu cultists, despite their reverence for the Great Old Ones, briefly regained their sanity long enough to realize the shoggoth was not a god to be worshiped but an enemy to be feared. In unison they raised their weapons against the massive blob and opened fire, firing hundreds of rounds with their automatic weapons. One of them even had a P17 rocket launcher, which he used to fire straight into the shoggoth's central mass.

All of it was ineffective.

Gunfire, grenades, and even P17 rockets just were absorbed into the greater mass of the monster's body. The explosions seemed to cause the shoggoth no stress at all. From what the *Necronomicon* described, the Elder Things had created this race to be one of the most highly adaptive organisms in the universe. It was not going to be stopped by anything as trivial as human weaponry.

The shoggoth retaliated faster than could have been imagined. Its tentacles reached out to crush, maim, devour, impale, or simply absorb whatever cultists it could lay its pseudopods on. To call it a battle would be stretching the definition, instead it resembled what my grandfather used to call an "old-fashioned curb-stomping."

"Never waste a good distraction," I muttered under my breath. Ignoring the plight of the dying cultists, I searched for something to open the massive stone doors at the end of the garage. A few yards away, I saw a large stone pillar topped with an oyster-like shell.

Hoping fortune was with me for once, I saw glowing holographic lights appear above the shell as I approached. I hoped the strange Elder Thing machine was a control panel for the doors. The symbols were nonsensical, vaguely resembling a few I'd seen in Doctor

Ward's lectures on pre-human species but none of which had any real meaning to me.

"Too late for 'Eeny, meeny, miny, moe,' I guess," I muttered before guessing what buttons to touch at random. I was rewarded by the sound of the doors grinding open. The sun shined in through doorways, revealing the extensive desert outside. If we could get to one of the vehicles, start it, and peel out then we were home free.

"Captain, it's done eating the cultists!" Jessica shouted at the top of her lungs.

"Yeah, I guessed that would happen!" I called back, turning around to look for an appropriate vehicle to steal. I was rewarded by nearly being conked on the head by a flying human torso. Apparently, the shoggoth hadn't liked the taste of that particular cultist.

The shoggoth's terrible piping noise grew louder and louder as it proceeded to raise itself up to the entire height of the massive door we'd run through. Staring at it, I felt the first true and lasting fear I'd ever experienced in the presence of an E.B.E. The shoggoth was magnificent, terrible, and godlike at once. It was every bit the dragon described by Jessica, a creature more powerful than anything I'd ever seen, excluding possibly the Color.

Having endured so much torture and pain at Doctor Ward's hands, my mind felt on the brink of breaking. Seeing it about to bear down on me, for a brief moment—very brief—I was ready to let it kill me. It was one of the few moments of genuine despair I'd ever experienced in my life. In that moment, I understood how some Wastelanders desired nothing more than to throw themselves into the mouths of the Great Old Ones. Thankfully, I was with someone who was a little stronger-willed.

"Go back to hell, bastard!" Jessica shouted as she pulled a blessed Dunwych spear from one of the arsenal piles. She hurled the weapon into the shoggoth with tremendous force, the tip penetrating one of the creature's many eyes. Almost immediately, the shoggoth reared up, letting forth a cry that sounded distinctly like pain.

"It *can* be hurt," I whispered before staring at the arsenal piles around me. Amongst their contents, I saw the same golden revolvers Doctor Ward had used to fight his monstrous creations. Before the shoggoth could recover from its minor wound, I scooped up the golden revolvers.

"Huh. Well that's good," Jessica said, more amazed than proud by her action. She saw me charge right at it. "Captain! What are you doing?"

I was beyond listening to reason by that point. My momentary cowardice combined with the days of torture I'd endured, the loss of my squad, and the very sanity-shaking nature of the shoggoth itself, was too much for me to handle. My mind broke and all rationality vanished, replaced with a blood rage fueled by anger and hatred.

Lifting the two guns in my hands, I fired the R'lyehian weapons through one of its tendrils, severing it cleanly. I could see the chambers for the revolvers and they did not miss any rounds. The tentacle turned stark white and crumbled to pieces before I fired into another one. The battle fury filling my heart led me to shoot everything standing between me and the central bio-mass which stood before me.

Somewhere, deep in my ancestry, there was a long line of grim-faced berserkers and bloodthirsty gunslingers which had waited generations to be unleashed. It was a romantic sentiment for what amounted to simply a fight-or-flight response gone horribly wrong, but I felt no pain or fear while I fought.

The hefty recoil of the ancient guns should have slowed me down, but instead my attacks became as fast as the beating of a hummingbird's wings. The laws of physics were defied as adrenaline, madness, and the chemicals Doctor Ward pumped into my veins combined to form an inhuman strength equal to anything the legendary god-kings of old possessed.

Despite the fury of my assault, the shoggoth was not overwhelmed. Quite the contrary, it probably wouldn't have even noticed my attacks if not for the strange properties the revolvers possessed. Each of my shots struck a piece away from the monster. These pieces burned away in the air as if dissolved by acid, the strange sorcery woven into the folds of the guns' strange metal being antithetical to the science which had spawned the shoggoth.

Seeing my attacks were causing it harm, I threw myself further into the folds of the monstrous thing, watching it back away and allow me more room to deliver brutal blows to its bulbous flesh. In any sane world, I would have been killed within seconds.

But this was not a sane world.

I felt two of my ribs crack, followed by a kneecap, as the shoggoth finally started retaliating, using its whip-like tendrils to land blows against my body. The attacks barely seemed to slow me down, my pain just giving me incentive to continue my relentless assault. Ancient berserkers would often die after they finished their blood rage, their wounds catching up with them after their fury ended.

If that was going to be the case, I cared little, because I only wanted to see the monster killed. All that was John Henry Booth, honorable soldier and family man, disappeared in the trauma of the man who had failed his squad before suffering unspeakable tortures. In that moment, the shoggoth became the embodiment of all the indignities inflicted upon me by Doctor Ward.

The brutal swath of a hundred or more bullets I put into the shoggoth were not enough to kill it, though. Stun it? Perhaps. The creature backed away, shifting its terrible mass as I tore away more chunks of it with every blow. The shoggoth did not remain troubled for long, though. Extending a half-dozen tentacles with thick shark-toothed mouths, the shoggoth bit into my legs and shoulders with a savage ferocity. I barely felt them before swinging my revolvers to shoot away more of its black tentacles. The pain was almost enough to shake me out of my fury, but I instead focused more on my desperate need to kill it.

If I was going to die here, I intended to make it a glorious end.

Blood poured from the wounds where I'd been bitten, slowing down my attacks despite my efforts. Still, I kept shooting into the side of the creature. A blow from one of the monstrous, oil-slick-looking tendrils landed against the side of my face and caused my vision to blur, possibly causing a concussion. I almost laughed, the mad, twisted sort of laugh the cultists routinely exhibited, life and death having no meaning in this battle.

The shoggoth's countless mouths opened, screaming a single word over and over again. "Tekeli-li! Tekeli-li! Tekeli-li!"

The creature proceeded to grab me by the leg with one of its tendrils, breaking my ankle with its crushing grip. Bringing my left pistol around once more, I shot myself free even though it sent me spinning down to the hard stone surface twenty feet below. Slamming against the floor hard, I could barely move when the shoggoth once more reared up its amoeba-esque form to attack. It was simply too powerful for any single human being to defeat, no matter how determined.

"Die already!" I spit blood from my mouth before struggling to my feet and spinning around like I was hurling a discus. Throwing my right revolver into the center of its bio-mass, I fell to the ground and collapsed. It was a final gesture of hate, brought up by a need to spit in the face of death before it struck me down.

"Tekeli-li! Tekeli-li! Tekeli-li!" the shoggoth shouted, almost sounding alarmed. Of course, it was impossible to read emotions into the strange piping noises it made.

"Jessica ..." I muttered, my palms pressed against the stone surface beneath me. "I'm sorry."

I wasn't able to see much once I did so, my body having no more left to give. Yet, the creature didn't finish me off. The shoggoth shuddered as the revolver sunk deep within the monstrous beast's folds. It burned away the top of its oozing, gelatinous form before slinking towards the ground. The shoggoth's frame transformed itself into a white powdery substance before exploding all over the walls.

"John!" Jessica shouted, running up behind me. "I don't believe it. You killed the dragon!"

I couldn't really hear her, my entire mind having collapsed in on itself. Dropping my remaining gun, I let loose the kind of mad laughter I'd seen a thousand times on the broken prophets of the desert, "Ha, ha, ha, ha, ha!" It was the kind of mad chuckle of a person who had seen too much of what man was never meant to know, the sort of glee which would have probably sounded very similar to the cries given by Abdul Alhazred himself when his villagers had stoned him to death.

The shoggoth's death left me unable to think or feel beyond the current situation. Destroying the thing should have liberated my mind but it left me completely empty, unable to muster the willpower to try and escape. The fact the door was open meant nothing to a broken man, for I was lost in the recesses of my tattered sanity. Jessica had to heft me onto her shoulders, carrying me to a car in order to drive us into the desert. The Hand of Nyarlathotep, even now active inside my body, kept me alive but it didn't heal my shattered sanity. That would take both time and vision-quests worked by Richard while I was in my semi-comatose state.

I had only the barest knowledge of what happened to my body during this time, though I could vaguely recall spells worked over me by Richard to draw together the broken parts of my consciousness. From there, I eventually awoke in the middle of the night and walked from Scrapyard to New Arkham.

In my gibbering madness I had one desire and one desire only: to return to my family. I crossed the desert from Scrapyard to New Arkham on foot, strangling a nine-foot-long desert snake on my way.

A short re-enactment of the most recent events of my life followed, opening with Mercury interrogating me in a chair before ending with Ward holding a blade over my chest.

As the memories became present-time reality, I soaked in the sights and sounds around me. My body was lying bruised and battered on its back, ravaged by the Elder Things' attacks. The sky was still raining blood around me, filling the ground around us with gore and crimson puddles. Shockingly, I was still alive as reliving my lost memories had taken less than half a second.

Ward finished bringing down his sword cane towards my heart. "Goodnight, Sweet Prince."

Fueled by memories of torture at his hands, my eyes blazed.

CHAPTER TWENTY

Slapping my fingers against the edge of his weapon, I prevented it from impaling me while he struggled to force it down.

"Not today, *Doctor*," I said, hate in my voice.

Doctor Ward stared at me, his eyes boring into mine as he shouted, "You irritating little maggot! I tried to give you immortality and you threw it back in my face! You even killed my shoggoth! Do you have *any* idea how rare those are?!"

Spinning my leg around, I knocked his legs out from under him and ripped the sword from his hands. The blade spun in the air and landed in the gore nearby. Throwing myself on top of the insane scientist, I proceeded to deliver a repeated series of blows to the madman's face. Blood poured out from where I struck him, his teeth shattering from a particularly powerful blow.

The brutalized doctor reached up for the Elder Sign amulet hanging around his neck but I grabbed it first and tore it away, tossing the talisman over my shoulder.

"I am going to squeeze the damned life out of you!" I shouted at the top of my lungs, wrapping my fingers around his neck.

Ward's face was already a blood-stained mess, his nose broken and several teeth missing from the force of my earlier blows. It was my hope to throttle the life out of him, letting him know exactly what was happening to him as he died. The Necromancer was far from helpless, however. He raised his palm, and I was thrown backwards with a blast of telekinetic force that sent me hurtling through the air. I ended up bouncing for ten feet across the muddy, blood-soaked ground.

Ward had a cocksure smile on his face as he said, "John, surely you could have come up with something better than that. They don't really serve as appropriate famous last words for a man of your caliber."

Ward walked over to pick up his amulet as I reached into my jacket and pulled out the Dreamlands representation of the golden knife Martha had given me. Hurling the weapon forward, it pierced both the Elder Sign and the hand which held it.

Letting forth a terrible scream, Doctor Ward stared down at the terrible wound he'd suffered. The Elder Sign promptly caught fire before exploding, leaving a burning, flaming stump in place of the man's hand.

"I prefer to let actions speak louder than words," I said, barely managing to stand up. Hobbling, I took a deep breath as I prepared to finish off the psychopath, fully intending to kill him. "If you die here, I'm pretty sure you'll die in the real world. Prepare to meet whatever gods you worship, Doctor."

Ward just stared at me, biting his lip and saying, *"Adieu,* John Henry Booth. It has been amusing."

Rushing at him, I hoped he would be too disorientated to cast any more of his black magic. Unfortunately, I failed. I watched Doctor Ward's body transform into a flock of deformed crows, the myriad disgusting birds scattering to the four winds. I slid across the mud, watching my quarry escape into the night.

"Ward!" I called out, sinking down into the bloody mud around me. The crimson rain continued to fall upon me, occasionally joined by organs and other disgusting hail from the surreal clouds above me. I could barely breathe, my body injured from the fragments of stone lodged within my knees.

Though I could barely feel it, I also knew the Elder Things had scorched parts of my body with their crystalline rods. The wounds weren't lethal, yet, but they would kill me without proper medical attention—medical attention which was not exactly available in the Dreamlands.

Knowing what happened to my squad did nothing to alleviate the pain; it only heightened the outrageousness of the situation. Doctor Ward, my former professor, was going to mutilate hundreds of children to turn them into monsters.

Struggling to get up, I failed, unable to move any farther. My body was battered, exhausted, and spent. I tried to wake up, to end the vision-quest and return to my mortal body, only to find my mind was trapped within the confines of the Dreamlands. The *Necronomicon* might have contained some spell or ritual to free my mind, but I hadn't finished reading it. The book also lacked any astral reflection, left in my orange pants back on Earth. Even attempts to will into existence exits failed, leaving me alone in the shadow of the Elder Things' tower.

If there was a small mercy to the situation, it was that no more Elder Things came out to finish me off. The loss of two more of their brethren probably told them it was suicide to try and risk any more of their lives to retrieve my body. It was ironic, given I couldn't have resisted them in my present condition.

Instead, I just lay there as minutes turned to hours and I expected to die at any time. In the end, I regained enough force of will to make one last attempt to save my life. Knowing no one else would be able to stop Doctor Ward, I turned to forces I never expected to—sorcery. I had to survive, though, to win justice for Jimmy and Stephens. To protect every single life Doctor Ward would take in his plan to transform the human race.

Sticking the tips of my fingers into the mud, I drew an elaborate circle before surrounding it with crudely drawn arcane runes. Each of the glyphs was dedicated to one the Great Old Ones worshiped by the Dunwych. I didn't know where the Dunwych had learned of the Other Gods or the Great Old Ones spoken of by the *Necronomicon*, but for once I allowed myself to believe they were worthy of worship. I wasn't a psychic, not like Martha, but perhaps in the Dreamlands it was possible for a normal man to work magic. It was ironic that I, who hated magic, desperately hoped now to use it.

The process took over an hour, my body collapsing several times during the procedure. Finally, I drove my fingernails hard into my palm in order to draw blood. Tossing the contents into the central circle, I called out, "Ia Cthulhu! Ia Shub-Niggurath! T'yanna Shub'Niggurath Naw'tecan! Ia Hastur! Uh'ah aja'fyanna Hastur gna Kadath! Yost Nyarlathotep!"

The spell, spoken in an alien language nearly impossible to speak with a human mouth, caused the world around me to shake. Like the tearing of paper, the sky split in half before the ground beneath me shattered into multiple pieces. Both above and below me were starry expanses leading to constellations I did not recognize. The Elder Things' tower leaned and tottered before falling downwards into the infinite blackness surrounding me. Everything else similarly dissolved, reducing the once vast graveyard to nothingness.

Soon, I found myself standing on a shaft of earth rising out of an alien asteroid belt with naught but floating bits of the tower's wreckage surrounding me. I imagined I could breathe in space, knowing that if I stopped believing it for a second I would suffocate in the vast blackness around me. I tried desperately to tell myself it was all a trick of the subconscious, but I knew my dream had long since run away from me, becoming something far beyond anything my conscious mind could come up with on its own.

Stepping out of the emptiness of space, walking across the astral infinity as if it were a paved road, was a man in black. Wearing a midnight-colored duster and Stetson identical to my own, he possessed skin as black as coal mixed with features close enough to be my twin's. He was a being I recognized instantly as the Black Soldier, one of Nyarlathotep's countless forms. He walked with a kind of otherworldly majesty that was neither good nor evil but terrified me to the bottom of my soul. I was in the presence of a god.

The figure removed his hat and put it over his heart before bowing. "Hello, John. It's been a long time."

"I don't recall meeting you before. You've made a strange choice for an avatar," I said, coughing. Standing upward, I felt strength returning to my limbs. Pulling off my blood-soaked shirt, I saw the scars in the shape of a hand glowing.

"You conjured me this way," the deity answered. Reaching over, Nyarlathotep placed his hand on my scar, where it fit perfectly. The god's touch was cold, like ice, but it burned like a branding iron. "There, that should put you to rights. All it required was a dozen or so inconsequential lives to repair you."

For a second, I felt and knew the names of all of the people across Earth's ruins who Nyarlathotep killed to heal me. Ruby a shopkeeper, Tom the caravan driver, Eldoc the Deep One, and others whose lives ended in an instant for the purposes of giving me a little more life.

I stared at him, horrified. "I didn't ask for you to do that."

"No, but it's what you think gods do. They strike down the

innocent and the guilty alike, never bothering to explain why. Azathoth was born in primordial nuclear chaos, the Big Bang being one of his baby-like belches, but it was *sentience* which gave birth to gods like me. You wanted a reason for all the horrible things that happen to people, a meaning for your impotent, unimportant little lives to strive towards. So, here I am."

I looked straight at him, whispering, "Mankind didn't dream you up."

"No, of course not. The races older than Cthulhu's people did. Humans aren't the only ones to have begged for *the Answer*." Nyarlathotep's voice became mocking, insulting every being of faith throughout history. "I adopt whatever forms are needed though, to give you all the knowledge you mortals beg for, the secrets that will make your dull existence bearable."

I was tempted to ask, shaking my head. Then I realized that Nyarlathotep was a trickster, a being who could not be trusted, and I guessed what sort of stories he provided to those who saw him in their visions. "The answer is whatever people want it to be."

"Of course," Nyarlathotep said, transforming into an Egyptian pharaoh with skin the color of obsidian. "*The Answer* is always what they want to hear. After all, what else would they dream of a god telling them?"

It wasn't lost on me this was exactly the kind of thing that I expected Nyarlathotep to say. I could not trust this strange deity, whether he was a product of my dreams or genuinely a god, but I needed him. Hell, it was possible I wasn't speaking to the real Nyarlathotep, if such a creature existed at all. The *Necronomicon*'s summoning rituals drew creatures from the Dreamlands into the physical world but gave them shape in accordance to the wishes and prejudices of the wizard casting the spell. That didn't make them any less powerful and the least of them was powerful beyond imagination.

I shook those thoughts away, lest they lead me to madness. "I summoned you. I need you to take me back to my body. I need to stop Doctor Ward and avenge my squad."

Nyarlathotep transformed into a flying wasp-like creature that seemed as much fungus as insect. His next words entered my mind rather than my ears, "You do not have to do anything. It is your choice to be hero or villain or valueless drain on humanity's resources."

"I choose to try and do what's right." I felt strong again, better than I'd felt in years. It made me sick to my stomach to think it had come at the cost of other people's lives.

"By whose standard?" Nyarlathotep changed into a black Elder Thing. "And for who?"

"My own and for me," I said, trying to avoid thinking about the fact I'd long since given up on notions of right and wrong. "I have some things I need to ask …"

Nyarlathotep, however, had already moved on. "I can take you to distant R'lyeh, Kadath, or the very heart of the universe. There you may join the ranks of the many prophets I've made immortal. Your race will be dead in three generations, no matter what you do. Life is an insignificant and ephemeral thing. Think carefully before you waste your meager years left on a dying race."

"Humanity has only three generations left to live?" I asked, stunned.

"Of course." Nyarlathotep became the image of a man-sized Cthulhu, a cephalopod skull necklace around his neck. "I'm surprised your race is going to last that long. You were always such a self-destructive little species."

Hearing Nyarlathotep's words was like a sock in the gut, confirming my worst fears about humanity's future. Then I remembered my speech to Mercury, telling her the importance was in struggling against death rather than triumphing over it. Taking a deep breath, I recited one of the most famous lines of the *Necronomicon*: "With strange aeons, even death may die. I will not give up. I *will* save my race."

Nyarlathotep assumed the form of my father, his color still darker than black. Grinning broadly, he snapped his fingers. "Very well, soldier, I shall take you back to your body."

My body caught fire.

CHAPTER TWENTY-ONE

I screamed as I woke up, a scenario I was rapidly becoming accustomed to. Feeling someone's hands on my chest, I grabbed them by the arm and went for my knife, only coming to my senses when I realized the person touching me was Jackie.

Blinking her large eyes, Jackie was surprisingly calm for a girl with a golden knife at her throat. "Uhm, hello."

"Jackie, I'm so sorry." Dropping the knife, I let go of her arm. From the feel of it, she didn't seem to be injured. "Are you alright?"

Jackie looked down at her arm, flexing it a few times to make sure it was okay. "I'm okay, sir. Why is Mister Jameson dead?"

Turning my head, I stared across the room at Richard's body. My canine companion was lying on the floor, his mouth open and eyes staring upward. Any hope I had for Richard's survival was dashed: he looked like he'd had the ghoul equivalent of a massive heart attack. Reaching over, I closed his eyelids and said a little prayer. I doubted Richard worshiped my god, but it was my hope there was a heaven equivalent for ghouls.

"He was killed by ancient aliens living in the Dreamworlds," I said, taking a deep breath and getting up off the floor.

"Oh," Jackie said, looking horrified. "Was his sacrifice worth it?"

"No," I answered her honestly. "It wasn't."

"I see," Jackie said, staring up at me.

"Yeah, I suppose you do." Checking the R'lyehian knife's blade, I saw it was covered in blood. Apparently, some things physically transferred to and from the Dreamlands. It gave me hope I could eventually drive the gold thing into Ward's black heart.

"What does this mean for me?" Jackie asked.

"Don't worry, little one. I'll take you with me to Kingsport," I said, placing my hand on her shoulder. "I'll take you with Mercury and we'll find you both a home."

Jackie looked down. "Thank you."

"You're welcome." I pulled the sheets off the crumpled bed in the guest room before throwing them over Richard's corpse. It was the closest thing to a funeral shroud I could provide my friend.

"Farewell, my friend," I prayed aloud, shaking my head. "May byakhees ferry your soul to Tsathoggua's caverns with swift wings."

Jackie tugged on my shirt. "Uh, there are some things you need to know."

"Yes?" I looked away from Richard's corpse, my eyes damp. I would never be able to forget any of my times with Richard, the Elder Things' tampering making each memory extraordinarily vivid. Certain neurological conditions gave similar perfect memories and often caused extraordinary distress to their bearers, but I was glad for it now. I would never forget Richard and for now, that was enough.

"Ms. Jessica is awake and Ms. Mercury has been kidnapped." Jackie looked over her shoulder as she spoke, as if expecting me to explode.

"What?" I asked, unsure if she was serious.

"Ms. Jessica woke up just a few minutes ago," Jackie said, looking up. "That's why I came in here to talk with you. As for Ms. Mercury, Lady Katryn came here and said Peter had taken her and to tell you when you woke up. I tried to wake you up earlier but it didn't work. I was hoping to try again and then you almost stabbed me."

"I'm so sorry about that."

"Please don't. It's okay." No child should have to say that.

I blinked, shaking my head. "Goddamn you, Peter."

"It'll be alright," Jackie said. "You're going to go to Kingsport and get them back, right?"

"They're going to Kingsport?"

"That's what Lady Katryn said, yes."

I took a deep breath. "Alright. Is she still here?"

"Yes," Jackie said. "She said the journey required provisions and should be undertaken with you if at all possible."

"Thank God for small miracles," I said. "Jackie, it might be dangerous to go to Kingsport now. Are you sure you want to go with me now?" I said, fearing the sort of fate which might await a girl brought into the intrigues Peter was involved in.

Jackie looked outside one of the nearby windows into Scrapyard, a look of revulsion passing across her face. "I would rather go with you straight into the jaws of any Wasteland beastie than stay here."

"I see. Did any of the villagers ever ..." I searched for a word appropriate to the outrage I felt, "*hurt* you, Jackie?"

Jackie seemed hesitant to answer, which only confirmed my suspicion. "Never my Da. His wife, though, used to. She hit me with her hand, wooden spoons, and even tried to drown me once. My Da found out though and drove her out of the village. None of the other Scrapyarders ever forgave him, driving out one of their own for a demon child."

I absorbed that information, deciding that I would never help this community again. "I admire your father."

"Did you have a Da you loved?" Jackie's voice was wistful, as if finally touching on the raw emotion having her father killed must have instilled in her.

"No," I said, my father's mentioning triggering a host of memories both good and bad. "No, I didn't."

"I'm sorry, Mister Booth." Jackie was trying to comfort me, which struck me as an obscene reversal of the natural order.

"It's alright." I leaned down and placed my hand on her shoulder, watching her flinch. Reaching around, I gave her a gentle hug. "I've finally put that ghost to rest. You know, you remind me a lot of my daughter, Anita."

"Is she pretty?" Jackie asked a question which almost made me laugh.

"Yes, she is." I didn't mention that she'd inherited too many of my features. Martha was, by all accounts, the most beautiful woman in the Remnant. Anita, on the other hand, had been a tomboy growing up with very little feminine about her. She was pretty as opposed to gorgeous, but I doubted Jackie wanted to hear that. "Someday, I'll take you to meet her and your new brother Gabriel. They'll love you."

They might indeed, Gabriel was morbid and arcane enough that he'd have no difficulty acclimating to the fact she was a ghoul-human hybrid. Anita might have a bit more trouble with the concept but at heart Anita was a good little soldier. She'd trust my judgment that Jackie was no threat.

Jackie patted me on the back, seemingly a little uncomfortable. "So, when do we leave?"

"Soon," I said, patting her on the back. "I have never left a child behind in distress. It is my one saving grace in a damned world."

It was another reason why I was going back to the Black Cathedral, why I had to return there no matter the cost. There were still children held prisoner by Doctor Ward, close to a thousand of them if my restored memories were accurate.

They might or might not be transformed by his experiments yet, but either way they had to be rescued. It was the right thing to do. Afterward, should I somehow survive, the world would become murky again and the only remaining goal would be survival. It made hoping we triumphed difficult.

"Thank you, Mister Booth." She looked on the verge of tears. "You remind me a bit of my Da."

"He sounds like he was a wonderful man."

Jackie's toothy grin brightened the room. "He was."

I heard the approach of a woman's footsteps. By the sound, she was athletic, built, and of medium height. Seconds later, I heard her voice at the door. "Geez, Captain, you're starting a family out here? I knew you liked the Wastelands but this is a bit much."

I rose up, turning to Jessica. She was wrapped up in a bed sheet and drinking from a red Christmas mug with a bull terrier in a Santa hat on its side. Despite her ordeal, she looked much better than before.

"It's good to see you alive," I said, rubbing Jackie's hair. It felt like a dog's fur and I immediately stopped.

Jessica took another drink from her mug. "So what's the short version of everything that's happened since I suddenly felt like someone hit me with a tank?"

"Events include being found guilty of treason, having my execution faked, and being forced to sneak out of New Arkham with Doctor Mercury Takahashi. I killed a nightgaunt, killed an Earthmover, and went on a vision-quest where I killed a bunch of pre-human alien demigods where I'd lost a good friend. Then I summoned either the Devil, Son of God, or both, and he brought me home. We need to go to Kingsport and get Doctor Takahashi back. She's apparently been kidnapped."

"Alright," Jessica said, nodding as if all the insanity I'd just blathered made sense. "Who's the kid?"

"Jackie Howard, Mercury's ward. If you choose to disregard most of my words, understand the bit about being exiled is true." I took a deep breath, staring down. "There's something else you should know—I was tried and convicted for the murder of my squad, you included."

Jessica didn't say anything for a second before replying, "Wow, the Council of Leaders is full of idiots."

"Yeah," I said.

"Want to go kill them next?" Jessica asked.

"Peter Goodhill first, Ward next, and then we can worry about anyone else we need to murder."

"Understood," Jessica said.

"Taking a look at me and then one at Richard's corpse," Katryn said, "I take it your dream-quest did not go well?"

I looked over at the body before glancing back at her. "No. Richard's loss is one that diminishes the world."

Jessica looked down at the sheet-covered body, apparently noticing it for the first time, before saying, "Richard's dead? That stinks. He was a nice guy. You know, for a ghoul."

"For anyone," I corrected her. "To answer your question, Katryn, it went. That's all that needs to be said. Are you alright? I heard about the situation from Jackie."

"Betrayal leaves scars, John," Katryn said, her voice bitter and cold. "I am most definitely not alright. I apologize for allowing your slave to be taken. I will compensate you for her loss."

"She is *not* my slave." I was surprised by her choice of language, though I suspected she was just expressing her disapproval of Doctor Takahashi.

"I know. I just didn't like her," Katryn said, giving a half-smile before continuing. "In the meantime, I've been treating your confederate to make sure she's healed enough to help you recover the Doctor before she's raped and murdered."

Katryn had such a lovely way of phrasing things.

"Yeah, the crazy savage lady makes a mean cuppa mud." Jessica lifted her mug, swirling around its contents a bit. "What's in this stuff anyway, Hun?"

"Ghoul urine," Katryn deadpanned.

Jessica started choking and rushed out of the room, presumably to vomit. Jackie watched the entire scene in silence, barely managing to stifle her laughter.

I raised an eyebrow at Katryn, biting my upper lip in order to prevent myself from laughing. "That was unnecessary."

"Blame the fact I'm a crazy savage." Katryn's voice didn't waiver or change. "John, if you need to talk, I'm willing to be your spiritual advisor. I sensed Richard's death and some change in your fundamental nature. The Hand of Nyarlathotep is a heavy burden."

"The Hand is no longer there." I didn't like where this was going. "I had it removed."

Katryn removed my shirt, exposing the hand which had become a deep shade of black. It now burned with the same power the R'lyehian knife did.

"The Hand is eternal, John."

CHAPTER TWENTY-TWO

I took one look at the blackened-hand imprint on my shoulder, larger and more prominent than ever. The thing looked like a tattoo, only it now seemed to twist and turn as if trying to dance across the surface of my skin.

"Dammit, dammit, dammit," I cursed, putting my shirt back on.

Jackie looked up to it. "Does this mean you're still immortal, Mister Booth?"

"No!" I snapped at her, causing her to take a step back. Seeing her reaction, I winced and looked away, feeling ashamed. "I broke the spell. Jessica's awakening is proof enough of that."

"The Hand of Nyarlathotep is more than that," Katryn said, almost resigned. "You have been marked by the attention of the God-Who-Walks. His presence will follow you no matter what."

I couldn't help but feel the pangs of fear. Nyarlathotep was a god; no other word could properly describe the extra-dimensional *thing* I'd summoned. I'd stupidly thought I could use the *Necronomicon* to make him obey my commands, but instead I'd become a source of amusement to the twisted deity. I wanted to take a knife and cut the offending mark off my body, to cast the excess skin into a fire and watch it burn. I could feel the magic burned my skin now and imagined the mark's sorcerous energies leaking into my blood, slowly transforming me into something horrible. "Does this mean I'm doomed to become a monster? To go insane? To die screaming? What?"

Katryn looked down, speaking softer than I expected. "I don't know, John. The last person who bore the Hand of Nyarlathotep disappeared centuries ago. I only know of it from hearing the holy diaries of Wilbur Whateley. One can never say the final fate of those who have attracted the attention of the gods, sometimes it is glorious and sometimes it is horrible beyond imagination."

"Can't you *guess*?" I confess, as rebuttals went, it wasn't my finest.

"The mark has been reinforced. It is now many times more powerful than it was before. You have been touched by the Trickster directly. I …" Katryn trailed off, which spoke volumes about the situation. She wasn't the sort of woman to shy away from uncomfortable truths.

"Go on, please." I felt my head, feeling helpless before the curse afflicting me.

Katryn didn't respond for several seconds. "Without someone to draw the breath of life from, the Hand of Nyarlathotep will in all likelihood turn in on itself."

"You mean, it's going to kill me." I dropped my hands to my side. It made sense in a twisted sort of way: I'd summoned Nyarlathotep and he'd repaid me for my hubris by condemning me to a slow death by the same method I'd had my life extended.

"In all likelihood, yes." Katryn's words were meant to sound clinical and detached but she couldn't keep the emotion out of her voice; it was a deep and welling sadness. I felt flattered she felt so much for me. "You may have a few years but more likely nine months to a year. Eventually, the Hand will drain away your life as it did Jessica's. Then you will die."

My shoulder stung, which only made the horror I felt all the worse. "Is there anything to be done?"

I was acutely aware of Jackie's presence at my side. It was staggeringly unfair the little girl was being orphaned again, on the same day she'd lost her first adoptive father no less. I was prepared for death; I'd made peace with the fact I was going to die fighting the Great Old Ones long ago. It wasn't right or fair for a little girl to suffer through that, however.

Katryn's prognosis wasn't good. "The Hand of Nyarlathotep earlier laid upon you by the Necromancer is one thing, but I can tell this one has been done by the Trickster himself. I cannot think of anything mortal which could undo it."

Honestly, we didn't know for sure that Ward had placed the Hand of Nyarlathotep on me and Jessica. However, who else could it be? Richard certainly couldn't have done it, such magic was beyond him. However, it was a moot point now. My own stupidity was to blame for transforming the mark from a threat to Jessica's life into a death sentence for me.

"I see." There was little more to say.

Jackie tugged on my pants leg. "Mister Booth?"

I looked down at her, realizing I was scaring the child. "I'm sorry, Jackie. I didn't mean to frighten you. I'll be fine."

Jackie furrowed her brow. "Mister Booth, you're a horrible liar."

I burst out laughing at the absurdity of it all then gave her a pained smile. "I won't lie to you, Jackie. This is very frightening, even for me. However, I will face whatever threat comes with dignity and courage. I will not go quietly into the night but shake a fist towards heaven until the very end."

I resolved to find some way to survive for Jackie's sake more than my own. It was a foolish thing to do, one could not simply will oneself to live longer, but I would not roll over and die either.

Katryn placed her palm on my shirt where the hand was. "I believe if there is any being who is capable of defying the will of the Other Gods, John, it is you."

I knew Katryn was lying, she was just better at it than me. The Dunwych believed very strongly the will of the gods was immutable, that they existed in every moment simultaneously. If Nyarlathotep had condemned me to death, it was impossible for me to defy him in her mind. Worse, it was blasphemy to do so. Thankfully, I wasn't Dunwych. I didn't know how I would defy the will of the Great Old Ones but I'd try.

"He's lucky I've got other things to do right now. Otherwise, I'd be summoning him right now to beat him within an inch of his life for this." It was an empty boast. I wasn't sure if it was possible to fight a being like Nyarlathotep, but it sure as hell felt good to say.

"I'd help!" Jackie piped in.

Katryn actually gave a half-smile, a rarer thing than me doing it. "I half-believe you could."

I was tempted to tell Katryn about Nyarlathotep's prophecy, his statement that humanity had less than three generations to live, but I hesitated. I didn't have enough information regarding it yet. He might have meant humanity had less than sixty years left to exist or he could have been speaking in terms of three human lifetimes. Either interpretation was unacceptable to me.

Instead, I reached over and kissed Katryn again, our bodies pressing against one another as her hand pushed down hard on my scar. The wound burned when it was touched, still aching from where the nightgaunt had pierced me. There was no affection there, no love, but I could pretend for the sake of keeping an ally. "Thank you for that, a little support goes a long way. We've already lost a lot of time, however. We need to prepare."

"For curing you?" Jackie asked.

"No, Jackie, for rescuing Mercury. Don't worry about my condition."

"Sir ..."

"Don't."

"It is a treacherous path you walk, John." Katryn pulled away, turning to look out the door with a longing look on her face. "I also realize how well you played me. Together we will retrieve Mercury and avenge any indignities she may have suffered. Then I will offer up Peter's heart to Shub-Niggurath. From there, we will go on to kill the Necromancer and spread his entrails on a tree consecrated to Yig-Seth."

"Good," Jackie said, gritting her teeth.

"Don't mind Katryn, the Dunwych just have a very visual way of expressing their displeasure." I heard my stomach growl. "Let's go get something to eat first."

Jackie nodded. "Sounds good. You're pretty stoic about this whole dying thing."

"I'm not dead yet and where there's life, there's hope," I said.

"That's what I said." Jackie looked up, cheerfully. "You promise you're not going to die?"

"I promise." For a moment, I was able to forget all about the various evils assailing my life. "Katryn, I'll need your help planning the assault on Peter in about two hours."

"With pleasure, John." Katryn bowed her head reverently. "What will you be doing in the meantime?"

"After I eat? Burying Richard's body," I said. "Just because we must always struggle for life doesn't mean we can't take time to honor the dead."

"Can we visit my Da's grave too?" Jackie said. "I never got a chance to say goodbye."

"Of course." I didn't tell her my promise not to die was a lie. The Necromancer's power was unbelievable and even if I did rescue Mercury, I had no idea how to stop Ward.

But I would.

And I would make it painful.

CHAPTER TWENTY-THREE

The next couple of hours were spent in the Scrapyard graveyard. The villagers normally would have objected to burying a ghoul there but I kept my sniper rifle prominently displayed during my digging. Jackie got a chance to visit with her father while I interred Richard's remains. The sheriff was buried fairly reverentially by the locals despite his adoption of a ghoul child. I don't know what she said to her father but it calmed her.

Later, I spent a good three hours looking over Richard's maps while everyone else ate and scavenged supplies. From my evaluation, I determined Peter Goodhill was several hours ahead of us and direct pursuit would have been fruitless even if I'd gone after him as soon as I woke up.

Instead, the most optimal strategy for us to pursue them would be to ambush him in Kingsport. The only consolation I had from this unfortunate situation was Peter was unlikely to harm Doctor Takahashi; she was too valuable as a hostage or slave to sell. Even so, I worried about her every other thought. I was surprised how much her kidnapping affected me.

Despite my best efforts to dislike her, Mercury's treatment of Jessica and desire to help Jackie had softened my feelings towards the torturer. I wasn't attracted to Mercury beyond the physical but I was starting to believe she hadn't really had a choice in doing the things she'd done. No, I couldn't quite believe that. There was always a choice. However, I could not blame her for her actions at gunpoint. I, too, had done horrible things under those same circumstances. Unlikely as it was to happen, I wanted to rescue her and bring her to some place safe so she could find a new life free from evil. If such a place existed in this world.

I was brooding about that when Jessica interrupted me. "Captain, you in?"

I was standing over a map of Kingsport, crudely drawn but accurate. Somehow, Richard had acquired it from traders. "I'm just working on some last-minute strategies. There are several places where Peter Goodhill might take refuge and I want attack plans for all of them, along with appropriate escape avenues."

"Sounds good. I brought you something for tomorrow's trip." Jessica walked in wearing an outfit much better suited to her personality. Having found some clothing in her size, she'd replaced her lost Stetson and was now wearing a faded set of jeans with a plain blue button-down shirt topped with a brown leather vest. In her arms was a set of folded men's clothing that I doubted had belonged to Richard.

"Thank you." I marked a possible point of egress on the map below me, using a wooden stylus with an inkwell.

"I thought you'd like some duds other than the kind soldiers wear." Jessica shook the clothing in her hands.

"Thank you." I smiled, looking down at the prison fatigues I was still wearing. "I am rather eager to get out of this outfit."

"Good to know. You hungry, Captain? We've still got some leftovers from dinner, too. That Katryn lady is quite the cook despite being a *native* type," Jessica said, making air quotes as she said the word "native."

"I had some beans earlier. Richard has a surprisingly well-stocked pantry," I said, ignoring her comment about Katryn. I wasn't sure if Jessica yet knew about my condition and I wasn't about to tell her.

Jessica frowned, wrinkling her nose. "By the way, Sir, you might want to take a shower before you change. You're starting to smell a wee bit ripe."

I sniffed the side of my lapel, near the blackened burn mark of the Hand. It reeked of something akin to sulfur and rotting meat. A shower probably couldn't cure that but I could cover up the smell with an oil-soaked bandage. "I probably should."

Jessica put the clothes on a nearby shelf before taking a deep breath. "That's the understatement of the year, up there with 'The Great Old Ones woke up temperamental.'"

I smiled at her joke. "How are you holding up, Corporal?"

"You're asking how *I'm* holding up?" Jessica seemed shocked by my question.

"I wouldn't have asked if I wasn't curious," I responded, putting away the maps. I'd done about as much planning as was possible without actually seeing the buildings in person. No plan survived contact with the enemy anyway and Peter was a wily foe. He'd be prepared for any attack by an R&E Ranger. I had to think like someone different and that was a harder task than it sounded.

Jessica blinked, amazed at my ability to compartmentalize. "Do you mean mentally or physically, Captain? Or do you just want me to call you John now, since we've both been discharged?"

"Either is fine," I answered. I had more important things on my mind than proper forms of address, especially from friends.

"*O Captain, my Captain,*" Jessica quoted a poem by Walt Whitman. "I think I'll stick with that one, you always did love poetry."

"Nothing wrong with poetry, it's been the province of military officers since time memorial. I even wrote a sequel to *Ozymandias,*" I said, smirking. "It was terrible."

"I'd still love to hear it sometime," Jessica said, leaning up against the wall. "I hope I at least got a military funeral. Do you think we got the full twenty-one-gun salute or do you think they thought it would be wasting ammo?"

"Almost certainly the latter. We'd be lucky if they remembered to write our names down, and that was before I was judged to be an abomination against God and humanity." I walked out to the Blue Meanie, looking at the car appraisingly. It was now fully outfitted for our trek across the Great Barrier Desert. "Though I imagine they'd take you back if you presented yourself and denounced me."

"You're hilarious, Captain." Jessica snorted. "Did anyone else ever tell you that?"

I'd heard it a few times before, not the least from friends and loved ones. "My wife for one."

"Ah, the wicked witch gets something right." Jessica gave a thumbs-up before looking at the Corvette. "Nice machine."

"Yes, it is."

"So, ready to talk about what happened to you?" Jessica gave a brief snort. "I'd like to hear the whole story. About your exile, dying, coming back, all of it."

"Telling the whole story would require a couple of hours and a great deal of alcohol. Suffice to say, it's a consequence of my actions and I'm not overly concerned."

"You're not overly concerned with *dying*?" Jessica stared at me.

"We're all dying, Jessica, every single day of our lives." I said, picking up a wrench and heading out past Jessica into the garage.

"That is the worst way to cheer up someone I have *ever* heard." Jessica looked away, trying not to gaze directly at me.

"Funny, I thought you were trying to cheer me up," I said before raising the hood of the car to make sure everything was working properly. I had only a limited amount of knowledge regarding automobiles, but I could tell the machine hadn't been touched by our erstwhile traitor.

"I was. I'm just bad at it." Jessica gazed down at the floor. "I'm sorry, Captain, it's just you're a rock. You managed to survive things no other person in the Remnant could ever dream of. You're a hero, no matter how much you deny it."

"There are no heroes in the Wasteland." That was one of the first lessons I learned away from New Arkham. "You didn't really answer my question, though. How do you feel?"

"I'm dealing," Jessica said, realizing I genuinely didn't want to talk. "The other Gammas dying was a blow to the gut but casualties happen. Remember when we lost Private Jenkins?"

"Yes, man ran straight into the mouth of a … well, I have no idea actually, but whatever it was, it ate him whole."

That particular mission had been a general disaster, Private Jenkins being promoted to the Rangers before he was ready. I had no idea what the creature had been; it had been little more than a free-floating hole in reality, but I'd spent a week tracking it down afterward. Two-dimensional gaping maw or not, M-Rad grenades were capable of killing it.

"I'm having a harder time dealing with you dying. Well, dying and not coming back, I mean," Jessica said, gazing at me with a kind of reverence that disturbed me. It was halfway between love and worship. I would have much preferred she look at me as an equal and friend. "Tell me, Captain, is this really the end? Are you going to die?"

I decided lying was the best course of action. I didn't want to be pitied or babied in the last months of my life. "I'm going to force Doctor Ward to reverse what's been done to me before I kill him, Jessica. Seriously, I'll be alright. A few well-timed punches and he'll cave. Then we'll hang him together."

Jessica visibly relaxed, exhaling a deep breath. "I *knew* you weren't going down without a fight."

Given the ease with which she believed my transparent lie, I debated telling her Santa Claus was real. Of course, for all I knew, he was flying around somewhere in the Dreamlands. "I can try and make some arrangement to get you back into the Remnant, Jessica. We both still have friends in the military, even if they did declare you dead and brand me a traitor."

"I'm glad to be free of the Remnant." Jessica's voice was surprisingly harsh. "You might not understand that but it's true."

"You'd be surprised." After taking in Peter's, Mercury's, and even my own reactions to leaving the Remnant, I was starting to realize that more people hated living in our homeland than I'd ever suspected. "Still, leaving your old life behind is never easy, especially when it involves entering into a world where the Great Old Ones rule."

"My husband died a year ago, fighting the Color. My children? Well, they died worse and there wasn't a damned thing I could do about it." Jessica trailed off, looking frustrated. "Do you think Ward was really behind it?"

"Yes."

"Good. Then I'll pay back this universe for taking them from me."

"Yes."

"John, do you remember the Yellow Spore Crisis?"

I did. The Yellow Spore Crisis had been triggered by cultists of Hastur, killing the youngest and most innocent of the Remnant first. Jacob O'Reilly had wanted to have more kids but Jessica had never gotten over the loss, transferring from regular army to the Rangers a month later. "I'm sorry."

"It's not your fault. You helped kill the cultists after it happened."

I was about to say something when she continued talking. "The

Great Old Ones rule in the Remnant just like in the Wasteland. We just refuse to acknowledge that big damn aliens own this planet now. I'd give anything to make that not the case anymore."

"We never owned this planet, Corporal. We just thought we did." I walked over and placed my hand on her. "Ward doesn't either, though, and I take comfort in that."

"It's about the only comfort I've got left."

"You're just a bastion of joy, Sir." Jessica looked almost happy as she spoke. Revenge was a poor substitute for those taken from you but it could keep you going. It was all I had right now, despite Jessica being in front of me. I would rather spend that time going after Ward than be here with her. It rather sickened me to realize that. I loved hate more than I did love and friendship. Perhaps we weren't so far from the Old Ones after all, but they didn't hate or love. They just existed, and in that, I envied them.

"What are you going to do after?" I asked, hoping to change the subject. "After killing Ward."

"There is no after, Captain, you know that. I accepted death when I joined the Rangers." Jessica rolled her eyes. "Isn't that what it's all about? Spitting in the eye of Cthulhu before it's all over?"

I knew exactly how she felt but I wanted her to lie to me the same way I'd lied to her.

"I'll accept fighting monsters is what we do." I paused to let a single beat past. "But I don't intend to die at all, neither should you."

"That's the spirit!" Jessica said, laughing. "Embrace your inner cowboy!"

"I will."

Jessica then made a serious misjudgment. "So are you and the tribal lady together?"

I closed my eyes and remembered the revulsion I'd felt during my time with the Dunwych as their slave. "No."

Jessica picked up on the subtext or at least some of it. "So not much future there, huh?"

"I don't think so."

"Right," Jessica said, punching me in the arm. "Come on. Let's go rescue your psycho-torturer friend."

"Agreed."

CHAPTER TWENTY-FOUR

Driving under the blazing sun across the Great Barrier Desert in a 1964 Blue Chevrolet convertible with trunk full of automatic weapons and three passengers was probably the most normal thing I'd done in the past month.

I'd changed from my earlier attire into the cowboy clothing Jessica had provided me after showering. Now I was wearing a pair of jeans and a button-down shirt like Jessica, a vest tight around my shoulders. I felt a little silly, even putting aside the hat. Still, wearing clothing other than the prison fatigues left me feeling a bit better about myself.

Jackie was sitting across from me as Katryn and Jessica shared the back seat. It was amusing to watch the two of them struggle not to look at one another. In a way, the two warrior women were a great deal alike, but I doubted either would ever feel that way.

The Blue Meanie was an excellent vehicle, even if it was important to keep it on the half-broken and shattered highways of Old Earth. I would have preferred the jeep belonging to the Remnant, but the Earthmover had taken care of that. The convertible, in a way, would also be lower profile because there were still many people who came to Kingsport for recreation as well as trade.

We were currently passing through the shadow of the Great Idols, a region which was even more telling of humanity's fall from power than the ruins of its former cities. Massive alien pyramids, their black surfaces smoother than anything that human hands could construct, stretched out amongst gigantic statues of the Great Old Ones which dwarfed the size of the Sphinx. Whoever had erected these chthonic monuments was obviously a worshiper of not only Dread Cthulhu but the entire twisted pantheon of the Great Old Ones.

Describing the various creatures I saw depicted in the enormous statues would have taken hours, and human language would fail to convey their innately disgusting nature. The greatest of the Old Ones' statues was, in many respects, the easiest to talk about. I, of course, referred to the statues of Great Cthulhu. The most powerful of the Great Old Ones was, in many ways, the most human-seeming. It possessed such recognizable traits as two arms, two legs, and a head with eyes. Its leathery bat-like wings and squid-like tentacles hanging from its face gave it a demonic appearance to be sure, but even that was not so far removed from human mythology as to shake one's sanity. Truly, he looked like nothing so much as an aquatic-themed representation of Satan.

I had to wonder if the Great Old One was truly so similar to us in appearance or if the designers of those massive statues had merely designed their depiction of him to be similar to them in form. I suspected the true face of Cthulhu was nothing so easy to look upon as the squid-faced dragon his idols routinely depicted him as. Another possibility was all of human's myths regarding gods and devils derived from dreams of the Great Old Ones. Given I doubted the builders of the Great Idols were human, especially given their gigantic size, the latter theory was likely. A disturbing thought, really. Just how much of humanity's mythology was nothing more than half-remembered glimpses of the alien beings living underneath us? I kept to my faith but it was like a leaking boat in the middle of Deep One-infested waters.

Regardless of my musings, the statues jutted out of the desert haphazardly. They extended from the ground as if a tremendous earthquake had forced them up from miles-high caverns deep beneath the Earth. Lightning storms and weird, strangely colored lights crackled between the titanic monstrosities, doing so whether there were clouds to produce them or not.

It was whispered amongst Wastelanders that hordes of Cthulhu cultists routinely made pilgrimages to the region in order to pay homage to their dark gods. There were even rumors of unnatural cities built in the region and directly underneath the monstrous idols. I couldn't help but gritted my teeth at the knowledge that one of the buildings near these idols was the Black Cathedral. We were less than forty miles away from it. My restored memories gave me its precise location here in the desert.

It was all I could do to keep myself from turning the car on a course to it in order to kill Alan Ward, forgoing the whole trip to rescue Mercury. I only stopped myself because Jackie was in the vehicle and I wouldn't risk her life for my vengeance. I hated myself for that because I'd grown fond of Mercury in our short time together.

Finally, hours into our drive, Jessica spoke up and ended the oppressive silence our group had been laboring under since leaving Scrapyard. "So ... Katryn is it? How exactly did you and the Captain meet?"

"I took him as a slave," Katryn said. "I decided he would make a good sire for my child. Dunwych women are expected to birth strong warriors in addition to being them. So it reads in the writings of Whateley."

"Huh. Well, that explains a few things," Jessica said, looking to me. I could tell she wanted to slit Katryn's throat then and there.

I shook my head, not wanting to talk about it. I'd lied through my teeth about my time among the Dunwych and did my best to make it sound like a grand adventure. The only person I hadn't kept it from had been my wife, who considered me weak for allowing myself to be captured.

"So you're friends now?" Jessica asked, more to me than Katryn.

"Our current relationship is limited to shared cooperation in casting down the Necromancer." Katryn shrugged. "Then time will tell if I kill him or he kills me."

"Ah," Jessica said, looking embarrassed. "You, Captain?"

"Oh, we're friends," I said. "Best buddies."

"Please don't kill anyone while I'm here," Jackie said, staring out into the valley. "I've had enough of that for a lifetime."

"Right," I said, deciding that this was as good a time as any to move on with the conversation.

"So, Mister Booth, why exactly did you wait so long to go after Ms. Mercury?"

"Pardon?" I didn't look at her, trying to keep my eyes away from the idols. I didn't want any further temptations to go after Alan directly. During my shower, the Hand of Nyarlathotep had begun to start itching, little black lines appearing around the edge as if they were creeping into my skin. I had no intention of dying before I sent

Alan to an early grave.

"You waited until you buried Mister Jameson's body and also did some other stuff before going after her. She's my friend, so I was wondering … why?" Jackie, in that moment, proved herself to be a very sharp young woman.

I said automatically, "He had too much of a lead on us. It was better to just wait and pursue him after we'd better prepared ourselves."

It was true, mostly.

"Yeah, but it just didn't feel right." Jackie leaned on her palm, resting her elbow on the car door. "There's more to it … isn't there?"

Damn, that girl could sniff out any evasion, couldn't she? Unfortunately, the truth was a bit more complicated than I wanted to get into right now. I'd needed a few hours to get ahold of myself after the events in the Dreamlands. Actually, I probably needed a few *years* to get ahold of myself. Hours were all I could spare though. I'd lost my squad, my family, my vocation, my closest friend, and my longevity in rapid order. The fact I could remember it all in perfect clarity just by thinking about it didn't help the matter one bit.

I wasn't sure if my ability to keep going in the face of such things was a sign of strength or incipient madness. I'd suffered a psychotic break fighting the shoggoth. It, combined with Richard's crude attempts to patch my mind together thereafter, was possibly responsible for my hallucination of Azathoth's court fighting Peter Goodhill. The other option was the Hand of Nyarlathotep was somehow linking me to that foul deity and his father. I was either going mad or being corrupted into something inhuman. Explaining *that* to a little girl was more than I was capable of pulling off.

Thankfully, Jessica spared me the trouble. "The Captain has a lot on his mind now."

The Great Old Ones waking up temperamental indeed.

"I guess. I was just wondering how he was going to bring her back."

"He's probably—" Jessica started to say.

"I'll think of something," I interrupted. "I promise."

"Don't make promises you can't keep," Jackie said, falling silent.

"Oooo, look at that!" Jessica said, pointing. "That's one cuss-ugly mother."

I glanced to where she was pointing and saw a particularly

blasphemous statue dedicated to the Unspeakable One. That particular member of the Great Old Ones was literally too bizarre and disturbing to describe.

Katryn clung to the spear she'd given me, holding the sacred weapon like a totem, thankfully ignoring the blasphemy to her god. "When we reach Kingsport, John, we should make an effort to link up with the army the Dunwych have assembled."

"I agree," I said. Though it was not for the reasons she thought. I intended to warn away the army.

I didn't think any number of soldiers would be useful against Alan Ward. If the least of his disciples could summon a monster like the Earthmover I fought earlier then human soldiers would be useless. I didn't even want to think about what sort of entities Ward himself could bring to bear. A small force to locate and terminate the Necromancer was infinitely preferable—as long as I was part of it.

"Mister Death would be interested in hearing what you have to say." Katryn's voice had a trace of wistfulness, almost mischief.

"Mister Death?" Jessica said.

"Her father," I said, not looking back. "He's the High Priest of Hastur."

"Who?" Jackie asked.

"The Lord of Disease and Despair," I said.

"Even the Dunwych's *names* are amazing." Jackie's eyes widened.

"That they are, Jackie-girl."

"Eh, fuck Hastur," Jessica said.

"You should not blaspheme," Katryn said.

"Or what?" Jessica said.

Katryn said, "They may hear you."

"I doubt they care," Jessica said. "It's the humans in the world who give a shit about pride, not the giant aliens who destroyed our world."

Katryn looked ready to argue, stopped, then looked away.

"Can you tell me anything about Kingsport?" I asked her, wishing this car ride would end. Richard had surprisingly detailed plans for the city, including a map of the sewer system. However, I knew very little about how the community was run. Knowing things like who was in charge could mean the difference between life and death.

Katryn didn't disappoint. "Yes, I can. The Dunwych have many dealings with Kingsport's traders."

"How's that?" Jessica asked, leaning back into her seat.

Katryn smirked. "They allow us to use it for trade and entertainment. In return we do not burn it to the ground."

"A bit of a running theme with you guys." Jessica closed one eye and stared at her with the other.

Katryn smiled at Jessica, a rare sight. "We try."

"We're almost to the city," I said, glad we were finally passing the shadow of the Great Idols. Many of Cthulhu's mile-tall statues would be visible for some time in the distance, though. I wouldn't feel entirely safe until they had completely passed out of sight. I couldn't escape the feeling, despite the size and age of the statues, they'd been constructed specifically to watch for me.

"Good," Jessica said, giving a furtive glance over her shoulder at the eldritch statues behind us. "I've got an itch to play some poker."

"We're not going gambling," I said. "This is a mission of mercy, nothing more."

"I can gamble *and* be merciful," Jessica said, huffing.

"Katryn, go on with your description, please."

Katryn gave me a brief overview of Kingsport's power structure, "Like the Elder Sign, the city has four points. Specifically, four ruling families: The Marshes, the Kings, the Cashes, and the Wyatts. They're all descendants of the warlords who rose in the aftermath of the Rising. Only the Kings and the Marshes should concern you, though. They are the strongest of the families, using the occult to guarantee their supremacy."

"The city runs on a feudal structure?" I asked, wondering how such an arrangement worked.

Shaking her head, Katryn said, "More like a kleptocracy. They intimidate all businesses for a cut of the profits but offer no real structure to the city. Everything is for sale in Kingsport and the only law is 'Don't offend the Four Families.' They keep a peace built around whatever is good for the flow of trade that lines their coffers. The populace just attempts to make do."

I couldn't say I was surprised. It wasn't so different from many other self-styled nations spread across the land. Civility was impossible without civilization.

"Do you think Peter is going to seek refuge with one of them?" I didn't think Peter Goodhill was the type to face me without a stacked deck. Then again, I would have thought him smart enough not to try and piss off an R&E Ranger who *wasn't* a coward.

"Peter has helped sell many slaves to the Marsh family. He also trained many of their soldiers," Katryn said, shaking her head. "It is a family strongly allied with the Deep Ones. Some say its patriarch is a member of that race, born human in a small village on the East Coast before the Rising. This will make any conflict with them difficult; they have the loyalty of the city's entire inhuman populace."

"God, I hate Deep Ones. They're stinking fish-men out to enslave the world, eat children, and horde all women into rape camps." Jessica's tone was positively venomous, expressing her loathing of the largest inhuman species on Earth after ghouls. I couldn't entirely blame her; we'd had several unfortunate encounters with the aquatic race.

I, myself, had met more than a few Deep Ones in my time. I could even understand their strange speech, even if I couldn't speak it. The desert wasn't a particularly good environment for them, so they mostly stuck to the lakes and marshes along the East Coast, but the ones I'd met ranged from psychotically insane to fundamentally decent. In other words, they were much like humans once you got past the scales.

"I'm fairly sure Deep Ones don't do any of that," I pointed out.

"What?" Jessica said, surprised.

"Well they are fish-men and I'll be honest, they don't smell very good to human nostrils. However, I'm fairly sure the whole eating people and rape camps thing is Remnant propaganda."

"Oh." Jessica paused, apparently surprised by my reaction. "They do breed evil human–fish-men hybrids, though. Right?"

"Hey! That could be consensual!" Jackie said, defensively.

I wondered where a girl like Jackie had learned a word like consensual, then I realized it had probably come up whenever her parentage was discussed. "Yes, it could be. Probably is, in fact. Sex and breeding has always been a commodity humans have been willing to trade for protection or wealth. How far are the Marshes likely to go in order to protect him?"

"Far enough," Katryn said. "The Marshes hate humans but if Peter's ties to the Necromancer are known they will not betray him. It is well known the sorcerer possesses power to rival the Great Old Ones."

"He doesn't. The Great Old Ones can rearrange the stars in the sky. Ward can only do parlor tricks by comparison," I said, remembering how his hand had exploded when struck by my knife. It gave me the confidence to believe I could kill him.

"Perception is what matters, John. You will have to learn that if you are to survive. Humanity has illusions of importance to the universe; the Deep Ones are not so different from us in that regard," Katryn said, surprisingly eloquently. "In truth, they are no more relevant than mankind but believe themselves chosen of Cthulhu. They believe Ward is blessed by the First of the Great Old Ones, and that attitude must be attacked if you are to escape Kingsport unharmed with your prize."

Mercury was more than a prize. "I'm not a very good speaker. So I suppose I'll just have to kill them all then."

"Good." Jackie balled her fists.

Katryn frowned.

"Not to shoot down all of the fun vigilante plans you've got, Captain, but why don't you ask your *best buddies* assembling an army to help?" Jessica asked, sounding like I was overlooking something obvious.

I had been and it was a good question. After all, we were going to a city where a whole army of technologically-adept and supernaturally-blessed warriors were gathering. As a priestess, Katryn could easily order any number of them to assist in Mercury's rescue if she were so inclined. Given Mercury had assisted in saving her life, even if it was only in distracting the Earthmover, I had no doubt she'd do it, too. I didn't want to owe the Dunwych anything, though. So, I made up a story that sounded plausible. "Brute force has its place. Quantity, after all, has a quality all its own. However, I'm a fan of small-unit tactics. If we were to show up at Peter's door with an army, he'd slit Mercury's throat, either that or attempt to escape. I intend to retrieve Doctor Takahashi alive and Peter Goodhill decidedly less so."

"What if she's not, though?" Jackie said, "What if he's killed her?"

The chances of that were higher than I really wanted to admit. As much as I wanted to believe that Mercury was not going to be harmed, I couldn't really gauge how much my brutal beating of Peter Goodhill had offended the former R&E Ranger. Some men gained sexual gratification and self-confidence from the abuse of women; I didn't want to think that was the sort of thing she was currently undergoing.

My answer was the same for dealing with Ward. "Then we have to kill him."

"Aren't we going to do that anyway?" Jackie pointed out the obvious flaw in my plan.

"Yes," I admitted.

"Not much of a plan then." Jackie sighed, not at all comforted.

"No, not really."

That was when we came into view of our destination. It was daytime, so Kingsport was not at its most visually distinctive, but clouds of smoke came up from its factory district as a great wall of welded-together scrap surrounded the vast community of two hundred thousand. A few damaged skyscrapers still stood amidst novelty-themed buildings which had been constructed during the city's glory years.

Kingsport resembled old, crumbling photos I'd seen of Las Vegas and Reno. However, it was obvious no matter how much construction had been done to make it reminiscent of those two, it was still a pale imitation. Indeed, it looked like a smaller version of a modern city combined with a Bronze Age city-state. I could see large numbers of caravans built around the edge and miles of mud farms stretching behind them.

"And lo I beheld Babylon," I said under my breath, appreciating both the good and the evil of the city that had risen from the desert.

"Babylon grew." Katryn shook her head. "This is a city which *festers.*"

I disagreed. "It lives. That, by itself, is an accomplishment."

Even if I had to make a deal with the Old Ones' worshipers to do so.

CHAPTER TWENTY-FIVE

Kingsport was a surprisingly well-organized anarchy. The original inhabitants wouldn't have recognized the city, the founding warlords and Four Families having done their best to make it into a garish traders' town. While it didn't approach the glories of old Earth, it was impressive how much sleaze they'd managed to jam together into one tiny area.

Neon signs scavenged from across the countryside were fused to older buildings made into gambling halls, brothels, drug dens, distilleries, food stands, and hotels. The bright pink and red paint jobs were painfully flamboyant but there was still grandeur to the place. Despite how crude the industries propping up the city were, it was still a place which had emerged triumphant and alive from the Rising.

None of the city's few skyscrapers were terribly impressive; the tallest stood no taller than a few dozen floors. Yet, they'd been maintained as much as humanly possible with scavenged parts from other ruined cities scattered across the countryside. In Medieval Europe, many ancient Roman sites had been cannibalized for the building of castles and towns. It was interesting to see the modern-day variant.

The city lacked the resources to power itself with solar energy the way the Remnant did, but myriad windmills and the methane smell that clung to the air showed they didn't want for power here. Indeed, it was lit up like a Christmas tree. All of my earlier complaints about the waste of power in New Arkham paled to what was being done in Kingsport, *during the daytime.*

I was especially impressed by the roads. They were composed of cobblestones, replacing asphalt that had long since turned to powder. We weren't the only car on the city streets but we were the most noticeable. We drew attention wherever we drove, people marveling at the Blue Meanie. I took the time to stare at them back, looking at the populace of the first major city I'd visited other than New Arkham.

The populace was a fascinating mixture of humanity's survivors: a group of a hundred or more refugee populations which had come together under the warlords who settled Kingsport and promptly interbred. There were individuals of African, Caucasian, Chinese, Hindi, Korean, and even Native American descent. All of the Pre-Rising humanity in the former state of Massachusetts had banded together to survive—and had.

Their clothing and mannerisms had over a century to develop along its own lines and I could observe, but not fully comprehend it, at a glance like so many other Wasteland communities I'd seen. Some individuals were dressed like they'd stepped out of the 1940s, with significantly more grime, while others were full-on punks. I wished there were anthropologists left to record the phenomenon.

On a purely emotional level, Kingsport reminded me of a detective story's setting. I'd seen several such movies back at New Arkham, made with posters on the back of the wall and patch-worn costumes. The crumbling but functional buildings had a sense of seediness clinging to their every curve. The signs were mostly written in a pidgin form of English combined with Chinese and Arabic writing, giving a sense of otherworldliness.

Steam pipes linked everything together, filling the air with random spurts of white smoke. Storm clouds had moved in over the city as we entered and a light rain was now falling on us, a few of the citizens surrounding us pulling out patched and worn umbrellas. It was the sort of place you could open the description of with the words, "The city had a million stories."

"Wow, Ms. Mercury would hate it here," Jackie said, looking over the car door. "It's not nearly science-y enough."

"I'm not sure science-y is a real word," I said, keeping a shotgun firmly placed on my lap in plain sight. A substantial number of the pedestrians around were armed. I guessed many of them would kill for a tenth of what the car contained, be it passengers or the weapons in the trunk. Others, I suspected, would kill just for the car.

"Of course it is, she made it up," Jessica corrected me.

"*Touché*," I said. "I think Mercury would like it, actually. Once she got a hand on the environment at least."

"Sell everyone and your mother out to survive?" Jessica said.

"Exactly."

We continued to drive slowly down the streets, my eyes darting to the various windows above us. I surveyed for any sign of a rifle sticking through, unlikely as it would be to spot one from my position. Any of them could contain Peter Goodhill. Sniping was just his style; it minimized his personal danger while allowing a stronger opponent to be killed.

I tried not to let it make me paranoid.

"So where's this army of Dunwych?" Jackie said. "I haven't noticed any pretty white-haired tribals running around yet."

"My family is unique," Katryn said, moving her hand to a tiny bone charm bracelet on her right wrist I'd barely noticed before. It contained hundreds of little grotesque idols to the Great Old Ones. Only by listening in intently could I hear her muttering unintelligible prayers to each of them.

I did not know what sort of magic she was doing but I felt automatically more secure. As much as I disliked magic, it having burned me rather badly, I put faith in Katryn's ability.

"To answer your question, Jackie-girl, it seems there's the army of Dunwych," Jessica said, pointing down at the end of a side street I turned the Blue Meanie into. The same sort of strange organic-seeming piping music I'd heard playing in Azathoth's court, though significantly less surreal, was playing on the other side.

Passing down the street was a parade, if such a description could be applied to a Dunwych religious ceremony. Thousands of Dunwych stood on the sidelines, even more diverse-looking than Kingsport's population. Hundreds more of the Dunwych's best warriors carried idols on sedans and walked down the street, covered by flower petals flowing down on them from nearby windows. Naked flute-players and horn-blowers of both sexes accompanied the procession, continuing their surreal offerings to the aliens who had annihilated the world. I recognized the parade as a ceremony called the *Karrab-Jaffan*, a Dunwych ritual devoted to warriors making their peace with death.

They thanked the Great Old Ones, also gods like Azathoth and Yog-Sothoth, for destroying the world and thus giving them the chance to prove themselves against great adversity. The ceremony would end itself in eating, drinking, and lovemaking as they all prepared to meet their end at the hands of the enemies they would soon engage. The ceremony was never performed save in the direst of circumstances. I'd first witnessed it right before my last confrontation with the Color. In a way it was strangely moving, highlighting that ancient need of humanity to personify those forces that were beyond its control. For good or ill, Great Cthulhu cared nothing about humanity, so worshiping him was pointless.

Yet, his effect on humanity told us much about our capacity for good and evil. The cult serving Alan Ward had been driven to madness by their need to act as if mankind's near-annihilation was part of a greater plan. The Dunwych confronted the disaster as if it was a way to prove their strength. I had to say, I much preferred the Dunwych's version.

Even in fatalism, there was beauty.

That was when a group of men with shotguns and pistols came around the corner of the street behind us. Apparently, they were trying to sneak up on us. It was insulting, really, when groups tried to do this. First, I was an R&E Ranger and trained to notice this sort of thing. Second, I didn't put much stock in getting up close with an opponent if armed with a gun. These jokers looked like they were trying to get right up in our face with their weapons. Seriously, if you were going to kill a person with a firearm you should take advantage of the whole "range advantage" thing they'd been created for.

"Dammit," I muttered under my breath, not turning around. "Jessica, do you see them?"

"Hmm?" Jessica asked, sounding confused. Apparently, she hadn't.

"Don't move, Jackie," I said, expecting her to turn around. After all, she was just a child rather than a trained soldier.

"What?" Jackie said, not bothering to turn back. Instead, she was engrossed in the festival before her. I supposed for those who had never seen a parade before, especially one as eerily lovely as the Karrab-Jaffan, the sight must have been bewitching.

"I sense them, John. Do you wish them to die?" Katryn alone seemed to have detected the presence of our coming attackers. Yet, she hadn't looked around either. She just stood there looking forward, an amused expression on her face.

"Not yet." I kept my tone even. "I just want everyone to be prepared for the time we *might* have to kill them."

"Yes, Captain." Jessica straightened her back and concealed her six-shooters underneath her legs.

Looking into the vehicle's rearview window, I got a good look at our attackers. They were composed of four men and two women. All of them were dressed in Kingsport's fashions, though a slightly higher class than the rest of the surrounding citizenry. They also sported garish jewelry in the form of gold medallions, rings, and teeth. It made them look simultaneously rich as well as trashy.

Their numbers bothered me; sending only six after us was downright insulting. If they'd truly intended to kill or intimidate my group, they should have sent at least twelve. Six could possibly kill or injure one of us but it wasn't likely. It made me wonder if this group was a random group of hijackers or just a group of overconfident fools who didn't know who they were dealing with.

Waiting for the greasy-haired figure leading the annoying little posse to get close, I wished I had some gum. When he finally arrived, he pushed a home-made shotgun to the side of my face. This particular man stood about five foot eight, weighed two hundred and twelve pounds, and wore a striped business suit with a number of well-sewn patches. His teeth, unlike the others in his group, were almost entirely gold and he had a glimmer in his eyes. I instantly took a dislike to him, taking him for the sort of man that got his thrills by bullying others.

The shotgun itself was a shoddy piece of workmanship with two pipe barrels, a pair of triggers on the back, and leaky re-usable shells as likely to explode in someone's hands as take out the enemy. My distaste for the man grew. There were a fairly large number of talented gunsmiths in the Wasteland. The fact that he stuck with such a crude weapon told me he either liked the loud noise such a gun would make or simply had no decent knowledge of firearms. I suspected both to be the case.

The man's language was as coarse as his manner. Poking me

in the side of the head with the ends of the shotgun again, he said, "Listen, you piece of shit. I've got a gun pointed right to the side of your stinking New Arkhamite face. You make one move and I'll blow your fucking brains out. Do you got it, you little queer, so … oomph!"

I slammed the car door onto his genitalia while Katryn moved like lightning with her spear, knocking three of the others on their backs. Jessica shot the guns out of the hands of two more aggressors, causing them to probably lose fingers in the process. Grabbing their leader by the throat, I stuck his own shotgun into his mouth, holding his hands above the trigger. If he moved an inch, I'd force him to blow his own head off.

"You, sir, will learn how to behave in front of children. I also strongly suggest you avoid insulting a person because of their sexuality. I've known many honorable men and women who've favored the same sex," I said, fully prepared to splatter his brains across the back of the Blue Meanie's windshield. The difference would be, I'd tell Jackie to avert her eyes.

"Mmmph!" the gangster tried to scream, panicking. I just shoved the rifle butt a little farther into his mouth.

"I do not operate according to the rules of other men. I am the product of a hundred years of humanity winnowing away the fat off its military doctrines. I was trained under conditions which would kill most men. I was forged in situations where it was me or the other man, repeated endlessly." I kept my finger on the trigger, visibly so. "Now, you are going to behave. Tell me who you are and why you've come or I'll just have the women behind me kill your associates. Then I will kill you."

I was fairly sure the man was about to do something stupid when we were interrupted by a man walking into the alley from the street where the parade was passing by.

He stood six feet in height, strongly resembling Katryn in terms of face and body type. The figure sported long silver hair, covering it with a brown safari hat that made him look like a big-game hunter. He was dressed like one too, wearing a long brown trench coat over his khaki pants and lightly tanned shirt. Several necklaces made of Deep One and Ghoul bones hung around his neck as his hands sported bracelets similar to the one Katryn wore. The man's left eye was missing, covered with a black eye-patch decorated with an Egyptian falcon. I recognized him as Mister Death.

"You do not have to kill him, Captain Booth. He is stupid but only following his orders. Blame the dog's owner, not the dog." His voice had inflections of indeterminate origins, neither Dunwych nor any other culture in the world. The closest reference point I could put was South Africa by way of New England.

"You also put down rabid dogs," I replied to the Dunwych mystic. "I have had a seriously bad day, Your Eminence. I do not need this sh—arbage." I corrected myself before I swore in front of Jackie. It wouldn't do to set a bad example for her.

"Hello." Jackie waved to him. "Could you please keep Mister Booth from killing this guy? Not because I like the guy threatening us but because I think it'd be really gross and ruin Mister Jameson's car interior."

"Certainly, child. John, would you be so kind as to not kill this man?" Mister Death stepped forward, raising a hand which was tattooed with the yellow eye of Hastur. "I consider it a favor to both me and my flock. Besides, I do not believe you want to blow the head off a man in front of a young girl."

"I'm not a young girl," Jackie muttered.

"I won't kill him once I have some answers, provided he doesn't pose a threat." I grabbed the gangster's hand as he reached for a pistol in his jacket, showing he was even stupider than he looked. Mister Death was right though, no point in avoiding foul language if I was going to cover the walls in the man's blood.

Taking the thug's pistol, I slid it into my own jacket pocket as I looked to see what the girls were doing. Jessica and Katryn were already out of the car, having seized the other members of the group's weapons. The two were holding the other five at gunpoint, a sensible move. Jackie was watching the ordeal as if it were a particularly exciting television show.

"I will answer your questions," Mister Death said softly, his voice low and almost melodic.

"Fine." I pulled the shotgun out of the gangster's mouth and threw him against the side of the nearest building in one easy gesture. The gangster attempted to regroup only to be knocked down again by the car door hitting him in the groin followed by a swift punch in the jaw. Stepping out, I put my foot on his chest to hold him down before turning to him. "You were saying, Your Eminence?"

"Please, John, call me Mister Death. All my friends do," the Dunwych high priest said. "As for who they are, they are 'Made Men' of the King crime family. Very highly placed members of Mister King's organization."

I looked over at them. "They're not terribly impressive."

"Compared to a bear, the dog doesn't look that vicious, but the rabbit is still afraid of him," Mister Death said. "Few they face are seasoned warriors."

I wrinkled my nose, remembering the old man's "mysterious sorcerer" routine when I'd first encountered him. "Mister Death, kindly abstain from the folk wisdom. I'm not here to enjoy the local atmosphere."

"Fair enough." He proceeded to walk over to me and placed his hat over his heart. "Lord King wishes to speak with you."

"He actually calls himself Lord King?"

"What else would he call himself?" Mister Death raised an eyebrow.

"What does he want with me?" I asked.

The gangster underneath me struggled a bit, so I twisted my foot on his chest before placing my finger on the trigger of his shotgun. The man with gold teeth stopped moving, realizing just how close he was to death.

Smart man.

Katryn held the end of her spear underneath the neck of a female gangster, looking as if she was waiting for a reason to kill her. "Lord King is an old friend to the Dunwych, mostly due to his willingness to pay tribute rather than futilely fight against us. He would be a powerful ally, provided he forgives us for humiliating his minions."

"He should be grateful we haven't killed any … yet." Jessica added, kicking one of the men in the jaw when he made a move for his gun.

Mister Death let out a belly laugh at Jessica's comment, despite it not being terribly funny. "Unfortunately, Ezekiel King told me of this desire only after he sent his men to fetch you. I would have warned him otherwise. You are not individuals who respond well to force, at least if my daughter's descriptions of you in her psychic messages to me are any indication."

While the idea Katryn had been talking to her father psychically was troubling, I was more concerned with how Lord King had learned of our presence. The occult arts were one possibility. So, was Katryn informing him through her father? The most disturbing possibility was Peter Goodhill spreading the word I was coming. I had enough troubles without him hiring mercenaries to go after me. "I admit his methods don't incline me to talk with him."

"Will you, though?" Mister Death asked. "Preferably, without taking any more of his men's dignity."

I wasn't sure it was possible to remove the dignity of criminals. After all, being criminals they automatically didn't have any. Still, the Kings obviously were no friend of Peter Goodhill and as an associate of the Dunwych he had to have some honor (choice of servants aside).

"Alright, I'll do it."

CHAPTER TWENTY-SIX

The trip to Lord King's headquarters didn't take very long, especially since most travel in the city was done on foot.

The place was slightly less garish than the rest of the city's buildings, having a simple neon sign which proclaimed it to be King's Casino. The establishment looked like it might have once been a bank, its large Greek archways and solid, durable presence giving a sense of timelessness in an otherwise fragile-looking city.

The people walking in and out of the casino were a fairly diverse lot. Some of them looked to be Wasteland traders while others appeared to be inhabitants of the city. I was unnerved to see what appeared to be New Arkham citizens scattered amongst them, citizens who didn't look like they'd fled the Remnant but were on a day trip. The casino exterior was guarded by a number of bouncers armed with crude machine guns and bulky melee weapons. They looked considerably more impressive than the poorly armed band sent to retrieve us.

The Blue Meanie pulled up right in front of the casino's revolving doors, causing a couple of the thugs to back away before immediately training their weapons on us. Mister Death had taken Jackie's place on the passenger's side while Jackie moved between Jessica and Katryn, giving her the safest position in the vehicle.

I wasn't sure how welcome we were going to be given the cold reception we'd given the slime which had tried to ambush us. We'd left those thugs tied up back at the street where they'd attacked us, using a rope they'd intended to use on us. After my meeting with Lord King, presumably he'd send someone to fetch them. Sparing them probably wasn't the best solution and I suspected Katryn wished she could have just slit their throats. However, I didn't want to kill them. With any luck, they wouldn't hold a grudge once we'd spoken with their superior.

Yeah, fat chance of that.

"We're here to see the Boss." I gave a short wave to the guards around me, keeping the weapons I'd hidden all over the car out of sight. I didn't intend to start a fight but I sure as hell didn't intend to rely on the honor of criminals for my safety either.

"Please allow us to pass," Mister Death said, waving his hand in front of them. His smile was at once gentle but also deadly.

"And don't you disagree!" Jackie said from the back, cheerfully shaking her fist.

I looked at the chief of the bouncers, a large Caucasian man dressed in a business suit. His arms and forehead were covered with a number of Elder Sign-like tattoos. The bouncer seemed caught between his desire to blow my head off and to let me through. I doubted he was used to people asking to see his boss. Crime lords summoned you, not the other way around (at least if the records in New Arkham were anything to go by).

Finally, he said, "Go on in, the Lord is expecting you."

"Understood," I replied, nervous about the amount of firepower we were facing. They might not be E.B.E.s but they were still dangerous.

Parking the vehicle in a nearby cordoned-off lot, I armed myself rather heavily from the trunk. Richard hadn't had access to the same sort of weapons that had been available in New Arkham but he had a number of semi-automatic weapons and even a few grenades. It would be suicide to start a firefight in an enemy's territory but we wouldn't go quietly.

Jessica and Katryn also helped themselves to armaments, and Katryn's father merely stood to the side. Jackie just watched the entire sight with a kind of perverse interest, as if she was in a story.

"Mister Booth, are you going to kill these people or talk to them?" Jackie asked, looking up at me.

"Talk, hopefully," I answered her.

"With guns?" Jackie asked, hopefully.

"No," I told her.

"Oh." She sounded almost disappointed.

I turned to Jessica. "I'm charging you with Jackie's protection while we handle this."

"Hey! I want to meet the bad guys!" Jackie complained. "Do you think they have secret treasure vaults filled with gold?"

Jessica frowned at me, taking Jackie by the arm. "I'm not sure I'm comfortable letting you go in there alone."

"I'm not going to be alone," I said, looking to Katryn and Mister Death.

Jessica frowned, indicating she wasn't exactly sure that they weren't part of the problem. "Uh, Captain?"

"I'll be fine," I reassured her.

Katryn bowed her head. "I will kill anyone who threatens him."

"Uh, thanks." Jessica looked awkward and uncomfortable with the whole thing. "Well, good, I guess."

"Stay safe." I nodded to Jackie. "We'll find you a home here afterward. This city is considerably safer than the Wasteland."

"Yeah, sure, Mister Booth." It was obvious Jackie didn't believe it. I wasn't sure I did either.

Kingsport was a decadent, evil, and thoroughly unsafe location. Other possibilities existed, like the Crow Kingdom in the distant British Isles across the Atlantic Ocean. There were also rumors that Boston had reconstituted itself, as well as York. All three were potential havens for a child in need. I wanted Jackie to enjoy all the fruits of human life before undergoing her metamorphosis. However, I wasn't sure if they were really realistic choices. I needed to find an appropriate guardian for her in case of my death. As much as I knew Jessica was undyingly loyal to me, I wasn't sure how she'd react to discovering Jackie would eventually become a ghoul.

"Good luck, Captain." Jessica looked hesitant. "Try not to get killed."

"I'll see what I can do," I said,

Turning around and heading to the casino doors, I saw Katryn and Mister Death followed close behind me. I felt oddly comfortable between the two magicians, one who worshiped life and the other death. If I was a superstitious man, I'd say their presence was a positive omen.

It was Katryn who spoke first. "Jessica is exceptionally loyal to you. She will follow you to the ends of the Earth."

"Yes, we grew up together," I said with just the barest hint of a smile. "We were in the same school grouping. We played 'Smash the Mutant' together as children, and as teenagers we took turns distracting the proctors to get alone time with our romantic partners—at least before the breeding exams."

Katryn narrowed her eyes, probably wondering exactly how "breeding exams" worked. In many ways, I admired the Dunwych practice of just choosing their sexual partners. Too bad their non-Dunwych partners didn't have a choice whether to participate or not. "Loyalty is what my father wishes to talk to you about. I can see it in his eyes."

"Yes," Mister Death said. "I am curious what you are willing to give for the future of humanity. What is your loyalty to your race?"

"I would give anything for it," I said. It was a stupid question to ask, and an insulting one. "Anything at all."

"Including your life?" Mister Death asked.

"Easily," I answered. Anything was anything after all.

"And your loved ones?" Mister Death raised an eyebrow.

"They are why I do it." What was the old wizard getting at? "Why do you ask?"

"In due time," Mister Death replied, smiling. "In due time."

That was one thing I had not missed about dealing with the Dunwych: they were maddeningly obtuse.

The three of us passed the entrance guards into King's Casino. I was almost immediately overwhelmed by the smell of Devil's weed, Ghoul powder, marijuana, and opium that clung to the walls. The place was dark and musty with yellow wallpaper, stained yellow carpet, and even the dealers wearing some shade of the color gold. I saw a few small statues of the King in Yellow, a Dunwych god often associated alternatively with the Unspeakable One or Hastur, resting on various gambling tables. It was a curious deity to associate with gambling.

Despite the abysmal smell of the place, it seemed to be doing good business as its rusty slot machines were almost all occupied and the place was packed to the gills. There were blackjack tables, roulette wheels, slot machines, and a few games I didn't recognize. The casino used old-time bank teller stands to run some sort of pawn shop, exchanging goods for yellow poker chips which looked like gold coins.

A number of the gamblers were not entirely … human. Some had skin corrupted by M-radiation, others looked like they carried the lineage of some unsettling, otherworldly entity, and a few sported deformities ranging from unnaturally long digits to no eyes. The dealers, while visibly disgusted by these beings, simply let them play as a normal man might. If nothing else, the Kings ran an equal opportunity business and I had to applaud them for that.

Serving the various mutant and trader gamblers were a rather pathetic looking set of waiters and waitresses. They were a skinny and frightened lot, forced to wear revealing attire designed to accent their meager sex appeal. I could see the hopelessness that rested behind their eyes, an all-too-common sight in the Wasteland. I had no doubt they were part of the establishment's many "entertainments" for sale.

Anxious to get out of this place, I looked to Mister Death and asked, "Where is our host?"

"There." Mister Death gestured to a set of glass doors nearby by the casino floor, apparently leading to some sort of restaurant. "Move cautiously and do not seem like an enemy. Mister King employs the local thugs to guard his casino, but to guard his person, he employs Dunwych."

"I'll take that under advisement," I said, moving through the strange room. "Now, what did you mean? About whether or not I was willing to sacrifice my life, I mean."

"I do not see your beginning or end, John. You are an ouroboros to my magic. I think it is because you are touched by the gods. I think you may be capable of killing the Necromancer, though only if you are willing to die in the process." Mister Death took off his hat, revealing his shaven head.

Katryn frowned. "He is capable of doing it without dying, Father."

"I found you in the Wastelands, Katryn. You were a gift from Shub-Niggurath and a child of two worlds," Mister Death spoke, shaking his wrist at her as if putting a hex on her. "But do not interrupt me again."

It was a strange revelation, especially given how much they resembled one another. It made me wonder if Mister Death was just trying to pass off an inauspicious birth as an accident of fate. Ignoring it, I told him, "I am willing to die to kill Alan Ward, Mister

Death. I may not have much life left in me anyway, but even if I did, it is a life well spent to sacrifice oneself for others."

"Ha!" Mister Death said. "Individual lives are often worth more than the lives of the herd. The Dunwych will die by the hundreds attacking the Necromancer. All that matters is a single life is taken, that of the corruptor."

We hustled our way past several patrons, trying to make our way through the crowded casino to the restaurant doors. No one was paying any attention to our conversation, drowned in the din of winnings and arguments with the dealers.

I didn't like the way Mister Death causally dismissed the lives of his fellow tribals. "I can get into the Black Cathedral without your people needing to sacrifice themselves. This fight is between me and Ward. I've made him bleed, I can kill him."

"It is too late for that. The Dunwych have already made preparations for war. We are a people who must either conquer or turn upon one another," Katryn explained. "Take advantage of the distraction it will provide."

I should have been surprised but I wasn't. "You'll just send them to their deaths by the thousands?"

"If necessary," Mister Death said, his voice low. "The Dunwych are a divided people. The Whateley line is no more, so we have no king. Instead, we have many chiefs, chieftesses, and priests. This would not be the first time one leader or another has sought to unite a race by making a conflict larger and more violent than it has to be."

"Is there nothing I can do to dissuade you?" I asked. Their cavalier disregard for human life bothered me more than their reverence for the Great Old Ones.

"No," Mister Death replied. "What is done is done. Besides, you have your own role to play. A hundred Dunwych would also fail where one might succeed. My daughter insists the one might as well be you. Personally, I think she is just infatuated."

"I'll try and kill him quickly."

"Let us hope," Mister Death said, approvingly. "We don't want the entire army to die, just enough to make the victory worthwhile."

Truly, madness reigned in the Wasteland.

The three of us finally entered into the King's casino. Despite it being daytime, the place was dark with all of the windows boarded over and covered with heavy yellow curtains. The place was illuminated by candles with numerous skulls and animal bones hanging from the walls. In a strange way, I could "feel" the wards against otherworldly entities built into the room's walls.

In the center of the disturbing restaurant was a white table where a man of Asiatic descent was sitting. He was surrounded by six or seven Dunwych warriors, who each wore slightly fewer weapons than a small army. He had long black hair and was wearing a pair of tinted glasses despite the already visibly low light provided by the candles. His attire was an actual honest-to-God tuxedo of the kind not seen outside of a movie. Despite his strange attire, I could tell he was taller than me and extremely well-muscled.

Walking forward, I saw them raise a number of automatic weapons towards me. Casually ignoring them, I pulled out a seat in front of the Asiatic man and sat down across from him. "Mister King, I presume?"

"Ezekiel Tobias King. I've been hearing quite a lot about you, Mister Booth." The gangster's voice was surprisingly low and guttural, as if his throat was full of gravel. "I've been hearing a lot about you from my sources near the Marsh family. You're also quite the celebrity back in that crazy survivalist compound you call the United States Remnant. All of my tourists from there have been talking about your hanging; apparently it was quite controversial."

"I'm surprised anyone can remember my name," I said honestly. "The Remnant citizens I remember were more concerned about who won the local ration lotteries that week. Oh, and who was sleeping with who, especially on television."

"Their trade is good, which is all I care about." Ezekiel removed his sunglasses, revealing slit-like serpentine eyes. "Are the men I sent after you dead?"

"No," I answered, leaning back in the chair. "I thought killing them might be construed as … impolite."

Ezekiel laughed before smiling. His teeth were mostly gold, like those of his followers. "I like you, John. You have more class than the average Remnant thug I deal with."

"Like Peter Goodhill?" I asked, deciding to ignore his baiting. Pride could get you killed in the Wasteland and the humble man often laughed last.

"No, I don't deal in slaves." Ezekiel said, reaching into his jacket pocket and pulling out two hand-rolled cigars. "Do you smoke?"

"I occasionally indulge," I said, taking one and smelling it. The aroma contained hints of Ghoul powder, which made me hesitant to smoke it. Still, it was important not to show weakness in these sorts of situations and I instead just broke off the end and allowed him to light it. "What do you want from me?"

"A moment, please," Ezekiel King said. He then started puffing on his cigar, filling the air with a strange corpse-like aroma.

Katryn and Mister Death took a protective place behind me, which made the Dunwych guards around Ezekiel uncomfortable. The Dunwych were a very spiritual people and they undoubtedly would take any orders from Katryn and her father more seriously than orders from Peter Goodhill. Hopefully, it wouldn't come between religion and money, since one could never tell where someone would fall in that decision.

Ezekiel continued, "Are you familiar with sorcery, Mister Booth?"

"The Remnant practices Arcanothology, which teaches that there's an underlying science to all so-called supernatural beings. I admit I've had my view in it shaken a bit. I still cling to its fundamental truth, however."

That was one way of explaining I wasn't sure what I believed after meeting the messenger of the Blind Idiot God who created the universe. That was the sort of thing which changed a person's worldview.

"That's not what I asked," Ezekiel said, blinking his yellow eyes.

"I know a little," I answered him. "Back at the Remnant, I read *Unknown Cults* and *De Vermis Mysteriis.* I'm currently reading a rather famous work which has opened up many new vistas regarding the manipulation of unusual energies."

Ironically, it had been Doctor Ward who had lent me those particular tomes as part of my studies. I had treated them as little more than research material for a book on the Brotherhood of Yith.

"You're reading the English translation of the *Necronomicon,*"

Ezekiel smiled. I wondered if he'd lured me here to steal it. Many people had done much worse for knowledge half as potent as what lay within its pages.

"Yes." There was no point in denying it.

"You're an educated man. I like that," Ezekiel said before taking several puffs on his cigar. "I was born a slave here in Kingsport. My grandmother taught me to read, though. I spent days sneaking into the ruins of the old municipal library, learning everything I could. Even then, it wasn't until I found a copy of *The Black Keys of Solomon* in the archives that I realized the true power available to a man in this world."

I thought about mentioning the hand on my shoulder, but realized Ezekiel undoubtedly knew the drawbacks of sorcery and just didn't care. So I said, "I'm glad you've done well for yourself."

"I fed my former master to a thing with eight million mouths and six dimensions. That's not well, that's *spectacular*." Ezekiel let out a laugh before putting out his cigar and placing his shades back on. "However, I have a problem. No matter how much I learn in the ways of sorcery, I cannot kill a certain man."

Events were starting to fall into place. I wasn't being brought here for any great purpose; I'd just been brought in because I was a new factor in a gang war. "Do you mean Alan Ward or the leader of the Marsh Family?"

Ezekiel leaned back in his chair, crossing his arms. "Ward is just the latest in a long line of Wasteland messiahs. You may be the next one. I keep my ambitions realistic. I just want to be the sole trade baron in Kingsport. Obadiah Marsh is a Deep One with his own copy of the *Necronomicon*. As such, he can repulse anything that I conjure against him. His Deep One hybrids are also the equal of any Dunwych warrior."

"That is a lie," Katryn growled, stepping forward. Her father placed a hand on her chest and gently pushed her back.

I found it rather amusing humanity had gone through an extinction event which had destroyed almost the entirety of our race, discovered magic was real, and had the very laws of physics upended—yet we were still feuding over things as silly as who got to control the flow of goods in towns. That they were willing to use spells which could alter the shape and nature of reality to fight over something so petty. Perhaps this, more than anything, justified Ward's decision to give up on humanity.

No, I couldn't let myself believe that.

However tempting it was.

"You want my copy of the *Necronomicon*?" Honestly, he was welcome to it. The book had brought me nothing but pain.

"I wasn't aware you had a copy until you stupidly implied you had one. However, no, I don't. I want Obadiah Marsh's copy." Ezekiel placed his hands together. "Peter Goodhill has placed a thousand pieces of green gold on your head. That means he fears you. This is why I wanted to tell you I would be willing to give you an equal amount if you were to take care of his employer."

"I'm not a mercenary," I said, quite glad to have my suspicions about the Marsh family confirmed. I took several more puffs on the cigar before putting it out beside Mister King's own. He had an ornamental obsidian ashtray, classy.

"You will be if you want to survive in the Wasteland, Mister Booth." Ezekiel didn't move a muscle, staring at me through his opaque glasses. "The question is, if I can set you up a meeting with the Marsh family to get your little girlfriend back—the one that Peter Goodhill entered the city with, will you kill Obadiah Marsh for me? I'll consider the *Necronomicon* copy in his possession a bonus."

This was almost too perfect, which is why the whole thing smelled of a trap. Minutes upon arrival in the city, I was being given the keys to my enemy's house. Keys which, coincidentally, would take me right into the heart of an enemy stronghold with my guard presumably lowered. It was the perfect scenario to kill me without any danger to Peter. After all, if I failed, Ezekiel King could just claim he was doing them a favor by sending me to them.

Unfortunately, it wasn't like I had any other immediately available options. "Make the meeting."

"I'm glad you see it my way, John." Ezekiel clapped his hands together. "Please, dine with me now. We're having … fish."

CHAPTER TWENTY-SEVEN

The meeting with the Marsh family took only a few messengers to arrange. I would venture to their quarter of the city, unarmed, and be escorted to Obadiah Marsh's penthouse. There I would be allowed to negotiate for Mercury's release. Yeah, in no way did this stink of a trap.

Despite my best efforts to convince them otherwise, Jessica and the others insisted on accompanying me to the Marsh family's headquarters. I appreciated their loyalty but the Blue Meanie was starting to get a little cramped. I sat in the front seat across from Jessica while Mister Death and Katryn took the back with Jackie between them.

The five of us were now traveling down near-empty cobblestone streets towards the Marsh district, a region avoided by most of the city's purely human inhabitants. It was unnerving to see abandoned buildings in a community so terribly cramped for space, but it seemed no one wanted to get too close.

Except us.

Jessica, currently playing with a cat's cradle, looked over to me. "I suppose you have a plan for getting out of this mess."

"Not really," I admitted.

Jessica blinked. "You're kidding, right?"

"At some point, I just had to start making up shit as I went along," I said. "Believe me, it is better this way. It gives me an out when everything goes to hell."

Katryn seemed surprised by my devotion, "I am wondering why you are wasting so much effort on a woman who has admitted to using torture and murder for your Council of Leaders. The John I knew was not a man to forgive such things."

"Maybe you don't know me as well as you think you do," I said, coldly.

Jackie looked between us, clearly uncomfortable.

"Revenge, pain, hate, and love. Even those emotions will pass from humanity in time as we become more like the Old Ones," Mister Death said coldly, looking over at the abandoned dwellings around us. "They are the example we must strive to be like if we are to transcend this half-dissolved dreamworld they have left us in."

"You're a weird man, Mister Death," Jackie said.

"Thank you," Mister Death chuckled.

"I explained my reasons to Jackie, Katryn," I said. "I have a promise to uphold."

"I'm sure the fact she's a petite, attractive, redhead has nothing to do with it." Jessica glanced over her shoulder at Katryn before making a clawing gesture.

Katryn rolled her eyes. "We have arrived."

The Marsh district was *felt* before it was seen. My hands felt clammy and I started sweating profusely, the mark of Nyarlathotep on my shoulder burning. Every instinct in my body told me to turn around and drive away. I forced myself to continue onward, passing through an arched entranceway with a pair of skeletal corpses suspended over it as a warning. That was when we entered into a place utterly dominated by the influence of the Great Old Ones.

It was easy to tell the Marsh district from other parts of the city. Whereas the other districts' buildings had been rebuilt with meticulous care, the ones here existed in a state of near-collapse. Nearly all of the windows were boarded up and most of the structures looked like they'd been gutted by fire.

The worst victims of this all-pervasive decay were the inhabitants themselves. They moved through the streets with an empty, soulless gait. All of them were deformed in some way: possessing scales, enlarged eyes, or pale skin that hung off their bones in unnatural ways. Deep One ancestry ran through the veins of the majority, though the ones who were purely human were even more unsettling. They followed around the Deep One hybrids with a kind of toadying obsequiousness, most being slaves of one sort of or another.

Truly I'd never seen such pervasive oppression. Slave quarters, built to resemble stables, were everywhere. Humans were herded by dozens into tiny iron pens while armed Deep One hybrids kept watch. Passing by a particularly large slavers' compound, I saw a six-year-old girl ripped from her mother's arms as they were shoved into different cages. I made a mental note to return to this place after my mission and tear it down brick by brick. It was a hollow promise since I intended to die but one which made me feel slightly better.

Eventually, we reached the heart of the district. There stood the Marsh family headquarters, a once-luxurious hotel which had been converted to a casino. It was a casino with no gamblers, however. Half of the upper floors had collapsed walls with a kind of coral-like substance growing up the side of the building.

Most of the building's windows were shattered with not even the token attempt to hammer boards over them like the rest of the district. Despite its state of disrepair, the casino was a center of power. I could feel it was the source of the choking sickness I'd felt upon entering the district. It rivaled anything I'd felt outside of the Black Cathedral. I realized, in an instant, the hotel had been consecrated as a temple to Great Cthulhu.

"This just keeps getting better and better," I muttered, staring at the building. A fading neon sign hung over its arched entrance, reading THE BLUE OYSTER INN.

Katryn reached over and placed her hand on my shoulder, "The Necromancer has been here, John. He has filled it with objects of power. Beware, the Marshes have powers you might not be able to counter."

"If you try and wrestle with a bull, prepare to get your bones broken," I said to her.

"I beg your pardon?" Katryn blinked, confused.

"I think he means John doesn't intend to confront them head on," Jessica said, feeling the back of her neck. "Though what he intends exactly to do instead, I have no idea."

"Win." I pulled out my golden knife and copy of the *Necronomicon* before handing them over to Katryn. "Watch over these."

Katryn blinked as she took both, stunned at the generosity of the gift. "As you wish."

"May the Yellow Sign never drive you insane or waste your

lineage with disease," Mister Death said, waving his hand as though blessing me.

Mister Death's eyes glanced over at the *Necronomicon* longingly. If he'd asked, I would have let him look over the Devil-touched manuscript, but I had no doubt he'd try to sneak a peek through his daughter. I had confidence Katryn wouldn't let him see it; her honor was too great for that. Katryn would reserve that privilege for herself.

"Try not to get killed, Captain," Jessica said. "You still owe me money from our last card game."

"I'll see what I can do," I smirked, remembering she'd cleaned up in ration cards last time. "Next time, I'll remember never to try and bluff you."

"You better!" Jessica replied.

"Good luck," Jackie said, smiling.

"We make our own luck." I gave her a thumbs-up before heading into the Marsh casino.

Immediately, I was assaulted by the disgusting nature of the building's interior. The Blue Oyster Inn was a casino, but only in the loosest sense of the word. Video poker machines were scattered about, all of them nonfunctional and rusted to uselessness. The carpets were stained with a layer of slime and the wallpaper was peeling off. The lights were functional but gave off a sickly fluorescent hue instead of anything resembling brightness.

A half-dozen or so Deep One hybrids were scattered about the lobby, all at a much more advanced stage of metamorphosis than the "mostly" human ones outside. They looked like the missing link between human and fish, as troubling in their own way to me as the ghouls were to the average person. I'd dealt with Deep Ones who didn't disgust me before, but they hadn't been gangsters or slavers.

The pure-blooded Deep Ones I'd met resembled nothing so much as a bipedal two-armed barracuda, their faces a twisted mix of human and aquatic ancestry. The ones around me, offspring of humans bred with pure-bloods, wore clothes but were well on their way to becoming full members of their race. I didn't know why the children of E.B.E.s with humans inevitably became identical to their supernatural forbearers, but the transformation was as inescapable as it was inevitable. The Deep Ones, ghouls, and Serpent Men were slowly breeding humanity out and some thought it was an improvement—I just thought it was biology in action. Humanity had gotten the short end of the stick evolutionary-wise, which was why we had to try extra hard to survive.

The six hybrids in the casino moved to intercept me as I walked to the semi-functional elevators at the end of the lobby. A five-foot-even man, covered in scales across his skin and cursed with webbed fingers, grabbed me by the wrist as I attempted to press the UP button.

Turning to him, I saw he possessed a pair of catfish whiskers that resembled a mustache. I found it made him look rather funny, more comical than terrifying. The Catfish Man wore clothes, a leisure suit of all things, but it was covered in filth and looked like it was rotting off his back.

"Good evening. I'm here to see Obadiah Marsh," I said, trying to be as polite as possible.

The Catfish Man didn't bother replying, instead throwing a punch at my face with the force of a locomotive. The other five Deep One hybrids attacked as well, charging at me like they were going to tear me to pieces. According to my father, the average hybrid possessed double the strength of a normal man and was three times as durable. Sixty seconds later, they were all lying on the ground with broken kneecaps and shattered jaws.

"I hate this city and everyone in it," I muttered before heading into the most functional-looking elevator.

As I pressed the button for the penthouse, the doors closed and I felt the machine rock and shudder as it traveled up the decrepit structure. I was getting annoyed at being attacked by so many amateurs lately. The least the city's gangsters could do was send a group of professionals.

Finally, the elevator reached its destination and opened its doors to a decadent court the likes of which I'd never seen. The humidity was appalling, closer to a jungle than desert with my face feeling wet just from just breathing in the air.

Obadiah Marsh's penthouse was in a far better state of repair than the rest of the casino. It had clean white wallpaper, fine hardwood floors, and numerous New England antiques spread around the room. The antiques were almost all covered in pieces of gold, mostly R'lyehian artifacts but also things which looked harvested from the ocean floor—Spanish treasures and such.

Pornographic Deep One statuary and pictures hung on the wall while a grand hot tub stood in the center of the chamber. The bubbling basin contained blackish green water and a singularly revolting figure: a Deep One pure-blood wearing a small fortune in gold jewelry. He looked like a caricature of a drug lord from the late 20th century crossed with a fish.

The man I presumed to be Obadiah Marsh was grotesquely obese with a round face which resembled a piranha's. He was completely hairless and his unnaturally large eyes focused onto me with a mixture of surprise and disgust. Obviously, he'd not expected me to make it up here alive.

"Get your guns on him!" Obadiah shouted, shaking a fruity drink at me.

Yeah, this was going to go well.

My eyes quickly took in eight other figures. With one exception, they were all Deep One pure-bloods wearing no clothes. All but one was armed, wearing leather harnesses to hold pistols and shotguns. A single one sported robes and a staff which made him look like an Eastern Orthodox priest crossed with a sorcerer. I presumed him to be a magic-user, which just made my situation even more desperate.

"Maybe I should avoid asking to be attacked by professionals whenever I'm feeling cocky," I muttered under my breath.

Sitting in the back of the room, however, was my quarry. Peter Goodhill was still wearing his combat fatigues but had abandoned his shirt to reveal a number of hideous new tattoos—I recognized some to be glyphs from the *Necronomicon*. Ironically, he was as unarmed as me, just watching the entire situation with a kind of wary amusement.

He did, however, say, "Don't underestimate him. He's tougher than he looks."

Raising my hands as if surrendering, I said, "Lord Marsh, I presume? I'm here to talk."

Obadiah paused a second before letting out a deafening laugh. He started to speak, possessing an Old Earth Bostonian accent of all things. "Ha! You've got testes, I'll give you that. It must come from all the dirty blood in your veins."

I was tempted to ask where he got off talking about dirty blood, but I wasn't feeling suicidal. "I try."

"Peter, do you think he has testes?" Obadiah looked over to my rival, who smiled. Peter had already replaced his missing teeth with gold ones.

"I believe, Lord, that he's got testes. It's just brains he's missing," Peter said, putting his hand over his chest and smiling.

The Deep One pure-bloods walked over and checked me for weapons, their slimy webbed hands patting me down quite invasively. After a second, one of them looked to Obadiah Marsh and grunted, "He's clean."

"Are any of my nephews downstairs dead?" Obadiah said, sipping his drink.

"No," I said, remembering my mission for Lord King. "Where I'm from, it's considered impolite to kill the associates of your host."

I was beginning to feel a sense of *déjà vu*. Apparently, beating up someone and dragging them to your boss's feet was just how they said hello around here.

Obadiah Marsh finished off his fruity drink before setting it aside. "So, you've been sent here to negotiate, have you?"

"Not really. Mister King sent me here to try and kill you. I have no desire to do so, however, because I've got no interest in playing power politics between mobsters." I stretched back my neck and gestured to the room. "May I come in?"

Obadiah Marsh looked at me, before glancing over at Peter, then back at me. "Most people would balk at letting in someone who has admitted to being contracted as an assassin."

"You're not most people."

It never hurt to play on the vanity of those you encountered. The truth was, seeing the slavery outside of the Blue Oyster Inn, I was determined to eliminate Obadiah Marsh. I didn't trust or like Ezekiel King but I'd seen no sign of slavery in his territory. It seemed to be the main source of income for the Marshes.

There was no sense in letting him know that, though.

"Alright, come in." Obadiah gestured with his webbed hands. "Just know that if you try anything, I'll blow your fucking brains out."

Peter looked appalled at his latest master, “Are you fucking serious?”

Obadiah shot him a glare. “Watch your mouth. You work for me but you’re not of the blood.”

“He ultimately takes his orders from Alan Ward,” I said, fully believing Peter Goodhill incapable of winning over someone’s complete trust. “I have no doubt he’s relayed every little secret about your organization to the Necromancer and is undoubtedly just using you as a means to an end.”

“You bastard!” Peter shouted, unaware I took that description as a point of pride. Turning to Obadiah, he said, “You don’t believe this, do you?”

“On the contrary, Peter, I know you. So, I have no doubt Mister Booth is telling the truth.” Obadiah gestured for the robed Deep One to bring him a pitcher of fruit juice, refilling his drink. “The problem is, Mister Booth, I don’t necessarily care. Alan Ward, inferior human slime ball that he is, is powerful and blessed by my god. He’s also good for business. We’ve sold more children to him in the past few months than I’ve sold in years.”

“He’s a prick just out to rescue his female. She’ll fetch a high price, trust me, Obadiah.” Peter was overplaying his hand, which helped me.

I was glad that Peter had undoubtedly put into Obadiah’s head that I was some sort of giant Boy Scout. It would help my credibility when I started lying my ass off. “Alan Ward is planning to take over the Wasteland. The whole Dunwych army attack is a lure to get them to be wiped out by his summoned monsters. He then intends to take over Kingsport and purge the nonhumans. It’s all a Remnant plot with Mister King.”

Peter just stared at me, as if I’d sprouted six heads. “You lying son of a …”

“A plausible story,” Obadiah said, continuing to sip on his drink. “But I’ve heard many plausible stories in my time. Why would you turn against your own people?”

“The woman is pregnant with my child,” I said, staring at them. “I am touched by Nyarlathotep and she would be killed if it was allowed to come to term.”

I lifted my shirt and exposed the mark, causing all of the Deep

Ones to exchange looks of fear and confusion. Peter was shocked himself, though I doubted he knew the mark's true significance.

"I believe you," Obadiah whispered, gurgling as he talked. "The question, John, is how exactly am I going to benefit from turning over Mister Goodhill and your little honey to you?"

This is where the riskiest part of my plan entered into the equation, the plan I'd completely made up on the spot. "Do you have a radio in your possession?"

"Several," Obadiah leaned back in his hot tub. "Why?"

"I serve the Opposition Party in the Remnant." I made up a story I hoped would sound plausible to the power-obsessed mobster. It never hurt to assume people believed the worst of everyone. "We'll benefit from seeing this current one collapse. Contact a Major Martha Booth on a frequency I give you and we'll have a trade. A set of heavy assault rifles, enough for you to eliminate all of your competition, in exchange for Doctor Takahashi's safe return and Peter Goodhill's head. She has converted to the worship of our gods."

It was, all in all, a suicidal gambit. In all likelihood, the Remnant would send R&E squads for the express purpose of exterminating *me* as well as Doctor Takahashi. However, they were also very likely to go along with any deals until they arrived. The fact the Marshes were E.B.Es., however, would work in my favor. In the confusion, it was quite possible Doctor Takahashi and I could sneak out.

If it worked.

Obadiah Marsh paused, before looking at Peter. "Looks like you're just out of luck, Peter."

The Deep Ones turned their guns on him, which caused him to stare at me with pure hatred. Hatred turned into a kind of admiration. "You do realize Ward's going to kill you, right?"

"No," I said. "I don't have the brains for it."

Peter made a rush for one of the Deep One's guns, using him as a shield as he shot one and then another before I grabbed the gun of one of the fallen ones and blew his head clean off. Peter died like a warrior, an R&E Ranger.

Tossing my gun onto the ground, I said, "Show me Mercury."

CHAPTER TWENTY-EIGHT

Of course, they made me send a message to the Remnant first. It was strange because I got the distinct impression the operators on the other line were distracted by something, almost as if they had a gun to the back of their head. Certainly, they didn't react as if my call was unexpected or in any way abnormal despite my supposedly public execution.

Whatever the case, it seemed to satisfy Obadiah Marsh and he ordered me to be taken to Doctor Takahashi. The Deep Ones led me down a blackened ash-filled staircase for two or three stories, eventually bringing me to a floor which looked like it hadn't been cleaned since the Rising.

Almost all of the walls separating the former hotel rooms had collapsed, with the entire north side of the building opening to a surprisingly majestic view of the city. You could almost forget the Marsh quarter was a pit of scum and slavery.

Sitting in the center of this view was Doctor Takahashi, still wearing her clothes from earlier and tied to a chair with rope. A gag was stuffed down her throat and she looked positively broken by her experience. There were a few bruises on her face but no sign she'd been manhandled in a more … unpleasant manner.

Walking up to Mercury, she looked up then looked down, uninterested in what she was seeing. A second later her eyes bulged as she did a double take.

"Mm mph!" Mercury bounced in her chair, trying to speak.

Struggling to speak through her gag, I placed my hand over her mouth and whispered, "Stay calm. I'm here to get you out. I convinced Obadiah Marsh to release you and kill Peter in exchange for the assistance of the United States Remnant in destroying the city's other crime lords."

"Mm mph?" Mercury raised an eyebrow before saying, "Mmm."

I nodded, knowing she understood the situation to be ridiculous. "I'm going to remove the gag now."

Pulling the gag out of her mouth, Mercury took a deep breath. Her eyes darting to the Deep Ones and then back to me, she said very softly, "You know, I'm no longer upset at you for being a liar. Apparently, it's quite a useful talent."

"I try," I said, before walking behind her and starting to undo her bonds. "Are you unharmed?"

"I really need to use the bathroom but I'm not injured in any serious way. They threatened me with rape and torture but I managed to talk my way out of both. They're really awful at interrogation, too," Mercury said, looking anxious to get out of the chair.

I blinked. "Really? Impressive."

Mercury nodded. "I learned quite a bit from them, like Goodhill is working for Ward, the Black Cathedral is going to be coming under attack soon, and Ward is prepared for the Dunwych with an army of tribals he's deluded into believing Cthulhu will protect during the battle."

This was all very useful information. "Thank you, Mercury."

She took a deep breath. "Booth, I've had a lot of time to think and I want you to know a lot of things."

"Okay."

"I've killed a lot of soldiers over the years," Mercury said, staring up at me. "I've witnessed incredible amounts of suffering. I've never enjoyed it, though. I want you to know that. I need you to know that."

I had a nasty retort waiting for her about how that was surely a comfort to all those she'd killed before I realized no one's hands were clean in this world. Also, I'd rather have someone like her at my side who regretted it than someone like Katryn who didn't even know such things were wrong. "I believe you."

Mercury nodded, looking to the Deep Ones who were approaching us. They got within six feet, holding their shotguns close.

We were both prisoners now.

"Well, crap," I muttered.

"Uh, what are we supposed to do now?" Mercury asked.

I reached over and grabbed one of the shotguns before forcing the Deep One holding it to shoot his comrade. The massive fish-man left alive blinked its huge bulbous eyes, stunned at the act before I grabbed his neck and snapped it. The fish-man's body proceeded to fall onto the corpse of his friend.

"This," I said, rubbing my hands. "God, does no one teach that guns are supposed to be used at a *distance*?"

"I guess not." Mercury looked down at their bodies.

"Let's focus on getting out of here." Shaking my head, I picked up one of the shotguns on the ground and proceeded to smash in the heads of the two Deep Ones on the ground. Their race did not regenerate, at least to my knowledge, but there was no point in taking any chances.

"Okay, Booth," Mercury took a deep breath. "I'd like to work with you. I mean after this. Maybe we can make this world a bit better—you know, before it ends completely."

I looked at her. "I'd like that too. Recent events have caused me to question whether I have any right to cast stones. We all did things we had to in order to survive. In this world, we're all Children of the Great Old Ones, Doctor Takahashi."

"Halsey," Mercury said.

"Pardon?"

"Mercury Anne Halsey. It was my name before Geoffrey took me as his wife." She looked over her shoulder. "Could you call me that instead? You know, if you're still going to avoid calling me by my first name."

"Alright," I smiled. "Mercury."

Mercury then leaned over and kissed me, lightly. "Do you know any way out of this place?"

Mercury nodded, "We can go down the next floor and use the servants' elevator. I saw it coming up. It's Obadiah Marsh's kitchen so we'll just have to deal with some Deep One cooks. When I last saw them, they were preparing human beings for tonight's meal."

"Mercury …" I trailed off, finding the idea ridiculous.

Her eyes looked desperate as she grabbed me by the shirt. "Booth, *we need to get the hell out of here*!"

I realized she'd been serious. "Oh. I see. I will, I promise."

"And give me a gun," Mercury said, letting go of my shirt.

I tossed her one of the shotguns that had been lying on the ground.

"Thank you," Mercury said, cocking it. "I've never been so happy for mandatory training."

Before we could do anything else, the sounds of patch-work cobbled-together helicopters were heard over our heads. Blinking, I sucked in my breath. "Those are Hunter-13s!"

"Oh shit," Mercury's voice resounded in the room. "The cavalry has arrived."

"For the other side."

Grabbing Mercury by the arm, I prepared to make a dash for the downstairs as I heard the sound of assault-rifle fire. That meant they were already closer than the penthouse. Almost as soon as we reached the stairwell, a group of armored infantry troopers came into view from above. They wore thick, heavy body armor, metal helmets, and environmental masks which were tough enough to stop a bullet. In their hands were heavy assault rifles with laser sights that immediately covered us both. They, noticeably, kept their distance as they aimed.

"What do we do now?" Mercury turned to me, panicking.

"Stand perfectly still and surrender," I said, calmly.

"What?" Mercury's voice sounded like she was going to do something desperate. I imagined her going down, guns blazing.

I placed my shotgun on the ground and raised my hands, noticeably covering the gun with my foot to keep her from trying to grab for it. "I don't think so."

"Why?" she asked, right before I put my hands on her and held her tightly.

I whispered in her ear, taking a deep breath and speaking as gently but firmly as possible. "Because, Mercury, if that were the case, then we'd already be dead."

"Okay," Mercury said, reluctantly raising her hands. "Good point. I guess there's no point in panicking."

"Panic can make you do or say things you regret," I said, keeping my hands up. "I've said much worse."

I recognized the Armored Infantry unit as the Red Wolves, Sergeant Major Aaron's unit. She was a stone-cold, brutal, and merciless soldier who I'd long admired as one of the Remnant's best. Given I'd long considered her a friend, it bothered me to feel her put a gun to my back. She led Doctor Takahashi and me up the stairwell into Obadiah Marsh's penthouse. There, every single one of the crime lord's Deep One followers had been blown to pieces. Obadiah, himself, had been riddled with bullets before being left to float in his pool. It was a poetic place for a Deep One to die.

Ezekiel King would have to wait for his copy of the *Necronomicon,* but it looked like I'd fulfilled half our contract.

Albeit inadvertently.

"I don't suppose you'd be willing to let me go for old time's sake?" I asked Aaron.

"Sorry, John," Aaron's voice echoed through the gas mask on her face. "Not happening."

"Hey, why does she get to call you John?" Mercury asked, clearly trying to calm the mood. That was right before a gun was shoved into her back, hard.

Leading us onto the rooftop, I saw two Hunter-13 helicopters had landed. To my surprise, I saw my wife and General Ashton-Smith standing beside them.

Martha was still dressed in the same clothes she'd worn two days ago and looked somewhat frazzled, a tremendously off look for a woman I'd never known to miss a day's sleep even after spending an entire day rewiring someone's brain.

General Ashton-Smith, on the other hand, looked poised and confident. He was a tall, balding, toffee-skinned man in a thick black coat over a military uniform covered in countless awards, enough to make me look like a rank amateur. Unlike some in the Remnant's top brass, he'd earned every single one of those awards too.

Karl Ashton-Smith was the very epitome of an R&E Ranger, a man who had turned down repeated promotions to the General Staff in order to remain the head of Gamma Squad until the battle with the Color left his left leg crippled. He was even leaning slightly off his cane, trying to hide his infirmity. They were two of the last people on Earth I expected to find here, let alone arrest me. I'd made peace with Martha on the cliff face, sort of, and General Ashton-Smith was my aunt's husband. He'd been like a father to me after my actual one's suicide.

"General?" I asked, hesitantly. I wasn't sure if it was appropriate to salute a man representing the government who'd betrayed you, but I did it anyway. I owed Karl Ashton-Smith my life many times over.

"President, actually." He returned my salute.

"Excuse me?"

"I'm now President of the United States Restored," Karl said, offering his hand for me to shake. I took it before he said, "The old Council of Leaders has been dissolved."

"It has?" Mercury blinked, skeptical of both his claim as well as the grandiose name for a city in the middle of the desert.

President Ashton-Smith looked at her as if she was something unpleasant underneath his shoe before gazing up at me. "Yes, the Secretary of Finance was found bludgeoned to death in his office by *parties unknown*."

I grimaced. The late Geoffrey Takahashi wouldn't be missed, but it was unlikely President Ashton-Smith approved of murdering one's husband. "How did that result in the Council's fall? Surely, he can't have been that vital."

"The amount of blackmail material he had in his files revealed enough 'indiscretions' by the old Council to remove them from office and some from the mortal coil. The files were presented to me by Major Booth." The newly elected President gestured to my wife. "Not a moment too soon either. The files indicated the Council had some insane plan to annihilate the Wasteland's civilian populace."

Martha just smiled at me. "The revelation of Doctor Ward's treachery provided the perfect justification for overthrowing the Council of Leaders."

In a way, it was disgusting. With only a thousandth of the original size of humanity left on this Earth, mankind was still fighting over who owned the rights to what. None of this was going to help in the battle against Ward, but undoubtedly they'd taken advantage of the power vacuum from Mercury's husband's death to paint them as collaborators with the man who'd imperiled the city a dozen times. I wondered how long Martha had been planning this. Was this why I'd been framed or just convenient timing for her to paint herself as the bereaved widow wronged by the Council of Leaders? In the end, it didn't really matter, did it?

Martha just flashed me an enigmatic smile. It was her way of letting me know I'd never know the truth.

"I see," I said. "Thank you."

President Ashton-Smith beamed proudly, clearly unaware he was Martha's puppet. "Needless to say, I was happy to extract some personal vengeance for your execution. I must say, you're looking very well for a dead man."

"Thank you," I said. "May I ask if this new government is meant to be … permanent?"

"Excuse me?" President Ashton-Smith asked, seemingly confused by my words.

Martha sighed, undoubtedly reading my mind. "He's asking whether or not you intend to rule by fiat."

President Ashton-Smith smirked. "Yes. We need strong leadership to guide us through this crisis."

This crisis, presumably, being Post-Rising life.

"I see." I paused, aware our lives hung in the balance. "Congratulations."

Martha smiled. "Which brings us to the matter of you. You have no idea how surprised we were when we received reports from our operatives in the city that you were here, even more so when you radioed us in order to make an arms deal."

"I … assumed something different would happen," I said, uncomfortably aware there were still guns pointed at my back. "I am curious, however, where this leaves me. Doctor Hals … Takahashi as well."

"Your 'execution' was unjust, John. I'm prepared to offer you a two-rank promotion to the position of Colonel in charge of the R&E Rangers." The President made air quotes as he said the word execution. "There's going to be a substantial number of revisions within the New Arkham government. We need men like you, men of vision, to carry out the transition."

Mercury coughed into her fist. "And me?"

"If you ever step foot in New Arkham again, you'll be shot." President Ashton-Smith didn't even bother looking at her.

"Understood," Mercury said, quickly.

It was everything I'd ever wanted, especially with the implication my uncle was grooming me for a position on the Council of Leaders. Unfortunately, it was too late. Looking at my shoulder, I turned back to him and said, "I'm afraid I'm going to have to decline, Sir."

President Ashton-Smith raised an eyebrow. "Oh?"

"Due to extenuating circumstances, I don't believe I'll be able to perform the duties you want me to. I am flattered by the offer but I believe …" I trailed off, thinking about the few months I probably had to live. "I would be better suited to continuing the Remnant's mission of assisting in the recovery of humanity out here."

If it had been any other officer in the Remnant, I'd have put my chances at walking out of this conversation at around fifty percent. Instead, President Ashton-Smith just looked at me and nodded, "Very well, *Captain*. Consider yourself on indefinite leave. We owe you our lives in the Remnant and that hasn't been forgotten."

"I've found a threat that needs to be dealt with." I wasn't sure if I should press my luck but this was too good of an opportunity to miss. "Professor Ward is assembling an army to deal with the surrounding countryside."

I neglected to mention his plan of wiping out all of humanity. If I did that, no one would believe me. It was one of the problems when facing true depravity. You often couldn't convince rational people that anyone could act so insane.

"I always knew he was too ornery to die out here." President Ashton-Smith gestured to the Hunter-13s beside us. "You can make use of these. I've got another seven coming here to help make a big impression on Kingsport's residents. The Remnant is now adopting a new policy in place of isolation: friendly outreach and elimination of threats."

"Recon and Extermination writ large," I said, believing they would murder most of humanity before they found humans pure enough to be accepted. That or they'd get themselves wiped out in a stupid war with Wastelanders not nearly as weak as they believed. "I see."

"Uh, are we free to go now?" Mercury asked.

"I'm entrusting your care to Captain Booth," the President said under his breath, barely trying to hide his distaste for the torturer. "Enjoy your freedom, Doctor. You certainly haven't earned it."

"Noted, Sir." Mercury breathed a sigh. "I understand."

The President took a deep breath and leaned on his cane. "Before I let you go, John, is there any tactical advice you'd like to give me for dealing with Kingsport's leadership?"

Walking over to the edge of the hotel, I looked down on the streets at the slavers' pens. There, there were probably hundreds of humans penned up like animals. "I think I have the perfect way for you to make a big impression."

CHAPTER TWENTY-NINE

An hour later, all of the slaver dens in the Marsh district were on fire and hundreds of slaves had been freed. Surprisingly, President Ashton-Smith's forces didn't appear to be exterminating the district's Deep One hybrids.

I knew he'd never really believed in the innate evil of E.B.E.s, but the fact that no one was objecting showed me the Remnant had changed on a fundamental level. Seemingly overnight. The slavers themselves, of course, were shown no mercy. Watching the entire process from atop the rooftop of the Blue Oyster Inn, Martha stood to my left and Mercury to the right.

Martha sighed, looking down at the burning buildings below. "You do realize this is an empty gesture, right? Slavery isn't going to disappear and the Remnant isn't even against it in practice, just principle. All you've gotten is a bunch of slavers killed."

"I know," I said. "I'm okay with that."

It wasn't about justice, what they were doing out here, or even winning the Remnant some points with the locals. No, this was just a final fuck-you to people I loathed. I was already feeling like I was running out of time and suspected my chances of killing Doctor Ward and rescuing the kidnapped children were slim to nonexistent. Stabbing at the nightmare the world had become was my only real pleasure left.

A part of me wasn't quite ready to accept defeat, though, and already I was thinking about consulting the *Necronomicon* for alternatives. Nyarlathotep, or the projection I'd conjured of him, had saved my life in the Dreamlands. Maybe it was possible it might heal me again. The idea of dealing with that monster again made my skin crawl but also made me remember the sense of power I'd gotten summoning him. It was a sick realization discovering you liked the feeling magic gave you.

"Figures," Martha said. "I thought you'd be pleased."

"I am," I said, thinking about the hundred and seventy people I'd found out they'd murdered in their coup. I expected I knew a lot of them. These were never as clear cut as the stories described them. I just hoped the General—sorry, *President*—was able to do some good in the next sixty years. "Is it time to go?"

I checked my watch. I'd sent Sergeant Major Aaron's team to fetch my associates and they should be arriving any time now.

Before I could even begin to speculate about what exactly Doctor Takahashi was thinking about, my companions were led in by Sergeant Major Aaron. The group consisted of Katryn, Mister Death, Jackie, Jessica, and Ezekiel King of all people.

"Captain, you want to explain what's going on?" Jessica said, shooting a dirty glare at Sergeant Major Aaron. The Sergeant Major's gas mask hid her face but by her stance, I gathered she wasn't happy with Jessica.

"I've been exonerated by the Remnant. The Old Council has been overthrown. I've rescued Doctor Takahashi. We have two new helicopters." I paused. "I think that about summarizes it."

"Good to know," Jessica deadpanned. Looking between Martha and Doctor Takahashi, she asked, "Do they know about the whole dying thing?"

"What?" Mercury said, shocked.

"I'm not dying," I lied.

"You're not?" Jessica blinked before Katryn elbowed her and I shot her a withering glare. "Oh, right."

"Subtle, Jessica," I muttered under my breath.

Mercury rolled her eyes. "Of course you'd lie about this."

"It's alright, John. I already knew," Martha said in a voice surprisingly devoid of emotion. "For what it's worth, I will miss you."

Mercury grumbled and stared at my shoulder. "Seriously, how could you keep this a secret?"

"We didn't exactly have time to discuss it," I said, frowning at her. "But I'm glad you're alright."

Mercury blinked then said, "Thanks."

I was about ready to start praying for Dread Cthulhu to come up when Katryn said to me, "The Dunwych army has started for the Black Cathedral."

I cursed under my breath. It was too soon. "On foot?"

"On horseback and in cars," Katryn said. "It occurred hours ago, so we do not have much time."

"Dammit, dammit, dammit," I muttered under my breath. "Okay, everyone who is going to be involved in taking down Doctor Ward, into the Hunter-13s. I have an old score to settle and I intend to make sure it's paid in blood."

"Yes, sir!" Jessica gave me a salute and headed right for the co-pilot's chair. The two of us were definitely going to get our money's worth out of Ranger flight school.

Mister Death and Katryn looked at each other before the former took his daughter off to the side to speak while Jackie tried to get on board, only for me to pull her off.

"I'm going to be entrusting you to Martha Booth and the soldiers here." I put my hands on her shoulders. "Where we're going is dangerous. I need you to promise you're going to stay out of trouble."

"I'll try, Mister Booth." Jackie looked at Martha before leaning in. "You realize she's touched, right?"

"I'm aware." I got up and rubbed my hands through her hair before walking back to Mercury and Martha. "Mercury, I'll explain everything once I'm back from the Black Cathedral. In the meantime, I'm going to just have to ask you to trust me until we manage to get all of this resolved."

"That's a lot to ask." I could tell Mercury wasn't entirely happy with my request, but she took three short breaths before saying, "Still, you saved my life, I owe you."

"Thank you."

"Wait, are we coming back?" Mercury asked.

"We?"

"Those children will need a doctor when we catch up with them."

I closed my eyes. "The chances of us coming back are very slim."

"I see. Well, I'm still coming. Perhaps it's time I actually looked after someone other than myself." Mercury gave a reluctant salute before heading off to join the group on board the Hunter-13s, leaving me alone with Martha as Jackie looked on.

I stared at my wife, realizing this was now where we probably parted ways forever. "I'm sorry for fostering this on you at the last moment."

"It's alright, I've come to expect your little twists and turns." Martha stuck her hands in her pockets. She closed her eyes and stood still for a few seconds. "I cannot read your mind right now."

I was surprised by that. "Oh?"

"It is growing darker and more opaque by the minute. You are changing, husband. Like a butterfly coming out of its cocoon."

"Or a death-moth."

"You don't need to continue this fight, John. If you are truly dying, you can come back to the Remnant and we can use our researchers to try and find some cure for your condition. I know more magic than anyone but Doctor Ward or the ghouls." Martha smiled; it was a rare look for her. I could sense the bitterness and concern behind her words, however. "I want to help you."

"I'm not the sort of guy who is just going to sit around and let myself get poked like a mole rat," I said before adding, "Besides, I knew what I was signing on for when I joined the Rangers."

"That's no excuse not to live."

"Perhaps. Perhaps not."

Martha looked down at the ground. "Very well, John. I don't agree with your choice, but I respect your right to it. It's one of the reasons why I chose to turn against the old Council."

"I'm glad I could be so inspiring." I was tempted to give her a kiss but hesitated. That part of our lives was over and I didn't intend to reopen it.

"I have a gift for you," Martha said, reaching into her jacket.

"What's this one? A revolver blessed by the Unspeakable One? A copy of the *King in Yellow* script?" I bit my lip then looked down, feeling a bit ashamed. "Sorry, I shouldn't mock your efforts. Your previous gifts saved my life on more than one occasion."

"I think you'll like this one a little bit better." Martha pulled out a picture of my children.

On the left side of the photo was a well-muscled, brown-skinned fifteen-year-old Anita Booth, wearing a pair of jeans and a tank top.

Her freckled face contrasted against her platinum-blonde hair. Her eyes were gray but she looked considerably more human than her mother. On the right, wearing a formal suit sized for his fourteen-year-old body was Gabriel Booth, his skin dusty bronze and his eyes a cat-like shade of yellow. He looked morose and somber, his usual attitude despite all my efforts to cheer him up. They were completely different in both personality and temperament but equally dear to my heart.

"Thank you," I told her. "I'll visit them."

"If you live," Martha said.

"Yes," I said. "If I live."

CHAPTER THIRTY

Minutes later, I was piloting one of the two Hunter-13s sailing through the air towards the Black Cathedral. The second was flying close behind us, carrying the Red Wolves team. Master Sergeant Aaron's team would serve as backup, giving us enough breathing room so we could sneak into the Black Cathedral and assassinate Ward before he knew we were coming.

It was an insane plan, really, but with the Dunwych army providing a distraction I was sure it had a chance of working. I didn't share my suspicion the Dunwych were going to get slaughtered to the man by Ward's monsters, but that was a price I was willing to pay to get my revenge on Ward.

I could tell myself I was doing this because I wanted to rescue the children inside the Black Cathedral but I couldn't bring myself to entirely believe that. There was a beast inside every human, every bit as callous and unfeeling as the Great Old Ones, and mine was hungry for Ward's blood. The fact I might have to die to get it, and sacrifice all my few remaining friends, was something I was still turning over in my head.

"Are you two sure you know how to fly this thing?" Mercury said, looking out the window as we passed across Kingsport's borders. The expression on her face was one of barely controlled terror. It was very similar to the one I'd worn during my first training mission in one of these.

"Nope," I said.

"Not a clue," Jessica said.

"What?" Mercury did a double take.

Jessica and I both laughed.

"Oh, fuck you," Mercury said.

For luck, I had the picture of my children prominently displayed on the dashboard. Jessica sat at my side, serving as my co-pilot, looking just as nervous as I felt. Katryn and Mercury sat behind us, occupying two of the passenger seats. Mister Death was absent, having apparently chosen to opt out of this mission.

Maybe he just didn't like flying.

"So can you fly or not?" Mercury said, digging her fingernails into the fresh black leather upholstery. "Well, I mean."

"Jessica is actually a better pilot," I said. "But I'm a better gunner."

"So he says," Jessica said. "Personally, I say I'm a better pilot *and* gunner."

"Then I guess I'm lucky I'm an officer," I said, not bothering to turn away from the vast desert stretched before me.

"Spoilsport," Jessica said.

The fact I was finally heading back to the Black Cathedral left me feeling queasy and anxious. I'd narrowly failed in avenging my squad in the Dreamlands. Had I been in better condition, I might have succeeded in killing Ward. Unfortunately, most of that had been the advantage of surprise. He would be ready for me next time and the odds were already heavily slanted against me.

"As long as we can get the drop on him, we'll be fine," I said softly, more to myself than anyone else.

Katryn countered, "You do realize the Necromancer knows you're coming, correct? If he has the slightest skill at divination, he will predict your actions three moves ahead."

"Yes," I said, wrinkling my brow. I hadn't meant anyone to hear that. "I figured that out when he sent a ghast disguised as my father to kill me in the Dreamlands."

"You're really going to have to tell me what exactly happened to you in the Dreamlands," Mercury asked.

"I will," I said, remembering Richard's head explode in front of me. "Eventually … and by eventually, I mean never."

"Now is not the time for levity," Katryn said. "My people are in danger."

"I thought you and your father were hoping the Dunwych would suffer a large number of casualties," I said, remembering our peculiar conversation outside King's casino.

"My father is High Priest of Hastur and a member of the Council of Elders. One does not argue with him in public or private," Katryn said. "Even if what he says is insane."

I regained a lot of respect for my lover's politics. "We're going to save them, Katryn, I promise. It shouldn't take long to catch up with the main column of the army."

Mercury pointed over my shoulder. "John, we have company."

Looking back at the windshield, I saw a terrible black *thing* coming towards us. Something so unnatural, it seemed to warp the very fabric of the air and sky around us. I thought for a moment it might be a gigantic nightgaunt, but I realized after a second it was something worse—a byakhee, a Devil of the Sky. One larger than any I'd ever seen before.

I'd faced the byakhee before and each time it had been a brutal and hellish battle. They were one of the most terrible threats existing out in the Wastelands, routinely pulling up humans off the ground and dropping their bloodless corpses down hours later. On rare occasion, they sang songs that could warp men's minds and turn whole villages to their twisted worship. This one looked like it could destroy a small city.

As the massive byakhee continued to glide across the air in defiance of all known laws of physics, larger than an Old Earth passenger liner, a chill went up my back as I took in the full size and shape of the monstrous abomination.

Byakhee resembled nothing so much as hideous skeletal gargoyles with massive wings and arms twice the length of their legs, creatures whose mouth and face were indescribable. Their features neither crow, mole, ant, nor decomposed human, yet existing in a state in between them all. Indeed, you could stare at their forms and not be able to take in their ever-changing looks due to the human eye's inability to stare into more than three dimensions.

This one possessed one recognizable pair of sensory organs, however. Eyes so terrible they might have been portals to hell itself. They were huge, free-floating, gaping holes in the skyline which burned like miniature suns, bloody red and oozing. Its arms ended in gigantic hundred-fingered talons each the length of steel poles.

"By the Black Mother," Katryn whispered, leaning forward to stare. "A matriarch."

"Who?" Jessica said, looking away from the monstrous soaring monster coming right at us.

"A mother of the byakhee race," I said, my voice trembling. I had read of them in the *Necronomicon*. "They can birth thousands of their kind in a single day and are summoned by only the most insane of magicians."

"Why?" Mercury asked, her scientific curiosity overcoming her fear.

"Because they can destroy nations," I said.

A byakhee matriarch starred in one of the more vivid tales dictated to Abdul Alhazred by Nyarlathotep in the *Necronomicon*. One particular creature born in nameless eons survived the destruction of its world by riding the solar winds to the Earth. Not a Great Old One, it was still an ancient being beyond anything humanity had the power to oppose.

Once it reached the Earth, it destroyed an entire continent of the old Pre-Babylon Lemurian civilization. The *Necronomicon* contained several spells for controlling and dismissing such creatures. Unfortunately, I was fresh out of the bone dust and human sacrifices necessary to do either.

"Shit," I hissed. "Incoming!"

"No kidding!" Jessica's accent dropped for a second, watching as I armed the weapons systems. "Do we have the kind of ammunition to kill this thing?"

"We're about to find out," I said, reaching over to the dashboard and engaging combat mode on the computers.

A holographic display listed the vital stats of the Matriarch, the Arcanothology sensors designed to record the makeup and weaknesses of nearly every E.B.E. found in the Wasteland. For the most part, the vitals read off of the Matriarch were listed as *Unknown*. The meters simply could not measure the strength, durability, and M-Rads radiating off the thing.

Dammit.

Taking aim with the Hunter-13's rockets, I was about to fire when the byakhee matriarch spat out a torrent of fireballs. The sensor readouts told me they were traveling as fast as missiles and were half as hot as the sun.

"Twelve o'clock!" Jessica shouted.

The number of flaming balls shooting forth at us was tremendous; they took up whole portions of the sky and it took every bit of my skill to avoid them. Mercury and Katryn bounced in the back but there was one advantage to the creature's size. It was damn near impossible to miss the gigantic thing.

Pressing down on the flight stick's missile controls, I shot forward two arcane-energy rockets. Ironically, designed by Doctor Ward, these missiles supposedly possessed the power to kill anything up to and including Great Cthulhu himself.

"Will those do any good?" Jessica asked.

"Probably not," I admitted, not even bothering to see if they'd worked. "Contact the Red Wolves and tell them to veer off."

The rockets exploded against the matriarch's chest, blue energy spheres exploding as the energy detonation washed over the massive byakhee's flesh. It was almost upon us now and I saw it wasn't the size of a passenger jet; it was much bigger and moving at incredible speeds.

We were also headed right at it.

"John, it's coming right at us!" Mercury warned me.

"That's the plan!" I shouted back.

As the rockets' energy seemed to pass harmlessly across the monster's chest, I swooped the Hunter-13 between its claws, exiting underneath its legs. The matriarch was not one of the most maneuverable of creatures, for which I was terminally grateful. It was about the only advantage we had right now.

Spinning the Hunter-13 around in mid-air, I gauged just how much damage was inflicted by the previous rockets. As the matriarch threw back its mouth and let forth an ear-splitting roar which threatened to detonate my eardrums, I saw it appeared completely unharmed.

"Oh, that's not good!" Jessica said, watching the visual feed from behind us. "Got any other ideas, Captain?"

"A few," I said.

"Are you lying?" Jessica asked.

"Yes," I said. "I have no idea what the hell I'm doing."

The pain in my shoulder exploded, causing me to temporarily lose control of the helicopter. Tightening my hands around the pilot stick, I struggled to stay out of the way of the creature that was descending on it. The matriarch's massive claws could easily reach around our transport and crush it to pieces.

Accelerating the Hunter-13 as fast as possible, the byakhee matriarch kept speed with us and even gained ground. Pulling sharply to the side, the matriarch passed over us while I felt nauseated. Falling back behind it as its momentum pulled it forth, I emptied every remaining rocket into the back of the monster. A process that only took seconds, but included every bit of hope I had for winning this contest.

The explosions detonated one after the other, burning harmlessly against the creature's sides before it let loose a shattering unholy scream that shook the metal carriage around us. I felt nauseous just being in its presence, the creature turning around like a great dragon. I was about to try and dodge under it when another series of rockets collided against the side of the matriarch, equally useless against its seemingly indestructible skin.

The Red Wolves had decided to join the fight. Under any other circumstances, I would have been ecstatic. Unfortunately, I knew it could only lead to ruin.

"We've got your back, Captain Booth," I heard the voice of its pilot proclaim. I regretted not knowing the name of the brave but suicidal soldier talking to me.

"Negative," I told him as I struggled to bring the chopper around. "This thing is after us. Proceed to the Black Cathedral. We'll distract it."

No sooner did I speak these words than the byakhee matriarch grabbed the other helicopter within its claws and crushed it to pieces. In an instant, all of the armored infantry on board and its brave pilots died horrifically. There was no triumphant explosion or glorious final battle, only tragic waste.

"Shit," I whispered, shaking my head.

Knowing we were outmatched, I pulled the chopper away and resumed our passage towards the Black Cathedral at top speed. Taking advantage of the momentary distraction afforded us by the Red Wolves' sacrifice felt cowardly but there was no other choice. We had no hope of killing this thing with mortal weapons.

I wasn't going to allow my squad to die for senseless heroics. Not again.

The byakhee matriarch was soon upon us again, however. It was determined to destroy us and resumed its attacks with a brutal fury. Sweat poured off my brow as the air around us exploded in more fireballs and the creature's claws swooped down on us again and again. Each time, we barely managed to avoid certain death, maneuvering away by a dozen or more yards at most.

"It's toying with us," Katryn said. "It wants to savor its kill."

"Let it," I said, as I felt the agony in my shoulder grow to tremendous heights. Worse, it was now spreading across my left arm and chest. "The longer it chooses to toy with us, the longer we live."

Katryn began muttering prayers to the Awakened Gods, making invocations to ward against evil. I wondered how effective any of them would be against a being as terrible as a byakhee matriarch. Certainly, it didn't seem to be any less effective in its pursuit. We'd need something a little stronger than prayers tonight.

"How much time do we have, John?" Mercury asked with a weak voice. It was foolish of her to interrupt my concentration, but I could understand her fear.

I just wished I knew whether she meant until we died or reached our destination. Unfortunately, the answer was probably the same. "Just a few minutes more."

Moments later, we came into view of the Black Cathedral. That magnificent bastion rose out of the Great Barrier Desert with the same twisted glory that I remembered from earlier. Battling on the ground in an almost Napoleonic fashion were the cultists of Cthulhu and the Dunwych. On both sides, terrible nameless monsters tore into one another and the troops, brought forth by the sorcerers to do war on their enemies.

The helicopter shook as the entire battlefield was covered by the matriarch's shadow. Zooming out from underneath its claws one last time, I proceeded to aim the chopper directly for the cathedral's tallest tower. We were going as fast as the vehicle was capable of moving and I had no intention of slowing down.

"John, what are you doing?" Mercury asked.

Tapping several buttons on the dashboard caused a series of alarms to start blaring across the Hunter-13's interior. "Secure your weapons, Jessica. We have eight seconds."

"Eight seconds until what?" Mercury shouted.

"John, are you sure you know what you're doing?" Jessica stared, realizing what I was doing.

"Not in the slightest," I said as I hit the EJECT button, causing the bottom of the cockpit to fall down along with the passenger seats.

A parachute popped out almost immediately as the Hunter-13 collided against the walls of the cathedral above us. The helicopter's engines and remaining arsenal simultaneously detonated as the matriarch slammed into the side of the building, impaling itself on the building's flying fragments and the tower it struck at full force.

Whereas rockets and flame did nothing against the creature, the extra-dimensional matter of the Black Cathedral's mortar tore through the byakhee matriarch's flesh like a knife through butter, shredding dozens of its redundant organs. Massive amounts of black ichor poured from its chest and arm wounds, while its wings were thoroughly shredded.

Despite this, the creature was not dead. In its agony, it smashed other towers and the building's upper levels. This only further widened its wounds and tossed up more fragments into its chest. Its apparent death throes would likely last for several minutes but the creature's defeat was now inevitable.

I, of course, had bigger worries at that moment. Hitting the ground at a fast speed and short distance, the parachute did little. Yet, Remnant efficiency was not to be denied. Instead of being flattened against the desert sands, we merely skidded across it and bounced several times. Had we not been thoroughly strapped in, we'd still have been killed instantly. Even so, it was a miracle none of us suffered broken necks or paralysis.

"Congratulations, John, you killed a second dragon!" Jessica shouted, staring up at the impaled monster.

I was too busy throwing up to respond. Mercury, meanwhile, held my head as my stomach emptied itself. Looking over at Katryn afterward, I saw even she looked queasy. I suppose even the invincible Dunwych had their weaknesses.

"John, that was beautiful. How did you know it would impale itself like that?" Jessica asked.

"I didn't," I admitted. "We're just lucky I guess."

"Is it possible to love and hate someone at the same time?" Mercury asked, stunned.

Katryn started un-strapping herself. "Yes."

"Good," Mercury said, giving me a few helpful pats on the back.

Looking to Katryn, she handed me my R'lyehian knife and I used it to cut myself free. We were behind enemy lines, within running distance of the Black Cathedral. Unfortunately, if we managed to draw too much attention to ourselves, we'd soon be overrun by cultists. Given the spectacle we'd made over the battlefield, I was anxious to get a move on.

Pulling out the heavy assault rifle I'd stowed underneath the front seat, I threw myself over the edge of the cockpit and waited for Jessica to join me. Katryn helped Mercury out of her seat and threw a knife hidden inside her leather attire into the heart of a Cthulhu cultist raising a rifle to shoot us.

"What now, Captain?" Jessica asked.

"We end this, or are ended."

CHAPTER THIRTY-ONE

Infiltrating the Black Cathedral proved to be surprisingly easy. The vast majority of the cultists had already poured out to engage the Dunwych, leaving the place largely unguarded. It was a seemingly foolish tactical choice but one I understood. The Necromancer's servants were nothing more than a liability once his new human race finished germinating. If the cultists suffered high casualties, it would make it easier for Ward to dispose of them later.

Still, there was a small garrison within and even with stealth there were a number of patrols we had to deal with. Thankfully, the Cthulhu cultists had become no more immune to bullets since the previous occasion Jessica, Katryn, and I had engaged them. This time, I made sure to shoot them in the head afterward. Hopefully, Mister Death had passed along that suggestion to the army outside. It would save them a lot of trouble.

The four of us were currently walking through one of the upper levels not crushed by the byakhee matriarch. The hallways around us were dimly lit by the Elder Thing free-floating illumination orbs and we were surrounded by a dozen deceased Cthulhu cultists. They were the latest victims of our increasingly bloody ascent through the temple. So far, we'd found no trace of Ward or his inner circle, but he was nearby.

I could feel it.

My shoulder pain had gotten to the point of being crippling, yet I was able to push it to the back of my mind. Somehow, I knew we were almost to the room containing this evil place's master. Using the Hand of Nyarlathotep as a sort of Geiger counter for evil was probably stupid, but it was the only lead we had. We could spend months exploring the temple and never find the insane sorcerer.

"He's close," I said, feeling the wound on my shoulder throb and ache with every step. "We just have to figure out where exactly."

I wasn't sure I'd be leaving this place alive. If so, I didn't care, as long as I managed to put down Ward. He'd become a living symbol of everything wrong with this world. Unable to strike at the Old Ones, I wanted to make him pay for the horrors my race had endured.

"I feel it as well, John." Katryn nodded, using a confiscated machete to decapitate the corpses of those she'd killed. On her back was an old-style M16 she'd used with deadly accuracy.

"We must be cautious," I said, trying to give a weak smile, but failing. The pain was simply too great.

Mercury, clutching a pistol close, looked up at me. "Are you going to be able to make it? Your left hand has red veins running all over it."

"I'll be fine." I took several breaths, not looking at my hand to confirm her words. "Really."

"Liar," Mercury whispered under her breath.

"In your next life, I hope you are a small god of the Earth," Katryn said to me, placing her hand on my shoulder. I suspected that was her way of saying goodbye.

Jessica just looked away, holding her heavy assault rifle close to her. She didn't want to confront the issue that I was probably not going to be making it out of here.

I couldn't blame her.

"Do you want me to pass along any messages to your children if you do not make it out?" Katryn said.

I thought about it for a long moment before saying, "No."

Stepping down the hall, I felt a particularly strong outpouring of otherworldly energy coming from behind an open doorway leading into a grand, pyramid-shaped hallway. The architecture of the Black Cathedral was different than I remembered, seemingly larger on the inside than it was on the outside. At this point, nothing surprised me, but I couldn't help but wonder just how much could really be relied upon in this world anymore.

The Dreamlands were a dimension where thought became reality and the Great Old Ones were linked to it somehow. Was it possible they were sucking the Earth into it, somehow? Was it possible they'd already done so? It would explain why the laws of physics were so damned screwy. If so, I wasn't sure there was anything to actually be done for humanity. We were already dead, effectively, and wandering around an afterlife we had just failed to realize we inhabited.

"So, do we have a plan for when we actually meet Ward?" Mercury asked.

"What do you mean?" I asked, feeling the hairs on the back of my neck stand up as we approached an octagonal door. The sense of power was growing all-consuming now. It was more than just Ward behind it. I really, really hoped it wasn't another shoggoth.

"Well, he's like a wizard, right?" Mercury asked.

"He's exactly like a wizard," Jessica said, looking over at her. "Mostly because he casts spells and shit."

"I used to not believe in magic, used to believe there was some rational explanation for everything, like psychic powers or ancient technology used by the Old Ones," Mercury said, her voice low. "I've seen enough since then to know even if there is an explanation, it's not one more scientific than 'they made it happen with their minds.' That kind of power is tearing up the Dunwych forces outside. If you're going to face down someone who has that kind of strength, then maybe we should have a plan."

"I'm not very good at plans," I said, keeping my fingers wrapped tightly around my heavy assault rifle. "I mostly play it by ear."

"And we've seen how that works," Mercury said.

"Maybe you'd like it back with the fish-men, Doc," Jessica said, frowning. "Who the hell gets kidnapped their first day out from New Arkham?"

Mercury stared at Jessica. "You were slowly suffocating under the ghoul's care. Your lungs were all but closed off thanks to whatever spell was cast on you. You'd have been brain dead if I hadn't done something, magic or no magic."

Jessica started to speak again before I raised my hand. We'd arrived at the iris door at the end of the hall. It was unlike any other door I'd seen in this place but very similar to the ones I'd encountered in the Elder Things' home. There was a kind of crystal growth on the wall I suspected was some kind of opening mechanism.

I didn't want to use it.

"Ward is a man," Katryn said, stepping up behind me. "What methods used to kill a man will be used upon him."

"He's less than a man now," Jessica said, a disgusted look on her face. "You didn't see what he looked like without his shirt. There's something living inside him now which has eaten him inside and out but left his still-walking-around corpse."

"Sometimes wizards invite other-dimensional creatures to share their flesh," Katryn said, looking down the empty hall from where we'd come. We were far from the battle now, and it seemed any remaining cultists had moved to join in the fighting. It disturbed me, though, because in a palace like this there had to be servants. I had seen neither hide nor hair of them, though. I'd also seen no sign of children or families despite the fact the Cthulhu cultists were an army larger than any outside of New Arkham or the Dunwych.

"What does that do?" Mercury asked.

"Allows them a bit more life and power," Katryn said, frowning. "The costs, though, are severe."

"No shit," Jessica said.

I lifted my right hand reluctantly to the crystal. "We'll cut off his head and burn his body to ashes. We'll also make whatever spells, blessings, or invocations to Katryn's gods necessary to keep him dead."

"I'm not going to use any heathen bullshit," Jessica said, growling. "Our squad deserves better."

"You can opt out, Jessica," I said. "A bit of paganism isn't going to damn my soul any more than all the sins I've committed."

"Sin is an illusion," Katryn said, putting away her M16 and pulling out her spear. "I am ready to deal with the Doctor."

"Guys," Mercury interrupted, looking down the empty hall the same way Katryn did. "I hate to ask, but … where do you think he's keeping the kids?"

"Excuse me?"

"I got the rundown on what you were originally here for, remember?" Mercury said, lowering her gun and putting it to the side of her leg. "That's why I'm here, to serve as an attendant to their needs. You said hundreds of children were kidnapped."

Mercury put a name to a nameless dread which had been haunting me since I'd started into this place. "Yes. Where are they?"

"It's a big cathedral," Jessica said, sounding about as convinced as I was.

"Not that big," I said, gritting my teeth. "There'd have to be a prison, cages, or something. We've seen none of that here. Just mostly empty temple rooms and chambers with a few spots obviously used by the cultist for sleep or storing their wastes."

"He wanted to turn them into super-humans, yes?" Katryn said.

"So he claims."

"Then they will be beside him."

I looked to the door. That was what I was afraid of. "Yeah, that makes sense."

I reached over to the crystal on the wall and placed my hand on it. It responded less to my touch and more to the presence of my thoughts, opening and revealing what lay beyond.

Cthulhu's Temple.

Full of children's corpses.

No. No. No! Dammit!

Stepping through the iris, I entered into a stadium-sized chamber which was as large as the Black Cathedral itself. There were massive rows of stone benches overlooking the central chamber, which was an acre long and dominated by a twelve-foot-tall stone relief of Cthulhu holding a spherical orb of light. The monster god looked down with four ruby-red eyes as the dragon-squid relief seemed almost human to me, staring down at us with a bemused expression. This representation of Cthulhu seemed almost saintly with a large, fat belly and its wings stretched around the globe as if enveloping it in a protective shield.

The top of the chamber was an onion-dome-like one with a holographic display of technology not belonging to any human source. It depicted an image of the galaxy and with thought rather than images, projected the origins of Cthulhu's people as they journeyed from their homeworld to this Earth in order to settle and construct their cities of eight-dimensional stone and thought.

The holograms showed Cthulhu's people doing battle with the Elder Things, warping reality with thought, before both were driven to the very edges of our watery third rock from the sun. As the Elder Things retreated to the frozen parts of the Earth and eventually the Dreamlands, so did Cthulhu's race enter slumber deep beneath the oceans or surface. I saw, to my horror, early humans and earlier races start worshiping Cthulhu's people and mistaking them for benevolent deities. They drew power from his sleeping form, confusing the Elder Things for deities and making an elaborate mythology as the psychics among them channeled his power to work amazing wonders.

There were no Elder Gods who opposed the Great Old Ones, or hostile powers to them. Cthulhu and his ilk were the divinities of mankind who inspired all magic as well as most religions. It was their presence that, ironically, provided humanity their few weapons against their servitors. Ward had discovered this and learned to harness that secret.

I didn't want to take my eyes off the holographic display above because to do so would mean acknowledging the horrific holocaust of bodies spread across the ground. Hundreds of children dressed in white baptismal robes and surrounded in chalk outlines with beatific smiles on their face, ranging from four to fourteen, of both sexes.

There were cups spread all around the room, the architect of their deaths no doubt, even as it was clear they'd all been given its murderous contents. The chalk outlines were surrounded with small sigils around them, invoking the names of the nonexistent Elder Gods and Cthulhu to protect them on their journey to a new homeworld in the Dreamlands.

"Death was his salvation for them," I muttered, staring down at them. "To send their spirits onward to a world in the Dreamlands away from us with no Great Old Ones to bother them. A place where they could live in wonder and glory forever."

"That sick bastard," Jessica said, looking on the verge of tears. "He was just crazy all along."

"Yes," Katryn said, looking down at the symbols on the ground. "I do not believe any of this will preserve their spirits. There is only a dream awaiting them."

Mercury checked the cup and sniffed it before shaking her head. "Shadowweed. It was painless at least."

"Small consolation to them," Jessica muttered, looking ready to start shooting everything in sight. "Where the hell is he?"

"He should be here," I muttered, approaching the stone relief of

Cthulhu. That was the source of the strange power I'd sensed.

Approaching the ball of light in the Cthulhu statue's unnaturally long webbed hands, I looked at it and saw it pulse with a strange blue-and-white aura. It was, in its own way, every bit as fascinating as the Black Cathedral had been to me when I first approached it. I could hear the music of Azathoth playing in my head as I approached it, only it was no longer the piping of violence or destruction, but a smooth, soft song of raw reaction. It was the song of creation, played by Azathoth's inhuman pipers at the beginning of the universe.

This universe at least.

I realized in that moment Katryn was wrong, at least partially. Looking into the glowing orb, I saw the blue-and-white Earth which Ward had created for his stolen children. I saw the moment frozen in time of a planet full of life as well as a race of man which would never know want, death, or disease. The world's entire history was contained in that bubble and it was possible to view it from the beginning to the end. I had never seen anything quite like it before.

"John, what are you doing?" Katryn called over.

"So beautiful," I whispered, reaching out to touch the glowing orb.

"Get away, Captain!" Jessica shouted, running over toward me.

I backhanded her across the face, sending her spiraling backward across the floor. It was an instinctive action and one I didn't have time to regret. That was when I saw Mercury holding her pistol in hand, aiming at my head. In that moment, I realized she was willing to kill me to prevent something horrible from happening.

I admired her for that.

But grabbed the glowing orb anyway.

"No!" Katryn called out, too late.

Mercury lowered her gun, unable to fire.

A wave of light passed over me and consumed my world along with everything else in the room.

CHAPTER THIRTY-TWO

As the light washed over me, everything was more vivid than in life. The sights, smells, and emotions. All of it.

I could recall the colors of the sky on the day I was born and remember what the taste of a meal was a decade ago. These were the memories the orb stored and shared among the human ghosts who dwelled within its folds. It wasn't limited to sharing memories either, but crafted dreams of stunning reality born from the most hidden desires of those souls it contained.

A girl named Marissa dreamed of her dead parents, abundant crops, and marrying the boy down the road.

A boy named Obed dreamed of becoming a great warrior, killing hundreds of opponents, then setting himself up as ruler of Kingsport.

Marcus dreamed of the Pre-Rising world he'd heard about in stories and swung from skyscraper to skyscraper on over a city long since dead.

The babe, Josefina, only a toddler, simply dreamed of growing up to become the woman she never would.

Camille dreamed of watching her parents die over and over again in the most horrifying manner possible.

James relived losing his virginity in a way which wasn't the clumsy manner of two newly pubescent children fumbling with each other.

Paradise.

But like all heavens, it belonged only to the dead.

I was alive.

Wasn't I?

The memory I relived was one I'd almost forgotten, so drowned out in the struggles of daily life it had been. It was five years ago; I was returning home from a riot suppression at one of the collective farms which supplied New Arkham and the Remnant with its food. I'd been involved in killing a dozen farmers and the burning of their houses. The smell of charred flesh and wooden buildings stuck in my nostrils and I remember throwing up like I'd still been a cadet. I was supposed to be an elite soldier but this hadn't been the work of a Recon and Extermination Ranger—it had been simple butchery.

Yet, what choice did I have? There were close to five hundred thousand citizens in New Arkham alone and any interruption in the flow of grain, mushrooms, rice, or other foodstuffs would mean mass starvation. My chief loyalty *had* to be to the people of the Remnant. The greater good trumped everything, even if I felt sick about it.

Right?

Walking through the front door of my single family house, a relative luxury when most had to bunk together in barracks, I saw the lights were off and my children were in front of the static-filled television. It was well past midnight and they should both have been in bed, but:

Fourteen-year-old Gabriel was sleeping on the carpet with his hands in his pajamas, his arms wrapped around my copy of *Unspeakable Oaths* with his head resting on the cover. It wasn't the kind of reading material my wife or I encouraged him to read, but he'd been sneaking into my private book shelf since he was ten. The white-haired boy had always been a troubled child but I loved him anyway.

Sitting on the couch was the half-awake form of my platinum-blonde-haired teenaged daughter Anita. She kept her hair cut short and was wearing a pink t-shirt with the R&E logo on the front and a pair of black bicycle shorts. Anita blinked when I opened the door and smiled at my arrival. "Hey, Da."

"Hiya, Scout," I said, smirking. "What are you doing up so late?"

"Waiting for you," Anita said, keeping her voice low. She was fifteen now and about ready to take up a trade. Anita had made no secret of the fact she wanted to join the military and had aced every possible test for advanced long-term training.

The possibility frightened me. I didn't want my daughter getting herself killed in a misguided attempt to make me proud.

"Where's your mother?" I said, putting my finger in front of her mouth and walking over to sit down beside me on the couch.

Anita gave me a sour look then turned away. "She's staying at a *friend's*."

"Ah," I said, knowing what she meant. I didn't blame Martha Booth for having taken up with other men. Our relationship had been forced on us by the Council, an attempt to breed psychic soldiers as if humans were just another animal to be husbanded. Neither of my children had displayed Martha's gifts, though it was still too early to tell with Gabriel. It wasn't like I could cast stones either. I spent time with prostitutes as well as a number of married Remnant women in similar situations. I'd thought about explaining that to Anita but, well, where the hell would I even begin?

"Who's been taking care of you in the meantime?" I asked.

"Aunt Eliza," Anita said, flipping off the television with a tape-covered remote. There was still a little light coming in through the windows from the moon outside.

"Ah," I said, thinking about the General's wife. "We're lucky to have her."

"Yeah," Anita said, turning back around. "She took us shooting."

I blinked. "Really?"

"Well, she took me shooting. Gabriel spent the entire time reading your creepy books."

I snorted. "Yeah, that sounds like him."

"I'm getting good," Anita said, brightly. "I think I'll be the best at the tryouts next month. They may put me straight on the path to becoming an R&E soldier!"

Gabriel stirred in his sleep a bit before turning over and continuing to slumber. He was muttering in his sleep. "T'hyahaha Shub'Niggurath N'awtqnk. Ia Hastur. Uyyh'aagh."

I looked at Gabriel, recognizing that chant from when I summoned Nyarlathotep in the Dreamlands, but dismissing it as a trick of the dream. "Before you take those tryouts, I'd like to mention something."

"What?"

I thought of a man trying to shield his wife and child while bullets flew through the air and chemical bombs were thrown. I thought of the burning houses where other soldiers from neighboring squads hadn't bothered to force the inhabitants out first. That was just what I'd seen today, not even a fraction of what I'd had to do in order to protect New Arkham.

Had to do.

"Being a soldier isn't the only way you can make me happy," I said, looking at my hands. I'd cleaned off the blood but the stains were still there in my mind.

Anita looked like I'd hit her, something I'd never do regardless of how often my father had done the same to me. "I just want to make you proud, Daddy. I want to protect people."

How did I explain to her that wasn't what it was about? That there were monsters in the Wasteland but also people? That preserving order in New Arkham was as often about being the boot that kept down those who were supposed to be in your charge?

It was too important *not* to tell her. "I'm just trying to prepare you, Scout. Being an R&E Ranger, being any kind of soldier really, is hard and dangerous work. I've lost a lot of friends over the years. Sometimes on missions which weren't heroic. You've been taught in school the people outside of our borders are dangerous, evil savages. The truth is they're just people. People who are hungry, afraid, or desperate will do things they wouldn't normally. This doesn't make them bad people. It just makes them less fortunate."

Anita seemed to hear what I was saying. "What about the monsters, Dad? They took over our world."

It was treason to say you sympathized with the creatures outside. "They're a different story. Still, they've been on this planet a very long time. In many cases, longer than us. They're also powerful. I've seen a lot of soldiers high on patriotism and vigor rush into situations where they think they can start taking the planet back from the monsters. That kind of arrogance gets them killed."

"Shouldn't we be trying to take back the planet?" Anita asked, surprised.

I took a deep breath, pondering how to explain what I was worried about. "Anita, I'll support you in any endeavor you choose to take. However, if I can impart any single piece of advice to you, it's this. Don't worry about the Great Old Ones, mutants, monsters, or demons."

Anita looked confused. "Excuse me?"

I pointed at Gabriel. "Worry about him. The job of a soldier isn't to destroy the enemy, despite what you've heard in class or read in storybooks. The job of being a soldier is to protect those under his care. It's what separates us from warriors and bandits. Those people who use violence to intimidate others. You won't always be able to make your own calls either, as that's what the chain of command is for. Sometimes you'll be asked to do the wrong thing, though, and you'll have to do it because that's the way the system functions. If you remember Gabriel, your spouse in the future, your friends, and others—and let them be the ones you think of—then you'll be able to be a good soldier. What helps them is to stay alive and keep your fellow soldiers alive."

It wasn't the best advice, full of holes really, but I'd always muddled through fatherhood.

Sometimes it worked, sometimes it didn't.

Anita put her hand on my mine and I put my arm around her. "I think I understand."

I gave her a kiss on the forehead. "You're the person I think of when I'm out there, Anita. You and your brother. As long as I have those I love, I'll be able to endure anything."

Anita gave me a hug and I held her tight.

That was when I heard the sound of an explosion and watched as Gabriel and Anita disappeared in flames. The memory was twisted and deformed even as I stood among their burnt skeletons in the ruins of our home. Turning upward, my heart beating so fast I felt like I was going to die, I saw the form of a Cthulhuoid horror standing over New Arkham.

It was a hundred feet tall with leathery bat-wings, the tentacled mouth of its ancient father, and a body both fat and repulsive. The creature drove men mad by its mere presence, causing them to kill their wives and children or be killed by them. In its terrible grandiose presence I realized I was not looking at a dream but reality. Not a precise vision of events but, even now, New Arkham was being destroyed by one of Ward's creatures.

Unharmed by the explosion, I raised my arms to the air and screamed before falling to my knees. I begged in that moment for madness to claim me, only for laughter to ring in my ears behind me.

"It is your dream," Nyarlathotep said, behind me. "If you do not like its contents then you should simply change the parameters."

I looked over to him. "This is reality."

The Black Soldier was standing among the ruins of my former house, looming over the bodies of Anita and Gabriel. "What is reality? Everything you experience exists in that tiny little brain of yours, a collection of wet matter and electricity. A dream is no less valid than reality as there is no way to tell the difference, really."

I gritted my teeth. "Is that what you told Ward? Is that why he murdered those children and sent them to this place?"

"Yes," Nyarlathotep said. "They live with the Small Gods of the Earth now. You could go there with your children now and dream for them the life you always wanted."

"They're dead."

Nyarlathotep stretched out his hand and they became alive again before I saw a vision of them being evacuated by Hunter-13 craft as the rest of the city fell.

"How many died for that?" I asked, remembering his price for healing me.

"Does it matter?" Nyarlathotep asked.

"No," I said. "We're all doomed anyway."

"Yes." Nyarlathotep smiled. "When I was dreamed into life, I was given a terrible need to know your every little thought. To intervene in your prayers, dreams, and aspirations. To be the god humans wanted for me. Terrible, all-loving, all-present, yet sadistic enough to let all of the horrors of this world happen."

I stared at him. "You're like a kid with a magnifying glass."

"Yes."

"Why are you here? Why me?"

"There is no answer to that," Nyarlathotep said, walking forward and staring at me with his deep, soulless eyes. "So, why don't you tell me why you are."

"To kill Ward."

"Not good enough."

I closed my eyes. "To save the children."

"Who you suspected would be dead from the beginning or, at least, beyond recovery. You even admitted killing Ward was more important. It's just not important enough that you would come back to this place the first opportunity you could."

I looked down at my shoulder. "To learn the secret of this. Ward didn't put this on my shoulder, did he?"

"No. I did. I linked you and Jessica so she could survive. It was what you wanted and when you summoned me, it was what I performed retroactively. I turned back the clock and placed my mark on you both."

"Then why did she awaken?"

"Doctor Takahashi's work. Richard's understanding of human anatomy has atrophied over the centuries."

"I see."

I closed my eyes. "Then the reason I survived the shoggoth, walked through the desert naked, and lived through the nightgaunt is … why?"

"The mark reflects what you are. What you were born to be."

"A monster?"

"Yes."

The Mark of Nyarlathotep wasn't killing me, I realized that now. It was changing me. That was when I closed my eyes and looked into the past, searching not just my memories but my mother's and I saw the terrible THING which appeared to her and brought about my birth. The thing whose touch had driven my mother to drink before a tearful confession of the truth drove my father mad. The Thing was inside me and the reason all of this was happening.

It was what I was becoming.

I screamed and awoke in Cthulhu's Temple.

CHAPTER THIRTY-THREE

I slowly climbed to my feet, struggling with the vision I'd seen. I wasn't human, had never been human, and my children were an unholy mixture of this world and other.

Oh John, Nyarlathotep's voice echoed through my mind. Your race was never pure of such things. Apes evolved thanks to the Elder Things' tampering and their dreams were warped by Cthulhu to create your race. Even the primordial slime which all life on this planet comes from came from another world as part of the body of a Great Old One.

I tried to force Nyarlathotep from my mind but found only echoes and shadows. I wasn't sure he even existed as anything other than a reflection of my own insecurities and suspicions. This world was a nightmare which humans couldn't wake up from.

Perhaps literally.

Once I stood, I saw Jessica, Mercury, and Katryn were twitching on the ground around me even as the children's bodies lay still. They were still caught in the same dream I'd unwittingly plunged myself into and had not yet awoken—if they ever would.

Looking down at my gun, I considered putting it underneath my chin and pulling the trigger. It was a simple enough choice: life as a monster or merciful death as a man. Even that choice was an illusion as I wasn't sure I could die. Glancing over at the Hand of Nyarlathotep, I saw it had already started to sport chitin patches which I knew would eventually spread to form an unnatural carapace. I clenched my right fist and concentrated, causing the chitin to sink into the folds of my skin and be replaced with the appearance of human flesh. It was a disguise, but wasn't that what monsters did? We cloaked ourselves in the appearance of normal humanity in order to pretend we were still people. It didn't matter anymore.

I'd made my choice.

I took my heavy assault rifle and placed the butt against the floor before resting my chin against its muzzle. Reaching down, I closed my eyes and prepared to end my existence. I had no idea what sort of afterlife awaited monsters or whether there would simply be cold oblivion, but it was a better choice than becoming the thing in my vision.

That was when Katryn stirred on the ground and climbed to her feet, lifting her spear and offering a better alternative than suicide. "Monster. You're a monster. A filthy alien creature from another world."

I let the heavy assault rifle drop to the ground. "Yes, yes I am."

I didn't want to commit suicide but the thought of living further was unbearable. Death at the hands of Katryn was perhaps not my preferred method of death, but it would at least be a warrior's end.

"I saw what you were in my vision," Katryn said, a look of disgust on her face. "I cannot believe I let you touch me."

"Don't flatter yourself," I said, tossing the gun to one side. "You imagined yourself as the great warrior race that would redeem this world with your knowledge of the Old Ones, but your people are being massacred out there the same as the rest of humanity."

"Fuck you!" Katryn hissed, assuming a battle stance with her spear.

"Oh, and I was kept a slave. I was never anything to you but a tool and I despise you for it. I just needed your help. Which I don't anymore."

Katryn launched herself at me, charging with her spear. I positioned myself to move out of the way then held myself still and waited for the inevitable. I just hoped her blessed spear was capable of killing me. I never got the chance to find out because Katryn was shot three times in the back. Katryn fell to her knees and collapsed, face forward on the ground, her spear falling out of her hand.

Mercury was behind her, still on the ground, holding her pistol and breathing short, quick breaths. "You're welcome."

I stared down at where Katryn was lying, watching a pool of inky-black blood pour from her body. It was proof Mister Death's claims she was not entirely human were true, but, whatever her inhuman ancestry was, it hadn't done much to save her. Mercury climbed to her feet and then walked over Katryn's corpse before emptying the rest of the magazine into her.

"That wasn't necessary," I said, looking between them.

"Better to be safe than sorry," Mercury said, her hands trembling.

"First time you've killed someone?" I asked, holding my hand out. I wasn't sure how to react having my attempt at suicide interrupted by someone shooting the weapon.

"Second," Mercury said. "Not counting those I gave a lethal injection."

I took the gun, pulled out a magazine from my belt, and reloaded it before I handed it back. "I forgot about your husband."

"I won't, as much as I want to."

My emotions were a whirlwind as I struggled with how I felt about Katryn's death. She'd never been my friend, only my enemy, but I still felt pain at her loss. I also didn't know how I was going to continue knowing what I did now. The moment to kill myself had passed, though, and I suddenly felt an overwhelming urge to live.

It was a qualified emotion, though, because of what I had to say next. "New Arkham is gone, Mercury."

Mercury blinked. "What?"

"Ward destroyed it," I said, swallowing my next breath. "The orb showed it to me. I don't know how I know it's true, that it's not a hallucination, but I do. The only survivors are a few evacuees and whoever came to take over Kingsport."

Mercury took a step back, holding her face.

"I'm sorry," I whispered, unsure what else I could say.

"Why be sorry?" Ward's voice echoed through the chamber. "You didn't choose to free their souls from this miserable decaying mess of a world."

I looked around the chamber, too exhausted to hate him. "Spare us the theatrics, Ward. If you're here to kill us, then go ahead, but I refuse to indulge your fantasies any further."

Mercury snorted. "Screw that, I intend to kill this child-killing bastard."

"You wound me," Ward said, stepping out from behind Cthulhu's effigy. He had his staff in hand and his eyes were completely blackened. The Doctor had cast aside his shirt and the monstrous mouths were in full display as a set of hideous new insect-like legs were growing out of his back.

"Only if I miss."

Mercury proceeded to start shooting at Ward, firing just as many shots as she put into Katryn, only with much more force. All of them went into the monstrous wizard's chest but he barely seemed to acknowledge them. Finally, after the last of her bullets left the pistol, Ward extended his hand and drew her gun from her hands.

"Shit," Mercury muttered, almost tripping over the corpse of a child.

Ward crushed the gun in his hand, dropping its useless fragments and pieces from between his hands. "You've killed my servants, destroyed my shoggoth, brought an army to my doorstep, and have come to kill me. In the shadow of Great Cthulhu's idol, though, Father of the Elder Gods and First of the Great Old Ones, you can walk away."

I stared at him, incredulous. "*Walk away?*"

"You murdered all these children!" Mercury said, stepping toward Katryn's body.

"Murdered? What does that word even mean," Ward said, scratching at his skin and pulling away a large chunk of it to reveal an armored surface underneath. "The world as we knew it was destroyed with the Rising and we are trapped merely in the shattered remnants of its dream. I set them free and placed them in a paradise. To live wondrous and free beyond the nightmare of this world."

I stared at him. "They're still dead."

"And what about you, John?" Ward said, his face starting to crack. It looked like he was wearing a mask now and the horrible thing beneath him was starting to poke through. "Isn't death preferable to what you are? Or is life, any kind of life, better? Humanity has had its day and now we both move onto the next stage of it."

Mercury was hunched over Katryn's body with my copy of the *Necronomicon* in her hands. It was a rather desperate ploy, especially with Ward standing right there, but I couldn't blame for her for trying to do something.

"Mercury, throw me the spear."

She didn't even look up, tossing me Katryn's weapon as I took it hand. It felt wrong, as if I was defiling her body to take it in hand. Still, if her angry ghost hated me for killing her, then I suspected she'd tolerate me taking revenge on her behalf.

"We are *nothing* alike," I said, growling.

Ward's body looked ready to fall apart, literally, and an extra set of arms burst out of his side, turning him into something I didn't recognize. It was yet another alien creature, from Earth's distant past or future, transforming what little human remained of the old wizard into something else.

"Are we?" Ward said, his voice becoming a guttural and monstrous thing which could barely produce human vocals. "We are both products of the magic we have worked, robbing us of what we treasured most to make ourselves something more. The only difference is I was born human while you were always a thing impersonating one of us. No different from that ghoul who desperately wanted to live among the apes his kind were born to feed upon."

The last of Ward's human body exploded to water, muscle, and flesh on the ground. The creature which stood in its place was almost twelve feet tall with a dozen spider-like legs sticking up from the main part of its body as the chestful of tongues transformed into a disgusting set of tubes on the bottom of its belly. The creature's head emerged from the top of its shoulders, looking like some hideous combination of an ant's with a crustacean's. There was something still undeniably human about it, though.

Which made it all the more horrifying.

In the dismal, dark, alien portion of my mind I recognized the creature as the Zglaoth which existed on the surface of a world which had worshiped a Great Old One known as the Living Sun, a creature which had made a million-year pilgrimage to consume its world before setting itself toward other intelligent life-bearing worlds. This one, somehow, had been plucked from its extinct race's fate before being physically, as well as mentally, bonded to Ward.

I almost pitied him.

Almost.

Hefting Katryn's spear, I charged at the alien abomination only for the creature to send me flying across the room with a burst of kinetic force it generated through will alone. In my mind, I heard Ward's mocking laughter and realized it was still him.

Mercury was struggling with the *Necronomicon* but another surge of alien energies flowed from Ward, and the corpses around her, hundreds of children murdered before their time, began to rise.

Fuck.

Ward's mocking laughter filled my mind. "This is a pointless display. None of what you have done this day or before has mattered in the slightest. We dwell in a cosmic void stretching across infinity, full of terrible things which care nothing for humankind's existence. When our former race perishes in the next six decades, there will be no one who remembers us with anything more than a passing interest. The Deep Ones, Ghouls, and Dreamwalkers will look back upon humanity as nothing more than an ugly, ill-formed race of weaklings. Like *Homo sapiens* did the Neanderthal, they will congratulate themselves on how well-evolved they were and never think it could happen to them."

I knocked away three of the Reanimated children who caught fire once touched by Katryn's spear and then a half-dozen others even as they huddled around Mercury but could not reach her, the doctor having used Katryn's blood to draw a circle around herself. Somehow, she'd learned that bit of sorcery in the time it had taken to get the book and a few moments glancing at it. I would not have thought human blood would be able to hold the horde of Reanimated back but Katryn hadn't been any more human than me.

Not really.

A berserk killing frenzy consumed me as I struck at the hundreds of attacking Reanimated around me. They were soulless, mindless, and empty. Whatever had been inside them had been ripped away, only to be replaced with fragments of Ward's malignant will and hatred, but their state only fueled my fury. The spear staff functioned like a ball of fire which consumed the magic within them, seemingly strengthening it with every hit.

The chants of Azathoth once more filled my head as well as the haunting alien music existing at the heart of the universe. One of the older-looking Reanimated grabbed hold of my right arm before being joined by a half-dozen others, pulling on it with the strength only one of the dead could muster before ripping it clean away.

The blood poured out, only for it to turn into a hideous whip-like tentacle. I ignored my horrific transformation to begin swinging the spear with my left hand while slashing with my tentacle into the crowd of monstrous children.

"What …" Ward's voice echoed in my mind, *"are you?"*

"Death!" I shouted, my voice sounding almost like Ward's before I charged at him with spear and inhuman appendage … only for a flaming Elder Sign to appear in front of him, the hideous star causing me to back away as an irrational fear of its power filled my veins. The Elder Sign had been created by the Elder Things thousands of years ago, infused with the psychic power of their race, and then had been appropriated by those who worshiped the Great Old Ones as the Elder Gods. Ironically, a weapon formed to fight them.

It was now working on me and not Ward.

"Damn …" I said, feeling blood start to form in my mouth before I began throwing it up onto the ground as it poured out of my eyes, ears, and other orifices.

"I banish you creature of Nyarlathotep," Ward said, chuckling. "You, spawn of the Great Old Ones, I shall send to the farthest reaches of the universe. You will dwell in the darkness and void forever alone until even insanity will be a welcome friend."

That was when Ward's psychic presence disappeared and there was only a terrible blankness around us. It was as if the room had been a terrible fire of light and energy, only to have that smothered in a wet blanket of some other force. The blood ceased to pour from my body even as the tentacle receded into my shoulder and human flesh grew over it.

Several feet away was Mercury, on her knees, reading from the *Necronomicon* as the remaining Reanimated struggled fruitlessly against her barrier. She was reciting a spell I did not recognize but was filled with a force which was every bit as powerful, if not more so, than Ward himself.

Hers was a bloodline which contained some ancient Atlantean, Mu, or Stygian which could channel magic every bit as much as a creature from another world. Even so, I could tell how the action was straining her. Her body was covered in sweat and the words she was forming with her mouth were obviously difficult. A single syllable misspoken could bring about her death.

Ward made a hideous series of noises which were nothing approaching English but whose intent was clear as he roared then skittered across the ground toward her. While Mercury's barrier kept away the Reanimated, I somehow doubted it would be able to hold against the several tons of monster which was presently barreling down on her.

Spitting the last of the blood in my mouth to one side, I lifted up Katryn's spear one last time and charged through the crowd of Reanimated children which made a few scattered attempts to claw at me. The spear slammed through the side of Ward, pushing out the other side, even as his entire body caught fire. A blue-white flame of other-dimensional energies exploded across the Zglaoth and it made noises enough to drive a man insane. Thankfully, I was well past the point of insanity and only cared that it killed him.

Which it did.

Several long seconds after the spear had been plunged into the monster's heart, Ward's frame collapsed to the ground and melted into an inky-black goo which I would not touch for all the food rations in New Arkham. Well, New Arkham before my enemy had destroyed it. The Reanimated collapsed to the ground around me, grabbing their heads and convulsing while Ward burned, only returning to death with his final demise. It was almost comical, some of the moves they made.

And then, finally, there was silence.

The Necromancer was dead.

Mercury ceased her chant and collapsed, dropping the book on the ground. "Okay, remind me never to do magic again."

"I don't think that will be a problem," I whispered.

Mercury slowly crawled to her feet, clutching the *Necronomicon* against her chest. "John, the things I saw you do—"

"I'm sorry."

Mercury said, "I don't care."

"What?" I asked.

She walked over and dropped the book before clutching me. "Just promise me we'll pretend to be human from now on."

"I promise."

I looked over at the glowing white orb in the Cthulhu idol's hands. It was glowing even brighter now and I saw Ward's soul was now imprisoned within. He was living the life of a human scientist in the 19th century. He had a wife, children, and an entire circle of friends all conjured from his dreams. The perfect heaven for a man who wanted nothing more than to be in absolute control of his destiny—it was close to my hell.

Oh and Katryn's body was missing now.

Lovely.

"What do we do about Jessica?" Mercury said, looking over at Jessica's fallen form. She still hadn't awakened from her dream.

I looked down at her and found myself staring into her blank, expressionless eyes. Her face, however, was covered in a beatific smile. My mind had opened to new possibilities with the awareness of its inhuman nature, so I attempted to look inside her mind. It opened up for me like a flower to the sun.

Inside, I saw her with her husband and children. They were in a still-standing New Arkham, living a life where peace and democracy had been restored by the General's ascension to President. The R&E Rangers went out on missions but no one died, and it was the beginning of a new age for humanity. I was there, with Anita, Martha, Mercury, Stephens, Parker, Garcia, and others.

An impossible dream.

But a beautiful one.

"Take her with us," I said. "We'll keep her until she wakes up."

"And if she doesn't?"

I closed my eyes. "We let her dream."

TO BE CONTINUED IN:

THE TOWER OF ZHAAL

ABOUT THE AUTHOR

C.T. Phipps is a lifelong student of horror, science fiction, and fantasy. An avid tabletop gamer, he discovered this passion led him to write and turned him into a lifelong geek. He is a regular blogger and also a reviewer for The Bookie Monster.

BIBLIOGRAPHY

The Rules of Supervillainy (Supervillainy Saga #1)
The Games of Supervillainy (Supervillainy Saga #2)
The Secrets of Supervillainy (Supervillainy Saga #3)

Esoterrorism (Red Room Vol. 1)
Cthulhu Armageddon
Lucifer's Star
Straight Outta Fangton

CROSSROAD
PRESS

Made in United States
Orlando, FL
29 June 2024

48425541R00162